PETER SMITH

Peter Smith was born and raised in the Black Country and educated at King Edward's School, Birmingham and Oxford University where he read Engineering Science. Following a research degree, he joined the academic staff of the Royal Military College of Science, now the Defence Academy of the United Kingdom where he wrote a number of academic books. In 2011 he retired from his post as Reader in Protective Structures. He lives in Oxfordshire, is married to Elizabeth and has two daughters and two grandsons.

ALSO BY PETER SMITH

BASIC Hydraulics, Butterworth and Co., London. 1982, ISBN 0-408-01112-2

BASIC Idraulica, CLUP, Milan, 1985, ISBN 88-7005-661-9

Mecanica de fluidos e hidraulica, Anaya, Madrid, 1988, ISBN 84-7614-170-X

Blast and Ballistic Loading of Structures, Butterworth-Heinemann Ltd., Oxford, 1994 ISBN 0 7506 2024 2
(with JG Hetherington)

Blast Effects on Buildings, Thomas Telford, London, 1995, ISBN 0 7277 2030 9   (with GC Mays *et al*)

Military Engineering Vol. IX: Assessment, strengthening, hardening, repair and demolition of existing structures. Secs 3.2, 3.7, 3.8, 4.4. Ministry of Defence, 2003

Blast Loading, Structural Response and Design, Centre for Research and Professional Development, Hong Kong, 2005, ISBN 962-86246-9-5   (with TA Rose)

Blast Effects on Buildings [Sec Edn], Thomas Telford, 2009, ISBN 978-0-7277-3403-7   (with D Cormie, GC Mays *et al*)

Tall buildings: Design Advances for Construction, Ch11, Saxe-Coburg Publications, Stirling, 2014,
ISBN 978-1-874672-25-8   (with TA Rose)

PETER SMITH

ACADEMIC LICENCE

A sort of mystery with engineers

Copyright © Peter Smith 2017

ISBN-13: 978-1542725002

ISBN-10: 1542725003

This novel is a work of fiction in which names and characters are a product of the author's imagination. Any resemblance to actual persons, either living or dead, is entirely coincidental.

To Elizabeth, Caroline and
Rachel (who designed the cover)

PROLOGUE

WO2 Simon Davies picked up the green ammunition box in his right hand and, with his left, took the Shrike that was hanging from the hook behind the door of his office in the Ammunition and Explosives Wing. He slung the Shrike – used to initiate the detonators that he and his Wing colleagues used to detonate explosive charges - in its green canvas case over his shoulder. He picked up the Land Rover keys from where they were lying on the corner of his desk and went out of his office towards the main door of the Wing.

'I'll be back by twelve at the latest. I'm doing a demo for a couple of the MSc courses first and then some instrumented tests for a PhD student - if he's got his experiments set up properly, that is. When I get back we'll look at the draft programme for next month's courses,' he said as he passed the open door of Sgt Mike Brown's office which was just a few yards from his own.

'OK, Si – see you later,' replied Brown, who was seated in front of his computer monitor. 'I'll try and get most of it sorted now, so there shouldn't be much for you to do on it later.'

Simon Davies nodded and continued walking. The Land Rover was parked in its usual place to the left of the main door of what was a sizeable building which housed a large range of light weaponry and ammunition types used for teaching on the various munitions courses for which Simon and his colleagues were responsible. The Rover started first time and he set off to drive the half-mile or so to the Explosives Demonstration and Experiment Range, usually known as the 'EDER'. He stopped the vehicle in front of the EDER's large steel gates, unlocked them and pushed both open. He got back in the Rover, drove another hundred yards and stopped again. This time he took hold of the rope running up the white-painted flag-pole and pulled on it. A large red flag attached to the lower end of the rope rose up the pole. The flag served to indicate that the range was in use and that access would only be permitted to those with the necessary authorisation. With the flag raised and hanging limply from the top of the pole – this September morning was crisp and clear but with no hint of a breeze – Simon got back into the Land Rover and drove the remaining two hundred yards to the group of buildings that were essential to the operation of the EDER. There was a small structure where charges were prepared for firing, a small covered 'grandstand' where the various demonstrations about the use of explosives could be safely viewed by participants on various munitions-related courses and a small demonstration hall - a steel-framed, steel panel-clad building - that housed various display boards. It was this building that students carrying out projects, or members of staff conducting research, often used to prepare their experiments.

Simon unlocked the preparation room door, went in and placed the Shrike and the ammunition box containing a couple of sticks of plastic explosive and a short length of explosive specially shaped to enable it to cut through metal on a small table located beneath the only window. He reached into the large patch pocket on his right trouser leg and took out a small box containing twenty electric detonators. These he locked in the small security cupboard attached to the wall of the room – detonators and explosives were always kept apart until the final moments of charge preparation.

He then opened the door to the demonstration hall and was relieved to see evidence that the student he was to assist today had indeed been preparing test pieces for the trials that morning. There were a number of strain-gauged panels in a variety of shapes and sizes made of a new high-strength composite material that the student - a Ministry of Defence-sponsored civilian - was assessing for its suitability to improve the level of protection for troops when they were on operations. He'd arranged to meet the student after the demonstration at about nine forty-five and it was now eight-fifty. The MSc students were also due to arrive in a few minutes. Before the instrumented tests, he would do the cutting charge demonstration in the hardened reinforced concrete building that was one of the most important features of the EDER. The instrumented experiments were also to be conducted in the hardened building because, in both cases, there was a possibility of fragments being created, either from the charges being detonated or from the materials being assessed. The building's layout meant that there was an extremely low probability that any fragments could escape from the building.

Simon walked the thirty yards to the building's entrance, unlocked the adjacent box which contained switches to the hardened lighting system inside, turned the lights on, entered the test chamber and stopped. In the centre of the chamber, lying on the foot thick layer of coarse sand that covered the floor was a body.

1

Monday 5th September am

Dr David Burgess looked across his desk at his friend and colleague Dr James Schofield.

'It seems like a century since the summer,' commented David.

'You've only been back two days! How can you say that?' asked James.

'Well, it takes me a little while to get back into the swing of things and, while that's happening, my enthusiasm tends to rather less than unbounded!' joked David as he took a sheaf of papers from the stacked in-tray on his desk and prepared to extract the few bits of information of relevance that it contained.

'When I turned on the computer, I found over 200 e-mails in my Inbox,' said David, 'of which only about 10% were worth reading and of those only about half a dozen needed a reply. But even so, it does take time to go through them all. Anyway, I think I've dealt with the vaguely important stuff. I was just starting on the things I found in my pigeonhole in the Department Office. Most of it is rubbish, of course, but I ought to go through it just in case I miss something that might be important.'

Across the desk, lounging in one of the office's two easy chairs, Schofield gave a smile of commiseration and took a sip of coffee from the mug he was holding.

'I had upwards of 150 e-mails too, and a pile of stuff in my pigeonhole. I've sorted most of it but it'll need another hour or so to go through it all,' said James, before adding, 'You'll find that the timetables for the new term are a bit of a mess that'll need some action on your part. There still doesn't seem to be any coordination between the undergraduate, postgraduate and short course timetables – you'd have thought that, with the timetabling software the Academic Coordinator uses, a lot of the more glaring errors could have been resolved before any draft was published. I noticed you'd got a clash on Tuesday every week and I'm sure you'll find more. My programme has lots of mistakes as well.'

James Schofield was a man in his mid-forties of somewhat stocky build. His greying dark hair fell over his forehead above a face set with deep green eyes and a mouth that always seemed to be on the point of breaking into a broad grin. This outward appearance of general easygoing bonhomie disguised a penetrating mind well capable of dealing with tough analytical problems. His special academic interest was the behaviour of complex structural elements under the action of the dynamic loads that were produced by impacts or explosions or even earthquakes. Academic colleagues held his work in high regard. Outside of his work, James had an active interest in antique furniture with a special liking for long-case clocks. Several such time-pieces were a feature of the thatched cottage that James, his wife Laura and two teenage children – Sam who was just 17 and Harriet who was 14 - occupied in the small village of Leddington which was about 20 minutes drive from the rural campus of The Defence University of Technology and Management where David and James were both senior lecturers in the Department of Civil and Military Engineering.

Like most of the University's academics, returning after what most regarded as an all too short summer recess, James was also finding the process of easing back into university routine a rather unwelcome effort. He drained his coffee and rose from his seat.

'I must go and finish sorting out those e-mails and my pile of papers – I can't understand where it all comes from,' he said. 'You'd have thought that people would have been discouraged from sending so much stuff out in August knowing that they'd get no response until September – if then!'

'See you at about eleven in the Common Room,' said David as James walked to the office door and went out leaving David alone with the unopened e-mails, the unanswered memos, the company circulars, the publishers' blurbs about newly-published and forthcoming texts and the pile of university-generated documents that had amassed during his four or so weeks away.

The next item on the top of the pile was the August issue of 'Recent Library Acquisitions' – he still liked to have this information in hard copy format as well as electronically. It usually extended over several pages – and hence was largely unread by the majority of staff – but this particular issue was a mere two sides of A4 paper. Only a dozen or so new books were listed together with about six reports.

'*Dynamic finite and boundary element methods*. Georgiadis K., Ellsworth, New York (2nd ed 2016)', he read.

'Might be worth a look,' he thought, 'The first edition has been useful over the years.'

The next entry was '*Management systems modelling*'. Blythe RT, Beechwood Press, London (2016).

'What on earth can that be about?' wondered David, whose opinion of any book with 'management' and 'systems' in the title was invariably low.

He glanced down the list of the few contract reports. The first was '*Radiographic techniques in ceramic armour assessment*. Report No 317/2016 Brown PJ *et al* US Defense Department, Anderson Proving Ground, June 2016' and held little interest for him. The next entry, however, did cause him to pause.

'*A novel method for protection against ballistic attack*. Wright SR, Neville G. Final report on Grant ARD/192 July 2016 TDU/MG'

'So!' thought David. 'It's all finished - I wonder how Stephen is getting on with selling the system to a commercial outfit, now that it's been shown to work so well?'

The entry referred to the completion of work on a research council grant that Stephen Wright, one of David's colleagues and also a senior lecturer, had been awarded about four years ago. The research council funding had been augmented by significant contributions from three or four commercial sponsors and had enabled Wright and his team to acquire some sophisticated equipment with which to carry out dynamic loading tests on the materials he was working with. The outcome of the research was a novel system that used materials found in standard armour packs but configured in a unique way that produced a significant enhancement in protection level without any increase in mass compared to existing products.

'I remember that, before the summer break, Stephen said that his sponsors were falling over themselves to acquire the licence to manufacture the designs commercially. A licencing contract will be a real boost to TDU – it would bring in a lot of revenue with a commercial partner on board to manufacture and market the system. They'd be able to promote it for civilian use as well as the defence applications,' mused David. 'I must ask him how the competition for the licence is going.'

David made a mental note to have a word with Stephen Wright about how commercial exploitation of the new system was progressing when they next bumped into each other.

David placed the Acquisition List along with the other items he'd scanned, into his 'Out' tray and reached for a few more from the now perceptibly-diminishing 'In' pile.

The first was 'Draft Timetable – Michaelmas Term'. As always when he saw the word 'Michaelmas', David smiled inwardly at the University's sometimes too overt desire to be thought of as 'Oxbridge-like' by naming its three terms 'Michaelmas', 'Hilary' and 'Trinity' as the University less than a couple of dozen miles away did and had done for centuries, rather than using the rather more straightforward 'Autumn', 'Spring' and 'Summer' labels. David took out his pocket diary and proceeded to note lectures and laboratory sessions scheduled for the coming term. Although the University authorities were keen that academic staff should maintain electronic diaries that could be remotely-accessed both by the registered user and also the Computer Centre, David preferred to keep a written note of his commitments. This 'old-fashioned' approach was much less open to undesirable scrutiny and avoided the possibility of someone entering a meeting date and time on the electronic system without ever consulting him as to his availability or, more importantly, checking whether he actually wished to attend a particular event.

Several clashes became apparent where he was meant to be lecturing to two groups simultaneously on different topics in different parts of the campus. With a sigh, David reached for the phone and called the Academic Coordinator's office to start the process of sorting out the confusion. The line was engaged.

'Must be others discovering the same nonsense,' he thought as he turned to his computer keyboard and began an e-mail to the Coordinator's office. He started to itemise the clashes and suggest ways that they might be resolved without having to undertake a complete rewrite of the timetables.

*

The Defence University of Technology and Management - TDU - was an institution with an interesting history. Though not a conventional university, it held a Royal Charter to award its own degrees and bore favourable comparison with a number of well-regarded UK universities.

Set up in London by military equipment manufacturers in the 1795 as the School of Military Manufacture, it designed and built field artillery pieces before being annexed by the Ministry of War and renamed as the Royal Artillery Training Academy – RATA for short. RATA expanded considerably over the next hundred and forty years and, by the mid-1930s, desperately needed new premises. In 1935 the Ministry acquired the Buckley Hall Estate in South Oxfordshire near the village of Sherington. Staff moved out from London and the new RATA opened in 1937 under the directorship of Professor William Butler, occupying a refurbished Buckley Hall and a number of new office and laboratory buildings. The onset of the Second World War led to an expansion of research and development at RATA with specialists in the field of military vehicles, communication systems, explosives and munitions being drafted onto RATA's staff. At the end of the war end, scientific and engineering staff numbered over two hundred.

After the war, the army wanted to maintain its technological expertise and sought to develop a stream of technically-competent officers: the Army Science and Technology Initiative - ASTI - was born. British Army officers came to RATA for a year of education and training in a wide range of military technologies. Butler also initiated a suite of first degree courses in engineering and science to attract both experienced officers who had missed out on a degree because of the war and also newly-commissioned officers.

In the 1950s and 1960s RATA flourished as officers from many countries flocked to the establishment. ASTI was renamed the Military Technology Course and British military personnel rubbed shoulders with officers from around the world together with an increasing number civilian students sponsored by UK defence industries.

However, in the 1970s, numbers on the many courses offered by RATA began to decline as a result of a shrinking British Army coupled with general defence spending cuts. Increased fees for overseas students led to a decline in their numbers also.

In the early 1980s RATA was in crisis. Too many staff were servicing an undersubscribed programme of courses and research was severely compromised by spending cuts and there was talk of a large number of redundancies and even closure of the Academy.

In an attempt to maintain its viability, the then RATA Provost, Professor George Nicholson, sought to appeal to the current government's liking for privatisation. A contract was drawn up between the Ministry and a newly-formed Academy Board of Governors that maintained the aspects of RATA's activities that were considered militarily essentially, but also allowed for greater operational and financial freedom. The Academy was effectively part-privatised and its staff ceased to be civil servants. Ministry presence on the campus was maintained, working in partnership with the privatised component of RATA. Freed from many constraints, the Academy competed for research and development work in a now much wider marketplace and expanded its range of teaching activities into a larger number of defence-related areas.

In 1985 the reconstituted Academy acquired its present name. TDU's new freedom triggered a huge expansion in the income derived from teaching and research. This came from both the Ministry contract and, increasingly, from 'private venture' activities – a burgeoning portfolio of short courses, research contracts and consultancy work. The bottom line of any TDU activity was the net income that it yielded and success was measured by the income it produced.

*

David Burgess had been on the TDU academic staff for almost eighteen years now. He had arrived at the University at about the same time as James Schofield and they had become friends during their first few weeks when both were finding their feet in a new environment. David had joined TDU straight from Durham University where, after a first degree in engineering, he had been engaged on a doctoral research programme into boundary layer flows. Though boundary layers were an integral part of TDU's research remit, particularly in relation to the aerodynamic performance of bullets, shells and other missiles, his knowledge of compressible air flow had led him, soon after his arrival, to take an interest in the subject of the blast loading of structures produced by the detonation of high explosive charges. His Durham undergraduate degree in Engineering Science had provided him with good basic knowledge of structural analysis which had enabled him to develop a level of expertise in the interaction of blast waves with structures. Now, about to start what would be his seventeenth full academic year at TDU, he had gained a respected international reputation in the area of blast loading, structural response and design.

David was a little older than James Schofield, somewhat taller and slimmer. His thick head of fair hair had, on numerous occasions, drawn comment from James about his appearance being rather akin to that of a slightly unkempt and ill-dressed window display dummy – likening David to the character in the 'Man at C&A' television ads of the 1980s was the commonest joke. David bore these remarks with good humour – he was usually able to respond with a suitable rejoinder to such banter. Like James Schofield, he was of a generally easy-going disposition, only inclined to anger when faced by some bureaucratic stupidity where a situation could have been quickly resolved by the application a modicum of common sense and not got bogged down by the apparent need to engage in a set of cumbersome procedural requirements.

David glanced at his watch.

'A few more e-mails to deal with and then coffee,' he thought.

There was a knock at the door followed immediately by it opening.

'Hello, David – good holiday?' asked the figure in the doorway.

'Yes, fine thanks, Alex. How about you?' said David.

'Much too short, I'm afraid,' replied Alex Simmonds. 'I could easily have spent another couple of weeks doing nothing.'

Alex Simmonds was, like David Burgess, James Schofield and Stephen Wright, a senior lecturer in the Civil and Military Engineering Department, one of the smaller units in the Military Technology School with a complement of eight academics headed by Professor Frank Hargreaves, one of the country's leading experts in the field of soil dynamics. George Hambidge, a surveyor, was the one other senior lecturer in the Department. Michael Carswell, in the grade of lecturer, was the seventh academic. A new member of staff, Chris Wells, had recently been appointed as a lecturer and was expected on campus that day.

'Ready for coffee?' asked Alex.

'I certainly am!' replied David as he rose from his chair and moved towards the door as Alex retreated into the corridor.

The two walked past a couple of closed office doors – colleagues still unable to take the plunge back into the reality of a new academic year and thus still holidaying – down a couple of flights of stairs and out into the open. The Common Room was in the TDU Headquarters building, an adjacent block about two minutes stroll away. This was an arrangement that was fine on a dry day but occasioned some discomfort on a winter morning with a wind-driven rain blowing across the nearby TDU sports fields.

As they walked David and Alex, slightly built and a bit younger than both David and James, exchanged a few pleasantries about their respective vacations. Alex had just returned from delivering a paper on his specialist area of vehicle ride mechanics to a conference in Switzerland and was enthusing about the scenery in the vicinity of Interlaken where the gathering was held.

'A beautiful setting for a conference – whenever the going got a little dull, you could always look out of the conference hall windows and admire the mountains,' said Alex. 'The family enjoyed the trip, too – we found an excellent camp-site about ten minutes drive away from the Rathaus – they dropped me off from the camper van at the start of each day and spent their time doing touristy things. They visited an open air museum, a cheese factory at Emmenthal, went for a sail on the lakes – you know the sort of thing.'

Alex was well-known in the University for his skill in choosing attractive conference venues both in Europe and the wider world to deliver a paper just sufficiently different from his previous contributions to merit its inclusion in the published proceedings. More often than not he was able to take his wife, Meriel, and their two young sons, Philip and Paul, skilfully offsetting their costs with the fairly generous subsistence allowances that such 'detached duty' was afforded to the travelling academic. Return journeys in the family camper van from European venues were invariable characterised by the purchase, in France, of substantial amounts of decent cooperative wine *en vrac* which was transported in the van's water carriers. The amount varied but was usually significant – it might even have been deemed a little excessive for a single family's consumption. Alex's standard joke was that if his cache was the subject of customs enquiry he would claim that, somewhere on the road, a miracle had occurred involving the van's water supply.

By now they had reached the Common Room, a large and well-proportioned room that was part of the building usually known as 'HQ' which housed the administration centre of the University. They both bought coffee and went over to the area of the room that the academics from the Civil and Military Engineering Department habitually occupied. This insularity extended campus-wide. Only very rarely did mathematicians socialise with electronic engineers, or physicists with chemists. The computer scientists seemed very reluctant to engage even their own kind in conversation. Each group seemed to preserve its own jealously guarded territory, though there were exceptions on occasion when an academic would edge into an alien group, usually to discuss a matter of business. Although there was a considerable amount of interdisciplinary project work undertaken University-wide, such fraternisation seemed limited to technical matters, despite exhortations from a long line of Common Room chairmen to reverse the trend.

Most of the Department members were already seated in their customary positions in what was known as the 'Civils Corner'. James Schofield, who was well into what was undoubtedly his second cup of coffee, was chatting animatedly with Michael Carswell. The talk was clearly of a technical nature. Michael Carswell was known to be a very able mathematical modeller in the field of structures and stress analysis who, once involved in a particular problem, was unable to give his attention to much else until the essence of a solution had been formulated. He'd been awarded a sizeable contract earlier in the year and was keen to refine the methods he'd been deploying to meet the requirements of the project. This involved the modelling of a complex structure subject to some even more complex forms of dynamic loading. James' opinion about adjustments to the idealisation of the structure that Michael was using was being sought and the talk was all of bending stresses, shear forces and strain energies of distortion.

Alex sat next to Michael Carswell while David found a vacant seat by George Hambidge who was idly leafing through a back number of the Times Higher Education Supplement. George put the paper down and greeted David.

'Have you seen the list of new undergraduates?' he asked.

George was not given to small talk, so there was no enquiring about David's vacation activities. George himself had probably spent most of the holiday period on some Scottish links with his wife Mary, also a keen golfer. He was little concerned with the social activities of his colleagues. Indeed, apart for his enthusiasm for golf – George was President of the University Golf Union – his fellow academics knew little of his life outside the University. He was a competent surveyor who had been responsible for a number of innovations in the use of remote sensing techniques in military survey. Indeed he had recently published a book on just that subject.

Without waiting for David to reply, George began to vent his frustration.

'Only ten! Ten! I can't think what the Department is coming to. We'll have to give serious thought as to whether we can continue with the degree if we continue to get only ten or so intake each year. Last year it was just twelve and one of them failed his Part One exams last summer. I'd hoped for at least fifteen, if not more – the admission panel offered over twenty places in the hope of getting a decent number. Some withdrew – one's gone to Bristol, another to Exeter and another has decided to have another year off before starting at any university. Three had such awful A-levels that they'll be lucky to get in anywhere – we certainly couldn't take them. So we're down to ten – not a happy start to the year. Even the Applied Technology degree's got a dozen and a half – most from clearing, it's true, and semi-literate to boot, but at least they've got them! And, of course, the new level of fees isn't helping to increase our civilian student numbers. It's all well and good the government saying that there'll be no 'up-front' payments, but the prospect of saddling yourself with tens of thousands of debt isn't to be taken lightly.'

David smiled to himself. It was usually the same story from George at this time every year: George's hopes for a huge intake were generally unrealistic and unrealised. Ten was really not too bad a number – at least an even number of undergraduates made the creation of pairs for laboratory work a simple task.

'Never mind, George,' said David. 'Ten is not too bad. It was down as low as eight three years ago and seven before that. What is it the government says about unemployment figures when the number goes up in a month? They look at the previous five or six years and proclaim that 'the trend is still down'. In our case the trend is definitely on the up! We ought to feel quite pleased about it, really. You've forgotten to mention that we've also got six entrants onto the Master's course – we've even got a Brit this time! That is good news –

though I know you don't have much to do with the course, they will bring in quite a bit of money to the Department.'

The situation with undergraduates was not good but, as David had indicated, it could have been worse. The number of Master's students was encouraging: the Master of Science degree in Protective Structure Analysis and Design - David had been a key figure in its development and was the Academic Coordinator for what was a very specialised course - had been running for ten years now with about four or five participants each year and had built up a good reputation both in the UK defence community and internationally. To have an intake of six this time was very pleasing. George merely grunted and sipped his coffee.

David became aware of a figure standing by his chair. He looked up and saw the tall figure of Professor Frank Hargreaves with a person that David did not immediately recognise.

'Gentlemen,' said Hargreaves, getting the attention of the group of academics before continuing. 'May I introduce Chris Wells – he's joining us as of today.'

George Hambidge rose and shook the newcomer's hand.

'Hello again, Chris. I was on your interview board last June,' he said.

Chris Wells smiled. The newcomer was a man about twenty-five or twenty-six years old, of medium height and build. He was dark-haired with a rather serious-looking face, with an aquiline nose on which a pair of metal-framed spectacles sat. His rather studious appearance was reinforced by a thoughtful manner of speaking though, from what he said, he seemed nevertheless to be in possession of a gentle sense of humour.

'I'm afraid I can't recall much of what happened that day. I remember Professor Hargreaves was Chairman of the panel and that there was a physicist who asked me very complicated questions about inter-atomic forces in amorphous materials which completely floored me, I'm afraid. I honestly can't remember anyone else!'

'Never mind,' said George. 'Despite old Arnold's questions – Dr Arnold Price was your tormentor – you did pretty well overall.'

'I didn't think so at the time,' replied Chris. 'I was sure I'd made a complete mess of the board.'

At his side Hargreaves smiled.

'This is James Schofield, our structures man,' said Hargreaves. 'I'm hoping that, once you've settled in you'll be able to collaborate with James on a new contract we've just been awarded from United Aerospace Industries that will need a good bit of input from both a structural analyst and someone who knows about new materials.'

James rose and greeted Chris with a friendly smile and a firm handshake.

'Don't frighten him off, Prof, before he's even got himself sorted out. I'm sure that between us we'll be able to do something useful on the contract. It'll be good to have someone with a new area of expertise in the Department. I understand that you've been working with some pretty advanced material modelling techniques. They could be useful on this project.'

Before Chris had time to reply, Hargreaves gently manoeuvred Chris away from the rest of the group.

'While he's here, just come and say hello to the Provost – then you'll be in the clear! He doesn't come down to coffee very frequently, so it would be as well to take the opportunity to meet him now.'

Hargreaves approached the Provost of TDU, Professor James Nightingale, and effected the necessary introductions. Nightingale was the University's second Provost, having taken over from the first, Prof George Nicholson, on his well-earned retirement some fifteen years ago.

'Very pleased to meet you, Dr Wells,' said James Nightingale. 'I know Professor Hargreaves was very pleased that you agreed to join his department. You'll find your colleagues a very pleasant bunch – I'm sure you'll enjoy working here.'

'I'm looking forward to it,' replied Chris. 'The University..........'

Chris stopped. The Provost had turned away from him and was now engaged in deep discussion with a rather portly middle-aged man. Chris's conversation with the Provost was over.

'The Chief Finance Officer,' said Hargreaves into Wells' ear as they moved back to the Departmental group.

'The Provost comes down so rarely,' continued Hargreaves,' that he's very much in demand when he does put in an appearance – though I'd have thought that Carter – that's the Finance man – would have had ample opportunity to speak with him almost any time – their offices are almost adjacent upstairs!'

'No matter,' said Chris. 'I quite understand.'

They were now back with the Civil and Military Department academics who had been joined by Dr Stephen Wright who, as well as sharing a number of academic interests with both James Schofield and David Burgess, sometimes drank his coffee with the Department of Explosive Ordnance Group. Hargreaves introduced Chris to Stephen and the members of the group whom he hadn't met.

'David?' said Hargreaves. 'Would you take Chris and show him the office he'll be in and help him to get hold of any stationery, library users card, computer account and anything else he needs, please?'

Turning to Chris, he continued, 'Then ask David to bring you along to me and we'll talk about the lecture course we'd like you to take over. It's not due to start until the second half of the term so there'll be time to prepare.'

'Yes, of course, Prof,' said David. 'I just want a quick word with Stephen.'

Hargreaves went over to get a second cup of coffee and, when he returned, found David in conversation with Stephen Wright.

'I saw the final report on your armour system listed in Library Acquisitions,' said David. 'You must be pleased to have got that out of the way.'

'Well, it had to be done and there was quite an incentive to complete it because of the interest the work generated,' said Stephen.

'That's what I wanted to ask you about,' continued David. 'How are negotiations to licence the design going? I'd heard that most, if not all, of your sponsors were keen to bid. It must be nice to feel that your work is in demand.'

James Schofield, who was sitting next to Stephen, joined in the conversation.

'Was it four companies interested?' asked James.

'Yes, that's right,' said Stephen. 'There's an Italian, an American, a Brazilian and an Australian firm and all were represented on the advisory panel. During the summer they all put in their bids and there's been a lot of to-ing and fro-ing about money and timings. Anyway, a decision about who's actually going to get the licence has been made. Just a few details to clarify.'

Stephen paused.

'Don't ask me who's going to get it – you'll hear soon enough!' he continued with a smile.

'OK, I won't press you,' said James, 'but I'll be interested to know.'

'I think I have a good idea – I've heard one or two things on the grapevine,' interjected Frank Hargreaves.

'Well, if you do think you know, I'd be grateful if you could keep mum for a little while longer, please, Prof. It's all a question of preserving commercial confidentiality until everything is signed and sealed,' said Stephen. 'Keep whatever you think you know under your hat!'

'Don't worry, Stephen, my lips are sealed,' replied Hargreaves with a smile. 'In any case, I might be completely wrong!'

'Well, whoever gets the contract, make sure you let us know so, you can buy us all a drink to celebrate!' added David with a grin as he rose to take Chris to the block where all the Civil and Military engineers had their offices.

'When is this famous contract due to be signed?' asked James with a smile.

'All being well, in about a fortnight's time – maybe a little less,' replied Stephen.

'Come on then, Chris,' said David. 'Let's see if we can get you fixed up.'

The two left the Common Room and walked back to the Department.

2

Friday 9th September am
The Friday following Chris Wells' arrival was the last before the official start of the Michaelmas Term. Staff in the Civil and Military Engineering Department had spent the week in preparations for the arrival of a decent number of both new undergraduates and master's course students. Although only ten were coming to read Civil and Military Engineering or 'C and M', as the Department's specialist undergraduate degree was known, there were in excess of a hundred new undergraduate arrivals who would join the two hundred or so students who were in their second and third years to make an undergraduate body of getting on for over three hundred. They were coming to read subjects as diverse as Aerospace Technology, Applied Military Science and the obscurely named Information Technology in Command and Control degree, the newly-devised and impressively-sponsored course administered by the Computing Technology Department. In all, the University offered six first degrees with greater or less 'defence' bias.

Perhaps even more important, particularly in the context of the University's revenue stream, were those students enrolling on a range of defence-oriented Master's degrees - year-long courses that involved both taught modules and an element of research - that would lead the successful candidate to the award of a Master of Science degree. There were upward of 140 post-graduate students embarking on Master's degrees. About 60 were starting the MoD-sponsored Battlefield Engineering and Technology course while others were enrolling on courses in Explosive Ordnance Technology, Dynamic Loading of Munitions Systems, Electronic Guided Systems Engineering, as well as the Civil and Mechanical Engineering Department's Protective Structure Analysis and Design Course.

Master's course fees were much greater than those associated with the undergraduate programmes – by as much as a factor of five or so – and the University spent a lot of time and effort in attempting to recruit students to these courses both nationally and internationally. Students from Australia, Canada, Germany, Sweden, Chile and Singapore as well as from the United Kingdom were among the nationalities due to register this September.

In addition to the undergraduates and masters students, there were about 20 or so other students embarking on pure research degrees – typically three years of work that would lead to the award of a doctorate. The University prized such students, not only for the fees they brought, but also for the prestige and standing their sometimes impressive work – which complemented the efforts of the academic staff – conferred on the University. The world of defence-related research was pleasantly surprised by the University's output: though small, The Defence University of Technology and Management often punched above its weight.

The new, and predominantly male, undergraduates were scheduled to register at the University's second largest lecture theatre – the Butler – by eleven o'clock on Friday morning. After a short welcome address from the Provost, they were to be taken by volunteers from the second year student body to their rooms in one of the several halls of residence and thence for a short meeting with the academic staff member designated as the student's 'Adviser' for the duration of the degree course. The afternoon was devoted to a 'Fresher's Fair' where University sports clubs and other societies tried to tempt the new cohort with various escapes from study. With only ten new C and M students, each member of the Department's staff, with the exception of Frank Hargreaves, expected to be allocated a couple of the new arrivals. There was general amusement among the Departmental staff that Hargreaves had opted not to take under his wing the two new female undergraduates due to register that morning, as he had done on previous occasions when women had elected to enrol on the C and M degree. The opinion was that perhaps Hargreaves was keeping his chores to a minimum so that he could devote all his energies to his bid to take over the Provost's post when Nightingale moved on up the academic ladder the following spring to become head of the government's newly-formed University Finance Committee. In the event, each of the five senior lecturers in the Department had two of the new intake to look after, meaning that each academic had about five or six advisees spread over the three years of the undergraduate degree.

In the case of the new Master's students, they too were provided with an Adviser for the duration of the course – usually drawn from those academic staff with greatest responsibility for delivering the taught modules and supervising research projects. David Burgess, in his capacity as Academic Coordinator of the MSc in Protective Structures, allocated students to C & M staff. Of the six in the new cohort, he would take on two – he'd picked the two Australians - while James Schofield, Alex Simmonds, Chris Wells and Michael Carswell would each have one of the other four.

With a number of students coming from overseas and who sometimes only arrived on campus on this first day, it had always been the practice to start the induction process after lunch. Therefore, a welcome address by the Provost was scheduled for 2.00pm in the newly-refurbished Wavell Lecture Theatre – the largest on campus - that could easily hold the 160 or so new post-graduate students. Registration was scheduled to take place afterwards in the Theatre's large entrance foyer. At about 3.15pm, when formalities had been completed, Burgess planned to collect the six new Protective Structures students and take them to meet with their respective advisers over a cup of tea in one of the small lecture rooms that would be used for the taught components of the course. There he hoped that any initial problems relating to the course - or indeed any other pressing matters - could be addressed in an informal and friendly manner so that the students would feel comfortable and welcomed in their new situation.

The separation of undergraduate and post-graduate students at this early stage in their respective University careers with registration at different times and places, tended to persist throughout the academic year. Generally, the only limited point of contact was in the University sports teams, though they tended to be dominated by the undergraduate students who formed the largest body on the campus. Age difference was a significant factor. Masters' students tended to be well into their service careers, most likely in their late twenties or early thirties and were often married with families and sometimes living in accommodation off the campus. They had a somewhat different outlook on life to the younger, more 'carefree' undergraduates: the two groups tended to keep apart. However, despite their differences, relationships between the two groups were generally good, it was just that they had little reason, desire or indeed opportunity to mingle.

The morning had gone well. The ten new C and M students – eight young men and two young women, all of whom were either junior officers or officer cadets – had been duly registered and introduced to their academic advisers. David had enjoyed a friendly chat with his two new students – a couple of officer cadets, both of whom hoped to join the Corps of Royal Engineers after graduation - and sent them off to lunch in good time with encouragement to see what the Freshers' Fair had to offer. He had no doubt that they would take full advantage of the many clubs and societies being advertised – 'extra-mural' activities were an important part of any army officer's CV and officer cadets were always keen to get involved – sometimes more than was advisable and to the detriment of academic work, or so David sometimes thought. With a free weekend ahead, David knew that the new undergraduates would lose no time in orientating themselves to their new environment and more than likely having a good time.

*

Friday 9th September pm

It was just before two o'clock and David was standing in the entrance foyer of the Wavell Lecture Theatre beneath a prominent sign with the words 'MSc PROTECTIVE STRUCTURES' attached near the top of the notice-board behind him. On his jacket lapel he had pinned a name-tag with the words 'Dr David Burgess Academic Coordinator MSc Protective Structures Analysis and Design' printed on the card it held. On the array of notice-boards in the foyer were similar signs with the names of the other master's courses and beneath them the respective Academic Coordinators. Uniformed students milled around, seeking out the Coordinator for their particular course of study. There were many different uniforms from all parts of the world on view – a lot of khaki of various shades, a fair sprinkling of air force blue and a few naval uniforms. David had already met five of the six new Protective Structures students and had told them that, after the Provost's welcome and a briefing from TDU's head of security - a retired Logistics Corps major - they would find that the foyer had been set up with a number of tables where Academic Registry staff would complete the registration process and issue each student with a 'Welcoming Pack'. This contained both information specific to the course they were about to embark on and of a more general nature about TDU and the local area. David had told them that, when they'd completed the process they should seek him out again – he said he'd be standing under the notice – and he'd take them to meet with some of the staff with whom they would be working in the coming year.

David glanced at his watch – ten minutes to two – and was wondering what had become of the sixth and final student. The lobby had almost emptied of students now as two o'clock approached. He felt a tap on his shoulder.

'Dr Burgess? Sorry I'm a bit late – I misjudged the traffic – I'm Major Miles Cowley. I'm here for the Protective Structures MSc.'

David turned to face the voice and his eyes were met by the steady gaze of the speaker, whose shoulder tabs indicated he was a Royal Engineer.

'Good, glad you made it Miles,' said David shaking the proffered hand.

Recalling his last visit to the Royal School of Military Engineering at Chatham in Kent, the main centre for education and training for the Corps of Royal Engineers, David added, 'I think we met when I was down in Chatham a few months ago to discuss whether the Corps would be sending anyone on the MSc this year. I think you hosted me at lunch.'

'Yes, that's right,' replied Cowley. 'I was keen to get on the course and I think your visit added weight to my argument that I should come and do it.'

As he was saying this the Provost entered, briefly stopping to have a word with Susan Thornley, the Academic Registrar, who was standing in the centre of the foyer with a number of her staff, preparing to set up the tables for registration after Nightingale's address.

'OK – we can talk later,' said David. 'But now you need to go into the lecture theatre for the Provost's welcome. You've just got time to go in and find a seat.'

Miles nodded, turned away from David and went into the lecture theatre. David, for his part, rather than listening to the Provost's welcome which he'd heard a number of times before and the security briefing which, though he acknowledged the need for it, he always found rather dull, decided to return to his office to pick up various pieces of detailed information about the MSc. He planned to give this material to the students to augment the items that the Registry staff had issued earlier after the Provost's talk. David reckoned he had about a half an hour or so before he needed to be back at his post under the MSc notice.

David's return to the Wavell foyer just before 2.40 coincided with the end of the briefings and students were already entering the lobby. They sought out one of the eight tables that had been set up to allow the Registry to complete the necessary formalities. A prominently-displayed card printed with a pair of letters - 'A – D', 'E – H' etc – was held on a small board mounted on a support at about eye-level behind each table. The Academic Registrar was known for her efficiency and, by checking the nominal roll, had prepared the letter cards to ensure that about the same number of students - in this case about twenty - would use each desk. The registration process took only about two or three minutes, sometimes less, so there wouldn't be any prolonged waiting and the process would be completed in about 30 minutes or so.

David positioned himself beneath the MSc PROTECTIVE STRUCTURES notice and waited for the first of the new cohort to join him. It wasn't too long before FLTLT Grant Thompson of the Royal Australian Air Force strolled over to him carrying a blue plastic wallet containing what David hoped was useful information. Others soon joined him by the notice and, while the growing group waited for all to have registered, the students chatted with each other and with David as introductions were made along with a general exchange of pleasantries. To David's relief, all six of the new cohort were ready to leave after only about twenty minutes following the end of the briefings.

David raised his voice a little to be heard over the surrounding hubbub.

'OK, gentlemen, I think it's time we made a move. We're going to the lecture room which will be a more or less permanent course room for you where there should be some tea and biscuits as well as a number of my colleagues for you to meet, so follow me.'

On the walk over to the lecture room, David pointed out a few of the features of the campus such as the recently-refurbished library, the well-equipped gymnasium and the computer centre which housed an impressive array of high specification desk-top personal computers.

The group arrived at the door of the lecture room in the Horrocks Building just as the caterers were finishing laying out items for tea. James Schofield and Alex Simmonds were already in the room, sitting near the back and chatting in low voices. Shortly after David and his party had entered, Chris Wells arrived accompanied by Michael Carswell. David was glad to see these four who, together with himself, were to be the academic advisers to the 6 students.

'OK, help yourself to a drink – there's coffee and tea – though both will likely taste the same – and biscuits for those who didn't get lunch. I guess that might be you, Miles,' said David. 'Then take a seat.'

As he was saying this the lecture room door opened and three more people entered. The first was Dr Stephen Wright who was to present one of the earlier modules concerned with the principles of various types of armour systems. He was accompanied by Dr Gill Neville, his former research student who had been recently appointed as a Teaching Associate and who would be contributing to Wright's module. The third member of the trio was Dr Kevin Varney who was the leader of the first module to be taken by the cohort and which was concerned with the chemistry of explosives. Unlike Stephen Wright and Gill Neville, Kevin

Varney was from the Department of Explosive Ordnance which was responsible for the MSc in Explosive Ordnance Technology. The six Protective Structures students would be joining with Explosive Ordnance students for the first of the ten modules that comprised the taught component of the MSc.

David put down the cup he was holding and, standing at the front of the lecture room, began to speak.

'Firstly, let me give you two or three more pieces of paper to add to the stuff in your blue 'Welcome' folders. There's information about the drinks party tonight, a list of contact details for those of us who'll be teaching you this year and a block timetable for the entire course giving important dates in the calendar – like exams!'

At the mention of this last words, and almost as if on cue, the six students gave an involuntary groan. David smiled.

'You'll have something similar already in your 'Welcome' folder, 'he continued. 'However, this sheet is specific to your course alone.'

He paused while he passed out the sheets to the six students and started speaking again.

'Right - at last you're with the people you'll be working closely with for the duration of the course. I know it's been said to you already by the Provost, but this time on behalf of the staff of the Civil and Military Engineering Department – Welcoming! As you know, I'm David Burgess and I'm the Academic Coordinator of the whole degree course, so I guess I'm the person you come and talk to about any problems you may have – preferably of an academic nature,' he added with a smile that produced a ripple of amusement among the students sitting at the tables in front of him.

'I'm also responsible for a couple of the taught modules you'll be tackling later on Blast Loading Assessment and the Response of Protective Structures to Blast,' David continued. 'If the recent past is anything to go by, I'll also be supervising at least one of you when you embark on your research projects later in the year. Before hearing from you, I'll just ask my colleagues to introduce themselves briefly so that you'll know who they are and where you'll meet them in connection with the course.'

David sat down on the table at the front of the lecture room while James, Alex, Chris, Michael, Stephen, Gill and Kevin said a few words about who they were and what involvement they had with the MSc.

Kevin Varney was the last to speak.

'I'll be seeing you all first thing on Monday morning,' he began. 'Your timetable should show that the 'Introduction to explosive ordnance' module kicks off in Lecture Room 10 in the Horrocks Building – that's the building we're in now – where you'll meet the ten new students on the MSc in Explosive Ordnance Technology – we usually just call it the EOT MSc. There'll also be about seven or eight other participants taking the module as a stand-alone short course. We start at ten to ten to give the short course lot a chance to get here – some will be coming up from MoD in London and there are a couple from Abbeywood in Bristol. We also have three participants from overseas. They are due to arrive over the weekend and will be staying in a hotel in the village.'

Kevin sat down and David spoke again, addressing the students directly.

'Right – let's hear a bit about each of you, please. No need to go into great detail – just your name, where you're from, a bit on your academic background and what you've been doing recently, just so we get an idea about who you are. Let's do it in alphabetical order – so that means, Miles, you start.'

Maj Miles Cowley, seated at the front of the room, stood and turned to face the others seated beside and behind him. Cowley was of medium height – about five feet ten – and with a carriage that suggested that he kept himself in shape. He had short-cropped fair hair and strong features that suggested the high degree of self-confidence generally displayed by British Army officers.

'Hello – I'm Miles Cowley,' he began. 'I'm a Sapper Major with a civil engineering degree from Southampton University. I was sponsored by the Royal Engineers during the degree and in the seven years since I graduated I've had a number of postings, the most recent being at the Royal School of Military Engineering at Chatham where I've been for the last six months. Before that I did a six month tour in

Afghanistan based at Camp Bastion. I'm hoping this course will enable me to understand more about how to design and construct effective protective structures for the guys in theatre because there seemed to be a distinct lack of technical knowhow about this when I was in Helmand.'

'Thanks for that, Miles,' said David. 'Graham Dowell next, I think.'

'Hi, all – I'm Flight Lieutenant Graham Dowell, Royal Australian Air Force.' said Dowell who was a man in his late thirties, and very solidly built. He looked as if he might have been something of a rugby-player – probably Union rather than League and a forward to judge by his rather bent nose and ears that bore evidence of having seen action in innumerable scrums over the years.

'Before I came here I was a technical liaison officer with the Oz government's Defence Science and Technology Organisation - DSTO - in Salisbury, South Australia. I started in the RAAF with just school leaving certificates as an aircraftsman. I did a series of part-time courses with the Royal Melbourne Institute of Technology in general engineering to amass credits and eventually got a BEng. Then I took a few specialist courses in military construction techniques through the Australian Defence Force Academy – ADFA – in Canberra. I must have done something right because I was commissioned at about that time - the late nineties - and began a series of technical jobs at various bases in Oz as well as a tour in Iraq after Saddam had gone. I was part of the team looking at damage to the Iraqi military and civilian infrastructure.'

Dowell paused and smiled before continuing.

'Looking around, I think I might be just bit older than the rest of you – it took me a bit longer to get where I am now!'

From near the back of the room a French-accented voice was heard. The speaker was dressed in khaki fatigues. He was of medium height and build with short brown hair, a long, rather serious-looking face with a pair of piercing blue eyes.

'Good afternoon everyone. I'm Major Philippe Giraud from the Royal Canadian Engineers. I did my civil engineering degree at the Royal Military College in Kingston, Ontario - I finished it about six years ago – and since then I've done a variety of jobs, the most recent at Suffield – that's our testing facility in Alberta - assisting with large-scale explosive tests on protective systems. That's why I'm here really – my goal is to learn about the principles of protective structure design and how to ensure that these systems work properly.'

'Thanks, Philippe, I'm sure the course will be useful to you,' commented David.

'OK – Capt Leng?'

Capt Leng Ng Chong from the Singapore Defence Force stood up and turned to face the assembly. Leng, also dressed in khaki fatigues, looked to be in his late twenties and had an open, friendly face topped by dark hair cut short.

'Hello, everyone. Please call me Alfred – you'll never manage to say 'Ng Chong'!' began Alfred with a smile. 'I did my civil engineering degree at Nanyang Technological University, finishing in 2008 and for the last four years or so I've been working with MinDef – our Ministry of Defence – liaising with their Land and Real Estate Organisation which is responsible for military structures in Singapore. I've done work on airbases and naval facilities as well as army installations, looking at hardened structures mostly. Some of my colleagues have been here at TDU in the past doing either this course or the EOT MSc. I applied to come because I think it would be useful for me to have a better understanding of the principles about how to analyse and design protective structures, rather than just applying rules from a design manual.'

David smiled when he heard the last comment because he had always felt the same about the 'recipes' that were used to design protective structures: their blind application without a knowledge of the underlying engineering principles seemed a dangerous approach to adopt when designing a structure that was expected to protect personnel from potential harm.

'OK, Alfred, thanks. We enjoyed having your colleague Teo Lim Chee on the course last year and Leonard Wang was, I think on the EOT MSc last year.'

Kevin Varney nodded at the mention of the second name.

'Right – Grant, let's hear a bit about you,' continued David.

The second student in the uniform of the Royal Australian Air Force stood up and faced the room. He was fair-haired, of medium height, slightly built with a rather wiry frame. His face was weathered, making him look as if he'd spent a lot of time in the Australian sun.

'Hi, everyone! I'm Flight Lieutenant Grant Thompson and, like Graham, I'm RAAF. I did my civil engineering degree at ADFA in Canberra and have done a number of construction project jobs both in Oz and, most recently, in Afghanistan where I was based in Kabul working on training facilities for the Afghan Army. I'm on the course to help increase the knowledge-base on protective design within the Australian Air Force, rather like Graham, I guess.'

Graham Dowell nodded as Grant finished speaking.

'And lastly, Major Schmidt from the German Armed Forces,' said David. 'Tell us a bit about yourself, Karl-Heinz.'

The final member of the new cohort stood up and turned to face the rest of the group. He was a little over six feet tall, of slim but powerful build – he looked very fit. He was clean shaven with short dark hair and was dressed in the uniform of the German military. He started to speak in what was only slightly-accented English.

'Good afternoon, gentlemen – my name is Karl-Heinz Schmidt and I'm a major in the German Army. I have a civil engineering degree from the German University of the Armed Forces in Stuttgart. After I graduated I did two or three years with various construction units based in Germany but, for the past three years, I've been based in Bonn working for what we call the Infrastructure Group which is concerned with the design and testing of military structures. I've been responsible for organising a number of trials of new designs at our test facilities and I thought it would be a good move to come and learn more about the analytical techniques behind the development of protective structures.'

'Well, thanks, all of you,' said David as Karl-Heinz sat down. 'That's been very useful for me and my colleagues and, I hope, for the six of you as well. Has anybody got any questions about the course or anything else you're not quite sure about?'

There was no reaction from the six students, so, after a pause, David continued speaking.

'I'm sure you'll get to grips with things pretty easily – if you do have any problems then give me a call – my number is 2340 - or drop me an e-mail – my address is on the campus intranet - or come and see me. My office is in this building – Room 2-13. The 'two' means it's on the second floor.'

'I do have one question,' said Grant Thompson. 'The drinks party this evening - is that just for students or are partners invited as well? The sheet with the location and timing doesn't say.'

'It's for both students and partners – the mess should have made that clear on sheet, sorry about that. How many of you are here with your wives and family?' asked David.

The two Australians both indicated they had their wives with them and, in the case of Graham Dowell, two school-age children as well. Philippe Giraud and Karl-Heinz Schmidt said their wives were back home in Canada and Germany respectively but both expected they would be spending some time at TDU during the year. Alfred Ng and Miles Cowley were both single, though Alfred said he hoped his girlfriend would be able to come over in the spring for a couple of weeks or so.

'I'll be coming to the party with my wife,' said David, 'and I think that Dr Schofield – James – will be coming too, so we'll see you there at about seven. It's due to last about an hour or so and it will give you a chance to meet some of the students on the other courses. Make sure you're wearing your name-tags. I think that's about it, really, except to remind you that the teaching programme kicks off on Monday with Kevin and his colleagues at ten to ten in Lecture Room 10 in this building. Kevin will, I am sure, provide a detailed timetable and information about assignments and exams and plenty of notes.'

Kevin nodded as David finished speaking.

'OK – let's call a halt now, though you might like to have another fix of tea and maybe another biscuit – if they're not eaten, they'll only be chucked out! I've got a few things to do before I go and pick up my wife, so I'll leave you to it now. See you later.'

David got up from his chair and, together with James Schofield who also indicated that he had to leave, left the students and the remaining staff members to finish tea and continue chatting.

3

Friday 9th September evening

It was getting on for six-fifteen when David eventually walked from his office to his car parked on what was once the RATA parade ground where, for many years, early morning drill had been practiced often with somewhat unwilling participants. David's journey home was quick – the market town of Farlington where David lived with his wife Anna was only about four miles from TDU – and he pulled into his driveway after a journey lasting only about ten minutes. Almost half of this time was taken up with the drive from the car park to the main gate of the sprawling campus, since he felt obliged not to exceed the 20mph site speed limit, mindful that the Ministry of Defence police might be playing with their newly-acquired 'speed gun'.

David opened the front door, dropped his briefcase by the telephone table in the hallway and called out to Anna.

'Hi – I'm home,' he called. 'Sorry to be a bit late but there was a late flurry of e-mails to deal with before I left.'

As he finished speaking Anna emerged from the kitchen, smiled and kissed him.

'I expected you'd be late,' she said. 'It's always the same when the MScs start up. Anyway, you're here now – time for a drink before we go out?'

David shook his head.

'No thanks. I think I ought to get ready. I need to put a suit on and a clean shirt. You look nice though – I guess you're already to go?'

Anna nodded. She was a woman in her early forties but looked younger. She was a good six inches shorter than David, of slim build with shoulder length brown hair. Though not perhaps beautiful she was nonetheless very attractive and David had been obliged to see off several competitors for her attention when they had first met at Durham University where she was reading mathematics. David was as besotted with her then as he was now. She'd never changed over the years and the raising of their two daughters – Rebecca and Charlotte – seemed to have left no mark on her. With both girls at university – Rebecca at Bath and Charlotte at Surrey – Anna had recently increased her hours working as a financial analyst for a marketing company based in a nearby town.

'Yes, I'm set. I'm just catching up with the newspaper before we go out.'

Anna had done an almost full day of work today and had left the house at about the same time as David, returning just before five o'clock.

David went upstairs to prepare for the Welcoming Party knowing that they'd need to leave before a quarter to seven to be there in the mess in good time to greet the students.

*

In the village of Leddington, a twenty or so minutes drive and about ten miles from TDU, James Schofield was also getting ready for the Welcoming Party. When he got into the house he found Laura sitting in the cosy kitchen of their cottage talking with Sam and Rachel about their day. Both children were at the local comprehensive school and both were doing well. Sam was showing a genuine talent for science and had done well in his GCSEs the previous summer. Rachel was young enough not to have had to make the choice between a more arts or science biased set of subjects as yet, though she seemed to have a talent for foreign languages; she was keen on French and had just started to study German.

James kissed Laura and was about to ask Sam and Rachel what homework they had to do that evening, when he was cut short by the almost simultaneous chiming of the cottage's four long-case clocks. The clocks were in the hallway, the sitting room, the study with the fourth in the dining room and all began indicating that it was six o'clock. James paused in what he was saying to listen to the sound. The clocks were his pride and joy and he'd personally restored them all to working order having acquired them cheaply from house-clearances and what Laura referred to as 'junk shops'.

'The one in the hall sounds a bit strange,' said James. 'The middle notes of the chime seem a bit 'off' – I must remember to have a look at the weekend – I noticed that it wasn't quite right a couple of days ago.

Sam and Rachel smiled. Their father was always tinkering with the clocks, and always being dissatisfied with the results of his work, even though they could rarely detect any change in the sound they made after his ministrations.

'No time for that now,' smiled Laura. 'It's time to get ready. You two need to get on with your homework, so go and make a start. From what you told me it shouldn't take you too long.'

This last comment was directed to Sam and Rachel who, with exaggerated sighs, got up from the kitchen table and went off to their bedrooms to tackle the work.

'We won't be late tonight,' Laura called out as they left the kitchen.

'At least I hope not,' she said in a quieter voice looking at James. 'These 'Welcome' dos can be a bit dull.'

'No, I don't think we need to stay late,' replied James. 'Just long enough to say hello to everyone and make sure that they feel 'Welcome'! I'll just go and put a clean shirt on.'

'I'll come up too and put on something different – working in the office for most of the day does make your clothes feel a bit grubby. I may have a quick shower,' said Laura.

'There's plenty of time. I don't think we need to be on the way until about a quarter to seven – it starts at seven but we don't need to be the first there,' commented James as both he and Laura went up the cottage stairs to their bedroom.

*

Dr Alex Simmonds stretched out his hand and picked up one of the three glasses of red wine that his wife, Meriel, had just poured. Meriel took the other two from the kitchen worktop and passed one of them to a woman sitting at the kitchen table.

'Here you are, Jill, there's the rest of the bottle, too, if you fancy it later. Why not come through to the living room and I'll remind you how to work the TV?' said Meriel.

Jill Bryant, Alex and Meriel's neighbour drafted in for babysitting duties for the evening, nodded, got up and followed Meriel out of the kitchen.

'The boys are playing some computer game up in Philip's bedroom,' said Meriel. 'I've told them that when it's finished they're to get ready for bed. They're normally pretty good about getting themselves sorted out, so you shouldn't have any problems. They can watch a bit of TV then, but it would be good to have them in bed by about 8.30 or so. We won't be very late – I hope we'll be back before ten.'

Jill nodded and sipped her wine. She'd done babysitting for Phil and Paul several times in the recent past and knew that they'd be no problem. She was rather looking forward to a quiet evening with a drink, some undemanding TV and a chat with the boys.

'OK,' said Alex, looking at Meriel. 'Drink up – I think it's time we were off. See you later, Jill.'

Five minutes later, dressed in warm coats to counter the chilly autumnal evening, Meriel and Alex set off on the fifteen minute walk from their house in Sherington village to one of pedestrian entrances to the campus.

'At least it means we can both have a glass of wine or two without having to worry about the drive home,' said Alex, as he took Meriel's hand. 'We're in good time – we should be at the mess by about ten past seven which is quite early enough.'

*

In the three-bedroomed married quarter on the TDU campus, Graham Dowell was busy getting into his suit – military students weren't required to wear uniform for the Welcoming Party – and quietly cursing as he did so. He didn't care for ties and he would soon have to put one on for the first time in many months. He'd tried to argue with Bronwen that he didn't need to wear one but she had insisted, telling him that he needed to 'play the game properly', at least for tonight.

'It's only for a couple of hours and you don't want to be the only bloke there not wearing the right gear. The invitation said 'lounge suit' and that means a collar and tie to go with it!' said Bronwen when he'd shown her the sheet with details of the party.

'It's still a bloody pain, though, Bron,' was Graham's reply. 'But, OK, just for tonight!'

'I've arranged for Carol to come in to keep an eye on the boys – she'll be here in about ten minutes,' said Bronwen, referring to the seventeen year old daughter of another of the new Australian students who was coming to watch over Rob and Chris, Graham and Bronwen's ten-year old twin boys.

Bronwen, a Tasmanian, had met Graham when she was working as an administrator at the Royal Melbourne Institute of Technology – RMIT - when Graham was doing his part-time engineering degree. They'd married about half-way through the period when Graham was building up his academic credits and, when he'd moved to a posting in Canberra and taken his commission, she'd moved with him. The twins had arrived in the first year of their time in Canberra and, though Graham had had various postings in the ten years since, they'd established a home there. Even though the city was not much loved by many Australians – they saw it as a place that gathered and then wasted the money they paid in taxes - it was a good place in which to raise a family. It was safe, had good schools and other amenities and offered a lot of sporting and cultural activities.

'Right, I'm ready when you are,' said Graham, as he managed to get his tie knotted and looking reasonably neat against his blue-striped shirt.

As he spoke he heard the doorbell ring. One of the boys ran to open it and there was a lot of excited chatter as Rob and Chris, who'd been joined by Bronwen, greeted Carol. Bronwen told Carol about the boys' bed times, where to find coffee making stuff and how to manage the TV zapper.

*

A few houses along the street, Grant Thompson, dressed in a smart pin-striped suit was ready for the Welcoming Party.

'Are you nearly ready, Jen?'

'Nearly done,' called a voice from upstairs.

A minute later Jen Thompson walked downstairs wearing a dress – a clinging knitted number in dark blue that hugged her slender figure - that she'd bought only that afternoon on a trip into Oxford with two of the other Australian wives.

Jen was in her late twenties, tall and blond and had been married to Grant for four years. She'd been happy to give up her work with an employment agency in one of Sydney's western suburbs and life in Australian army accommodation to spend a year in the UK, particularly as she knew one or two of the other wives accompanying their husbands on courses at TDU.

'You look great,' said Grant appreciatively, planting a kiss on her cheek. 'Time we were off.'

They both put on coats against the chill of the evening and set off for the short walk to the mess.

*

In the grand house on the edge of the campus, Professor James Nightingale slipped the notes he'd made for the short address he'd be giving at the Party – nothing too long or too formal – certainly not a repeat of the session earlier in the day. He really only needed to welcome wives and partners and hope they'd enjoy the 'TDU experience' as much as he hoped those preparing to study would. He buttoned up his overcoat, called to his wife Delia that he was ready to leave. Two minutes later they both left the house for the few minutes walk to the mess.

*

In his office in the Horrocks Building, Professor Frank Hargreaves logged off his computer and glanced at his watch. He'd told his wife that he wouldn't bother coming home and would go straight to the Welcoming Party and have something to eat when he got home. His wife, Elaine, was never very keen on TDU social events and he knew she'd not be sorry to miss the Party. He knew, however, that there'd be a good supper waiting for him when he eventually did get home.

*

A few doors along the corridor, George Hambidge was also closing down his computer. There was a knock at his door which opened immediately and his wife Mary walked in. He looked up and smiled.

'Hello! Everything OK?' he asked. 'Did you have a good day?'

Mary had just come from a day of golf with her friends, playing a new course that had only recently opened about fifteen miles from TDU.

'Yes, thanks. It's a decent eighteen holes and a nice clubhouse,' replied Mary with a smile. 'They did a good lunch, too! I've been home and changed so I'm ready to be welcoming!'

'Good,' said George. 'It's been a bit hectic here with the two new lots of students, and I could do without this party tonight.'

'You always say that,' said Mary. 'You'll enjoy it when you're there. Are you ready?'

*

Michael Carswell had finished his shower and was now dressed in a smart dark blue suit ready to drive the ten miles back to TDU for the Welcoming Party. Although he knew it was 'good form' to support his colleagues at these events, and it was useful to meet up with the new students with in a relaxed an informal atmosphere, he, like George Hambidge, could well have done without this evening. He would have liked to be putting the finishing touches to the conference paper he was writing – the deadline for submission was only a few days away and he still had to prepare some graphs for inclusion. His experience told him this would take longer than the writing of the text which was almost complete.

He also needed to do some more work on a grant application that had been returned to him by the Finance Office who had said they required some further details about proposed costings. He felt a little aggrieved about having to supply such fine detail, but knew that he'd have to flesh out some of the items in his budget if the application had any chance of success. It all took time which could be put to better use, he thought to himself.

Every time he'd been to a Welcoming Party, he'd come away feeling he'd rather not have attended. He couldn't really have much to drink because he'd have to drive home and the food on offer – what he called 'cocktail nibbles' - wasn't really any substitute for a proper supper. Normally he'd have enjoyed preparing a meal for himself in his neat kitchen in his cottage in Longstone, one of the several villages that surrounded TDU, but he knew he wouldn't feel much like making anything for himself after the party and was already planning a detour to pick up fish and chips from the chippie in Sherington on the way home after the party.

He checked that the kitchen door was locked and the cottage windows closed and with their security latches engaged – there'd been a spate of burglaries in the area these last few months - and went out to his car parked on the short driveway to the right of his front door. He glanced at his watch – ten to seven it said – and, as he started the car and set off for the drive to TDU, he knew that he'd be in good time for the Party.

*

Dr Chris Wells put on his dark green waxed jacket, glanced at his watch and estimated that, if he left now he should be in the mess by soon after seven. He wasn't quite sure what time was 'acceptable' for a member of staff to arrive but, as the new boy, he thought he'd better play it safe and be there pretty much on time.

He'd been lucky to find this first floor flat above the Sherington newsagents shop. It suited him well, being only a short walk from the nearest campus entrance, and he'd signed a rental agreement for twelve months. He thought that, if he liked the job at TDU and, more importantly, he passed his probation period, he'd then start to look to buy something in the area. After a couple of years working on short-term contracts after his PhD, it would be nice to think that he was on the threshold of a more permanent post.

The staircase from the flat took him to a door on the side of the building in a short passageway between the newsagents and the adjacent building. He emerged onto the village high street and almost collided with a couple walking hand in hand along the pavement. He was blurting out an apology when he recognised one of them as Alex Simmonds.

'Hello, Chris, no need to apologise, no harm done,' said Alex. 'Let me introduce you to my wife. Meriel, this is Chris Wells – he joined the Department last week.'

Meriel smiled at Chris as they shook hands and continued walking along the street.

'Nice to meet you, Chris. Alex has told me about you – I hope you're settling in to TDU life. You've come from Nottingham, I think Alex said?'

'Yes, that's right. I was on a one year contract in the Materials Department doing some work related to my PhD about the development of a new generation of ceramic materials.'

'So you might be doing some work with Stephen Wright, then?' asked Meriel. 'I think he uses ceramics and other stuff for his armour work. Is that right, Alex?'

'Yes, though I'm not sure what Stephen's current interests are. I think James Schofield is also looking for some help on the materials side of a new contract just starting,' replied Alex. 'I guess you could be in demand.'

The trio arrived at one of the three pedestrian entrances to TDU and, in turn, inserted their passes into the electronically-controlled turnstile gate.

'Good,' said Alex. 'It's about five minutes to the mess from here.'

*

Dr Gill Neville finished brushing her short dark hair, checked her make-up, picked up her coat and went out of the front door of the small house she rented in Farlington. David Burgess had suggested that he and Anna might give her a lift to the Welcoming Party but she'd declined, saying that she wasn't sure whether she'd even come home before going to the Party. In the event she had left TDU soon after five-thirty and, after doing a little shopping in the town's small supermarket, had gone back to her house on a small estate on the edge of the town to get ready. She'd thought that it would be good on this occasion at least to travel independently. That way she could choose her time of departure if things started to drag – she wasn't quite sure what to expect from what would to be her first Welcoming Party.

After three years as a research culminating in the award of her PhD last summer, she had been appointed as a Teaching Associate which would allow her to continue working with her PhD supervisor, Stephen Wright. It was Stephen who had encouraged her to come to the Party, saying it would be good for her to meet some of the students she would be teaching in the next few weeks. He had asked her to deliver a few lectures on her specialised armour research and take charge of some experimental work with the cohort. It would be her first lecturing work with the MSc students though she had done a little bit of laboratory 'demonstrating' during her PhD work and she was feeling a little nervous at the prospect. Perhaps meeting with the students in an informal setting would help allay some of her misgivings about her transition from student to lecturer.

She got into her car – an elderly but, so far, reliable Nissan Micra – and set off on the short drive back to TDU.

*

Dr Stephen Wright in his cottage in the village of Sixhampton, four miles from TDU, buttoned his overcoat and picked up his car keys from the small table in the hallway. He went into the living room where Giles Mitchell, his partner of many years, was sitting watching the evening news on the television in the corner of the room.

'OK – time to go. I don't expect to be too long. I'll try and leave by eight-thirty– I only need to be there for an hour at most,' he said to Giles. 'Are you going to wait for me to get back before you eat?'

'Of course,' replied Giles. 'It's no fun eating alone. I won't start to cook until about eight – I'm doing sea bream with new potatoes and beans with the remains of the apple pie we had yesterday for afters. It won't take long to cook, but let me know if you're going to be late.'

'Right – I'll make sure I'm back in good time. See you later,' said Stephen.

He got into his car parked behind Giles' on the driveway, started up and backed out onto the road. He glanced at the clock on the dashboard – 6.50PM it read. That's good, thought Stephen, about an hour and a half at the Party should be more than enough.

*

In a good number of the single officers' rooms in the mess, MSc students were getting into their civvy suits for the Party.

Karl-Heinz Schmidt finished the telephone call to his wife back in Bonn. Annaliese was used to him being away from home but she still didn't like it. Karl-Heinz had already arranged a flight back to Germany for a weekend at the end of the month.

Philippe Giraud pressed 'Send' on his laptop computer and his daily e-mail to his wife Monique in Edmonton was on its way.

Miles Cowley finished his call with the words, 'See you on Friday evening – not sure what time, but the last timetabled session ends at three so I'll get on the road then - but you know what the traffic's like on Friday!'

He was already looking forward to the weekend with Nicky.

Alfred Leng was ready for the Party. No point in e-mailing now – Wendy would be asleep – he'd send a message telling her about the Party later.

4

Friday 9th September evening
The tables and chairs in the mess dining hall had been moved to the side of the well-proportioned, high-ceilinged room. This was one of two such dining halls on campus. The other was operating two sittings this evening because the Welcoming Party would not allow for a normal dinner service. It was expected that the Party would be winding down from about eight onwards and those living in mess accommodation would avail themselves of the second sitting in the other mess hall starting at about quarter past eight; undergraduates had been instructed to eat at the first sitting.

It was just after seven and already the hall was pretty full. Students had arrived promptly at seven so as not to be seen to be lacking in enthusiasm for their new circumstances and at least some of the academic staff knew that the sooner proceedings started the sooner they'd end and they could 'stand down' from their welcoming duties. In any event, the mess manager wouldn't thank anyone for overly extending the gathering – the avoidance of overtime payments was never far from his thoughts.

Smartly-dressed mess staff carrying either bottles ready to refill empty glasses or large salvers with various 'finger foods' moved through the throng of students and staff and their partners, occasionally pausing while glasses were refilled and canapés selected. The lighting in the hall was subdued but bright enough to allow the name tags worn by both staff and students to be read without having to bend in too close to the wearer. The hall's full-length dark green velvet curtains were drawn. On the cream-painted walls between the covered windows were a dozen or so large canvasses, each lit from above, with portraits of distinguished military figures from the past. The hall looked both impressive yet surprisingly welcoming and was admirably fulfilling its role this evening in promoting relaxed informality.

At fifteen minutes past seven the mess manager banged loudly on one of the tables located midway along the side of the room. Silence fell and Prof James Nightingale, holding a microphone in his right hand, climbed the couple of steps onto the small platform that had been brought in from one of the mess storerooms especially for the Party.

'I think that everyone who is due to attend should be here by now, so let me start. First thing to say is that I'll not be speaking for long – a fair number of you heard enough of me earlier this afternoon,' he began. A ripple of laughter – possibly of relief - went round the room.

'I just want to say that the welcome I gave to all our new students this afternoon also extends to the many partners who are here tonight and who will have a key part to play as you embark on your courses here. My colleagues and I know that you will support your husbands – and for a number of you, your wives - as they engage on their various courses of study. We know it'll take you a little while to settle to life at TDU – particularly those from overseas - but, if the evidence of the past few years is anything to go by, all of you, both students and partners, will enjoy your time here.'

He paused and looked at his audience who seemed to be giving him the attention that he had hoped for and, in his position, he rather expected.

'The trick is to work hard at your courses and meet the deadlines your tutors set. I know it's easy for me to say this, but it's true and, if you do what I suggest, you'll have plenty of time to enjoy the other things that TDU and the area have to offer. So I wish you all well, confident that you will all make the most of your time here. Please, enjoy the Party.'

Nightingale finished speaking amid a generous round of applause both for the sentiment of his message and possibly for its brevity, stepped down from the platform and moved towards the group of staff and students nearest the platform where he spent a few minutes in inconsequential conversation with a number of TDU staff, students and their various partners.

David and Anna Burgess had been in the mess hall from just before seven and had managed to intercept each of the new students as they entered. By about ten minutes past seven they had managed to gather round them a 'Protective Structures' group comprised of not only students and their partners but also quite a number of the staff who would be teaching the course. Introductions had been made and the group had broken up into smaller knots of people and several lively conversations were underway. Though Professor Nightingale's address had brought talk to a temporary halt, the chatting soon recommenced after he had stepped down from the platform.

Nightingale finished talking with a number of people in the Explosive Ordnance contingent and, recognising the tall figure of Frank Hargreaves close by, moved towards the Protective Structures gathering which had gravitated towards the centre of the room.

Frank Hargreaves, who was engaged in conversation with Graham and Bronwen Dowell and Grant and Jen Thompson, stopped as he saw Nightingale approach.

'Good evening, everyone,' said James Nightingale as he joined the group. 'I hope Professor Hargreaves isn't being too serious about what he expects from you during the coming year!'

Frank Hargreaves gave a somewhat watery smile in return.

'Not at all, James, in fact we were talking about mutual acquaintances in Australia. This is Flight Lieutenant Graham Dowell and his wife Bronwen and Flight Lieutenant Grant Thompson and his wife Jen. Graham's just come from a stint at DSTO in Salisbury and Grant has just returned from a tour in Afghanistan, based in Kabul. Both Graham and Grant have ADFA connections.'

James Nightingale smiled and shook hands with the Dowells and the Grants.

'A great place, ADFA,' commented Nightingale. 'I first went out there to deliver a couple of courses soon after it opened back in the 1980s and I was there only last year when I was investigating the possibility of setting up a staff exchange programme. Although we've had a number of TDU staff go to

ADFA for short visits over the years – I delivered a couple of short courses on my first trip – we've never had ADFA staff here at TDU for anything other than a few quick visits. There's never been the sort of extended exchanges when some real collaborative work could be undertaken.'

'Yes, sir, I'd heard something about your visit,' said Grant Thompson. 'I did my civil engineering degree at ADFA and still keep up with a number of the staff there. When I said I was coming to TDU for a year, they mentioned that you'd visited.'

Grant turned to Frank Hargreaves.

'They also mentioned that you'd made contact when you were over in Melbourne, Professor,' Grant continued.

'Yes, I did have some dealings with one or two people at ADFA,' confirmed Hargreaves.

Turning to Graham Dowell, Grant Thompson continued, 'Did you know about Professor Nightingale's ADFA visit?'

'Yes, like you, I keep in touch with some of the ADFA guys – Bruce Brown is my main source of gossip these days,' replied Graham, referring to one of the ADFA Civil Engineering Department's more senior academics. 'I'd heard that you'd been over, Professor. Hope you enjoyed the trip and that things went off OK.'

'Well, nothing's been fixed yet, but I'm hopeful we'll have something in place early in the New Year,' said Nightingale who then turned to Hargreaves and, with a slight edge in his voice asked, 'So what's this about Melbourne University and ADFA, Frank?'

'Well, it's early days yet,' replied Hargreaves. 'The University of Melbourne – you know I went down there earlier this year for a conference - is setting up a Research Network in the general area of 'security' and part of the Network's scope is concerned with protective systems including protective structures. Since I knew you'd already been talking about a formal staff exchange arrangement with ADFA, I suggested that TDU could in some way liaise with ADFA to contribute to the scheme. I'm hoping that James Schofield might get involved. He already has some contacts in Australia.'

'That sounds as if it might have some useful possibilities in the context of exchanges. It would have been good to have known the details about your discussions when I was in contact with the Dean at ADFA a few days ago,' said Nightingale with a hint of annoyance in his voice. 'We ought to talk soon to make sure our ideas are both running on the same lines. Give me a call on Monday.'

Hargreaves nodded in response.

'Nice to have met you – I'm sure Prof Hargreaves and his colleagues will look after you well,' said Nightingale, turning to the four Australians.

With these words, Nightingale moved away to join another nearby group.

'I ought to go circulate a bit, if you'll excuse me,' said Hargreaves with a smile directed at the four Australians and moved towards where James and Laura Schofield were talking with Philippe Giraud and Alfred Leng.

'There seemed to be a bit of tension between those two,' commented Grant Thompson when Hargreaves was out of earshot. 'Maybe the Provost thinks that Hargreaves is stealing his thunder with the Research Network idea?'

'I thought Prof Nightingale was a bit starchy at the end there, too,' added Jen Thompson. 'What do you think, Graham?'

'Well, I'd heard from Bruce Brown that Prof Nightingale is expecting to be appointed to a big job outside of TDU. Apparently he was very full of the idea when he visited ADFA last year,' replied Graham. 'I think he's going to be head of something called the University Funding Council that works with every UK uni. He's apparently been doing a number of overseas visits in the last twelve to eighteen months. I guess he's aiming to show how outward looking he is and how his international experience will be a great asset when he gets the job.'

'Sounds like hard work,' commented Jen Thompson. 'There seem to be a lot more unis here than in Oz, that's for sure.'

'Bruce also said that he's got a bit of a loose tongue when he's had a drink,' continued Graham. 'Apparently, at the formal dinner they gave him at ADFA, by the time they got to the port, he was sounding off about how useless the current Funding Council is and how some of the guys here at TDU will need to smarten up their act if they want any Council funding when he's in charge!'

'I'd keep that under your hat, Graham,' said Bronwen. 'You don't want to stir anything up before the course has even started!'

'No worries – my lips are sealed,' smiled Graham. 'In any case Prof Nightingale is way above my pay grade for me to have any effect on his career advancement!'

*

James and Laura Schofield were engaged in a lively conversation with Philippe and Alfred as Frank Hargreaves approached. James introduced the two students who shook hands with Hargreaves. Hargreaves greeted Laura Schofield warmly, kissing her on both cheeks.

'How are you settling in?' Hargreaves asked the two students. 'I think you're both living in the mess?'

Both Alfred and Philippe indicated that they were pleased with their accommodation. They were living in one of the two recently-built blocks which boasted *en suite* study-bedrooms and which were provided with both television and internet connections. The rooms were a considerable step up from what used to be the mess norm at TDU; shared bathroom facilities and communal TV rooms were a thing of the past.

'Alfred was telling me about the latest multi-tonne explosive trial he attended at Woomera earlier this year,' said James. 'He was assisting with testing some Singapore MOD munitions storage systems and managed to do a bit of sightseeing when the trial was over.'

'Where did you get to?' asked Hargreaves.

'Well, Prof, I didn't have much time but I did see Adelaide and drove along the Great Ocean Road to Melbourne – a fantastic drive! I had a couple of days in Melbourne and then flew home from there,' replied Alfred.

'It's an interesting city, Melbourne,' said Hargreaves. 'I was there earlier this year on business at the University. I managed to do a few tourist trips – including a visit to a winery or two.'

'I'm not a wine drinker,' said Alfred, holding up a glass which looked to contain orange juice. 'I don't mind having a beer sometimes, though! It seemed that that was all there was to drink after work at Woomera!'

'Well, I'm keen on wine, too,' commented James. 'I've had a couple of visits to Australia during the past few years – I delivered two short courses at ADFA and managed to visit a few of the boutique wineries around Canberra – some of them produce some really good stuff.'

Turning towards Frank Hargreaves, he continued, 'I'm hoping that I might be able to get out there again if your Network discussions are successful.'

'Well, I hope they are,' interjected Laura, smiling at Hargreaves. 'A few weeks in Australia with James would be very welcome – make sure you seal the deal, Frank!'

'What about you, Philippe? Have you had cause to go to Oz?' asked Hargreaves.

'No, Prof, I'm sorry to say I've not had that good fortune,' replied Philippe. 'As you know, we have our own test facilities in Canada and there's really no need for use to travel to Australia for explosive trials. Of course, I'd like to visit and so would my wife – she likes the idea of all that sun! It can get too cold in Alberta!'

'Don't I know it,' said James. 'I was at a conference in Banff a year or so ago and stopped off in Calgary to visit an old friend who's head of the Structures Group at the University. Even though it was only just the start of autumn, it still felt pretty chilly to me. My friend said that the snow and ice sticks around till May sometimes – I'm not sure I'd like that.'

'You all need to come to Singapore,' said Alfred. 'It's always warm there!'

'I had a stopover on the way back from Melbourne earlier this year,' said Hargreaves. 'Ninety degrees Fahrenheit and ninety percent humidity nearly did for me – thank goodness for air conditioning!'

*

While these conversations were progressing, David and Anna Burgess together with Michael Carswell and Alex and Meriel Simmonds were engaged in conversation with the other two

Protective Structures students, Miles Cowley and Karl-Heinz Schmidt. It turned out that Miles and Karl-Heinz had an acquaintance in common in that, as part of his work at the Royal School of Military Engineering at Chatham, Miles had been liaising with one of Karl-Heinz's colleagues based in Bonn in connection with a seminar on Force Protection Engineering that was being planned at Chatham for the following spring.

Frank Hargreaves who was keen to meet all six new students, had excused himself from the conversation with the group gathered around James Schofield and introduced himself to Miles and Karl-Heinz.

'The other guys have been talking about exotic places they've been able to get to as part of their work – conferences, trials - that sort of thing. Do you get the chance to travel in your job, Karl-Heinz?'

'Sometimes, yes,' replied Schmidt. 'You probably know that we have an agreement with the Americans to act as joint hosts for the annual conference on systems for force protection which takes place in alternate years in Germany and America, so I had a few trips to the States in connection with the conference in San Diego last year. After the conference, which I attended with my wife, we decided to travel down to Australia for a couple of weeks holiday and flew back with a stop-off in Singapore. It was all very interesting.'

'I guess you went to Sydney – there's lots to see there and in the area round about – the Blue Mountains aren't too long a drive,' said David.

'Yes, we went to Sydney first, did some sightseeing in the city and a couple of coach tours and then we hired a car and drove to Melbourne. We had a couple of days in Canberra on the way, 'said Karl-Heinz.

'I've had two trips to Canberra when I was a visiting fellow at the Defence Academy – ADFA - in the Civil and Structural Engineering Department. Anna and the family came with me on both occasions – we had a great time. I think I was the first TDU academic to visit ADFA. I was asked to deliver a couple of courses and advise them on getting some work started on protective systems. They did get some way towards developing expertise, but they still like to send students to

TDU even so. I think a year in the UK is still a great attraction!' commented David with a smile. 'I keep up contact with a number of the students from Oz who've been on the MSc here as well as several of the ADFA Civils staff.'

As he spoke, David recalled one of the e-mails he'd found waiting for him on his return from holiday a week or so ago. One of his ADFA contacts – John Evans in the structural dynamics group - had told him both about the generally positive response to Nightingale's overtures about exchanges and his intemperate remarks over dinner. He'd also commented on the suggestions Hargreaves had made to ADFA - which he'd heard about from a friend at the University of Melbourne - about the new Research Network collaboration. John had remarked that it seemed odd that the two approaches hadn't somehow been linked – though he'd acknowledged that academics, particularly those with big egos, loved to 'do their own thing' and maybe both Nightingale and Hargreaves were keeping their cards close to their chests in what were early stages of the various discussions. John thought that the Hargreaves ideas seemed very ambitious and there'd need to be some proper analysis of the costs and effort involved soon or there could be some serious disappointment in Oz if Hargreaves' apparently firm proposals weren't - or couldn't be - fulfilled.

David made a mental note to keep this information under his hat at least for the present. It wouldn't do any good to discuss what were merely outline proposals at this stage, particularly if there was some competition between Nightingale and Hargreaves about how any schemes should progress.

'You get about a bit, don't you, Alex,' said Frank Hargreaves turning to Alex Simmonds with a knowing smile. 'I think you must be the most widely-travelled of all the academics in the Department. Where was it this last summer?'

Alex Simmonds was used to Hargreaves chiding him about how much travel he managed in any year and his response was swift.

'Interlaken, Prof, for the 5th International Terramechanics conference. I had a couple of papers to deliver and, before you ask, the money came from the Terradrive contract. No Department money was involved!'

'Glad to hear it,' replied Hargreaves with a smile. 'I bet you've got at least a couple of trips in the pipeline, knowing you.'

'Of course,' smiled Alex. 'I've got a paper accepted at a soil-vehicle interaction conference in Singapore in March and I'm hoping to go on from there to a conference in Adelaide on ride mechanics – I've contributed to others in the same series in the past. Oh, and there's a quick trip over to Germany in February – just a couple of days – for a seminar organised by Terradrive. Because of the contract, they'll be paying my expenses. It would be rude not to participate!'

'Will Meriel be going with you to Singapore and Australia?' asked David. 'I know she often accompanies you on trips to Europe.'

'No, I'll be on my own. It's a bit too far to go and, since it'll be term time we'd have to take the children out of school. I've always gone on my own when a trip is outside Europe.'

'My Head of Department at Leeds before I came to TDU always asked my colleagues the same two question before he'd approve participation and financial commitment to any overseas conference,' interjected Frank Hargreaves.

'What were they then, Prof?' asked Alex Simmonds, who already knew what the questions were but also knew that Hargreaves liked to tell this story when in new company.

'Well…..,' said Hargreaves. 'Firstly, he'd ask the chap who was pitching for funding to go to, say, Madrid for a week, if he was presenting a paper at the conference. If the answer was 'No' then the conversation would pretty much end there and then and the request was refused. If the answer was 'Yes', then he'd ask his second question which was: 'Would you still be pressing to participate if the conference was being held in Scunthorpe?''

At this, Miles chuckled and Karl-Heinz looked slightly puzzled. Michael Carswell, who up until this point had been rather quiet, came to his rescue, saying, 'Scunthorpe is a place in the UK noted for its heavy industry – steel-making – rather than for its charming architectural and cultural heritage.'

'Ah – I understand! It would be a bit like going on holiday in Dusseldorf then,' said Karl-Heinz with a smile.

'You've got it!' said Hargreaves. 'When it got round what to expect, my colleagues always used to answer 'Yes' to both the first and the second question and be ready with a good half-dozen reasons why they should go to Madrid or Stockholm or wherever!'

When he'd finished speaking, Hargreaves looked at his watch and cast an eye around the mess hall.

'It's gone eight and I think I might be heading home. Numbers seem to be thinning. I guess the mess staff would be grateful if we made ourselves scarce – you can always retire to the bar! I'll say goodnight to you all.'

Hargreaves left and it was clear that in only a very short time the mess dining hall would be clear of everyone except mess staff clearing away glasses.

'Right – who's for the bar?' asked Miles

David, Anna, Alex and Meriel all declined and said their goodbyes. From past experience of these events, David knew that there would still be a decent number of his academic colleagues and quite a few of the new student body keen to continue socialising over a glass, so he didn't feel any guilt about leaving – he knew that he'd be seeing quite a lot of the new cohort over the next year and he'd at least got to know a little about each of them today.

Michael Carswell also said that he had to go and, though he left the mess hall with the Burgesses and the Simmonds, he was quick say goodnight and make his was to his car as soon as they left the mess building.

He knew he'd not been at his most sociable that evening, but he had a lot on his mind. As well as needing to complete the paper he was working on and amending his funding application, the meeting with Graham Dowell this afternoon and again this evening - when he'd learnt more about Dowell's connection with DSTO - and all the talk of Australia this evening had made him even more worried about a piece of work he'd just completed for the MoD.

This was the development of a piece of software for use by commanders in the field for the rapid assessment of damage to framed structures that had been hit by a blast load from the detonation of something like a vehicle bomb. The idea of the software was that a military engineer would quickly be able to provide advice about whether a damaged building was safe to enter after it had been attacked or if, because damage was of such severity, the building should not be entered unless some repairs were undertaken. The contract was part of a much bigger one about structures for force protection that the MoD had let to a consortium of universities in the UK. He'd almost completed his work when, a couple of weeks ago - in an e-mail from an academic at another of the universities in the consortium - he'd become aware of similar research by a group at DSTO in Salisbury in South Australia. He'd made some enquiries of colleagues at other universities working in the area of analytical software development. He'd learnt that the Australians had produced something that seemed to be almost identical to that which he had written in both its analytical approach and in its use of intuitive graphical user interfaces. For the last fortnight, nagging away at the back of his mind was the thought that he'd somehow learnt about the Australians' approach – maybe at a conference or at a software seminar - before he started on his programme of work and that he had subconsciously incorporated their methodology into his own approach.

The possibly of plagiarism was something that was of continual concern to academics. The thought that he might – however unwittingly – have plagiarised the DSTO work was of great concern and, having learnt of Graham Dowell's DSTO connection, he feared that the similarity might well come to light. Although he had just about convinced himself that his work was completely independent of any outside influence, there could be, at the very least, personal embarrassment if the similarity came to light and - far worse – both significant contractual implications and personal career-threatening problems if DSTO were to pursue a plagiarism case in regard to the software.

He reached his car, climbed in and drove home.

5

Friday 9th September evening

The mess bar was itself quite a big room equipped with large leather sofas, low tables and a selection of daily newspapers. The bar was open for a couple of hours at lunchtime when, though a few people might have a beer before lunch, it was mostly used after lunch to drink coffee and read a newspaper before the afternoon programme of instruction commenced at two o'clock. In the evening it was open from about six thirty until eleven when it was a focal point for socialising by those living in mess accommodation.

A number of both TDU staff and students had made their way into the bar as the Welcoming Party had drawn to a close. George Hambidge together with Mary and Chris Wells were already at the bar and were soon joined by Graham and Bronwen Dowell together with Grant and Jen Thompson. Stephen Wright and Gill Neville weren't far behind them.

'What are you doing here, tonight, George?' asked Stephen as he reached the bar. 'I didn't think you had much to do with the MSc.'

'There's a first time for everything,' replied Hambidge. 'This year we've included some work on remote sensing in the module on damage assessment this time. We're going to used the techniques I teach to plot regions of damage on structures that have been hit by something like a blast or a missile. I thought it would be worth coming along to meet the new cohort. If I don't do it now I probably won't see them until I walk in to deliver my first lecture!'

Turning to Graham Dowell, Hambidge held out his hand.

'I don't think I've introduced myself – I got caught chatting to one of the computer science lot. I'm George Hambidge and this is my wife Mary.'

Graham introduced himself and Bronwen as well as the Thompsons.

'Is Steve Evans still on the ADFA staff?' asked Hambidge when all introductions had been made and it was clear that both Australians had some connection with ADFA.

'No, he's just retired, I think,' said Grant Thompson. 'He'd been there quite a while and when I finished my degree he was in his late fifties or early sixties and that was about five or six years ago now.'

'Yes, I suppose he would be about 65 now. I knew him a long time ago when we were both working for the Kenyan government doing some mapping work out in the sticks. He was responsible for one of several sectors that were being surveyed and I was leading a team looking after another. We used to meet occasionally in Nairobi when we were processing data. I knew he'd gone to ADFA after the Kenyan work was finished and I've been in occasional contact with him for about twenty years now.'

While the Hambidges was talking with the Australians, Stephen Wright turned his attention to Chris Wells.

'I think you might have met Gill this afternoon when we had tea with the students,' said Wright. 'Gill and I have been working together on armour systems these past few years.'

'Yes, we met briefly this afternoon,' said Gill smiling at Chris. 'When Stephen talks about us 'working together', he means he's been a slave driver these last here years while I've been the slave.'

'What she really means,' interjected Wright with a laugh, 'is that Gill has been using a piece of MoD contract research on a novel armour system as a vehicle for her PhD. The fact that she worked so hard is not my fault – she was just terribly keen!'

'And did the effort pay off?' asked Wells.

'Yes, I'm relieved to say,' replied Gill. 'I submitted my thesis in May and the viva was in early July. Luckily, I only had some minor corrections to make and the award of the degree was confirmed a week before Graduation Day at the end of July.'

'Congratulations,' said Chris. 'It's a very stressful time when you're writing up and, I guess, still having to do work on the contract?'

Gill nodded.

'When I was finishing my thesis – about a couple of years ago now – I remember thinking that I'd never complete it – there always seemed to be so many revisions and checks to make sure that I was presenting a watertight case that I could defend no matter what the examiners threw at me,' said Wells.

Gill smiled.

'She did pretty well in the viva,' said Wright. 'The external examiner was a bit sceptical about the merit of some aspects of the work at first, but by the time we came to the final discussion about how we should proceed, he was completely won over and 'minor corrections' was the outcome. They really were 'minor' and Gill managed to complete those to the satisfaction of the internal examiner within a week.'

'So, what now – are you going to carry on with work in the same area or are you looking for something different?' asked Wells.

'I think I'll be doing some more work in the same area, working with Stephen again,' said Gill, looking towards Stephen who smiled and nodded. 'But I've been appointed as a Teaching Associate, so I'll actually be doing some lecturing and laboratory work with students – on armour systems, of course! - as well continuing with the armour research. I think that there's going to be some development work starting soon.'

'Well, it's not quite resolved just yet, but I'm confident that the funding will be available,' responded Wright. 'But in any case, there are some surplus funds from the contract that's just finished that can tide us over for two or three months.'

Wright raised the almost empty glass of beer he was holding to his lips and drained it.

'I think it's time I was on my way. Giles said he'd wait to eat until I got back,' he said to the group gathered around. 'Just as well it's the weekend – it seems to have been a busy week. Goodnight all!'

He put his glass down on the bar and left.

'Who's Giles?' said Chris Wells, who was now standing alone with Gill and thinking what a pretty girl she was and how it might be nice to get to know her better.

'Giles is Stephen's partner,' replied Gill. 'They've been together for a long time, apparently. Certainly years before I came here to start my research. Giles runs an art gallery in Oxford. He buys and sells art. Some if it is quite expensive, though I'm not sure business is that good at the moment.'

Chris Wells looked at his watch.

'How about a bite to eat?' he asked Gill, who looked up at him with a surprised look that quickly turned to a smile. 'The Buckley Arms in the High St does decent pub grub and I don't feel like cooking for myself tonight.'

'Yes, why not?' replied Gill. 'That sounds like an excellent idea. I've got my car outside, so I can drive us there.'

With a few words of goodbye to the group still talking at the bar Chris and Gill left. Their departure prompted the Hambidges to leave also.

'Nice to have met you,' said Mary to the Australian quartet, 'but it's time we left. We're both playing golf this weekend – on both Saturday and Sunday – and George will need to get his beauty sleep!'

George Hambidge gave Mary a somewhat world-weary but affectionate look as she took his arm and led him away, leaving just the four Australians who ordered another round of drinks before moving to a group of easy chairs that had just been vacated by another departing group.

*

'Not a bad evening,' said Grant Thompson, as they sat down. 'But I think we may have missed any chance of eating in the mess – it's getting on for nine o'clock.'

He turned to Bronwen Dowell.

'When we've finished this drink why don't you and Graham come back to our place – we can fix up a bite to eat, can't we, Jen?' he continued.

'Not a problem – we can do a quick pasta or something and there's a nice bottle of red we can open,' replied Jen.

'Sounds good,' said Graham. 'You OK with that, Bron? We can check in at the quarter to see that all's well with the boys, if you like.'

'Yes, a great idea, thanks, Jen! The boys will be OK – I told Carol that we'd not be back until about eleven – I thought we might have gone to have something to eat in the village, but Grant and Jen's suggestion is a much better idea,' replied Bronwen with a smile.

'Well, I thought it was a very enlightening evening,' said Graham Dowell, emphasising the word 'enlightening'. The others turned towards him.

'What do you mean, 'enlightening' – I thought it was good to chat with academics and see what makes them tick, but you sound as if you got more from the evening than that,' said Grant.

'I picked up lots of little things beneath the surface,' said Graham. 'Quite a few tensions, I think. And there was one thing I discovered, quite by chance, which explains quite a few things that I'd not been able to work out before.'

'Sounds very intriguing,' said Jen. 'What have we been missing?'

'I guess your discovery must be more intriguing than just the academic sniping that went on tonight,' commented Grant. 'It struck me that Profs Nightingale and Hargreaves were a bit touchy this evening. I already knew about their various visits to Oz through my ADFA contacts. I think you've got it right, Graham, when you were talking earlier about the way they regard each other. I got the impression that Hargreaves isn't too keen to involve Nightingale in his Research Network plans while Nightingale wants to make sure he's seen as the head honcho in setting up the formal exchange programmes. I guess it's normal academic games – each trying to outdo the other to make sure they keep their profiles high. I think the fact that Nightingale's hoping for this big job outside TDU and Hargreaves is hoping to succeed Nightingale is all part of the game.'

'I guess you're right,' said Bronwen. 'The thing that struck me is how many of the staff and some of the guys on the course have Oz connections of some sort. Both James Schofield and David Burgess were both telling me at some point in the evening about courses they'd given in ADFA. George Hambidge seems to have been pretty pally with the ADFA surveyor at one time. Alfred seems to have done at least one set of trials at Woomera and even Karl-Heinz has managed to get a decent holiday in God's Own!'

'So what is it that's so intriguing that you discovered this evening, Graham?' asked Jen.

'Well, actually, there are two or three things,' replied Graham Dowell. 'I suppose that a couple are about putting a face to a name.'

'Come on then, Graham, spit it out!' said Grant.

'The guys at DSTO were telling me just before we left Oz about the research that someone in the UK has been doing on rapid analysis of blast-damaged structures,' Graham commenced. 'Last month they'd found an abstract for an upcoming conference paper that seemed to be using the same approach as they are developing. They were wondering how the guy who was doing it got the idea. Information on the technique shouldn't have got outside DSTO – up until a month ago, all the documents about the work were internal to DSTO. They'd not published anything outside the organisation until last month when they wrote a short paper about the method and talked about it at a seminar on computational analysis techniques in Adelaide. Then they thought that maybe it was they who were doing the copying - maybe someone in DSTO had come across mention of the approach somewhere earlier and, though at the time it hadn't registered as something useful, he might have logged the idea subconsciously and it resurfaced when the analysis project was underway. Both the UK work and the DSTO stuff seem to have started at about the same time. I didn't take much notice of what they said at the time but, seeing the name Michael Carswell on the Department's staff list it jogged my memory and, having had a chat with him during the Party about the sort of work he's doing, it's definitely him that the DSTO team mentioned!'

Graham paused and took a sip of his drink before continuing.

'When he found out that I've been doing work with DSTO he looked a bit uncomfortable. Up to then he'd been quiet and withdrawn – I'm not sure he was really enjoying the

Welcoming Party - but after he found out more about my DSTO links, he seemed keen to end our chat. Perhaps he's having the same thoughts about the work as DSTO – maybe they ought to talk!'

'It doesn't seem a big thing – surely you can have the same good idea about something when on opposite sides of the world and, anyway, I bet there'll be some differences in the way the two approaches work that mean the techniques aren't really identical,' commented Grant.

'You may well be right,' said Graham. 'But as we've seen, academics do tend to get very jealous of each other, even when what they're doing could be complementary rather than in direct competition!'

'So what was the second discovery this evening, Graham?' asked Jen.

'Well, again, it's putting a face to a name,' said Graham.

'Who this time?' asked Jen. 'Surely not another previously-undiscovered Oz connection on the part of the TDU staff!'

'Maybe!' said Graham. 'But I might be barking up the wrong tree, so perhaps it'd be better not to say anything at the moment. It's no big deal, but could be a bit embarrassing if what I think is true - I'd better make sure of my facts first!'

'It's not like you to hold back,' said Grant, smiling.

'Well, there's a first time for everything!' responded Graham. 'There was one other thing, though, that might be worth thinking about.'

'And that is?' interjected Grant.

'And that is – when is Stephen Wright going announce which company is going to get the contract to manufacture his new armour system?'

'That sounds really dull,' said Bronwen, 'and it's getting late and I'm beginning to feel hungry!'

'You're right –it is dull and I'm hungry too,' said Jen. 'Let's go and get something to eat. Drink up, guys!'

They finished their drinks and rose from their chairs and were shortly walking briskly back to their house.

6

Saturday 10th September am

Weekends at the Defence University were almost invariably quiet. TDU students were generally rather better funded that their impecunious counterparts in 'normal' civilian universities. TDU undergraduates often took weekends away, either visiting friends or engaging on military-sponsored sporting or 'adventure' activities, only returning on Sunday evening to put in a few hours of study before the academic programme recommenced on Monday.

In the case of post-graduate students, although some working towards PhDs liked to take advantage of the tranquillity afforded by the empty corridors and lecture rooms, most MSc students stayed away from the academic areas of the campus at weekends. They would generally use at least some of Saturday or Sunday to prepare assignments to be submitted to meet the various deadlines set by module tutors. However, there was always time for some recreation, particularly important for those with families living away from TDU. Quite a number of the UK military students on the Military Technology Course travelled back to their family bases – often leaving on Friday afternoons when academic commitments had been met – and sometimes before then! In the case of overseas students, the weekend provided the ideal opportunity for exploration. With London only an hour's train journey away and Oxford, Bath, Stratford and the Cotswolds within very easy reach, there was a lot for the first-time visitor to the UK to see and do.

At weekends TDU academic staff were only too pleased to be away from the pressures of university life. Although a few cars belonging to staff could occasionally be seen in the car parks at weekends, such visits tended to be short and made for the purpose of collecting some forgotten paper or lecture material for use first thing on Monday morning.

*

Chris Wells woke on Saturday morning at about eight, thinking about the evening he'd spent with Gill Neville, first over steak and chips and a glass of house red at The Buckley Arms and later at his flat where they'd drunk coffee and talked about, among other things, life at TDU.

Gill was clearly proud of her recent doctorate and was excited about the prospect of starting to do some lecturing in her new role as Teaching Associate. She seemed less certain about the direction her research would take now she'd got her PhD. Her project had, of course, been successfully completed and she finishing it and submitting her thesis had more or less coincided with the end of the Stephen Wright's contract that had provided some of her funding. Towards the end of her project, she'd told him that Stephen had seemed a bit distracted and a little vague about the prospects for her continuing with the same line of work. Though he'd said at the Welcoming Party last night that he was confident about further funding, she didn't think that anything had quite been decided yet, though she knew that negotiations with potential manufacturers of the new armour system were ongoing. Gill had said that Stephen had been involved in a number of discussions with Carter, TDU's Chief Finance Officer, presumably about contracts.

Anyway, as she said, the fact that she'd been appointed as a Teaching Associate meant that the pressure to secure funding for any post-doctoral work on her part had eased for the moment and her salary would be fully paid by the University rather than from the University and a research sponsor. Gill had said that she thought that the next few weeks would be a good time to step a little back from her research, which had taken over her life particularly during the past year, and devote some effort to the preparation of her lectures and tutorial material.

Chris for his part had told her about his work at Nottingham prior to his appointment at TDU. He'd been involved in work on new ceramic materials both conducting experiments and doing some numerical modelling concerned with their performance under high strain-rate loading conditions. This was the sort of work that he thought had led TDU to appoint him. He'd expressed the hope that he and Gill might get to work together.

Actually, after their evening, Chris hoped that they'd do rather more than work together in the future. He'd felt attracted to her and he thought his feelings had been reciprocated. Their conversation had quite quickly strayed away from research and other technical matters. They talked about their backgrounds and families and discovered that they both had shared interests in art – both loved to visit galleries and exhibitions – the cinema and theatre. It was Gill herself who had suggested that she might show Chris some of the art that Oxford had to offer and he had readily agreed.

He'd said that he would drive and had arranged to pick her up in his car from her house in Farlington and drive the two of them to Oxford. Gill had advocated using one of the City's out-of-town park and ride systems to get into the centre since parking was scarce and, even if it could be found, expensive.

As he walked to his car parked in the yard behind the flat, he was very much looking forward to the day which Gill had suggested should include a walk round the University sights in the City, a bite of lunch and a visit to the recently modernised Ashmolean Museum.

*

In the cottage in Sixhampton Stephen Wright awoke to find he was alone in the bed. He looked at the radio alarm clock and saw that it was just after 7.30. He heard the creaking of the cottage stairs and looked up as Giles Mitchell entered the room carrying a mug of tea.

'Are you going to travel in with me this morning?' asked Giles who was not yet dressed. 'Because, if so, I need to be in a bit earlier today so I'll be need to be leaving before about eight-thirty or otherwise the traffic will be murder.'

Giles' gallery in the centre of Oxford, in a street just off the High had relatively gentle opening times – usually from ten until four – so he usually left the cottage after nine, avoiding the worst of the commuter traffic into the city. Though 'normal' hours were relatively short, Giles on occasion had private viewings for potential clients when the gallery was closed to the general public.

'Yes, I thought I'd see if I can buy a couple of pullovers and maybe some cord trousers now that we're getting into autumn. I'll also pick up some fresh fish from the Covered Market which we could have for supper this evening and maybe something like a piece of beef for tomorrow. I thought we could cook in the evening, if we were to do that walk you were talking about earlier in the week.'

'Good idea,' replied Giles. 'The butcher right in the centre of the Market's best for beef, I always think. A walk tomorrow would be just the thing.'

Oxford's Victorian Covered Market was a favourite destination both for Giles and Stephen. Giles often bought food – meat, fruit and vegetables and good bread – from the Market during the working week. It was always of good quality, though rather expensive by supermarket standards. Later in the year, when pheasants were in season he would certainly buy a couple of brace – during the week a brace could generally be had for around six pounds.

'I'll have a quick shower first, and then you'd better get a move on,' said Giles as he turned to leave the bedroom.

*

Soon after eight thirty, they were on the road to Oxford for the twelve mile drive to the city. Much as the Oxford authorities would like to have excluded any and every car from the city centre, Giles was fortunate to have an off-the-road parking space behind the gallery, so didn't have to concern himself with Park and Ride buses or extremely high parking charges in the city's relatively few car parks. They arrived at the gallery soon after nine fifteen, having avoided the worst of the Saturday morning traffic, and entered via the rear door.

The gallery had been started by Giles and Edward Turner about ten years previously using money that Giles had acquired as a result of his redundancy from a medium-sized insurance company that had been taken over by one of the big players in the insurance market. The pay-off, though not vast, had been sufficient for him to buy into a partnership with Edward Turner, an old university friend, to set up a gallery business to allow them both to indulge their passion for fine modern art. Between them they acquired the lease on the gallery building and began, modestly at first, to stock it with interesting paintings by up and coming British artists. Over the years, the reputation of the gallery had risen and the 'Turner and Mitchell Gallery' boasted a client base that extended over a wide area with customers travelling to the gallery from London, the South-East, the Midlands and the West Country.

About three years ago and seven years into the partnership, Turner had decided that he wanted to start up on his own in Scotland, the country of his birth. Mindful that he and Giles had built up the business together, Edward had agreed to take out only a part of his share of the business, leaving in about a hundred thousand pounds. He and Giles had had an agreement drawn up which would allow Giles to repay Edward over a period of six years at a modest rate of interest by a series of monthly payments and a lump sum at the end of the six years. There was a proviso that, should Edward have need of the remaining money earlier than the six year term, he could demand the cash by giving six weeks notice to Giles.

For his part, though the notice term was shorter than he'd have liked, Giles had generally been comfortable with the arrangement. Edward Turner had always said that he would only, in the last resort, invoke the 'six week notice' clause. All Giles' projections indicated that the financial requirements could be met - and, indeed in the first year or so following Edward's departure, the gallery – now renamed 'The Mitchell Gallery' – had done well. However, the past two years had not been so successful with the economic downturn affecting even the deepest pockets and Giles' sales figures had taken on a rather less healthy appearance.

Giles turned the lights on and went to the entrance of the gallery where three or four items of post were lying on the floor behind the door. He picked them up and leafed through them, stopping when he reached the third of the four envelopes which had an Edinburgh postmark. Giles opened it and visibly paled as took out and read the two stapled sheets that it contained. He looked up at Stephen who was casting an eye over the paintings displayed towards the rear of the gallery near the desk on which sat Giles' computer together with a pile of gallery brochures and other items of paperwork.

'Stephen, look at this,' said Giles in a voice that carried more that a hint of discomfort. 'It's from Edward – he says that he needs the balance of his money by the second week of January.'

'But you'll be able to pay him, won't you?' asked Stephen. 'How much is it?'

'It's still over fifty thousand. You know I've been paying him about twelve hundred a month since he pulled out of the partnership three years ago and I've paid him about forty thousand or so in the last three years,' replied Giles. 'He says his new business needs an injection of cash, that's why he's calling in the loan. According to the terms of our agreement, I'm afraid that he's within his rights to demand the balance.'

Giles paused and looked at Stephen.

'But you've been setting aside other funds to deal with just this situation, haven't you?' asked Stephen.

'Things haven't gone as well as I'd hoped since he left – you know how the downturn has hit the market hard. I guess that's why he needs his money now.'

Giles paused before continuing.

'But, yes, I thought I'd be able to meet both the monthly payments and build up a cash reserve in the first half of the loan period enough to pay off the balance which would have been about twenty thousand at the end of the term. I was aiming to have a good portion of the money available by about now - even if he called in the loan early - though I didn't expect it, at least not quite so soon.'

Giles passed the letter to Stephen saying, 'The letter is almost apologetic, but he's been hit by the recession and it seems he's in a bit of trouble.'

Stephen frowned as he read Edward Turner's letter.

'Well, as you say, it sounds as if he's having some problems up in Edinburgh – probably the same sort of problems that you're experiencing here and, from the tone of his letter he's not making this demand lightly.'

Stephen turned his attention to the second sheet which was mainly taken up with a column of figures.

'If this account is correct, and I guess it is, you need to pay Edward about fifty-four thousand pounds early in the New Year. How much have you got in your reserve?'

Giles looked distressed as he answered.

'I had hoped that I'd have been able to put aside a good seven or eight thousand or so each year so that, by the end of the six years, I'd have getting on for fifty thousand or so available to pay him the twenty thousand at the end of the term with a good sum remaining – thirty thousand or so - that I was planning to use on upgrading the gallery. With the way things have been these last couple of years, though I've managed to make the monthly payments – and that's been a struggle at times, particularly recently - I've got barely eighteen thousand in my reserve. I can't see how I'm going to get hold of nearly forty thousand by January.'

Giles paused and looked at Stephen who was beginning to realise the seriousness of the situation.

'I really thought that sales would be good this year. There's some really fine work here, but buyers at the higher end of the market have been thin on the ground. I've not had the turnover of paintings or cash that I'd need to be able to pay Edward anything like in full. I'd be hard pressed, even if I managed to sell a dozen or so works in the gallery. It might mean that I'll have to consider selling the whole business to raise the money.'

Stephen consulted the letter and its attachment again, almost in the hope that he'd misunderstood what he'd read, but it was all very clear and very reasonable. Giles had entered into a binding agreement with Edward whose less attractive terms were now being invoked. The thought of his partner having to give up what he'd worked so hard for these last ten years filled him with sorrow – there must be a way of getting hold of the money.

*

The morning was bright though a little chilly and the TDU campus was looking particularly attractive in the autumn sun as Prof Frank Hargreaves parked his car in an empty bay close to his office in the Horrocks Building. The leaves on the trees that fringed the car park and formed an impressive guard of honour along the main traffic routes through the campus were just beginning to turn. There was just a hint of gold beginning to show and it wouldn't be more that two or three weeks before the campus would be filled with the sound of leaf-blowers as the ground staff sought to clear the considerable expanses of grass that were a feature of the TDU campus. Seemingly wrapped in his thoughts, Hargreaves walked the thirty or so metres to the entrance to the building and, as he started to climb the stairs up to his office on the first floor he was snapped from his reverie as another figure came towards him down the stairs.

'Good morning, Prof, nice day!' said the figure whom Hargreaves, after taking a second or two to recover, recognised as Dan Parker, one of the Department's research students.

'Good morning, Dan,' replied Hargreaves. 'What brings you here on a Saturday morning?'

'Experiments, Prof,' responded Parker with a rueful smile. 'I've got about four days of range time booked in a couple of weeks and the preparation of the samples to be tested and getting the instrumentation sorted out is taking much longer than I thought. I got to the stage of almost completing the third of my ten samples last night and thought it would be worthwhile coming in for an hour to finish it off. That means I'll be able to make a fresh start on Monday on the remaining ones and, with any luck should have broken the back of the preparation by next weekend. That'll give me the best part of a week to make sure everything's working before taking the stuff out onto EDER.'

'Sounds a good plan,' responded Hargreaves with a smile. 'I guess that you'll want to have this stage of your range work completed before the weather gets too bad?'

Hargreaves knew that Dan Parker, who was being jointly supervised by both James Schofield and Stephen Wright, was a diligent student who, he seemed to recall, had been trying to develop something more than just a friendly relationship with Gill Neville, though he might have got this wrong. He did remember that Parker's work on the structural use of composite materials subjected to dynamic loading had been the subject of a recent departmental research seminar. Hargreaves knew that Parker– he was just starting the final year of his project and would be thinking about starting to write up soon – had made a good presentation about his work and had dealt with questions from the audience at the seminar competently. He'd only once called on one of his supervisors - James Schofield he thought it was - for support and comment about a feature of the tests to which he was subjecting his samples – something about the justification for the samples' method of support – and overall he'd given a good account of himself.

'Yes, you're right, Prof,' replied Dan. 'Though it's not so bad even if it gets wet since the explosive testing is done in the hardened building. As long as the instrumentation stays dry, it's not too much of a problem. But you're right, it would be nice to be able to complete this set of experiments before the weather worsens and I have got a lot of instrumentation for these trials. There'll be a lot of data to analyse – I've got strain gauges and an accelerometer as well as pressure transducers for blast wave measurement and a high speed video camera to monitor the response of the sample. It would be good to have that available to work on during the winter! And of course I've got my numerical simulations to do as well.'

Hargreaves listened with interest to what Parker was saying. His was one of a number of PhD research projects in the Department of Civil and Mechanical Engineering well-funded from external sources. He felt that it could only help his bid to become the next Provost that he could say just how many projects were underway and how much money they were bringing into the Department and thus onto the University's books. Also, by keeping an eye – albeit at a distance – on these various pieces of research, meant that he was at least in a position to give the relevant supervisor a gently nudge if there seemed to be any problem with a particular piece of work.

Hargreaves recalled the uncomfortable experience a number of years ago now with a student who had absented himself from his master's course project at a critical stage in order to do the Hajj to Mecca. He'd disappeared off his supervisor's radar for getting on for six weeks and had returned with only just enough time to complete the second stage of what was meant to be a three phase study. He had, of course, been referred by the Examination Board at the end of the course before being considered suitable for the award of the degree. He had been obliged to carry out further work to satisfy the examiners at considerable inconvenience both to himself and, not least, to Department staff. Fortunately there was little or no outside sponsor's money involved in the project – the Department tended to supply the funding for MSc work – but it had sounded a warning to all the Departmental academics of the need to keep firm but friendly control over students, be they Masters candidates or working for PhDs.

'Well, good luck with your preparations – we'll have to arrange another seminar in the new year to hear about your latest results,' said Hargreaves. 'Excuse me now, but I need to get on – paperwork, always more paperwork!'

*

Dan Parker continued down the stairs while Hargreaves went up to the next landing and thence to his office where, after slipping off his coat, he sat down at his desk, unlocked the lower right-hand drawer using a key from a bunch that he took from his trouser pocket and brought out a card folder on whose cover were the words 'TDU Provost'.

This file, which Hargreaves had been compiling over the past months, ever since it had been known that Prof James Nightingale would be leaving TDU at the end of the academic year, round about August next year. In his quest to become the new Provost, Hargreaves had already submitted paperwork for consideration by the ten members of TDU's senior governing body, the University Board. This was chaired by the university's 'Visitor', a retired four star General, and was comprised of three emeritus professors from TDU, three senior professors from other universities and three senior serving military members. They would make the decision about who would be the new Provost and, as part of their deliberations, would undoubtedly seek counsel from the current incumbent. Additionally, there would be an extended interview of each candidate scheduled for late October with a view to making an appointment before Christmas, thus allowing any successful candidate about eight months before commencing as Provost.

Hargreaves knew of just two other candidates beside himself and both were from outside TDU. One was the head of an engineering department in a long-established Scottish university and the other was currently a senior manager in one of the MoD's equipment procurement organisations.

Hargreaves opened the file in which, sitting on the top of the pile of papers, was his submission to the University Board, compiled over the summer. This contained a comprehensive account of his career to date, emphasising the many successes he'd enjoyed both within TDU and as a well-regarded member of a number of committees outside of the University. This was all history, of course, and he knew he would have no difficulty in relating what he'd done, why it was important and the benefits that had accrued as a result of his efforts. He'd also been required to include a section in his submission about how he saw TDU developing and prospering if he were to be appointed Provost.

He knew that he could expect the interview to concentrate significantly on these ideas and, following his brief and slightly uncomfortable discussion with Nightingale at last night's Welcoming Party, he thought it would be worth reviewing what his so-called 'Vision' section looked like – what an awful term, he thought - and maybe adjusting one or two aspects of it, to diffuse any difficulty that Nightingale might feel about his ideas for research network involvement with Australia and any technical or personnel exchange programme between TDU and Australian universities. He wondered whether he should include in his submission what he was expecting to hear in relation to Stephen Wright's armour contract negotiations. When the announcement he was expecting was made, it could surely only enhance his case for his exchange programme. He made a note to include it, but only after any official announcement.

'It's a good idea to make sure that I've got my ideas as firm as possible,' thought Hargreaves as he read through what he'd written in his submission.

'The situation about the network and exchanges has moved on since I wrote this,' he mused, 'and with the way Nightingale reacted yesterday, it might be good to make sure that my ideas are seen as complementary to his rather than duplicating them. He doesn't like to feel that others can also come up with an idea or two!'

Referring to a second folder labelled 'Oz network' already sitting on his desk, Hargreaves made a number of notes on a clean sheet of paper. After about a half hour or so he reviewed what he'd written and felt a degree of satisfaction with the refinement of his plans and the details he'd been able to provide that had only really been available to him quite recently. He placed the new sheet next to the pages of his submission concerned with his plans to develop TDU, closed the 'TDU Provost' folder and locked it in the drawer of his desk.

'I should think I can convince James that I'm not stealing his thunder about Oz when we talk next week,' he said to himself as he took a Post-it note and wrote 'Monday am – Call JN re Oz'.

'It's important that I keep him sweet, at least until after the interview. After that I don't much care what he thinks!'

*

Saturday 10th September pm

TDU Headquarters next to the Horrocks Building at first sight seemed deserted. Though a few staff did occasionally come in on Saturday for an hour or so – mainly to finish off work without fear of interruption – the place was generally very quiet. However, one office on the floor above the Common Room was occupied. Most unusually for him, since he liked to keep his work limited to the working week, the Defence University's Chief Finance Officer, Robert Carter was seated at his desk on which lay a number of cardboard folders and sheets of paper arranged in five neat piles.

Carter was a man in his early sixties with rather thin greying hair. He was somewhat overweight and his rather prominent stomach meant that he seemed to be an uncomfortably long way from his desk even when his chair was pulled in as close as he could get it. This morning he was wearing a grey pullover over an open-necked shirt in stark contrast to the dark suit and tie he habitually wore during the working week. His florid face, with its large and protuberant nose, sported a surprisingly dark, neatly trimmed moustache. Carter was known in TDU as a man who liked a glass of wine both with his meals and, so the wags said, between and after his meals as well. These meals, the view was, were likely to be nothing less than hearty.

He'd been Chief Finance Officer for TDU for getting on for ten years now, having come to the post from a medium-sized company specialising in the manufacture of components for the defence automotive industry. He was known to be a stickler for 'procedure' and demanded that he be furnished with the appropriate and comprehensive paperwork before he would look at anything, whether a request for the purchase of new equipment, the appointment of new staff or the submission to a potential sponsor or grant-giving organisation for research funding. For all that, the general view was that his approach to dealing with the University's finances was sound – he was regarded as a safe pair of hands. Though TDU was not over-endowed with financial resources, Carter could justifiably claim that what funds it did have were well-managed.

In his right hand he held a pair of gold-rimmed glasses that he had just taken off after reading the document on the top of one of the piles of paper. This sheet was printed at the top with the logo of the American 'ArmorTech' company. He put on his glasses again and took the top sheet from the fifth pile, slightly separated from the other four on the desk: this sheet bore the rather elegant TDU logo and letterhead printed in red and blue. He put the TDU-headed sheet on the top of ArmorTech document and placed all the pages in the pile - perhaps a dozen in all – inside one of the buff-coloured cardboard folders with the letters 'AT' written in a neat hand in the top left hand corner.

On the top of each of the three remaining piles was a sheet with the company logos of Armacomposta, a Brazilian firm, Comparmour from Australia and Difesa Composita based in Rome. He took another sheet from the fifth pile, scanned it briefly and placed it on the pile topped by the sheet with the Armacomposta logo and slid the whole pile of papers into a folder with the letters 'AC' in the top corner. The third pile had a two-page document on top, the sheets being stapled together, with the 'Comparmour' logo at the top. After adding a TDU-headed sheet to the pile Carter put all the pages in the folder labelled 'CA'. He repeated the process with the remaining documents which related to 'Difesa Composita', placing them a folder labelled 'DC'.

He briefly wondered whether they might have approached another company besides these four, but quickly dismissed the thought. These four were among the biggest players in the manufacture of protective systems based on composite materials and he was sure that they offered the greatest potential. In any case, confidence that Stephen Wright's assessment that all four would respond positively to TDU's proposals had been well-founded and in less than ten days time the business would be complete.

Carter pushed his chair back from the desk and awkwardly stood up. He gathered up the four files, looking both on the desktop and on the floor, to ensure that no documents had fallen out during the course of his work with them. He took his briefcase from beside his desk and placed the files in one of several compartments within the case, closed it and set the built-in combination lock.

He picked up his coat and struggled into it before making one final check of his desk and its surrounds. He carefully closed the door of his office and made his way out of the building to his car. As he walked towards his vehicle he wondered how his colleagues would view the fact that he was breaking of one of his very firm procedural rules that no university business files should be taken off the campus unless approval had first been given by one's line manager who would then log their removal on the appropriate and secure university intranet pages. He comforted himself with the thought that there was a certain urgency about these documents and working with them at home was quite justifiable – he just wanted to make sure he'd not forgotten anything and he was certain that the Provost would approve of such a conscientious approach.

He eased himself into his car and drove off the campus, his thoughts firmly fixed on what to have for lunch and the couple of glasses of claret that might accompany it.

7

Monday 12th September am
Monday was the start of the teaching programmes for all the newly registered masters students. The weather at TDU was like at the weekend – dry and bright with some warmth in the air when the sun was shining. In his office in the Horrocks Building, Kevin Varney looked out of the window and thought how much nicer it would be to still be up on the downs doing the walk that had occupied him and his wife Joanne during most of Sunday. The lunch in the pub about halfway round the circular walk they'd planned had been very enjoyable, he recalled, and they'd got back to their car just as the sun was getting low in the sky and there was starting to be a bit of a chill in the air.

Kevin generally felt this way on a Monday morning and even more so when he was about to embark on the delivery of a course which would keep him totally occupied for the entire week. He also knew that, once he was under way, he'd enjoy the lecturing and the interaction with students who, this being the first taught module of the course, would be enthusiastic and attentive, at least for the first few sessions.

The module was entitled 'An introduction to explosive ordnance' and was really a vehicle for presenting detailed information about the chemistry of explosive materials. After a brief summary of how explosives worked, he usually started with a couple of sessions on the history of explosives and then introduced the principles of analysing the energy liberated when an explosive reaction was initiated. Later in the module, the emphasis would shift to individual explosive compounds and the way they were used to undertake specific tasks like producing a significant blast wave load on a target or, when in the form of a 'shaped charge', cutting through material.

He glanced at the first page in the folder of notes on his desk with the heading 'Explosive Processes', to remind himself what he was going to talk about to the class first. The notes began with a discussion of the all-encompassing term 'combustion', the word used to describe the oxidation of a fuel either using oxygen from the air or oxygen from within a chemical compound. Kevin read the first paragraph through quickly:

'*When applied to gun propellants, combustion is usually referred to as 'burning' with the burning reaction taking place on the surface of the material. Almost any explosive material can be made to burn. If the speed with which the burning layer moves is much less than the speed with which sound would travel in the explosive, the process is termed 'deflagration'. The gas liberated as a result and the heat generated both flow in the opposite direction to the advancing reaction front. It should be noted that deflagration is a rapid process and typically takes only a fraction of a second when occurring in a conventional weapon.*'

Kevin paused in his reading to wonder whether he really needed to include more about deflagration as a phenomenon at this early stage. After a few moments reflection he concluded that, although it was a process of considerable significance in accidental explosions in facilities like offshore gas production platforms like the Piper Alpha disaster in 1987 or the earlier explosion at the Flixborough cyclohexane plant on Humberside in the 1967, the process of 'detonation' would, at least initially, be of more relevance to this body of predominantly military students. He continued his reading:

'*'Detonation', however, is a much more rapid combustion process, with the reaction zone, maybe only about 200 microns thick, moving faster than the speed of sound in the material. Once initiated, a detonation reaction will sustain itself and will be accompanied by large step changes in pressure and temperature at the reaction shock front which, depending on the particular explosive material, can move at speeds of between 1500 m/s to 9000 m/s. This means that a detonation reaction can be considered as practically instantaneous. Within the reaction zone, the pressure can be as high as 300 kilobars – about 300000 atmospheres – with a temperature reaching 4000 degrees Kelvin.*'

The section ended with the words: '*Materials that detonate easily are referred to as 'high explosives' while materials that more readily deflagrate, such as those used for gun propellants, are referred to as 'low explosives'.*'

Kevin continued leafing through the file of notes and felt generally satisfied with what he saw. He'd spent a couple of days the previous week making a few amendments and updates both to these sections - which he'd used on this course several times previously - and to the PowerPoint presentations that he used to illustrate the points he needed to emphasise. In a separate pile were sheets labelled 'Tutorial Problems', while in a third stack were copies of the assignment that students would tackle and which, together with a written examination just before the Christmas recess, would comprise the assessment for the module.

Kevin looked at his watch and saw that it was just after half-past nine. The module was due to start at ten minutes to ten and he was gathering up his file of notes and the tutorial sheets when there was a knock at the door.

'Come in!' called Kevin and the door immediately opened to reveal David Burgess who was carrying a cardboard folder.

'Are you on your way to Room 10?' asked David.

'Yes,' replied Kevin. 'Coming along to make sure all your students have found their way there? I've got a list of the ten EOT MSc students and there should be someone from the Short Course Unit to make sure that the visitors are all happy. There are only six of them now – a couple apparently cried off on Friday afternoon.'

'Yes, I'll just make sure that all's well with the guys and that they had a good weekend,' said David. 'Then I'll leave you to get on with it – you must have them for most of the day, I guess?'

'That's right – we're in the lecture-room all morning,' said Kevin. 'This afternoon we're going out onto the EDER with Simon Davies from A&E Wing to demonstrate some of the ideas we'll be looking at before lunch. Let's hope the weather keeps fine.'

*

Lecture Room 10 was a recently refurbished tiered lecture room that could seat getting on for forty. This morning the room was about two thirds full and, as he entered, David Burgess saw that the six Protective Structures students were sitting together more or less in the middle of the room. There were other uniformed students sitting together in groups of three or four around the room whom David assumed were the EOT MSc students. The half dozen other occupants of the room – four men and two women – were sitting in pairs in the front couple of rows. A girl whom David recognised as Fiona Bryant, one of the Short Course Unit's staff, was collecting together papers on the table that stood next to the computer and projection system.

'All done,' she said, smiling at David and Kevin as they came in. 'You've got six taking the module as a short course. The two in the front row on the left are from Abbeywood, the lady and gentlemen on the right are both from DSTL at the Fort and the couple behind them are over from TNO in the Netherlands. I've completed all the paperwork for them and, as you see, everyone has a file with the notes you asked us to prepare. I'll drop in at coffee time to make sure that our visitors know about arrangements for lunch. I should also have log-in details so they can access the network.'

'Thanks, Fiona, I can take it from here,' said Kevin as he started to log onto the computer and access his lecture presentations. While Fiona was speaking with Kevin, David walked up the two or three steps to where the Protective Structures students were gathered.

'Good morning, gentlemen! Good weekend, I hope? We've been lucky with the weather so far this September,' said David addressing his six students.

His greeting elicited a friendly response. The two Australians mentioned that they'd been out and about in the Cotswolds on Sunday, as had Philippe Giraud who'd driven out to Stow-on-the-Wold with Alfred. Karl-Heinz had joined up with another German officer on another course and seen some of the sights of Oxford. Miles Cowley was looking a little tired, saying he'd driven back from Chatham just this morning and, to miss the M25 traffic had set off at 6.00am, but that another coffee would soon see him right.

'Glad you had interesting weekends,' said David, 'but I guess it's time to start work now – I'll leave you to a bit of TLC from Kevin and his colleagues for now but, if you need to talk about anything that's concerning you, you know here to find me. See you later!'

David said a quick goodbye to Kevin, who was just about ready to introduce himself and the module to the group, and returned to his office.

*

On the floor above, James Schofield was putting the finishing touches to the lecture on structural analysis that he was to deliver just after coffee-time to the newly-arrived civil and mechanical engineering undergraduate students. James was regarded as someone who would, by virtue of his personality and engaging lecturing technique, gain the confidence of the new cohort of undergraduates who were embarking on an approach to study that was likely to be very different to that which they had experienced at school.

One of the first things he planned to say to the class was that they'd be unlikely to learn much during the course of his fifty-minute lecture. He'd tell them that it would be delivered in a clear and approachable manner and that they'd enjoy it. He was also sure that at this point they'd laugh and look sceptical. He'd then tell them that 'learning' would take place afterwards when they were back in their study bedrooms, when they read through the printed notes he planned to issue, reviewed the additions to the notes that he would encourage them to make as he lectured, try the carefully constructed tutorial problems that he would distribute that complemented the notes and consulted the recommended texts to augment the notes and provide another slant on the subject material. He knew that this would provoke a somewhat disgruntled response. Nevertheless, he knew he was right and was certain that at least some of the class would, however grudgingly, come to acknowledge that his view was correct.

There was a knock at the door and, before James could respond, it opened and Michael Carswell entered.

'Good morning, Michael. How was your weekend?' asked James affably. 'Did you manage to finish the paper you were worried about on Friday?'

'Yes, I managed to make some decent progress on it – still a few graphs to annotate – but it's not that that I want to talk to you about,' replied Michael.

'Well, if it's about the new contract, I think we'll need more than the time I've got this morning – I'm lecturing in about three quarters of an hour,' said James.

'I guess it is and it isn't,' responded Michael. 'It's about the whole method that I've been developing that I've used both on the MoD contract – that's what the paper is about – and that I plan to use on the new pieces of work I hope you're going to assist with.'

'Come on, then, spit it out – what's the problem?' asked James who could see from Michael's face that whatever it was that was troubling him appeared serious.

'It's a combination of little things really,' began Michael, 'which, taken together, might be interpreted as indicating that my analytical methodology isn't really mine at all, but that I've pinched someone else's and not acknowledged it.'

Michael proceeded to recount to James the content of the e-mail that he'd received from one of the other academics involved in the MoD work and his reference to DSTO's analytical approach. He told James about the brief conversation he'd had on Friday evening with Graham Dowell who, it was apparent, had a good knowledge of DSTO's work in the area of force protection and seemed at least to know some of the numerical modellers there.

'What should I do, James?' asked Michael, clearly agitated by the situation. 'What if my method is the same as theirs? I'll bet that there are restrictions on the usage of their approach, just as there are on the stuff I've produced on the MoD contract. I can conceive of untold embarrassment for me, TDU and the MoD if it turns out that somehow I have appropriated an existing methodology and claimed it to be my own. If DSTO get wind of it and it turns out that I really have been using their method and calling it mine, it would be awful......'

Michael's voice trailed off as James stood up behind his desk.

'So, to put it simply, you're worried that you've plagiarised someone else's work and are using their ideas without acknowledgement? Is that it?' asked James.

'I suppose so,' replied Michael. 'I've been racking my brains to remember how I first thought of the approach I'm using. I really believed it was my own idea but now I'm beginning to have some doubts.'

'It seems to me that the first thing that needs to be done is to get hold of some hard facts. All that you've told me so far is hearsay and conjecture. You need to go back to the start of your work on the software and the principles it uses and trace its origins. You need to establish where you got the idea for the key feature of the program,' said James in a reassuring tone. 'Then you need to get hold of solid information about what DSTO are doing. Until you make a comparison you won't know if your method and theirs are similar. Even if they are, the chances are that there are some key differences between your approach and theirs.'

'I guess you're right,' replied Michael. 'But what if I really have pinched their idea? The consequences could be serious. The MoD contract I've just finished specifies that any software developed during the course of the contract belongs to them – though I can use it on this new piece of MoD work. They won't like it if it turns out that DSTO is the true originator.'

'My advice is not to worry,' interrupted James. 'When I first started publishing, I used to be concerned that some of my stuff was a bit too close for comfort to other research. There's bound to be some similarity between techniques that are designed to solve the same sort of problems, but equally there are likely to be distinct differences. The best thing to do is to find out exactly what DSTO are doing – maybe you need to talk to Graham Dowell and get hold of a contact in the section at DSTO which is doing the work you're worried about. If there is a problem, it would be better to sort it out before you go into print with your conference paper.'

'Yes, you're right, I can't undo what's been done,' replied Michael. 'It may only come down to having to acknowledge the DSTO work. I hope so – MoD can be very awkward about having stuff they think they've paid for and is exclusively for their use being run by someone else. Even worse if it's a foreign government – albeit the Australians.'

James looked at his watch, picked up the material for his lecture, and smiled at Michael.

'Again I say – don't worry – get some solid information and take it from there. It may be the start of a fruitful collaboration between TDU and DSTO that could complement the various Hargreaves and Nightingale schemes for Anglo-Oz collaboration. Why not come and have a coffee?'

'Coffee – good idea,' replied Michael. 'Thanks for your advice – I may be over-reacting, but you're right - it would be best to find out.'

*

Frank Hargreaves looked at his watch, saw it was about ten o'clock and thought it would be a good time to make the phone call to James Nightingale that the Provost had suggested at the Welcoming Party on Friday evening.

Hargreaves knew that Nightingale's first commitment every Monday morning was a session with some of the senior military staff on campus together with Robert Carter, the Chief Finance Officer and the Academic Registrar, Susan Thornley. The meeting was referred to as 'Morning Prayers' and offered a chance for both the military and TDU to review the previous week's business and look ahead to matters that had to be addressed in the coming five days. The meeting was almost always affable and, though there was a suspicion among some of the more senior TDU staff that it provided a golden opportunity for the military to snoop on TDU's plans, it did provide a forum where potential problems could be raised and possibly contentious issues given a preliminary airing. If there were any problems, they usually centred on the business of the balance between how TDU was servicing the MoD's suite of courses and the amount of effort the University was devoting to the generation of the complementary business essential to the balancing of the university's books.

Hargreaves dialled Nightingale's number and was immediately answered by the voice of Marion Jones, Nightingale's long-serving PA.

'Provost's office,' said Marion.

'It's Frank,' replied Hargreaves who had known Marion ever since she'd started working at TDU. 'I was hoping to have a few minutes with James this morning. He suggested we fix up a meeting.'

'Oh, right,' said Marion. 'He said that you'd be calling and suggested that you meet at about a quarter past ten. He finished 'Morning Prayers' before ten this time and he's just looking at his post.'

'That's fine - I'll be with you in about ten minutes,' said Hargreaves and put the phone down before picking up the file labelled 'Oz network'. He quickly scanned its contents before setting off to walk the short distance to Nightingale's office situated on the floor above the Common Room in the University's administration building.

He knocked on the door Marion Jones' office through which all visitors had to pass to get to Nightingale's well-appointed room looking out over the campus, and entered.

'Hello, Professor, he's expecting you – go on through', said Marion with a smile.

Hargreaves thanked her, knocked on Nightingale's door, waited for a shouted 'Come in' and entered. Nightingale was sitting behind a large desk on which sat a number of piles of papers and files. A file was open in front of Nightingale, who looked up as Hargreaves entered. Hargreaves sat down on one of the two chairs in front of Nightingale's desk. They exchanges pleasantries about their respective weekends during which conversation Hargreaves did not mention the Saturday morning annotation of his Australian file. Nightingale put down the pen he was holding with which he'd been making marginal notes on the paper he was reading and looked directly at Frank Hargreaves.

'Our conversation on Friday evening was unnecessarily embarrassing, Frank. I should not have been learning about your Australian plans in front of students who seemed to know both a good deal about my recent trip to ADFA and more than likely knew a fair bit about your plans for linking up TDU,

Melbourne Uni and ADFA through this new network,' said Nightingale. 'They certainly seemed to know rather more about your contact with ADFA than I did.'

Hargreaves shifted slightly in his seat.

'If you're going to succeed me as Provost,' continued Nightingale, 'you'll need to be a bit more careful about what you say in public and a bit readier to keep your senior colleagues informed about your schemes. Have you spoken to Robert Carter about the financial implications of such collaboration? Don't you think that Susan Thornley would need to be informed about the implications of having Australian students registered here for research degrees and for UK students to be working in Australia? I know that encouraging research student transfers is a key facet of these Networks and it has cost implications.'

Nightingale paused before continuing.

'And most importantly, I would have thought that you would have discussed your ideas with me well before now, instead of revealing them in such an unprofessional way that makes us both look as if the left hand doesn't know what the right is doing.'

Hargreaves was silent as he opened the file he was holding.

'It really is no big deal, James,' started Hargreaves. 'It's just unfortunate that we happen to have a couple of Aussies who know that we've both been in Australia recently and that both of us have had dealings with ADFA in one way or another. I haven't felt the need to discuss matters with you because it's early days yet. These things take time – you know that - and there are no firm plans in place at this stage. The Network funding for Melbourne hasn't been agreed with the Australian Research Council…..'

'All the same, I should have known about the possibility,' interrupted Nightingale. 'The military here are getting very touchy about activities that they think might mean we put less than 100% into our work for them here.'

'I've got my file here with some information,' said Hargreaves. 'I'd be very happy to talk it through with you but there's not that much detail yet, mainly my suggestions to

Melbourne and ADFA rather than anything concrete back from them.'

'That won't be necessary because I want you to prepare a written review of what course your discussions have followed so far, supported by some idea of the costs involved and the possible benefits – both financial and academic – that such collaboration might bring.'

'Yes, I can do that but it won't contain much by way of detail because there's some way to go before anything can be fixed,' replied Hargreaves. 'But, if that's what you want……..'

'Yes, it is, Frank and I'd like to have it before the end of the week, please. It's vital that I know about important initiatives my staff might be contemplating….' Nightingale paused before continuing in a rather more conciliatory tone, '….and it does sound a good idea. If it's meshed in with my proposals to ADFA –which are at quite an advanced state – the two schemes could be seen as totally complementary and good for TDU.'

'And good in furthering your aim to move to the UFC,' was Hargreaves unspoken thought. Hargreaves could quite see how well it would play at the interview board when Nightingale spoke about masterminding a prestigious tie-up between internationally recognised defence-oriented universities. He was sure in his own mind that there'd be little if any mention of any input from valued colleagues.

'OK, James, message understood,' said Hargreaves, managing to raise a smile. 'After all, I wouldn't want to throw a spanner in the works in connection with my application to occupy this office, would I?'

'Point well made,' said Nightingale, also with a smile on his lips, if not in his eyes. 'We seem to be on the same wavelength!'

Hargreaves rose, took his leave, said a friendly farewell to Marion, who he was sure had heard most of their conversation, and walked back to his office to commence his 'review'.

*

It was coffee time and the lecture room was empty. Kevin had delivered his first couple of lectures and one of his colleagues had come into the lecture room to set up equipment for a very small-scale demonstration of some explosive materials some of which would be further investigated at bigger scale on EDER after lunch.

A few doors along the corridor there was a room with a couple of coffee machines and all the class were there. As always, talk was about anything but what had just been presented in the lecture room.

Graham Dowell was leaning against the wall by one of the windows overlooking the car park and talking to Grant Thompson.

'I've been racking my brains all weekend about it,' started Dowell, 'and I'm sure that I've come across the name Alex Simmonds somewhere before – I think it was in connection with something going on DSTO, though I'm not sure in what context. There is one section at DSTO doing some work on vehicles that has some connection with his ride mechanics stuff, but I don't think there are got any formal links with TDU. I only had a brief chat with him on Friday, but I got the impression that he likes to get around to conferences and meetings all over the place. Maybe that's where his name came up – the blokes at DSTO seem to have pretty generous conference budgets. Perhaps someone mentioned his name as being at a conference somewhere. It'll come to me in time, I guess.'

'I think most academics like to get out and about,' replied Grant. 'It's one of the perks of the job, I guess.'

They paused in their conversation and sipped their coffees as Miles Cowley approached.

'Good weekend?' asked Grant. 'What did you it up to?'

'I was back in Chatham with my fiancée, Nicky. She's in the Royal Engineers as well – she's just started the Professional Engineer Course at the RSME and they seem to be working her hard. I'm hoping she might be able to get up here for the weekend in a couple of weeks time. Maybe we could meet up for a drink together one night when she's here?'

'Good idea,' replied Grant. 'You and Nicky could come and have something to eat with us.'

Graham glanced at his watch.

'I think we'd better get back in there,' he said. 'Kevin has got some sort of pyrotechnic display for us next.'

*

Kevin Varney's final lecture of the morning ended at five to one. Before the class left for lunch, he'd made sure that everyone knew that the afternoon would commence on the EDER for a series of explosive demonstrations. He arranged to meet the six visiting course participants at the entrance to the mess at two o'clock to walk them over to the range. The MSc students all felt confident about finding their own way there for the session that was to start at a quarter past two.

Though most of the rest of the class were going to eat in the mess, Grant Thompson and Graham Dowell were both going back to Grant's quarters for a bite of lunch. It was only a ten minute walk from the Horrocks Building and only about five minutes to walk from the married quarters to EDER, leaving plenty of time for a sandwich and a coffee.

Soon after a quarter past one they were in the kitchen of Grant's quarter and enjoying the ham and salad sandwiches that Jen Thompson had made for them before she and Bronwen had gone out for a shopping trip to Oxford.

'You were saying at coffee-time about Alex Simmonds and some connection with DSTO,' said Grant between mouthfuls. 'Well, you reminded me about another possible TDU connection with DSTO. Just before I left Oz, I heard from a guy at DSTO who'd been doing some work with Comparmour.'

'I've come across the name before – but remind me who they are,' said Dowell.

'They're one of only a couple of Aussie companies that do research and development into composite armour systems. They try and both develop their own stuff as well as manufacturing other systems under licence. They are also active collaborators with DSTO,' replied Grant.

'It was towards the end of my tour in Afghanistan,' he continued, 'that I heard that Comparmour was interested in selling some of their kit to the Afghan Army. The word was that they were bringing out a range of personal protection systems that incorporated some new techniques and material combinations that had been developed in the UK. They were apparently negotiating to acquire the licences for the system and I'm sure that the Stephen Wright was the name mentioned as being involved on the UK side.'

'Could well be,' replied Dowell. 'From what Dr Wright was saying on Friday night, negotiations with some firm with the aim of commercialising his system are at an advance state. Though he didn't say which firm, I guess it could be Comparmour.'

Graham looked at his watch, finished his second sandwich and drank the last of his coffee.

'Time we were off,' he said to Grant. 'We're due on the range in ten minutes.'

8

Monday 12th September am

Robert Carter had just settled his rather bulky form behind his desk when the phone rang.

'Carter,' he said. 'Oh right, yes, Stephen come on up. I'll get the paperwork ready. It shouldn't take more than a few minutes to complete it – most of it has been done already and it's just those few amendments we discussed last week that you need to check.'

Carter put the phone down and reached into the large drawer of his desk equipped like the drawer of a filing cabinet and which was filled with suspension files. He selected the file marked 'Armacomposta' and checked to ensure that the three other files he had returned to their suspension carriers when he arrived in his office that morning were towards the back of the drawer – he wouldn't be needing them for this meeting. He opened the file and took out the top sheet with its bold TDU heading. He scanned the document and had just picked up a second sheet when there was a knock at the door.

'Come in!' called Carter who looked up to greet Stephen Wright.

'Good afternoon, Robert,' said Stephen. 'Everything OK? These last amendments are very small and I think you've already spoken to Armacomposta about them. Their UK rep called me last week and said that they wouldn't provide any difficulties. Quite a relief at this stage in proceedings.'

'I agree – it'll be good to have matters finalised after all our negotiations. I spent some time reviewing them again over the weekend and I think everything is as it should be,' replied Carter. 'We've only really provided some clarification of terms – nothing else has changed. Here, have a read through the covering letter and then we'll both check to ensure that all of the various annexes are as they should be. If you're happy we can then get it all off to Armacomposta today – better to send it via someone like UPS or FedeX. They should have the stuff within 24 hours.'

'OK,' said Stephen. 'Pass me the file and I'll have a look.'

The novel composite armour project had been funded by the one of the UK's research councils. It had been brought to a very successful conclusion, resulting in the design of a system that provided an enhanced level of protection to personnel against ballistic threats – bullets and fragments – making use of standard materials already used in protective clothing. The innovative aspect of the system was the way these materials were put together in the protective garments. Commercial exploitation was actively encouraged by the research council and, though it was unusual for the results of projects like this to produce commercially viable output so quickly, the fact that the system's components were already available coupled with a perceived urgent need to reduce the risk to combatants, had led to the system's swift exploitation.

The project had benefitted from input by several sponsors who had provided worthwhile financial contributions to the research as well as 'support in kind'. Wright had found the financial inputs very useful, allowing the purchase of pieces of equipment that were ideally suited to performing the dynamic testing he required and which he might otherwise have had to make do without.

Perhaps even more valuable was the so-called 'support in kind' which was provided by representatives from various interested parties who attended progress meetings, commented on the course of the work, suggested ways the research might be advanced and improved and generally took a technical interest in the project. In this case, UK representatives from four firms specialising in armour technology had been invited to attend the quarterly progress meetings. They came from the Boston-based American company ArmorTech, the Italian firm Difesa Composita whose head offices were in Rome, Armacomposta, a Brazilian specialist firm in Rio and the Australian armour manufacturer Comparmour. All four organisations had shown interest in the project and provided useful input. Of the four, Armacomposta had shown serious interest in the work right from its inception and had made valuable inputs into several technical aspect of the project.

Under the very strictest terms of commercial security, it was Armacomposta who, since the end of the project, had been actively working with Wright and TDU - in the person of Robert Carter - to obtain a licence for exclusive manufacture of the new system at Armacomposta's factory in Rio di Janeiro. The deal that was about to be finalised would be of significant financial benefit both to TDU and to Armacomposta. Only those at TDU directly involved in the negotiations - Robert Carter, Stephen Wright and James Nightingale - knew about the details of the deal being set up. Armacomposta had insisted that no competitor should get wind of the agreement until it was fully in place. The licencing agreement that they were about to sign was worth somewhat in excess of £300,000 to TDU as an initial payment. With a significant number of sales already agreed in principle and more in the pipeline, Armacomposta were confident of being able to recoup this outlay within the first six months of production. TDU was, of course, always seeking to increase its income from whatever source – in the current financial climate its generation was vital to the University. There was also good news for Wright in that it had been agreed by TDU that, not only would some of the licencing money be allocated directly to his research group but that he, personally, would be financially rewarded for his efforts in developing the new system by the payment of an *honorarium* to the tune of 15% of the licence fee. The income to his group – the exact figures was still to be ratified - would be of considerable use in both furthering its research aims as well as raising Wright's personal standing both in TDU and beyond. The *honorarium* which, he calculated, would be about £30000 after tax, would be put to good use.

Giles knew nothing about this money but, with his imminent need for cash, Stephen thought that it would be a wonderful way to help his partner out of a difficult situation – it would go a long way to sorting out Giles' financial troubles. He'd not thought when he'd tell Giles, but felt it best to wait until the deal was fully signed and sealed. If all went to schedule, he estimated he should have the money towards the end of November, in good time to meet Giles' January deadline for payment.

Carter placed the two sheets that he was holding back on top of the other papers in the file and slid it across the desk to Wright. These first two sheets were a letter addressed to Armacomposta's chief executive setting out the contents of the package of papers, a timetable for the return of the signed agreements and the schedule of payments associated with the manufacturing licence. Much of the documentation had already been reviewed by Armacomposta's UK office and the expectation was that the various papers would be returned, signed by Armacomposta, well within a week of their receipt. The initial licence payment of £300,000 would be paid to TDU before the end of September so that the necessary steps towards manufacture could then commence. Armacomposta were keen that the first production units should available for sale early in the New Year. There was a rumour that they were already in preliminary discussions with the government of Afghanistan – and other organisations besides - about acquiring the new system though, for reasons of commercial security, they wouldn't reveal who their potential customers were.

Following this initial payment, annual licence renewal would be at a rather lower cost than the initial charge, but there would be further payments to TDU in the form of 'royalties': TDU would be paid a percentage of the income Armacomposta received for each unit of the armour system sold.

The negotiations between TDU and Armacomposta over the last two months had been lengthy and detailed and had meant that both Carter and Wright's holiday plans had been disturbed to some degree, though both felt the need to proceed as swiftly and efficiently as possible. These documents represented the last in a series of iterations and the prospect of 'closing the deal' with Armacomposta had been a powerful driver.

'The letter is fine,' offered Wright. 'I'll scan through the other documents, though goodness knows I've read them several times these past few weeks.'

'They're only marginally altered in one or two places in comparison with the previous set and I know we both read those very carefully at the time,' said Carter, 'but a final check wouldn't go amiss.'

While Carter turned to the computer screen sitting on the left side of his desk and responded to a couple of e-mails, Wright spent fifteen minutes scanning the contract document and its various annexes.

'It all seems absolutely correct in every regard,' Stephen said. 'They're as keen to get this agreement off the ground as we are, so I can't see any reason for them not to sign and make the payment according to the schedule. It'll be good news for James Nightingale to know there's a quarter of a million coming in before Christmas – should make for a good Christmas party this year!'

'Well, let's hope so,' responded Carter. 'I'll sign them now and get these to the courier before the end of the day. I'll keep you informed of developments. I'll send an e-mail the Armacomposta CO and to Armacomposta UK to let them know what we've done. I might open a nice bottle tonight to celebrate!'

'Good idea,' replied Wright with a smile, suspecting that Carter opened a 'nice bottle' most evenings. 'Must let you get on – keep me posted of developments.'

Carter remained sitting at his desk after Wright had left, thinking that it was a good thing that no further amendments were necessary to the documents which meant that they could all now be sent.

9

Monday 12th September pm

It was coming up to a quarter to two when, in the materials laboratory, Dan Parker looked up from the work bench at which he was seated to see Gill Neville approaching. She was accompanied by Chris Wells.

'Hi, Dan,' said Gill with a smile. 'I'm not sure whether you've met Chris Wells before – he's just joined CME Department.'

Dan, looking a little surprised and possibly a little put out, shook hands with Chris while Gill, casting her eyes over the several plates of ceramic material bonded to what seemed to be a woven substrate continued, 'Are these the next set of samples for your trials next week? You must be nearing the end of this phase of the testing, I guess?'

Dan, who seemed to have recovered his equanimity, returned Gill's smile before speaking.

'Yes, these are them,' said Dan. 'It's been a bit of a struggle getting them ready in time for the range. Some of the instrumentation has been trickier to deal with than I thought – the dynamic strain gauges particularly – and today I've had interruptions throughout the morning – at coffee time, between lectures and at lunch-time up until about a quarter of an hour ago.'

Gill looked and felt a little awkward as Dan made this remark. Seeing her discomfort, Dan tried to reassure her.

'Not your fault, Gill,' said Dan. 'I think this is the first time that I've seen you since I started to prepare these specimens. No, the interruptions have been from MSc students who've been coming in to ask me about the various projects that Stephen is offering this year. There was a list of his proposals issued with course documents last Friday – he must be the only academic to provide this sort of stuff so early in the courses - and the keen ones are anxious to suss out what's on offer as soon as they can. I think it's all a bit early, really, but I don't like to dampen their enthusiasm by suggesting that they should do a few modules to see what takes their interest before they start worrying about projects. He must have put my name down as the point of contact and indicated that I'd be helping to run a couple of them and they've been along to pick my brains about what might be involved. I don't really mind, but I could have done without them this week.'

'My name's down on a couple of Stephen's projects as well and I've had students along this morning,' offered Gill. 'There were two British Army students, one Chilean major and an Italian Air force captain all asking about project work.'

'I had the Chilean, one of the Brits and the Italian – Giovanni Corradi, I think he's called. He seemed very keen on one of Stephen's projects. I think he plans to put the one on composite armour as his first choice,' said Dan.

'He seemed quite knowledgeable about armour systems already - I think he works in the area at his base near Rome. He did say something interesting about one of the firms that he's had some dealings with in the past – Difesa Composita. The name rang a bell with me – weren't they one of the companies involved in your research with Stephen?' asked Dan. 'He'd heard some rumour they were about to sign an agreement to manufacture a new generation of armour system, though he wasn't sure who the agreement was with – maybe an American firm, he thought.'

'Yes, Difesa Composita were on the advisory panel for our project and they did provide some quite useful advice on occasion,' said Gill. 'If they have been dealing with another outfit in the States, it would make sense for them to see what we've been doing - I suppose it provides a sort of assurance for them that they're keeping up with all the latest developments in the technology.'

'Giovanni only mentioned Difesa Composita in passing,' replied Dan. 'I guess he was just trying to indicate that his enquiries about the armour projects are serious and that he'd be bringing some basic knowledge to the work. Next time you see Stephen, you might mention how much interest both you and I have had about the topics he's included on the list.'

Gill nodded in response to this comment before saying, 'The reason I called in is that I need a couple of pairs of ear defenders. I thought I'd go out onto the EDER this afternoon for Kevin's explosives demo and take Chris along – he's not been on a range before. Could I borrow a couple of pairs from the lab, please? I'll bring them back before the end of the day. You know how strict they've become recently about range demonstrations. I know they have some sets out on the range, but there'll be quite a few students who'll need to use them and it might be easier if we took our own along.'

'Yes, sure,' replied Dan. 'There are some in the box on the filing cabinet near the door – just write your name, the date and time and the numbers painted on the ones you take in the book which should be in the box as well. When you bring them back, put the date and time against the entries and just initial it.'

'Thanks, Dan,' replied Gill. 'We'd better be going – the demo starts just after two.'

Holding the sets of ear-defenders that looked rather like a pair of large headphones, Gill and Chris left the laboratory and set off on the ten minute walk to the EDER. Gill was thinking that she must remember to tell Stephen about the Italian's interest in his projects and, perhaps more interestingly, his comment to Dan about Difesa Composita.

Turning back to the samples on his work-bench, Dan resumed his preparations though he found that his concentration has been disturbed and not just by the interruption.

*

It was a quite warm and sunny afternoon on EDER, perfect weather for demonstrating the performance of different types of explosives and for making some blast pressure measurements without having to worry about keeping the expensive recording equipment protected from rain. The digital storage oscilloscope with its monitor could simply be set up on a table in front of the viewing area and the cables to the signal amplifiers run out to the concrete pad where most of the demonstrations would take place.

Gill Neville and Chris Wells arrived at the range just as WO2 Simon Davies from Ammunitions and Explosives Wing was about to start his briefing which, as required, always began with a few words about safety on the range.

'Good afternoon, everyone. My name is Simon Davies, this is my colleague Mike Brown and we will be running the demonstration this afternoon. The rules are simple – everyone remains at this viewing area while the charges are being set and will remain here until permission to move towards the test pad is given by me. Although the size of charges we'll be using is small – none are more than a hundred grammes – when the charge is ready to fire, everyone should be wearing ear defenders – we'd hate for you to end your first day of the course with you all deaf!'

There was a murmur of amusement among the approximately two dozen students, all dutifully clutching pairs of dark green ear defenders.

'Dr Varney here,' continued Davies turning towards Kevin who was making adjustments to the recording equipment, 'will explain the measuring equipment that's been set up and the measurements he's going to make.'

'OK, Simon, thanks,' replied Kevin. 'Well, firstly we're going to use a couple of piezoelectric pressure transducers to measure the overpressure produced at a range of about one metre and one and a half metres by the deflagration of a quantity of butane gas initiated by a simple match-head igniter. Then we'll measure the overpressure produced by the detonation of a small quantity of high explosive – Simon's using C4 – that has the same energy content as the butane. I've set up the transducers so they measure side-on pressure. Just to remind you - that means that the pressure wave will pass over the transducer which is in a streamlined mount so that it won't disturb the characteristics of the pressure wave. I've set up the recorder so that we should see all the important features of the pulses.'

Simon spoke again, saying, 'The butane will be enclosed in a simple cardboard box which has had all its edges taped up to prevent gas escape. The igniter has been pushed through the roof of the box to its centre and the hole has been sealed. To fill the box we're just using a canister of butane gas such as you might use to power the sort of blow-torch used by plumbers for soldering pipe connections. There's a hole in the box for the tube from the butane canister to introduce the gas. There's also a small hole left open in the top of the box and when the box is full of butane – Mike will be able to smell it when it comes out of the hole – we'll seal both holes with pieces of tape. Does anyone have any questions about this first demonstration?'

The question was met with a few murmured comments from the group to the effect that all seemed pretty clear so, without further ado, Mike Brown went off to prepare the charge and Kevin set his instrumentation to trigger when the igniter was fired. After four or five minutes Brown returned and nodded to Simon Davies.

'Ready to fire,' said Davies who looked round the group to see that all were wearing their ear defenders.

'Firing,' called out Davies as he pressed the button on the so-called 'exploder box' he was holding – generally known in military circles as a 'Shrike' after its manufacturer's name - that would initiate the match-head. Fifty metres away on the test pad there was a flash of light and a sizeable ball of flame visible as the gas exploded followed, almost instantaneously, by a loud noise.

Sitting in front of the recorder, Kevin pressed a couple of buttons and, on the monitor on the table, two traces appeared which were the graphs obtained by the two transducers showing the change of pressure as time elapsed.

'Not bad at all – quite a nice pair of traces,' said Kevin, turning to the group standing behind him. 'Come and have a look – you'll see we have a fairly gentle rise from atmospheric pressure – that's the horizontal line at the start of the record – up to a peak overpressure of about twenty kiloPascals at one metre away followed by a reduction in pressure back down to atmospheric pressure after about fifteen milliseconds. The second record starts a few milliseconds after the first, the peak pressure is a bit lower and the time to fall back to atmospheric pressure is a bit longer. I've saved these records and we'll do some analysis of them in our first session tomorrow morning.'

'If you'd like to inspect the test pad and have a look at the instrumentation, now would be a good time, while Mike and I prepare the next charge,' said Simon Davies.

Spotting Gill Neville towards the rear of the group, Simon said, 'Dr Neville, why don't you walk down and explain the set up?'

Gill smiled, pleased at being referred to as 'Dr Neville' rather than just Gill, nodded and set off with Chris Wells along the concrete path to the test pad, followed by the group of students. When they got to the pad, Gill pointed out what little was left of the cardboard box - just a few charred pieces – the remains of the match-head igniter and the cables that led back to the firing point both from the igniter and from and the two pressure transducers in their so-called 'mushroom' mounts designed so as not to disturb the characteristics of the pressure signal they were set up to measure. After a couple of minutes, Mike Brown arrived at the pad holding a small sphere of white material in one hand and carrying a green-painted metal box in the other and with a block of something white tucked under his arm.

'This is the charge for the second demonstration,' began Mike, 'which is a one hundred gramme sphere of C4 plastic explosive. In the box is an electric detonator which I'm going to push into the charge until the end of the detonator is at the centre of the sphere - but I can't do that until you have all moved off the pad. When it's ready, I'm going to put the charge on this block of expanded polystyrene foam.'

He let the white block fall to the ground.

'The height of the block is the same as half the height of the cardboard box used to ignite the butane and the block will be one metre and one and a half metres from the two transducers which are at the same level as the charge, so this demonstration will have pretty much the same geometry as the first.'

Mike paused before continuing, 'Gill, you could get everyone back to the viewing area, please, while I set the charge?'

Gill nodded her assent and the group started to make its way back to the viewing area with Gill and Chris bringing up the rear. The group was only back at the viewing area for barely a minute when Mike Brown re-appeared, telling both Simon Davies and Kevin Varney that the second charge was ready.

'Ready to fire!' announced Simon, again checking that all ear defenders were in place.

'Firing!' he called.

He pushed the button on the Shrike and, on the test pad, a bright flash was seen accompanied almost instantaneously by a loud bang, rather sharper and perhaps more intense that in the first demonstration. As before, after pressing a couple of buttons, Kevin produced two traces on the monitor and invited the group to observe the pressure against time graphs.

'Quite different shapes to those produced by deflagration,' commented Kevin. 'Here we've got almost instantaneous rises in pressure from atmospheric pressure because now, rather than the intense pressure pulse from the deflagration reaction, here we've got shock wave traces – or to be more precise since they've been produced by the detonation of a high explosive – blast wave pressure profiles. The peak pressures are about two hundred kiloPascals from the closer transducer and ninety kiloPascals for the one further away. The time taken for both records to fall back to atmospheric pressure – that's the positive phase duration, remember – is about two milliseconds. Again, I'll save these records so that tomorrow, we can try and do some analysis and see how well these measurements compare with any predictions we might make.'

Kevin paused and looked around at the assembled group before adding, 'Does anyone have any questions or comments about these two experiments before we move on to look at fragmentation effects and then the effect of charge shaping?'

One or two of the students asked questions about the characteristics of the instrumentation and the recording devices as well as about the two methods by which the charges had been initiated. Chris went to have a closer look at the traces on the monitor while Gill found herself standing next to Giovanni Corradi, the Italian Air Force officer she'd been speaking to that morning at coffee time about the projects that she and Stephen Wright were offering.

'Giovanni,' began Gill, 'you remember that we were talking with Dan Parker about one of Dr Wright's projects this morning?'

Giovanni turned to Gill and smiled before replying in excellent English, 'Yes, of course, I hope I wasn't too insistent in my questions about the projects, but I think it would be really interesting to do one of those that Dr Wright is proposing.'

'Not at all,' replied Gill. 'It's a good thing to show such a level of interest early on and you seem to have some knowledge of the subject already. But it wasn't that I wanted to ask you about.'

'What is it you want to know?' asked Giovanni.

'Well, it was your remark about Difesa Composita this morning and a new armour system that they might be planning to manufacture. I'm interested, because we had a representative from Difesa on our advisory panel for the project that Dr Wright and I have just completed which involved development of a new type of armour. He didn't mention anything about Difesa manufacturing any new system and I was just wondering what the system was – it might be of interest to us here. Is it an American development, do you know?'

Giovanni thought for a few moments before replying.

'I work in the equipment acquisition department for the Italian Air Force at a base near Rome and the Difesa factory is on an industrial park near our offices. My colleagues and I sometimes have a drink after work in a bar nearby and we see Difesa staff there occasionally. I can't recall exactly the details, but, over a drink in the bar not long before I came to England, I got the impression from one of their guys – quite a senior manager I think he is - that they were expecting to get the go ahead to start producing a new system sometime before Christmas. I'm not sure who the prospective partnership is with – it could be one of the American firms we deal with but I really don't know. I could try and find out, if it would help.'

'No need to do anything at the moment, thanks Giovanni,' replied Gill. 'I just thought it would be interesting for Dr Wright to know about what you'd heard. If he thinks it's worth following up, I'm sure he'll have a word with you – but thanks all the same.'

Gill stopped and looked round to see that Simon Davies was just about to introduce the third demonstration of the afternoon which was to be carried out in the very solid reinforced concrete building to the right of the viewing area. Simon was carrying a thick piece of card about a metre square.

'OK – can I have your attention, please?' began Simon. 'This piece of card is one of six similar pieces that we're going to use as 'witness screens' to look at the fragmentation pattern produced by a cased charge. This is the charge we're going to use.'

Simon paused and held up a small cylinder of steel in one hand and a small steel disk with a central hole in the other.

'As you can see, the cylinder is closed at one end and almost filled with 25 grammes of C4. The disk will fit tightly inside the open end of the cylinder and, when Mike is setting up the experiment, he'll push an electric detonator through the hole in the centre of the disk so that its end is in the middle of the cylinder. One piece of card will be on the floor and he'll place a block of polystyrene about 500 millimetres high in the centre of the card. He's then going to fix four more witness screens - he'll hold them together using duct tape – to make an open-topped cube. Once he's put the detonator in the charge, he'll place it on top of the polystyrene so that the charge is in the centre of the box and then fix the last piece of card on top of the cube. The wires from the detonator will pass through a small hole we've made in the top witness screen.'

Simon paused and looked around at the assembled group.

'Any questions before Mike gets on and does this?' he asked.

One of the group asked if the steel cylinder had any grooves cut into it to encourage the formation of uniform sized fragments to which Simon replied that the characteristics of the fragments would be determined only by the properties of the steel and the geometry of the charge. With no more questions forthcoming, Simon passed the charge components to Mike who made his way into the test building.

Gill took advantage of the delay before the charge was ready to seek out Chris Wells who was talking to Kevin about the records that had been obtained from the two explosions.

'Chris, I'll just wait till this next charge has been fired and then I think I'll have to leave – I've got a meeting with

Stephen about the new contract,' said Gill. 'You can stay till the end of the demonstration, if you like, it should be finished in a half an hour or so – there are two more tests after the fragmentation demonstration.'

'I think I'll have seen enough after this one,' replied Chris. 'I was most interested to see the instrumentation working and look at some real pressure-time records. The other experiments don't involve making pressure measurements - so Kevin tells me – just a look at the fragmentation pattern on the witness screens and then a couple of shaped charges tests. One is to make a hole in a piece of armour plate and the other is to use a commercial cutting charge to slice through a steel pipe. I'll walk back with you, if that's OK.'

Their conversation was cut short by Simon Davies calling out the 'Ready to Fire' warning. Everyone had put on their sets of ear defenders before Davies shouted, 'Firing!'

There was a dull thud from the building and a cloud of black smoke emerged from the entranceway. Simon turned to the assembled group and said, 'I'll just give the smoke time to disperse – there's an air extractor system installed in the building that should clear out most of it in a couple of minutes – then you can come in – perhaps groups of six would be best – to have a look and see what we've done.'

Gill caught Simon's eye just as he finished and told him that she and Chris would have to leave the range now, and thanked him for his clear explanations of the tests. A few seconds later both Gill and Chris were making their way along the tarmac road that led back to the main part of the campus.

As they walked they chatted and when they were out of sight of the group of students, Chris took hold of Gill's hand for the rest of the stroll back to their offices.

10

Tuesday 13th September am

Michael Carswell opened the door of his office and, as was his usual practice, went straight to his computer, turned it on and, after a delay of about thirty seconds during which time the various security firewalls were activated, logged in and immediately accessed his e-mail 'Inbox'. Several new messages had arrived overnight and the one that he was looking for with the subject line that read 'Re: Force Protection Software' was second on the list of those unopened. He clicked the mouse and opened the message in the reading pane on the screen.

Following his talk with James Schofield the previous morning, Michael had spent the rest of that day well into the evening reviewing the work he had been doing for the Ministry of Defence. This was on the development of software for the rapid assessment of damage to framed buildings that had been hit by the blast from the sort of substantial explosive charge that might be used in a vehicle bomb. His approach considered both steel and reinforced concrete structures and was designed to allow a military field commander, with only a minimal amount of data to input – such as building dimensions, material used for construction and typical member sizes - to make a rapid assessment of the structural integrity of the building. The output from the software was to be used to assist in deciding whether the damaged building was safe to enter or whether, because of the severity of the damage it had suffered, it would need strengthening and repair before it could be occupied.

Michael had been looking back over the work he had done in developing the software in order to determine just exactly how he had come to select the techniques he had employed in the analysis and what their origin was. He had gone all the way back to the analytical principles underlying the software and had managed to trace the key component of his approach back to a method first discussed in the 1960's. This technique made use of a combination of the peak overpressure at the blast wave front and the impulse delivered by the blast – that was simply calculated as the area under the graph of pressure variation over time – as a means of determining whether the response of an idealised structure had crossed a threshold of specified response as a result of a particular combination of pressure and impulse. He'd then been able to trace the development of the approach so that it could be used for the assessment of the performance of real structural elements. The method had become widespread and had been the subject of numerous journal and conference papers over the years and had been enshrined in a number of well-established design manuals prepared in the United States in the 1970s. In these documents, the methodology was based on representing these real structural elements for response assessment purposes as simple – so-called 'single degree of freedom' - structures that experienced the same amount of maximum deformation as the actual structural element.

It had been rather more complex to establish how the connection between individual elements to form a whole structure had been dealt with. It was a big step up from single elements and there had been a number of different approaches promoted by a number of different research organisations – both universities and government agencies – from around the world, with varying degrees of success. Michael had been able to establish that the basis of his connection methodology was both well-documented in a number of open source papers and reports during the past decade and was well-regarded by those who had made use of the approach in the early days of blast response assessment work: there had generally been decent correlation between the results of the analysis and experimental investigations. He'd been relieved to confirm that he'd given appropriate acknowledgement to these sources in the documentation accompanying his software: his report had included references to all the key papers.

When it came to the evaluation of the way the blast propagated through the building being analysed, he recalled how he had been faced with assessing approaches that were either far too trivial to allow accurate analyses or far too complex in their implementation. The simplest methods evaluated blast pressures and impulse using the same database employed for calculating blast loads from an explosion in free air remote from any building. Clearly this was far removed from the circumstances he was trying to assess. Then there were extremely complex methods that involved the detailed numerical modelling of the propagation of the blast wave through the building assuming that the building elements did not respond significantly as the blast passed through and interacted with the building structure. This approach effectively meant that the building elements remained undeformed during this time. The loading profiles so calculated were then used to assess the response of the building elements. The most sophisticated approaches were those so-called 'fully-coupled' analyses where blast wave propagation and structural element response calculations were carried out simultaneously.

Michael recalled how he had been obliged to discount these methods as not only being far too complex to be implement by hard-pressed field commanders but also extremely costly of both computing power and time. He knew that run-times for some of the most detailed fully-coupled analyses were measured in tens of hours and required access to very high specification computers. Very early on in his investigations he'd concluded that a field commander's laptop would have no hope of performing anything like these sorts of calculations.

Michael had eventually adopted what could best be described as a hybrid approach in which the loads obtained from numerical simulations of blast wave propagation through a number of standardised and idealised building geometries had been evaluated using a high-end computer. The results of these analyses had been used to form a database incorporated into Michael's software. Then, for a particular element in a particular building location, a series of dialogue boxes on the operator's computer screen prompted selection of the database file that best replicated the actual blast load. There was a neat twist to this analysis in that the dynamic forces generated between structural members connected together could be combined with a stored blast data file to better replicate the actual load that any particular element experienced.

It was this component of his programme that gave Michael most cause for concern. Was the use of a combination of loading from a built-in database with dynamic reaction loads his idea alone or had he extracted it from another source without acknowledgement? He recalled when he'd realised that the approach he had subsequently implemented would be a good one to try – it was in the first few weeks of the contract and he remembered how frustrated he'd been with the complexity of the task he'd been set. He remembered spending a few sleepless nights as he struggled with finding a way to address the complexity in an approachable manner and how, one morning while shaving, the mists of confusion had suddenly lifted and the way forward seemed blindingly obvious. He'd embarked on implementing the approach in the software that same day and, as the technique grew in scope and reliability, he'd put thinking about where the source of his approach lay well to the back of his mind.

Late yesterday evening with great relief he'd found what he was looking for: its discovery immediately lifted a weight off his mind. He was scanning through the substantial file of papers he'd built up during the course of the project and, in the section devoted to the numerical simulation of blast waves, he'd found the reference he'd been looking for. It came in a paper presented at a conference in Italy three or four years earlier by a Turkish academic from one of the Istanbul universities who was widely known among the numerical modelling community for his work on impact. This paper was his first foray into the field of blast loading and structural response and he had presented some elegant simulations of blast wave interactions with complex structural geometries using a sophisticated piece of commercial software that could be used for both impact and blast analyses. In the discussion and conclusions in the paper, there was a section speculating on the need, in every instance, for the sort of complete analysis that had been presented in the paper. The author offered a number of suggestions for simplification that, while preserving the essential output, would be swifter and much easier to implement. One of the suggestions included the use of a number of pre-calculated and stored load-time histories as a means of obtaining an acceptable response assessment. Another comment suggested the combination of a stored load profiles with dynamic support reaction forces and moments to produce an even better level of assessment without the use of excessive time or computing resources. The paper also outlined a couple of examples where the suggested approach might find application.

This, Michael recalled, had been the trigger for the method that he had implemented in his software. Though, of course, the detailed coding was his own, the principles he was using had been documented and, furthermore he had already referred to the paper in his report, including it in the 'Bibliography' rather than specifically referring to the paper in the text of the report.

The so-called 'front end' of the software – what the operator interrogated on the computer screen to run the program and access the output – was unique to the program. It had, of course, been assembled by Michael, but it made use of well-established Graphical User Interfaces - or GUIs as they were known – so there had never been any question about the integrity of this part of the software.

As relief had flooded through him, he realised how irrational he'd been in his concerns. He saw that, rather than panicking on Friday evening at the Welcoming Party, he should have carried out the review he'd just done immediately after he'd received that message from the research consortium member with its inference about plagiarism of work from Australia. He could have saved himself days of misery. He reminded himself that the key to successful and uncontentious research was that sources should always be acknowledged. It was quite acceptable to reproduce whole passages from papers by others provided the text was presented as a quotation between inverted commas and details of the source provided in full so that a reader could find the reference for himself, if necessary.

Michael's last act yesterday evening had been to e-mail Graham Dowell to ask if he could both provide him with a contact in the structural engineering section at DSTO Salisbury and also to suggest a time when he and Graham might have a chat about the work being undertaken in Salisbury.

*

Michael looked down the list of messages and found one from Graham Dowell whose reply was short and helpful:

> Hi Michael –
> Not a problem. I'm happy to chat. School doesn't start till 10.00 today so I could call in at about 9.15, unless I hear from you to say no. I'll come to your office.
> Cheers!
> Graham

The message had been received at just after eight that morning, suggesting that Graham had checked his e-mails on his laptop in his quarters round about breakfast time using the remote access facility that, for the past couple of years, the University had made available to students for when they were off-campus or were unable to make use of an on-site university computer.

Michael was pleased by the reply – it would be good to have a talk with Graham sooner rather than later – and glanced at his watch. It was just after nine o'clock which would give him ample time to jot down a few points that he wanted to talk with Graham about and which he'd been thinking about since his relief about the source of the techniques he'd been developing. He took out a pad of paper from his desk drawer and began writing notes to help him get his thoughts in order.

He was disturbed from his task by a knock at the office door. He glanced at his watch and saw it was just after ten minutes past nine.

'Come in,' he called.

The door opened to reveal Graham Dowell wearing his Australian Air Force uniform and with a rucksack slung from his right shoulder.

'Hope I'm not too early,' said Graham, 'but I need to have a word with Dr Burgess before the first lecture as well as seeing you.'

'No, that's fine,' replied Michael. 'Thanks for replying to my e-mail so quickly – I only sent it last night! Have a seat.'

Graham slipped the rucksack off his shoulder and sat on the chair Michael offered.

'I usually have the laptop fired up at breakfast – so I can catch up with the news from Oz with ABC News Online – and I noticed a couple of mail messages waiting for me,' said Graham. 'So, what is it you wanted to talk about, Michael?'

'Well, you recall our conversation at the Welcoming Party about the work I'd been doing on developing some software and about your work with DSTO?'

Graham nodded.

'A couple of weeks or so ago I had a message from another member of the consortium working on a different part of the same MoD contract I'm involved with. He said that he'd heard that there was a group at DSTO who are developing a software system for assessing building damage that seemed to have certain similarities with my approach. Since I got this message I've been worried sick that maybe I'd somehow pinched the idea at the heart of the analysis from DSTO or somewhere without realising it or acknowledging my sources.'

Michael paused and glanced at Graham whose expression gave nothing away, before continuing.

'Because I was putting the finishing touches to the MoD report and I had a conference paper to prepare and a lot of stuff to get ready for the start of term, I sort of pushed my concerns to the back of my mind. Our conversation on Friday night made me realise that I'd have to try and sort things out – if there was any question of plagiarism or me somehow improperly using someone else's ideas, then I needed to know.'

Graham shifted in his seat and, with a grin on his face, said, 'Well, we students all know about how to plagiarise work – we had a presentation on all the tricks during our induction sessions last week! I think the idea was to ensure we don't do it rather than encourage us in it!'

Seeing that Michael had more to say, Graham paused.

'Sorry to interrupt – go on.'

'After a miserable weekend, I decided to get some advice and spoke with Dr Schofield who managed to calm me down and suggested a number of things I should do to check what I'd been doing and how I came to be using the methods I'd employed. I spent most of yesterday from coffee-time on until late evening reviewing the stages of the project to clarify my sources. I should have done it when I was first alerted to the fact that there might be a problem.'

Graham leaned forward a little in his seat.

'So, what did you conclude?' he asked.

'It took a while, but I found the reference that triggered my development of the approach I used – I'd honestly forgotten just what it was that had set me off - and, to my great relief, found that I had included it in my report. I'd not, perhaps, emphasised the significance of what was a relatively small component of a much longer paper as much as I should have done. I intend to make a couple of editorial changes to my final report as a result of my review.'

'So, what's this got to do with me?' asked Graham, though he realised where Michael was heading as he described his concerns.

'It's really the work at DSTO that I need your advice and help about,' replied Michael. 'It seems that a team at DSTO have been developing a system to do the same tasks that my approach uses and I wanted to check to see if the approach actually was the same and just how they'd come to be using it.'

Graham leaned back in his chair and smiled.

'I thought this might be what you wanted to talk about ever since we chatted on Friday,' said Graham. 'In fact, Grant Thompson and I were talking about the conversation you and I had when we got back to our quarters on Friday night.'

'Oh, really?' said Michael. 'Do you know something about the work in this area that's going on at DSTO?'

'Yes, a little,' admitted Graham. 'Not long before I left Oz, I was having morning tea with one of the guys in the Defence Technology section who is part of the software development team. He mentioned that they'd seen an abstract for an upcoming conference that seemed to deal with the same problem and wondered where the author had got hold of the idea. I didn't really take too much notice at the time – I was more concerned with getting ready to come here – but seeing your name on the staff list and meeting you in person jogged my memory. My colleague was sure that the approach DSTO is using is their own idea. The only occasion it had been spoken about outside DSTO was in the last month when they presented some initial results at an informal seminar in Adelaide.'

'The conference abstract was published about five weeks ago,' Michael interrupted. 'During the past week or so I've been putting the finishing touches to the full paper. Maybe, like me, the DSTO team saw the same reference that triggered my approach?'

'That may be the case,' said Graham. 'Alternatively, they may really have come up with it themselves independently.'

Graham paused before he continued speaking.

'But does it really matter?' he said, 'If you're confident about the origin of your approach and if DSTO have either been triggered by the same reference or have really come up with the same approach 'out of the blue', isn't this a good result in any case? I bet the lines of code you use to implement the technique are different in detail to DSTO's. Even if the way data is entered and results presented are similar I'd guess there'll be some key differences. Both you and DSTO might be in a good position to combine your efforts to produce a program that is better than the two separate routines.'

As Graham stopped speaking, he looked at Michael who seemed to have visibly relaxed on hearing what Graham had to say.

'From what I heard from a number of people at the Welcoming Party last Friday, active collaboration between TDU and Oz – be it DSTO, ADFA or Melbourne Uni – sounds to be flavour of the month,' continued Graham. 'Quite a number of the staff I spoke with on Friday seemed very keen to go to Oz or at least work with Oz – why should you miss out?'

As Michael listened to Graham, he thought to himself that his concerns over the past couple of weeks had grown out of all proportion and, as Graham implied, matters could be turned to his, TDU's and DSTO's advantage.

'I guess you're right,' replied Michael. 'I know about the Research Network that Frank Hargreaves is pushing and the exchange links that the Provost is keen about. Perhaps a trip Down Under could be on the cards! Maybe the thing to do is get in contact with the DSTO team and put my cards on the table – I don't think I've lifted anything from them and they could well have just hit on the idea from having read around the subject. There are a lot of papers in the general area of blast damage assessment, after all and, like me, something they read might have triggered them to adopt the same method that I'm using.'

Graham reached into his rucksack and pulled out a tablet computer, turned it on and, after a few touches of the screen, turned it so that Michael could read what was displayed.

'This is the guy you might contact – Stuart Young – he's the bloke from the DSTO software team I was speaking with before I left Oz. I'm sure that he'd be pleased to hear from you.'

Michael wrote down the e-mail address shown on the screen and said, 'Thanks, Graham, that's a good idea – I'll get in contact straight away. It's been really good to have had this talk – I feel much better for having spoken about my concerns.'

'No worries,' relied Graham, looking at his watch. 'I've got to go – there's a lecture by Kevin Varney just about to start. Let me know if you need any more information.'

Graham turned off his computer, put it back in his rucksack and, with a final smile and wave to Michael, departed.

11

Tuesday 13th September am

Alex had eaten a swift but hearty breakfast with Meriel, Philip and Paul before the boys left the house at 8.15 to catch the school bus that would take them the five or six miles to Farlington Junior School where Philip was in Year 5 and Paul in Year 6. Meriel worked part-time as a member of the practice management team in the medical centre in Farlington, but her four hour stint didn't start until 1030 so she had no need to leave the house for the ten minute drive to work until after ten. Her hours were fairly flexible and meant that she could generally be home before the boys returned but, if they stayed on for after-school activities - which they did on a couple of days each week -she could work on a little longer and then pick them up from the school gate.

It was about a quarter to nine when Alex put on his coat, kissed Meriel goodbye and set off on the walk to TDU. For the second morning in succession as he strolled along Sherington High Street he was joined Chris Wells who caught up with him just after he'd passed the entrance to Chris's flat.

Alex and Chris exchanged greetings and commented on the fine weather that had persisted for several days now. Chris had come to realise from talking with that Alex, and from things that other colleagues had said, that Alex was a dedicated conference goer. There was nothing he liked more than a foreign trip of a few days to some congenial location to deliver a paper on his latest work in the field of vehicles – particularly military vehicles - and their performance on a wide range of different terrains.

'I had a bit of a result yesterday afternoon,' said Alex as the approached the TDU security gate, 'I received an invitation to be keynote speaker at a conference in Washington DC in March. What's more, the organisers are going to pay my travel and accommodation expenses, so the Department won't really be able to say no!'

'Washington DC sound better than Washington Tyne and Wear,' commented Chris with a smile. His most recent conference involvement had been at a Ceramics Association meeting in Coventry earlier in the year just after he'd applied for the job at TDU. 'Will it be just you going or will you try and take the family?'

'Just me this time,' replied Alex. 'It's in term-time and we don't like to take the boys out of school – it'll only be four nights away in any case.'

'What's the topic of the conference – vehicles, I know, otherwise you'd not be involved – but any particular slant?' asked Chris.

'Well, it's quite a big affair which has usually been limited just to contributors from the States. This time they're opening it up to a wider audience and inviting keynote speakers from around the world to encourage a more international participation. There'll be stuff on all aspects of military vehicle performance, including things like vehicle and personnel protection systems, vehicle mechanics and control systems as well as my stuff on ride. It should be good. American conferences tend to have a few plenary sessions for everyone and then so-called 'break-out' sessions which are more specialised. I've been asked to talk at one of the plenary sessions, giving an overview of developments in vehicle ride – just up my street!'

Alex paused as they reached the security gate and both he and Chris pulled out their passes to allow them entry onto the campus. They continued on the last few hundred yards to their offices with Chris offering congratulations to Alex on what seemed to be a prestigious invitation. They arrived at the entrance to the Horrocks Building and went their separate ways to their offices.

Once Alex had taken off his coat and turned on his computer he logged onto his e-mail account and was pleased to find a message with the heading 'International Military Vehicle Congress, Washington DC'. He clicked on the message and read:

Hi Dr Simmonds –

I got your message accepting our invitation – glad you're able to make it! We'll book you into the conference venue, the Marriott Hotel in MacLean, for four nights. When you've booked your flights, let me know your arrival time and I'll arrange for you to be met at Dulles and be driven to the Marriott.

The attachments to this message give the format to be used for your paper which will be included in .pdf form on the CD we'll be making of the Proceedings. I'll need your paper in its final form before the end of January.

We're looking forward to meeting with you, particularly now that the new TDU composite armor system – Dr Stephen Wright's name was mentioned in connection with it - is going commercial. It seems a very compact system with lots of potential. One of my colleagues who works in the field says he understands that one of our big defense contractors is acquiring the license to manufacture the new system. He'd like to talk to someone from TDU about the system's potential for use on vehicles as well as by personnel.

Let me know if you need any further information. There's a link to the conference website on one of the attachments which should answer most of the usual questions.

Regards
Mike Kuszczak
IMVC Administration Team

Alex clicked on the e-mail attachments which opened in another window on the screen. Nothing he saw about the required format gave him much cause for concern – he'd just have to select a US paper size for the final format of his paper. He re-read the e-mail from Kuszczak and felt a slightly puzzlement about the comment about 'the new TDU armor system'. He recalled the conversation at coffee time a few days ago where Stephen had declined to make any comment about which company might be about to acquire the armour licence. He was sure that Stephen wouldn't want the identity of the potential licencee to be in the public domain until everything had been signed and sealed.

'Might be worth just checking before I mention anything to Stephen about the conference and what I might say to any manufacturer who happens to be there,' he murmured to himself.

He clicked on 'Reply' and began typing.

Hi Mike –

Thanks for all the information – it all looks pretty clear to me. I'll start to make enquiries about flights now and will ensure you have my paper in good time.

You mentioned the TDU armour system – I'll pass on your comments to Dr Wright. Just so I've got my facts straight when I talk to him, what's the name of the company that is acquiring the licence?

All the best,

Alex Simmonds

Alex pressed 'Send' and looked at his watch – it was about 9.30, so it would be the early hours of the morning in Washington. The earliest he might expect to receive a reply to his message would be well into the afternoon. He put the question about the composite armour licence to the back of his mind turned his attention to the other unopened e-mails in his 'Inbox'.

*

Gill Neville put her head round the door of Chris Wells' office to find him staring intently at his computer screen.

'Am I interrupting?' asked Gill. 'It's getting on for eleven and I thought we might walk over to the Common Room for a coffee.'

Chris looked up and smiled at Gill.

'I can stop at any time,' he said. 'I've been putting together some lectures on materials for one of the undergraduate courses – the module doesn't start for another month and I've got quite a lot of the stuff sorted out already. It's a question of doing some decent PowerPoint presentations and preparing tutorial material. I used to assist with tutorials when I was at Nottingham and I've got a number of problems and exercises that I used there that I can adapt to use on this module. A cup of coffee sounds like a good idea.'

He rose from his desk and together they walked the short distance to the Common Room building where Chris saw that there were already a few people sitting in the 'Civils Corner'.

'It might be breaking the customs of centuries but, even though you are strictly not a 'Civil' lecturer, I think I could invite you to join this august group,' said Chris in a mock-serious tone, indicating the assembled group.

'Only if it won't disturb the established order of so many years standing,' responded Gill in a suitably acquiescent tone. 'It's only since I became a Teaching Associate that I've even been allowed to use the Common Room. Before that I used to grab a coffee in the lab - usually with Dan Parker. I feel a bit guilty about abandoning him, but it's good to have decent coffee from a clean cup after years of grotty instant in a chipped mug!'

Chris and Gill carried their coffees over to the group and sat down on a couple of the unoccupied chairs before extending a greeting to those already seated. A few general remarks were made about the continuing fine weather, the way the new undergraduate entry were shaping up and the enthusiastic way in which the students on the Protective Structures and Explosive Ordnance Masters courses had already been making serious enquiries about research project topics. Work in earnest on this important component of the courses was not scheduled or expected until after Christmas, but the consensus was that it was good for students to have engaged already with potential supervisors even though the allocation of projects would not be made until early November.

James Schofield put his empty cup down on one of the tables around which the 'Civils Corner' seats were grouped.

'I've had a couple of the Protective Structures guys come and chat about two of the topics I'm offering,' he said. 'There's one on dynamic finite element modelling and another concerned with conducting some small-scale blast tests on model structures on EDER. The Sapper, Miles Cowley, seemed quite keen on the one involving range work and Karl-Heinz Schmidt wanted to try his hand at running the new analytical package I acquired last spring, to see if he can correlate the analysis with some of the trials results he's got access to from his work in Germany.'

'Alfred Leng seems keen on doing something with me about internal blast propagation inside complex-geometry structures,' commented David Burgess who was sitting next to James. 'I think that one of the Aussies – it might be Grant Thompson – has been chatting with George about using the photogrammetric kit for assessing structural damage caused by blast and impact loads.'

'What about you, Gill?' asked James. 'I know it's early days, but I bet you'll have had some interest in your personal protection projects – a couple of those you and Stephen are offering look interesting.'

Gill smiled, pleased to have been included in the conversation, even though she still felt a bit of an outsider in this particular academic circle.

'Yes, that's right,' she replied. 'Both Stephen and I – and also my research colleague Dan Parker - have had three or four enquiries, mostly from EOT students. I think at least a couple of them will choose one of ours.'

'What's the situation with the licencing of Stephen's new system?' asked David. 'He told us at coffee a week or so ago that a deal was almost finalised, but he wouldn't say with whom. Do you know if it's been sorted out yet – you work quite closely with him, I know, and I wondered if he's let anything slip!'

'Well, I think the contract is almost ready to sign,' replied Gill. 'I really don't know which company is involved. You know that there were four armour firms in all represented on the steering group – ArmorTech from the States, the Italian

Difesa Composita, Armacomposta who are based in Rio and Comparmour from Australia. I don't know the details of any bid from any of them, though I guess whoever offered most would be likely to get the licence.'

Gill paused to sip her coffee before continuing.

'There was something that one of the Italian students on the EOT MSc said to me yesterday when we were on EDER. As I said, I've not been involved in anything to do with the licencing side of things – Stephen's been dealing with the contract with Mr Carter, the Finance Officer. Anyway, this student – an Italian Air Force officer - said that he'd heard that Difesa Composita were about to sign some deal for a new generation of armour system – he thought it could be an American development, but I've not heard of anything particularly different being developed in the States. But if it's 'Commercial in Confidence' stuff they might be playing it close to their chests. Or it could be that Difesa have become preferred bidder – I really don't know.'

As she finished speaking, Alex Simmonds sat down on a chair that had just been vacated by George Hambidge who muttered something about having to get equipment sorted out for an undergraduate surveying practical that afternoon.

'What did you say about licences?' asked Alex, turning to Gill.

Gill briefly repeated what she'd heard from Giovanni Corradi about Difesa Composita possibly acquiring a licence for the manufacture of novel composite armour and the possibility that an American company was involved.

'That's interesting,' said Alex. 'I've just been dealing with an e-mail about the conference I've been invited to in Washington next spring. My correspondent – one of the organising team – mentioned Stephen's work and how he thought that an American manufacturer was expecting to seal a commercial deal to manufacture it shortly. He didn't offer any names and it might all be hot air, but I e-mailed back him to ask if he knew which American firm he thought might be involved.'

'There are always rumours when it comes to who's won what contract,' interjected James. 'In my experience it's mostly just ill-informed chat with nothing behind it. I can't believe that anyone other than the highest bidder would acquire the licence if Robert Carter is involved!'

Gill shrugged before replying, 'Yes, I'm sure you're right and it may be that people are mixing up Comparmour or Armacomposta with ArmorTech – the names are a bit similar and they were all involved in supporting Stephen's project.'

James glanced at his watch and rose from his seat, saying that he had a Board of Studies meeting to attend. Most of the rest of the group finished their drinks and also left, leaving just Alex Simmonds, Gill Neville and Chris Wells.

'What does the rest of that day hold?' asked Alex, directing his question to both Gill and Chris.

'More lecture material to prepare,' replied Chris.

'Same here,' said Gill. 'I've also got some lab sessions to sort out. This evening Chris and I thought we'd go and see the new Meryl Streep film in Witney – it's had good reviews.'

'Sounds good,' said Alex, thinking that Gill and Chris seemed to be spending quite a lot of time in each other's company and how that was probably quite a good thing for both of them.

'Meriel and I thought we might go one night this week as well. Let me know what you think of it.'

*

Tuesday 13th September pm
It was getting on for five thirty and Alex Simmonds was just about to turn off his computer. He had promised Meriel that he'd be home in good time this evening since she was going to the monthly meeting of the book group that met in the village and he would be in charge of the boys. As he reached for the mouse to close the machine down, he heard the tone indicating that he'd received a new e-mail. He looked at his watch and decided he'd just about have time to open it, read it and still be home in good time. He'd said he'd aim to be back by six o'clock for an early-ish supper so that Meriel could be out of the house by a quarter to seven for her seven o'clock meeting. Alex clicked on his Inbox and saw that the new message was from the Washington vehicle conference. He opened the e-mail and read:

RE: RE: International Military Vehicle Congress, Washington DC

Hi Alex –

Thanks for your reply. Glad to hear that all the information I sent is clear. I look forward to receiving your paper.

I asked my colleague about the armor system licence – he said he thought ArmorTech had acquired it.

Regards

Mike Kuszczak
IMVC Administration Team

Having read the message, Alex clicked to close the e-mail window, logged off the computer and started to put on his jacket that he'd left hanging on the back of the office door. As he made a couple of checks to ensure the office window was closed and that his security cupboard was locked, he couldn't help thinking that the business surrounding the licencing arrangements seemed to be somewhat confusing. Probably no cause for concern, he told himself, but he made a mental note to mention it to Stephen when he next saw him. He looked at his watch which showed the time as twenty to six – a brisk walk would see him home at just about six, as he'd promised.

*

From the window of the materials laboratory overlooking the car park, Dan Parker watched as Gill Neville and Chris Wells walked hand-in-hand – somewhat self-consciously, he thought – towards Gill's car. As he watched, his shoulders slumped with disappointment.

12

Wednesday 14th September am

Michael Carswell logged onto his computer and went straight to his e-mail inbox where he immediately found the message he'd been hoping for from Stephen Young at DSTO in Australia. Somewhat apprehensively he clicked on the message to open it.

Re: Blast response assessment software development
Hi Dr Carswell –

Thanks for your message, the contents of which my colleagues and I found very interesting.

We're glad you've made contact with us – we were planning to e-mail you shortly ourselves having seen your conference abstract about the response software you're developing.

On the face of it, it sounds as if your software might be doing something very much on the lines of the program we're developing. I understand from your message that you thought that maybe you'd come across our work and were subconsciously using it as the basis of your program. We think that's unlikely because it's only recently that we've talked about our efforts outside DSTO when we presented some results at a small seminar in Adelaide last month.

We, for our part, were also concerned that somehow we'd latched onto your technique and were using it in our work without acknowledgement. After all, you are well-known in the field of dynamic loading and we wondered if somehow we'd 'pinched' your method. From your message explaining how you lighted on the approach you're using, we can see that we've both been consulting the same sort of papers and reports in order to assess what the software needs to do and we have both arrived at a similar way of achieving it.

I can tell you that, having read the description of your approach, we are, indeed, working on similar lines but there are differences. For instance, we only ever use the positive phase duration in evaluating impulse whereas you sometimes – depending on structure orientation – include the negative phase in your assessments. Also, from your description, it seems to us that your method of data entry differs from ours and, in some cases, the nature of the input about construction materials is different. For instance, you incorporate a variable dynamic increase factor to define your material properties whereas we use an averaged global figure. Attached are some 'grabs' of our input screens and a couple of examples of the way we output results. We'd be pleased to see what you do.

Carswell paused in his reading and sat back in his chair, relief flooding through him. His worst fears had not been realised and, indeed, it seemed that his work might complement the Australian work rather than duplicate it. In an easier frame of mind, he read on.

So, we hope that we have set your mind at rest – we, too, had been a little anxious that we'd somehow been guilty of that heinous crime of 'plagiarism', but we don't think that's the case and nor should you harbour any concerns.

In fact, in the light of the potential link-ups that we've been hearing about between TDU, ADFA, DSTO and Melbourne Uni's new Research Network, we wondered whether, subject to appropriate clearances, we might be in a position to either share our results or, better still, actively collaborate on developing a piece of software that uses the best of both our individual programs.

The fact that you've got both Graham Dowell and Grant Thompson with you on the Masters course – Graham has been working at DSTO and we've had a fair bit of contact with Grant over that past couple of years – might help in establishing a collaborative link that fits into the bigger picture.

What do you think about this idea? Looking forward to hearing from you.

All the best,

Dr Stuart Young
Head DSTO Software Development

Carswell looked back at the start of the e-mail and noticed that Young had copied the e-mail to Graham Dowell, which seemed quite acceptable in the light of Graham's involvement with DSTO and the possibility of assisting in developing a formalised basis for collaboration. He clicked on the attachments and images of the DSTO input and results screens appeared on his monitor. As he inspected them it was clear that – given that the two programs were designed to solve the same set of problems – there were similarities in the data required at input and in the content of the output. It was also clear that there were key differences. Some of what the

DSTO program appeared to do seemed to be better than his program, while he was able to identify aspects of the Australian work that seemed inferior to his own efforts. The possibility of genuine collaboration to produce a really comprehensive piece of software was something that quite excited him. It might even mean that – like most of his colleagues had done in the past and were continuing to do – he'd get a trip to Australia as part of the venture, a prospect that rather attracted him.

He saved the attachments he'd downloaded and began to type an e-mail in response to Stuart Young's message.

*

Wednesday 14th September pm
Michael Carswell was just finishing his lunch – sandwiches that he'd prepared at home before leaving for work and a couple of pieces of fruit – when there was a knock on the office door.

'Come in!' called Carswell. The door opened and Graham Dowell entered.

'Good afternoon, Michael. Do you have a few minutes for a chat before the afternoon programme starts?' said Dowell. 'I didn't have time to see you this morning – we had a full morning, mostly in the lab, and I didn't even get much of a coffee break.'

'Yes, of course.' replied Michael. 'Have a seat. I'm glad that you've called in – I was planning to e-mail you in any case.'

'Does that mean you've read Stuart Young's message?' asked Graham. 'It seemed to contain some positive news, I thought. Looks like whatever fears you might have been harbouring about similarities between the DSTO program and your software are unfounded. The suggestion of active collaboration sounds a good idea – might be worth trying to incorporate any future joint undertaking under the umbrella of the various TDU-Oz links that everyone seems to be keen on.'

'Yes, I've read it and I am pleased by what Stuart Young wrote,' replied Michael. 'What we've both been doing is similar in principle but the details are different. Our two pieces of work complement each other rather than replicate each other, which was my real fear and DSTO seem to be of a similar opinion.'

'The bit about a collaborative venture sounds good,' offered Graham. 'I'd be happy to help if I can. After I finish here I'll be back at DSTO for at least a year and it might be useful to have someone with a foot in both the TDU and DSTO camps, so to say.'

'That might be very useful,' said Michael. 'I'll need to talk to people here and also at MoD who are sponsoring the work I've been doing, but it would be helpful to have someone with inside knowledge of DSTO while something is being sorted out. Thanks for the offer.'

'No worries. Let me know if you need any further information or contact details at DSTO,' replied Graham with a smile as he rose to leave.

'There is one other thing,' said Graham as he picked up his rucksack that he'd placed on the floor between his feet. 'At the same time as I got Stuart Young's e-mail I received another message from another of my DSTO colleagues who works with armour systems. He's been doing some work with the Aussie firm Comparmour who'd hinted to him that they are acquiring the sole licence to manufacture the new system that Stephen Wright has developed. Stephen was talking about his system at the Welcoming Party though he didn't mention Comparmour.'

Graham paused as he slung the rucksack over his right shoulder, before continuing.

'Comparmour had also mentioned to my colleague that they'd heard that the Brazilian composite armour manufacturer – Armacomposta, I think they are called – are also in the process of gearing up to produce a new range of personal armour products. They were wondering if the new system – which they assume has been developed in-house by the Brazilians – would be in direct competition with Dr Wright's designs. I've tried a couple of times to talk to Stephen, but I've not managed to catch him yet. If you see him, maybe you could mention what I've just told you – he might be interested to see if he can find out what the Brazilians have produced.'

'I think Stephen's away for a couple of days – he'll be back by Friday, I think – and I'll mention what you've said about the Brazilians,' replied Michael. 'I seem to recall that Gill Neville said that Armacomposta had a representative on the steering group for their project. Maybe everyone's getting the names of which firm is doing what muddled up?'

'Yes, could be,' replied Graham, glancing at his watch. 'Sorry, I must go – there's a lecture due to start soon.'

Graham went out of the office leaving Michael feeling both pleased with the events of the day so far and a little puzzled by the rumours and misinformation that seemed to attend Stephen Wright's armour work. Probably just that, he mused – someone somewhere has got the wrong end of the stick and is making comments based on supposition and hearsay without any real foundation.

Michael checked the time and judged that he had a few minutes before a meeting with one of his undergraduate students to drop by James Schofield's office and let him know how his contact with DSTO and his discussion with Graham Dowell had turned out.

*

James Schofield clicked the 'Print' icon on the pc screen and sat back in his chair as the structural analysis notes he'd just completed for one of his undergraduate courses started to appear in the printer output tray, when there was a tap on the door. Before he'd had time to respond, the door opened and Michael Carswell came in wearing a broad grin on his face.

'You look as if you might have had some good news,' said James, as Michael approached his desk.

'You're right, I have,' replied Carswell. 'I'd have told you earlier if you'd been around this morning.'

'I had a Faculty Board meeting about undergraduate exam regulations that took up most of the morning as well as a dental appointment first thing in Farlington, so I've only been in my office since just before lunch. So – any news from Oz?' enquired James.

Carswell proceeded to relate how he'd followed James' advice and been able to confirm in his own mind the fully-acknowledged source behind his building damage assessment software and how, with Graham Dowell's help, he'd contacted

DSTO who had provided a reassuring and indeed positive response to his message.

'I'm glad things have been sorted out,' commented James. 'It's never worth getting too worked up about things like this before you've checked the facts. I know that when you get lost in the detail of a piece of work you can often lose sight of the important guiding principles that formed the basis of your efforts. It seems the DSTO guys also had similar thoughts – it can have done no harm to either of your investigations to have made this contact. It sounds as if both parties might benefit from a collaborative effort.'

Michael nodded in agreement adding, 'It's a great relief to me – the thought of being accused of some form of plagiarism had been playing on my mind. I'm glad it's been sorted out.'

Michael paused as James turned in his seat to remove the dozen or so pages sitting in the printer output tray.

'There was one other thing that Graham Dowell mentioned when he dropped by just now,' said Michael. 'It was from another of his DSTO colleagues and was about composite armour. It seems that Comparmour – the Australian firm that has dealings with DSTO and who were part of Stephen's advisory panel for his project – had dropped a hint that they were acquiring the licence from Stephen. Comparmour had also picked up some rumour about a Brazilian armour manufacturer – Armacomposta – that was also planning to go into production of a new personal armour system which they assumed had been developed by the Brazilians 'in-house'. I know that Armacomposta had a representative on Stephen's advisory group and it struck me that Stephen ought to know that either there's possibly a new competitor with a new product about to launch or that, at the very least, there's some confusion in the armour industry about who's doing what.'

James listened carefully to what Michael was saying, a frown appearing on his face at the mention of Armacomposta.

'There certainly seems to be some confusion, at least,' said James. 'The name of two other armour manufacturers came up in conversations over coffee yesterday. One of Alex Simmonds' US contacts mentioned to him in an e-mail about a conference Alex is due to speak at next spring, that he'd heard that the American firm ArmorTech were actually acquiring the licence to manufacture Stephen's new system and Gill Neville was telling us that one of the Italian MSc students had told her that he'd heard that the Italian firm Difesa Composita were possibly going into partnership with a US outfit with a new system.'

James paused while he started the process of printing a second set of notes.

'I think the confusion stems from the fact that all four of these companies have similar names and all had representation on the advisory panel for Stephen's project. The facts surrounding the roles of the advisors and the licencing arrangements have got twisted and muddled.'

'It might be worth speaking to Stephen, just so that he knows the rumours going the rounds,' suggested Michael. 'I don't think he's back on campus until Friday morning – he's gone to a two-day seminar in Newcastle, I think – and I shan't be around – I've got a meeting in Oxford all day on Friday. Could you speak to him, do you think?'

'OK. If he's back on Friday morning, I'll speak to him then. I can't leave it any later because I don't plan to be around on Friday afternoon,' replied James. 'I was hoping to get away early – we're going to visit Laura's parents in Devon for the weekend - and I was wanting to leave here at lunch time and head off as soon as the boys got back from school soon after three. It could wait till Monday, I guess, or, if I don't manage to talk to Stephen, I could have a word with Frank Hargreaves and ask him to speak to Stephen on Friday afternoon – Frank'll be here, I'm sure.'

'I think it would be better just to speak to Stephen first. Though Frank knows a fair bit about Stephen's project, it would be good to keep things among ourselves and just let Stephen know what's being said before involving anyone else. Frank might think he should go and talk to Nightingale. I think it would be worth avoiding that at least until any problem's been identified – and there's no certainty that anything's amiss. There just seems to be a bit of confusion about who's got the licence for Stephen's system and whether there are any competing systems coming on the market. It may just be hype on the part of the companies who've not got the licence trying to demonstrate that they're still in the game. It can't be long before the licence is in place and any confusion will disappear,' said Michael, glancing up at the clock on the wall above James' desk. 'Must go – I've got one of the second year undergraduates coming to see me in a couple of minutes.'

Michael left the office and James sat back in his seat mulling over what Michael had told him. He was pleased that Michael's mind was set at ease about his programming work and thinking, in connection with Stephen's licencing arrangements, that rumour and hearsay didn't help anyone and the sooner that the record was set straight, the better. He resolved to speak with Stephen first thing on Friday morning, but thought it would be wise to make sure he'd got his facts right first. He picked up the phone and dialled Alex Simmonds number.

*

The phone in Alex Simmonds office rang. Alex turned away from his computer screen, which was displaying the booking screen for British Airways flights to Washington DC.

'Hello,' he said. 'Oh, hello, James, what can I do for you?'

He listened to what James Schofield had to say, before responding, 'Yes, of course, I'll forward the e-mails to you. I agree that there seems to be some confusion in the air about armour systems. It's as likely as not a case of crossed wires. My contact in the States – Mike Kuszczak – was only reporting second hand what he'd heard, though when I asked him for clarification about his first mention of ArmorTech he did ask his informant again and got the same reply that ArmorTech were acquiring a licence for Stephen's system.'

On the other end of the line James thanked Alex and said that he thought he'd also check with Gill Neville about her chat with the Italian MSc student so that he had as much information as possible before having a word with Stephen on Friday morning.

'Good idea,' said Alex. 'Rumours and gossip aren't helpful – it would be good to sort it all out before any licence agreement is in force – that can't be long now and I'm sure that Stephen will know all the details about when that is due to happen.'

Alex put down the phone, quickly found the two emails from Mike Kuszczak and forwarded them to James Schofield before returning to the British Airways screen and the flight options for travel to Washington next spring.

*

Gill Neville was just about to leave her office when the phone rang. With a sigh and a smile at Chris Wells who was standing at the open door waiting to walk with her to her car and for her to drive them back to his flat, she picked up the receiver.

'Oh, hello, James,' she said, before covering the mouthpiece and saying to Chris that it was James Schofield and she wouldn't be long. 'What can I do for you?'

Again James explained the situation regarding the apparent confusion over armour licences and asked her to tell him again about the conversation with Giovanni Corradi about the possible Difesa Composita – ArmorTech link. This Gill did in a few sentences, more or less repeating what she'd said at coffee the previous day.

'There's no doubt that one of the four from our advisory panel is being awarded the licence agreement,' she said. 'Both Stephen and I were impressed by all four's commitment to the project. Stephen said that he was also impressed by the financial arrangements being proposed by each of the four – though I'm not party to the details. Whoever gets the licence will be paying a fair bit for the exclusive right to manufacture the system.'

Gill paused as James spoke, telling her his plan to speak with Stephen to apprise him of the rumours and confusions that seemed to have arisen.

'I do agree that it would be wise to clarify matters regarding all four companies involved in the project – I'm sure they'd not want to be involved in any convoluted stories!' said Gill. 'We got on well with all of them – if I had to plump for one of them, I'd say that Comparmour seemed the most committed to the development of the system commercially, but, as I say, all the negotiations have been done by Stephen and Finance.'

Gill put the phone down and looked up at Chris who was looking out of the office window at the golf course that bordered the car park, and beyond to the rolling farmland that surrounded the campus. It was a clear evening and the rising slopes of the downland hills were visible in the distance.

'It's a really nice place to work, here,' commented Chris, turning towards Gill. 'Although there is a lot of nice country around Nottingham, it's nowhere near as accessible as here – we could be up on the Ridgeway in about 10 minutes after leaving this office. It would have taken longer than that just to get off the campus at Nottingham!'

'Yes, it is a good working here – a bit isolated, perhaps – it's not so easy to pop out at lunch-time to do much by way of shopping, for example,' commented Gill.

'That's not a problem most of the time, is it?' asked Chris. 'You can always do a bit of food shopping in Farlingon on your way home, I guess.'

He paused before continuing, 'But no need to worry about that tonight – I thought we'd see what the food's like at the Queen's Arms in Kingston Barwell – it's the village just this side of Leddington where James Schofield lives. James was telling me over coffee a couple of days ago that they've got a new chef and the food has improved immensely in comparison with what it used to be. I've reserved a table for seven-thirty.'

'That sounds good,' replied Gill, glancing at her watch, picking up her bag and moving to the door. 'I'm sure we could find something to occupy ourselves before we need to go out……'

As she spoke she blushed, while Chris looked at her and just smiled.

'Possibly,' he said. 'It's definitely time to leave here, at any rate.'

13

Thursday 15th September am

James Schofield looked at the time showing at the bottom right of his computer screen. It read '9.15' and James thought to himself that he'd have plenty of time before his only lecture of the day, due to start at eleven fifteen, to write something to discuss with Stephen Wright concerning the various rumours and whispers about the armour licencing contract.

He'd arrived on campus in good time this morning – not long after eight-twenty – and had gone immediately to Lecture Room 10, where Kevin Varney's 'An introduction to explosive ordnance' module was based, in the hope of having a word or two with Grant Thompson and Graham Dowell on the 'Protective Structures' course and the Italian Air Force officer Giovanni Corradi who was part of the EOT MSc cohort. James hadn't met the latter before but, as he entered the room, where already four or five students were standing around chatting, he soon spotted what he knew to be an Italian Air Force uniform. After excusing himself for breaking into the conversation Corradi was engaged in with a couple of students in Royal Naval uniforms, James introduced himself.

'Sorry to break into your conversation, Capt Corradi……,' began James.

'Please, call me Giovanni,' interrupted Corradi in clear Italian-accented English.

'OK – thanks! And I'm James……. Giovanni, I just wanted a bit of clarification about a conversation you had with my colleague Gill Neville at the start of the week in connection with lightweight armour. I know you're interested in doing a project will Gill or Stephen Wright and that, before you left Italy to start the course here, you'd heard something about a new system that Difesa Composita might be developing.'

'Yes, I remember talking to Gill,' replied Giovanni. 'All I said to her was that, over a drink in a bar near where I work and which is close to the Industrial Zone where Difesa Composita is based, I'd heard one of their managers – one with responsibility for new product development and manufacture - say that they were expecting to be given the authority to start the manufacture of a new armour system, possibly before Christmas this year. It was the first I'd heard about it and wondered if it was a system that the Americans had developed – I know that Difesa do have collaborative agreements with several US firms. I haven't done anything about finding out anything more. I was expecting Dr Wright to get in touch after Gill had spoken with him, but I've not heard from him.'

'He's been away for most of this week,' said James. 'I expect he'll get in touch in due course. I'm interested in any new system that comes on the market because it may have some relevance to the protection of structures even though I would guess that whatever Difesa is interested in is likely to be mainly applicable to vehicle and personnel protection.'

Just as James finished speaking, a half dozen or more students entered the lecture room. Among them were both Grant Thompson and Graham Dowell. James thanked Giovanni for the information and, after a quick glance at his watch which indicated that there was still more than ten minutes to go before the lecture session was due to start, he approached the two Protective Structures students who were busy taking notebooks and writing implements from their backpacks.

'Good morning Grant, Graham,' began James. 'Just before the lecture starts could I have a quick word with you both, please?'

The lecture room was starting to fill up and the noise level was rising.

'Perhaps we could just slip out into the corridor?' suggested James. 'It's a bit quieter there and it'll be easier to talk.'

Once in the corridor James turned to the two Australians.

'It's just a small point that I wanted talk about in relation to some new armour systems due on the market soon. I think you might have talked with one or two of my colleagues about what the Australian firm Comparmour might be planning to do. Also, I think you might have mentioned the possibility of a Brazilian firm also being on the point of offering a new system. Is that right? I'm interested in any new system because it might have applications for structural protection.'

It was Grant who spoke first, telling James about what he'd heard towards the end of his tour of duty in Afghanistan, namely that Comparmour were hopeful of manufacturing a new personal protection system that had been developed in the UK.

'There aren't many Australian firms that are involved in this area,' continued Grant. 'Comparmour are the biggest in Oz and it sounds a good thing for us if we'll be able to get into the Pacific Rim market in a significant way. I didn't realise until a few days ago that the system Comparmour were involved with was developed here – at least that what I assume is the case after chatting with Stephen Wright at the Welcoming Party last week, though he didn't actually say which company had won the manufacturing licence.'

'That's what I assumed, as well,' said Graham. 'But it may not be as straightforward as that after what I heard yesterday from a mate back in Oz at DSTO.'

'Why, what have you heard?' enquired James.

'Well, again, it's nothing definite, but it seems that there's a Brazilian company, Armacomposta, who are also reported - on the grapevine at least - to be bringing out a new personal armour system themselves. My contact thought it was a system developed in-house by the Brazilians - they've been expanding their military R&D significantly these last few years.'

Graham paused and Grant continued.

'It may be that, in response to Stephen Wright's work, other companies feel they've got to get on the bandwagon or get left behind. I was talking with Giovanni after lectures yesterday and he mentioned the possibility of a new Italian system being available soon. I can't imagine they'll be a patch on Stephen's system, but maybe these companies feel that they've got to try and put something out there in competition, even though what they're offering isn't much different to what they already have on the market – just the same stuff, but sexed up, so to say.'

'You may be right,' replied James. 'Thanks for the information. I'll talk with Stephen when he gets back later this week. I'd be pretty certain that he knows all about these companies anyway – I think the two you mentioned acted as advisors on his research project. They'd see what his system offered, of course, but they couldn't make use of the technology it uses without the appropriate licences.'

As he finished speaking, Kevin Varney arrived at the lecture room door, carrying various files and a pile of what looked like handouts to support his lecture.

'Thanks a lot, guys,' said James, nodding to Kevin as he passed. 'Duty calls – enjoy your morning!'

Grant and Graham smiled their goodbyes and followed Kevin into Lecture Room 10.

*

Back seated at his desk, James opened the e-mails that Alex Simmonds had forwarded him and read through them. There certainly seemed to be a lot of rumour and confusion around. If Mike Kuszczak, Alex's contact in Washington, was to be believed, a third overseas company – the American outfit ArmorTech - also seemed to be on the verge of offering a new protective system. James was particularly struck by the line from the last message which read: '*I asked my colleague about the armor system licence – he said he thought ArmorTech had acquired it.*'

This was the first reference to a definite link between Stephen Wright's system and a particular manufacturer other than Comparmour, who, as James knew from his conversation with Gill, she felt might be favourites to win the licencing contract. But, he thought, maybe Kuszczak's informant was confusing Comparmour with ArmorTech?

James came to the conclusion that the best course of action was to send an e-mail to Stephen that summarised what he had learnt from his various conversations and which he could read on his return. They could talk about the content subsequently.

He clicked on the 'New message' icon and began to type:

Hi Stephen –

I thought it would be worthwhile letting you know about certain 'confusions' that seem to have taken hold about your armour system.

There are some rumours floating around concerning other new systems – besides yours - just about to become available.

Anyway, there's a rumour that Difesa Composita in Italy are buying a licence to manufacture a new system that my informant (Giovanni Corradi on MSc EOT) thinks might be an American system – though he has no firm knowledge about it.

There's also a rumour from an American contact of Alex Simmonds that the US firm ArmorTech are reported to be acquiring a licence from you. Alex doesn't know exactly where the rumour started, but his American contact thinks it's a quite reliable source.

Then it seems that the Comparmour in Australia have hinted to one of Graham Dowell's contacts in DSTO that they are expecting/hoping to acquire the licence.

Finally, Comparmour also said to Graham's mate that the Brazilian outfit Armacomposta are bringing out a new system that is thought to have been developed in-house.

I must stress that Gill has not made any suggestion as to who is getting the licence, though

she did express the view that she thought
Comparmour had made some useful inputs to the
project.

I thought it would be worthwhile you knowing
about these stories, particularly as all of these
companies – Comparmour, ArmorTech, Difesa
Composta and Armacomposta were on your
research advisory panel.

I guess there are a lot of crossed wires here and
you might want to consider taking some action to
clarify the position?

When you get back from you trip – Newcastle was
it? – I'd be happy to talk with you if you need any
more info.

All the best,

James

He read through what he'd written, corrected a couple of typing errors and clicked on 'Send'. He looked at his watch and decided he'd just have time for a coffee before his lecture.

*

Thursday 15th September pm
Stephen looked at his watch and saw that it was approaching 12.30. The current speaker in the two-day seminar on high strength composites was bringing his very dull presentation to an end – death by PowerPoint, as Stephen and some of his TDU colleagues referred to such uninspiring lectures. He was reading through his final two slides summarising his presentation that had been concerned with development in stab-resistant textiles for use in body-armour.

It was with some satisfaction that Stephen noted that lunch was due shortly and that the final session of the seminar was only scheduled to last for about ninety minutes and should finish before three o'clock. When making his flight bookings, Stephen had calculated that there'd be no problem in catching the five o'clock flight from Newcastle International Airport at Woolsington, just outside the city. The Metro journey from the city centre would only take about thirty minutes, so he should be at the airport in good time for check in. The flight was about an hour and a quarter so he'd reckoned that he'd be picking up his car at Heathrow by seven and be home well before nine o'clock, if all went to plan.

The speaker had finished with his slides and was responding to a couple of questions from the audience of about forty when Stephen's mobile phone rang. The screen showed that the caller was Giles.

'Stephen – thank goodness I've got through to you. I've been trying for the past hour.'

Giles voice sounded anxious.

'Reception here is a bit patchy,' said Stephen, who immediately noticed the strain in Giles' voice, 'particularly in this seminar room. Let me just go outside. Hang on.'

Stephen rose from his seat, which was on the end of a row, quickly left the seminar room, crossed the foyer where lunch was being set out and went out of the building.

'You still there, Giles?' began Stephen. 'There seems to be a good signal here. What do you want to talk about so urgently?'

'I've had a call from Edward about the money I owe him. It seems that things are rather worse for him than he indicated in his letter and his creditors are asking for their money before the end of October rather than in the New Year, which is what I was working to. Edward was very apologetic but it seems that he's no option but to accede to his creditors' requests to pay sooner. He's within the terms of our six weeks notice agreement.'

Stephen again noted the agitated tone of Giles voice.

'Giles – calm down. There's no need to worry. I've got some good news for you. I wasn't going to tell you this until later – I'd meant it as a sort of early Christmas present – but I'm planning to use the *honorarium* from the armour licencing agreement as a contribution to paying off the loan. It will be about £30000 and I think you said you've got about eighteen thousand available besides in the fund you've been building to repay Edward. I know that's still four or five thousand short of the fifty-four thousand due to Edward. I'm sure we can find that easily enough.'

There was silence at Giles' end of the phone.

'Hello, Giles, are you there – did you hear what I just said? There won't be a problem.'

Giles came back on the line sounding, if anything even more strained.

'That's wonderful of you, Stephen, it really is, of course.'

There was some sign of relief in Giles' voice but Stephen had a feeling that there might still be a 'but' from Stephen.

'It's not that simple,' continued Giles in a voice that trailed off to silence.

'What's the problem?' asked Stephen. 'If you're worried about the extra five thousand or so, I can lay my hands on that, too, if need be.'

'There are two things,' began Giles. 'The sum I owe Edward turns out to be nearer sixty-four thousand rather than the fifty-four I'd calculated earlier – he sent an e-mail after his call setting out all the details of our agreement, the payments made and the payments still due. I've checked and rechecked my sums and I must have made an error early on in my repayment calculations but didn't notice the slip until I compared it with Edward's accounts. But it's worse than that……'

As Stephen listened he felt his anger and apprehension rising. He couldn't believe what his partner was saying.

'What do you mean 'a slip' – surely you can't have made such a fundamental error? And what else aren't you telling me?' demanded Stephen, conscious that his raised voice he was attracting one or two glances from passers-by.

'It's the money I said I'd put aside – the eighteen thousand – I'm afraid it's gone,' replied Giles.

'What do you mean?' said Stephen. 'That money has been specifically earmarked for years. You said that you'd ring-fenced it from all your other gallery transactions – so where has it gone?'

'Two big sales went wrong these last six months. I was going to tell you, of course, but the time never seemed right. I had, I thought, agreed the deals and, on the basis that I was expecting about twenty or so thousand from these sales I committed myself to acquiring several Thurstons that came on the market. You know we've had his work in the past and it sold well?'

Stephen recalled the bold abstract oils by the Scots painter Alistair Thurston that Giles had enthused about last year. Not my cup of tea, Stephen had said at the time, but they'd sold fairly readily and at a tidy profit.

'Go on,' said Stephen, really already knowing what his partner was about to tell him.

'I thought it would be safe to use the ring-fenced cash to fund the Thurston purchases and that I could then replace it from the sales I mentioned. I took the eighteen thousand and a couple of thousand from the gallery account, but I've not been able to replace it. The Thurstons will sell, but nothing like as soon as I'll need if I'm to pay off Edward.'

Stephen took a deep breath and asked, 'OK, so exactly how much have you got to find by next month?'

'It's £63,500………,' Giles' voice trailed off.

Stephen paused before replying, quickly doing some mental arithmetic.

'So, if I can contribute £30000 from my licence *honorarium* - assuming that I can get hold of it in time – and if I can quickly lay my hands on, say another £5000 that still leaves you short of £28500. How much could you get hold of?'

'I think I could manage about £4000 or maybe £5000 more or less immediately. Of course, there's a lot of value in the gallery works, but I'd need to sell between a third and a half of the stock to get close to what I need and, in the time frame I'm now working to, it won't happen. Even if we had until January I doubt that I'd even get close.'

'I think you need to contact Edward again and tell him the situation – maybe if he had the guarantee of, say, £40000 – that's almost two thirds of what you owe him – he might be prepared to allow you more time to make up the shortfall. You should tell him about the Thurstons – maybe he'd consider taking them in lieu of the remainder of the cash?'

'Well, maybe, yes, I don't know,' replied Giles, sounding somewhat less distressed now.

'You need to calm down,' said Stephen. 'I expect to be back home by about nine this evening – we can talk more then and…..'

Giles interrupted as Stephen was still speaking. His voice had at least lost the panicky edge of their earlier exchanges.

'Your *honorarium* money is such a boost – a wonderful gift – thank you so much. Maybe we can figure out a way of paying after all. Your idea of cash and art is something I didn't even think of – I've been in such a funk - but with your contribution it might work. I'll get on to Edward now and see if he'd be prepared to do a cash with paintings deal.'

'OK – good idea. We'll talk tonight. We'll work it out somehow – don't worry! I've got to go – lunch is starting. See you later – about nine I should think.'

They said their goodbyes and Stephen returned to the seminar, turning over in his mind what Giles had said and making a mental note to talk with Robert Carter at TDU first thing in the morning about the timescale for paying his *honorarium*.

*

In the materials laboratory at TDU Dan Parker sat in front of his computer screen and completed the entry of the data from his most recent experiments – simple tensile tests on the new material he was planning to use in his next set of explosive trials. He clicked on the graph-plotting utility of the program he habitually used to record, store and manipulate his data. He annotated the vertical and horizontal axes of the graph that appeared on the screen as 'Force (N)' and 'Extension (mm)' respectively, and then highlighted the data-file he'd just created and clicked on the 'Plot' icon on the screen. A dozen or more small solid black triangles appeared, the first at the origin of the graph where the axes crossed and the rest at increasing values of force and extension. Initially, a straight line could have been drawn through the triangles, indicating that the material was behaving elastically. The data points then deviated from this trend as each subsequent increment of force produced a slightly greater increase in extension. The last triangle on the graph was at a force of 1240 Newtons when the sample broke. Dan saved that graph and look at his watch. It was almost one o'clock.

At another bench in the lab Gill Neville was setting out an array of different materials for use in an undergraduate laboratory session scheduled to start after lunch at half past two. Dan called over to Gill.

'Gill – do you fancy a quick bite of lunch at 'The Forum'?' asked Dan, referring to the on-campus coffee bar that both staff and students used for break and lunch-time socialising. 'They've got a new lunch menu this term and I thought you might like to come and try it out with me – my shout, of course.'

At the sound of Dan's voice, Gill turned away from her bench and was about to speak when the door of the lab opened and Chris Wells entered. He gave a friendly wave in Dan's direction before walking over to Gill.

'Are you all set?' he asked. 'If we leave now we can be at the pub in ten minutes and be back well in time for your lab. George Hambidge was saying at coffee that their lunch-time specials are really good.'

'Yes, I think so,' replied Gill, who then turned to Dan. 'Perhaps we could try The Forum another day, Dan? Sorry to mess you about.'

In response, Dan managed a smile and replied, 'Yes, OK, another time. It's not a problem. I'll probably just go and get a sandwich and bring it back here. Hope the pub's good.'

Gill put on her coat that was hung over the back if a chair by the bench and picked up her bag that was resting on the bench near her material samples, smiled apologetically at Dan and left the lab with Chris. Dan could hear her laughing at something that Chris had said to her as they walked down the corridor. He stood up from the bench and walked over to the window overlooking the car park to see Gill and Chris walking hand in hand towards Gill's red Micra.

Though Dan's face betrayed no emotion, inside he was feeling a mixture of anger and frustration. Although he'd never made his feelings known, he had long been attracted to Gill. They'd always had morning coffee in the lab and an occasional lunch at The Forum together over the last months.

From their conversations, Dan knew a lot about Gill and she about him. They had got on well and Gill seemed to enjoy his company. As the last summer progressed he felt he was getting to the point in their relationship where he could overcome his natural shyness and ask her out on a 'proper' date.

Then Chris Wells arrived and, in this last week or so, everything seemed to have gone sour. Gill's appointment as teaching associate had pitched her much more into the academic circle than she had been as a research officer and coffee sessions in the lab seemed a distant memory. Every day now found her in the Common Room accompanied by Chris. Today's lunch appointment with Chris was just another example of Gill drifting away from him. Chris seemed nice enough, but he'd definitely taken over Gill. Any thoughts Dan had about a deeper relationship with Gill seemed unfulfillable – and all because of Chris Wells.

Dan turned away from the window, and still with thoughts of what might have been, made his way over to The Forum to buy a sandwich to eat at his bench and give himself time to think how he could bring Gill back to him. The letter he'd received from the Finance Office earlier in the day had been pushed right to the back of his mind, but it too would likely contribute to thwarting any hopes he might have about himself and Gill.

14

Friday 16th September am
James Schofield glanced at his watch, saw that it was just after 9.15, picked up the phone and dialled Stephen Wright's number. After a couple of rings, Stephen answered.

'Wright.'

James responded with cheerily.

'Hi, Stephen, it's James Schofield here. I was just wondering if you and I might have a quick word about the e-mail I sent you yesterday.'

'I'm just dealing with e-mails now,'replied Stephen. 'I haven't got to yours yet. What's it about?'

'There have been one or two stories circulating about your armour licencing that have somehow got into the TDU rumour mill,' replied James. 'I think you need to know about what's being said. It didn't seem worth disturbing you while you were away - it's nothing serious, I'd say - but it would best be dealt with fairly soon, since you know what's what. Can I pop round to your office for a quick chat?'

At the other end of the phone Stephen heaved a silent sigh before replying.

'Yes, sure – could you just give me 10 minutes to read what you've written and deal with a couple of other messages? It's amazing how they pile up even after only a short time away!'

'Sure,' replied James. 'See you at about 9.30 then.'

He put the phone down and began gathering the notes that he would be distributing at his undergraduate lecture later in the morning.

Stephen also put the phone down and slumped in his seat, thinking to himself that he could do without having to deal with any more problems just at the moment, particularly after his discussions with Giles following his return from Newcastle last night. They'd spent a lot of what remained of the evening poring over Giles' finances and the gallery's holdings, to see how it might be possible to get together the sum of money that Giles required to meet his obligations. They'd been able to identify a possible way forward, but it would need some negotiation by Giles with Edward Turner and, even if Turner agreed to take a mixture of cash and art, there'd still likely be a significant shortfall in what Giles could offer.

He turned to his computer, found James' e-mail that had arrived in his Inbox last evening and proceeded to read it, his feeling of disquiet growing as he did so. He'd just finished when there was a knock at the door, swiftly followed by its opening and the entrance of James Schofield.

'Good morning again, Stephen,' began James. 'This won't take long, I'm sure.'

'Hi, James,' replied Stephen. 'What's been going on while I've been away? Your e-mail suggests that the rumour mill has gone into overdrive!'

James sat down on a chair in front of Stephen's desk and took out a folded piece of paper from his jacket pocket.

'I've printed off my message, just to make sure I get it right – a number of the companies you've been involved with on the armour project and the licencing contract do have similar names. I wonder if this might possibly lie behind the rumours that seem to be circulating?'

James looked up at Stephen as he finished speaking. Stephen, for his part, looked sceptical.

'Anyway, am I correct in saying that………..,' James paused to consult the paper he was holding, '….Comparmour, ArmorTech, Difesa Composta and Armacomposta are the companies that were part of your advisory panel on the research project, though the winner of the contract hasn't been announced yet?'

'Yes, you're absolutely correct,' said Stephen. 'All four companies were very useful in the input they made to the project. As I think Gill said to you, Comparmour were fairly pro-active both during the project and when it came to discussions about licencing after the project had ended. But so were the other three, in reality. All four were very interested in acquiring the licence. Of course, when we were sounding out all four of them about possible contractual agreements, separate negotiations were conducted with each company confidentially. When Robert Carter and I reviewed all of the proposals, we came to the conclusion that one of them was proposing something significantly better than the other three both in terms of financial incentives and the promotion of the armour system, so we terminated our discussions with the other three companies when we embarked on serious talks with the one we selected. Which company that is will be announced very shortly.'

'Well, that seems very straightforward,' said James. 'But the fact remains that there is some confusion in the armour world about who's doing what and with whom. It might be worth issuing a statement to clarify the position so that all the rumours can be laid to rest.'

'I agree,' replied Stephen, 'and indeed it is the plan to issue a Press Release once the contract has been signed. The winning bidder got the final contract documents on Monday and they indicated that they would return them signed before Tuesday 20th. The contract will officially commence on October 1st. In the light of what you've told me, it might be worth making it quite clear in the Press Release something along the lines of……..hang on a moment………'

Stephen paused for a minute or two while he wrote on a piece of paper that he took from his desk drawer. When he'd finished writing, he read out what he'd prepared.

'*Following serious and constructive negotiations with Comparmour, ArmorTech, Difesa Composta and Armacomposta, the licencing contract for the manufacture of the new system developed at The Defence University has been won by COMPANY A . COMPANIES B,C and D are thanked for their significant input to the project that led to the current licencing agreement...,*' Stephen paused and looked up at James. 'Or something like that, anyway. I can't tell you who Company A is just yet! That should be sufficient to clarify the situation, I'd have thought.'

'That sounds a good line to take,' commented James. 'I didn't know that the contract was so near signing. Once that's done and the Press Release issued, that should put a stop to any speculation.'

'I think I'd best go and talk to Robert Carter to put him in the picture,' said Stephen. 'He wouldn't know anything about any rumours – he seems to live in a world completely divorced from anything other than spreadsheets and bureaucratic procedures – certainly nothing of a technological nature!'

James stood up to leave, saying, 'I'm glad that I put that e-mail together for you – it seems very timely to move away from hearsay to something definite. Must go – a lecture calls!'

After James had departed Stephen sat for a few moments longer thinking about the conversation he'd just had, wondering how such rumours got started. It must have been a combination of the similarity of company names and the fact that they had been close collaborators on the research project that had conspired to generate what seemed to be world-wide rumours about the armour system.

He glanced at his watch and saw that a lecture and a meeting scheduled with one of his research students would take up most of the rest of the morning. He also wanted to do a bit more analysis of his finances before lunch to see how Giles' money concerns might be eased. But, he thought, a talk today with Robert Carter wouldn't go amiss. As well as the need to lay to rest any contract rumours with a well-worded Press Release once the agreement with Armacomposta was signed, he determined that he would also seek to extract a firm date from Carter as to when his *honorarium* would be paid. In the light of Giles' situation, early payment was paramount. Stephen decided to call in on Carter after lunch.

*

Friday 16th September pm

Stephen had spent more than two hours with his research student who, he was pleased to learn, was managing to progress his research plan more or less as agreed at their previous meeting and had already started to draft his interim review document. Once this so-called 'transfer report' had been submitted, there'd be the need to convene an interview panel to confirm – or otherwise – the transfer of the student's registration from an MPhil degree to that for a full doctoral programme.

Once the student had departed, Stephen had found a half-hour or so just before lunch when he'd been able to conduct a more considered review of Giles' financial predicament than had been possible last night when he'd been tired from his travel and Giles was in a state of acute anxiety. As he sat at his desk, Stephen reviewed the calculations of the previous evening. He had been able to confirm that Giles did indeed owe Edward Turner almost £63,500 and that this money was due by the middle of October. When Stephen's *honorarium*, assumed to be about £30,000, together with other cash input by Giles of £4000 and another £5000 from Stephen, the shortfall was over £24,000. Of course, Stephen had other financial resources, but most of it was tied up in various fixed term bonds and accounts that did not allow access until the term expired and certainly not in the time-frame that Giles' problems demanded.

He'd been disappointed, but not overly surprised, to find that Giles' resources were very meagre – almost all his money had been put into the gallery. His access to cash was very limited – only a few hundred more that the £4000 he'd already included in his calculations. The gallery stock was the single unconverted asset and a preliminary assessment last night had indicated that, were Edward Turner to accept a payment in cash and paintings, about a third of the shortfall could be covered. If this offer was acceptable and the time to pay the remainder extended to the original New Year deadline, it would give Giles the chance to sell some pictures. If, over the Christmas period two or three of the Thurstons could be disposed of at the prices Giles felt they were worth, the problem might be solved.

There was, of course, much uncertainty in all of these calculations and the prospect of Giles having give up the gallery and start all over again seemed a real possibility if Turner felt unable to accept Giles' proposals.

*

Stephen glanced at his watch, which showed that it was just after a twenty-five to two, and decided that it would be a good time for a discussion with Robert Carter before he got involved in any afternoon meetings.

Stephen strolled over to Carter's office in the TDU Headquarters building and entered the outer office where Jean Blair, Carter's secretary, was sitting behind her desk eating an apple and reading a magazine. She looked up as Stephen entered.

'Gosh, is it that time already? It only seems about ten minutes since I started my break,' said Jean, smiling at Stephen.

'It's nowhere near two yet – carry on with your lunch,' replied Stephen. 'I just wanted a quick word with Robert – is he in?'

'He just went out but said he'd only be away for a couple of minutes – he's got a meeting scheduled for two fifteen with Prof Nightingale, so he'll be back in good time to make sure he's got all the stuff he needs for that. Why don't you go in and wait?' suggested Jean.

'OK,' said Stephen. 'What I want to talk about won't take long.'

Stephen pushed open the door to Carter's office and went in, pulling it to behind him. Carter was noted among the TDU staff based in the Headquarters building for the sparseness of his office and the almost complete lack of any papers on his desk, even during the working day. Whenever he completed a piece of work, Carter always filed the documents away or, more likely, got Jean to deal with them. Stephen was, therefore, a little surprised to see something of a jumble of papers on Carter's desk and his curiosity at the unusual lack of order drew him towards the side of the desk where Carter's black leather upholstered chair was to look more closely at the array of documents. Most of them seemed to be concerned with financial projections for the various departments within TDU - forecasts for expenditure on equipment and personnel and the like over the next few months. Stephen knew he really shouldn't be looking at this stuff - there were probably things he shouldn't be party to – and he started to move away from the desk. As he was doing so, a sheet of paper partly covered by others caught his eye. Its heading was: 'CONTRACTUAL AGREEMENT BETWEEN DIFESA COMPOSITA AND THE DEFENCE UNIVERSITY OF TECHNOLOGY AND MANAGEMENT' which was followed by a paragraph all too familiar to him from his checking and re-checking of the Armacomposta contract document. Stephen lifted the sheet of paper obscuring the rest of the document and found that the page he had started to read was the top one of a small pile.

Stephen paused, thinking to himself that he should stop his prying, but a rising sense of alarm, given what he had come to discuss with Carter, drove him to pick up the sheets and start to read. The top one was, but for the heading, identical in wording to the Armacomposta contract document. Beneath it were several other pages where it was evident that the only difference between what he was reading and the Armacomposta contract was the substitution of the words 'Difesa Composita' for 'Armacomposta' and the total value of the contract which was given as £290,000. With a mounting feeling of apprehension, Stephen looked at the fourth sheet and saw that the spaces for signatures by Carter - who, Stephen knew, was designated as the official authorised to sign on behalf of TDU – and the contractor's authorised signatory had already been filled together with dates when the signatures had been added - Thursday 15th September.

Stephen's apprehension had now turned to a feeling of real concern as he continued to leaf through the bundle, all of which were on TDU headed paper. The fifth sheet was headed: 'CONTRACTUAL AGREEMENT BETWEEN COMPARMOUR AND THE DEFENCE UNIVERSITY OF TECHNOLOGY AND MANAGEMENT'. The following pages were identical to the Armacomposta contract documents except for the appearance of 'Comparmour' in place of 'Armacomposta'. The total contract value here was given as £275,000. The last sheet of the document was also signed and dated with yesterday's date. The ninth sheet was like the first and fifth with 'ArmorTech' in place of 'Armacomposta'. Carter's signature and that of ArmorTech's financial director together with yesterday's date were on the final page and the contract value was now £295,000.

'What on earth is going on here?' said Stephen to himself, his brain racing as he tried to make sense of what he'd read.

He looked up from the documents and his eyes met those of Robert Carter who was standing on the other side of the desk. The office door was closed.

'Found something interesting to read, Stephen?' asked Carter in a voice that betrayed no hint of concern, but had an edge of what Stephen could only interpret as menace.

Stephen's surprise at seeing Robert Carter rendered him speechless for a moment before, with his thoughts in turmoil, he found his voice.

'Well, I'm not sure,' began Stephen in a voice that he was surprised to find sounded relatively calm. 'I came over to talk to you about some rumours that seem to be circulating about just who *has* been awarded the armour licence – various sources seem to be involved and there seems to be some confusion. I noticed these papers on your desk – I know I shouldn't have been looking – but the heading on one of them caught my eye and I couldn't stop myself from reading what they contained. I was beginning to wonder......'

Stephen paused and looked at Carter who stood listening, his face expressionless.

'Go on, Stephen,' said Carter. 'Tell me what you were beginning to wonder.'

Stephen was taken aback by the Carter's manner and general lack of emotion before continuing.

'Well, I was wondering how you come to have on your desk three versions of the armour licencing documentation, made out in the names of the three companies who were unsuccessful in the bid to acquire the licence. Then I was wondering how all three of these sets of papers are all signed by you and by the appropriate authority in each company and dated with yesterday's date.'

Carter's expression didn't change as he listened.

'Excuse me just one moment,' said Carter before he walked to the office door, partly opened it and spoke to his secretary in the outer office.

'Jean, could you give Professor Nightingale a call, please? Offer my apologies and tell him that I may be delayed by about ten minutes or so but that I'll be with him before half past two. Tell him that I'm just waiting to receive the last bit of financial information that we need for our meeting.'

Carter closed the office door and sat in the chair behind the desk.

'Sit down, Stephen,' said Carter. 'Let me explain.'

Stephen sat in the chair on the other side of the desk to Carter, still holding the sheaf of papers. Carter began to speak.

'It's like this, Stephen. I have had enough of TDU and the whole business of trying to make financial ends meet for a university that never seems content even when the balance sheet has something approaching a healthy look to it. Every year it's the same – more squeezes on personnel, staff not being replaced, Nightingale always asking for more, but never providing the resources that might allow the generation of those precious funds that he uses as the measure of his success – and I've done with it.'

Carter paused and looked at Stephen who had never heard Carter talk like this in all the years he'd known him. He opened his mouth to speak but Carter stopped him.

'Just listen, Stephen. You can have your say shortly,' continued Carter. 'I'm sixty-four and, although I've said nothing about it, I have a condition – a rare and complex form of leukaemia that has remained infuriatingly resistant to any treatment - that means I'll most likely not enjoy what is often referred to as 'a long and happy retirement'. My consultant says that I might manage another year if I'm lucky. Under normal circumstances, I'd be retiring next year but I thought it would be nice to bring my retirement forward a few months and have access to rather more – indeed considerably more - cash to enjoy what little time I'm likely to have than my pension scheme will provide. When the armour licencing issue came along and I was essentially in sole charge of the financial arrangements – Nightingale isn't ever much bothered with detail, just the bottom line - I saw it as an excellent opportunity. I have been very careful to ensure that each of the four companies involved knows nothing of the bids made by the other three. When you, Nightingale and I decided that the Armacomposta bid was the best for you and TDU, you expected me – and indeed Nightingale told me - to inform the other three that they had been unsuccessful and to thank them for their interest…….'

'But you didn't,' said Stephen as he suddenly started to realise what Carter had done.

'No, I didn't,' continued Carter. 'In fact, my discussions with the other three continued to successful conclusions. Most of my negotiations were done by telephone and I've made good use of the University's secure e-mail service. Just before last weekend, I received confirmation from each of the so-called 'unsuccessful' bidders that they each accepted the terms of the licencing agreement that I had negotiated with them. The final stage needed original paper documents for signing, so I sent the documents to each of them by courier on Monday and received them back signed and dated this morning. It's a great pity that my carelessness just as matters are on the point of being finalised has allowed you to see what I have been arranging. I'm usually so careful about the way I deal with documents – particularly sensitive ones – and I'm disappointed with myself that I left these almost on view - I was checking each to ensure that everything was in order. I thought that, in the few minutes I was away from my desk – I needed to get some more of my medication from my car – that they'd be safe enough. Anyway, each of the three armour companies thinks they alone are getting the licence and all three are each paying about £300,000. I expect you saw that all three documents are signed and dated. As you know, because you were involved in drawing up the contract, the signing obliges the contractor to 'pay up', so to say, by noon on the third day after the date on the contract or it becomes null and void. This means that all three are obliged to transfer the money by twelve o'clock on Monday 19th September to secure and finalise the contract. There's really only one aspect where the agreements with Comparmour, Difesa Composita and ArmorTech and differ from that with Armacomposta. Their money is going to be transferred into a different account to that which Armacomposta will use next week. To the uninitiated it looks like a TDU account but is, in reality one specially set up by me, though it would be difficult to find out who actually arranged it. So, by noon on Monday at the latest, I will have received all three fees. In fact, I've already received notification from all three companies that the transfers are scheduled to be completed before 9.00am GMT on Monday 19th at the latest, and probably sooner. When the money is in the, shall we say, 'special' account, I'll be moving it somewhere even more secure, and you won't ever see me again......'

'Why are you telling me all this?' asked Stephen. 'I'm going straight to Nightingale and then to the police…..'

Stephen started to get to his feet, but Carter spoke again.

'You could do that,' conceded Carter. 'I'd find it difficult to deny what I've done, now that you've seen the papers and heard my story, but maybe you could just listen a minute or two longer.'

There was something in Carter's voice that made Stephen pause. He sat down again.

'Good. Thank you,' began Carter. 'Firstly, let me assure you that what I've done won't have any deleterious effects on the real agreement with Armacomposta. That's all above board and is fully on schedule to be completed early next week. I was talking with Armacomposta just this morning. They have the contract and will return it signed by next Tuesday when the money will also be paid over. You'll get your *honorarium* - which incidentally I have calculated to be just over £29500 when all deductions have been made – by the end of the month. But I know that £29500 is not enough, is it Stephen?'

Stephen's eyes widened.

'What are you talking about 'not enough'? What do you mean?' he said.

'I happen to know,' replied Carter calmly, 'that Giles needs rather more than you and he can quickly lay your hands on. You're forgetting that I offered some informal advice when Giles was setting up his partnership with Edward Turner and I know – more or less – the terms of the agreement. I liked Edward and kept in contact with him when he split from Giles. He's occasionally asked me for my views on his finances since he's been in Edinburgh – he was pleased with the set-up that he had with Giles, which was partly at my instigation - and he's been telling me about his need for an injection of cash into his business. To cut a long story short, I think you and Giles are going to need getting on for £64000 to meet Giles' obligations.'

Stephen was silent, his thoughts racing, wondering what was coming next.

'Before you go running to Nightingale, perhaps you'd like to give some thought to what I consider an attractive offer?' said Carter. 'If you delay speaking with the good Professor until, say, ten o'clock on Monday morning, I am prepared to be generous to dear Giles and transfer £40000 to his business account. I don't think that this sum would raise any eyebrows with Giles' bankers - it could easily be put down to the proceeds from two or three paintings that realised rather more than Giles initially envisaged when he acquired them for the gallery. I have his account details, of course, from when I was advising him. This transfer will be made just before I leave the country on Monday morning – I won't tell you where I plan to go. Electronic transfers are so much more efficient these days and you'll see the money as cleared funds in the account immediately.'

Carter paused. Stephen tried to speak, but such was the shock he felt that he was unable to say what he knew he should – namely, that he was immediately going to speak with the Provost.

'Just think, Stephen,' continued Carter. 'All your problems solved by one piece of simple electronic activity. Giles' gallery saved, Armacomposta still paying for the licence and for your *honorarium*, the people you work with able to continue and develop their research, TDU's coffers augmented. Who loses out? OK, the three firms I've conned, but in reality, they're small sums in the big picture for these outfits. I plan to leave a 'helpful' letter behind explaining that I acted alone, so no-one will be compromised by what I've done. As for the forty thousand that Giles gets – well, if he acts sensibly and allocates it to 'sales income', it'll be unquestioned.'

Carter again paused and again Stephen remained silent.

'I take your silence to indicate that you haven't dismissed my proposal out of hand,' continued Carter. 'You can still go to Nightingale and tell him what I've been doing - which would salve your conscience - and you could return the

£40k I'm paying for your temporary silence. You might even contemplate telling Nightingale most of what I've done, but keep hold of the money – wouldn't it be nice to still have Giles' problems resolved? It's entirely up to you. Just delay saying anything until Monday.'

Stephen's mind continued to race as he tried to assess the impact of what he'd been told. The thought he couldn't suppress was that, by maintaining his silence for a couple of days or so, he would be able to solve the problems of the person he held most dear in his life.

'I don't know about this, Robert,' said Stephen, at last finding his voice. 'I'm not sure I can do what you ask…….'

'Think of Giles,' interrupted Carter. 'Giles is the one who will benefit – surely that's worth a little mental discomfort for a couple of days?'

The mention again of Giles caused Stephen further consternation. Maybe he could accede to Carter's proposal. It would solve so many problems so quickly. Should he talk to Giles? Could he go along with this invitation to defraud? He needed time to think. He came to a decision that would, if nothing else, buy some time.

'I can scarcely believe what I'm hearing,' he said. 'All my instincts are to pick up the phone to Nightingale now. But I've known you and worked with you for a long time now and I think we've got on well in the way we've dealt with sorting out all those contracts and grants over the years and I've respected your judgment about the things we've done together. I'm really shocked to hear of your leukaemia – I had no idea.'

Stephen paused while he further gathered his thoughts. Carter still sat unmoving on the other side of the desk.

'I think you need to consider what you are about to do and see if you can't undo it,' continued Stephen. 'You could contact Difesa Composita, Comparmour and ArmorTech now and invoke the cooling off period that I know is specified in each contract. I know that any party can withdraw within seven days of the contract being signed, and all monies paid will be fully reimbursed. Tell each of the three that the situation has changed and TDU can no longer award them the licencing contract – I'm sure you'll be able to provide a plausible reason. Maybe something along the lines that the money Armacomposta is offering has been significantly increased at the eleventh hour and that TDU has decided to award the licence to them. They'll not like it, but they'll have to accept it, particularly as Armacomposta will be publicly acknowledged as the licencees next Tuesday, as we'd planned.'

Stephen paused and looked at Carter to see what his reaction might be. Carter's face remained impassive and he said nothing.

'So,' continued Stephen, 'I won't do anything straight away. You could deal with the situation and avoid any criminality. Is what you're planning really worth it? Please think about what I've just said - you could undo what you've started.........'

'Think about dear Giles,' said Carter, his voice cutting across Stephen's. 'Wouldn't it be so good to have all his problems resolved? You could still tell Nightingale all you've heard and, if you wanted to, pay back the £40k I'll be transferring on Monday. Or you could keep it................'

Carter's voice trailed off as he looked implacably at Stephen.

Stephen felt an overwhelming need to get away. He needed to regain his calm before he did anything he might later regret. He took a deep breath.

'OK, Robert,' he began. 'I need to give more thought to all of this. I'm going to go now, but the least I can do is to give you my word that I won't do anything about contacting Nightingale until Monday morning, or at least not before I've spoken to you. I hope I'll have no need to speak to him at all and that you'll tell me that you've thought better of what you're doing. When I call you, I hope that you'll have come to your senses and sorted out this filthy mess you've created.'

Carter smiled before replying.

'Thank you for that, Stephen. I can't promise that I'll be changing any of my plans, however, but I will think about what you've said.'

Stephen stood up and again made as if to say something, but thought better of it, before turning and making his way out of the office. He managed a perfunctory goodbye to Jean, still sitting at her desk, before making his way out of the building. He paused to take in great gulps of fresh air which seemed to help as he tried to come to terms with what he'd learnt. He looked at his watch – it was almost a quarter past two. It would be at least seven before Giles returned home – he had to talk to Giles in person at home rather than on the phone or at the gallery.

*

Stephen Wright spent an afternoon in which in his mind he ran and re-ran his conversation with Robert Carter. To try and distract himself from his dilemma he attempted to complete a paper that he was planning to submit to the International Journal of Armour Composites, but he kept returning to his conversation. He knew what he must do – either immediately – but he'd given his word he wouldn't – or later, after he'd talked to Giles. He had to talk to the Provost. But what if Giles wanted to accept the money – how would he feel then? Would he be able to resist if Giles wanted to do what Carter had suggested? Why was he even contemplating going along with Carter's proposals? He really needed to discuss matters with Giles face to face.

*

At the 'The Mitchell Gallery' in Oxford, Giles picked up the phone.

'Mitchell Gallery – Giles Mitchell here. Oh, hello, Charles, what can I do for you?'

Giles listened as Charles Garnett, one of his established clients with whom he'd had dealings since the gallery opened, spoke.

'OK, Charles,' said Giles. 'It's a bit short notice, but I can drive over to you this evening with those couple of landscapes you were interested in last week. I can see that it would be good to view them where you plan to hang them, though I think it would be better if you saw them *in situ* in natural daylight.'

Giles paused and looked at his watch before continuing.

'I can close the gallery a bit early this afternoon and be with you before six o'clock. There'll still be an hour or so of decent light to view the pictures and you and Dorothy can see just how they'll look.'

At the other end of the phone Charles Garnett asked Giles if he'd like to stay for dinner as a 'thank you' for his willingness to call.

'Well, thank you, Charles, that would be very nice,' replied Giles.' I look forward to it. I'll see you at about six o'clock.'

Giles put the phone down and smiled to himself. The prospect of a couple of sales was very pleasing – the Garnetts had shown genuine interest in the nicely executed pair of oils by Sebastian Pollock earlier in the week and he'd been half expecting them to call in for another viewing. Going out to their rather grand manor house in rural Oxfordshire was no great sacrifice, particularly with the prospect of dinner and the chance to sample something from Charles's extensive and highly regarded cellar.

He looked at his watch which showed it was almost five o'clock. The drive to the Garnetts would take about thirty minutes or so – he had to negotiate his way through Oxford's evening rush hour – so if he closed the gallery soon after five, only about a half hour before his normal closing time, he'd be there in good time. It was not unusual for Giles to make such visits to clients and on such occasions, Giles always let Stephen knew if he were to be late back home. He took out took out his mobile phone and composed a quick text message to Stephen.

'S - Back by 11. Taking Pollocks to Garnetts to view. Dinner (+ Charles' cellar!) after. G'

Giles pressed 'Send' and began the process of carefully wrapping the two pictures he was taking to the Garnetts' and closing down the gallery for the evening.

*

In his office a TDU Stephen's phoned beeped, signalling an incoming text. He opened and read Giles' message, briefly considered sending an immediate reply before thinking better of it – he'd be able to speak with Giles this evening, but just a bit later than he'd planned. A couple of more hours to think might be a good thing.

15

Saturday 17th September am

Giles left Charles and Dorothy Garnett's rather later than he had intended and it was just after midnight when he got home, still elated at having sold both Pollocks at a very decent return. The money would, of course, be of some help in paying Edward Turner. He was surprised to find Stephen still up, sitting in the living room watching a late night film.

'I thought you'd have been long in bed,' said Giles. 'I would have called to say I might be rather later than I'd intended, but when I looked at my watch it was already well after eleven and I thought you'd be asleep.'

'Don't worry,' replied Stephen. 'I couldn't have slept anyway. There's something we've got to discuss about Turner's money……'

'I've got a bit of good news about that,' interrupted Giles. 'I sold both pictures to the Garnetts – they took a while to decide this evening – and I think the net profit from the sales will be almost £7000. That'll help quite a bit!'

'I'm glad about that,' said Stephen. 'But there's something that you need to know and which you and I have to make a decision about very soon.'

Giles was surprised by the tone of Stephen's voice. He'd thought his news of a decent contribution to the money for Turner would have produced a more positive reaction. Giles had been buoyed up by the Garnett sales and was starting to think that, if he could persuade Turner to extend the deadline for complete payment, he might indeed be able to get all the rest of the money together from sales over the Christmas period. Instead, Stephen's reaction seemed rather muted.

'Sounds serious,' said Giles, hoping that Stephen's tone was as a result of tiredness and that whatever it was that Stephen wanted to tell him wasn't going to be bad news.

'Go on then, spit it out,' he said.

'Just sit down for a minute,' said Stephen, who then began to recount the details of his encounter with Carter earlier in the day.

Giles listened with mounting disquiet as the implications of what Stephen was telling him began to sink in. He felt a mixture of conflicting emotions as he assessed the full import of what his partner was telling him, but even before Stephen had completed his account, Giles' mind was made up.

'So,' concluded Stephen, whose voice had become increasingly strained as spoke, 'what it comes down to is this: no matter what we decide, I will say nothing to anyone about Carter until Monday morning. I gave him my word and I want him to have the chance to undo what he's set up. I can't believe that he's been so stupid in creating this scam. I will keep to my promise and speak with Nightingale on Monday only if Carter goes through with his scheme. I hope I'll find that he's come to his senses and sorted out the mess he's created – he has got the time and the means to resolve matters and, if he does, I'll say nothing. If he does go through with it then I suppose by Monday he'll have gone. I don't know where he plans to go with the contract monies - a country with no UK extradition agreement, maybe. I can either tell the University and the police everything on Monday or I could keep the business of the money in your account quiet. I could even say nothing and wait for Carter's shenanigans to come to light on their own – it won't take long for the three companies to realise they've been taken for a ride or.........'

Before Stephen had finished speaking, Giles broke in.

'What can you be thinking of?' he began. 'Are you quite mad? Are you really expecting me to allow you and, of course, me to become party to this? I know you're thinking of me and the gallery and I can't tell you how good that makes me feel to know you care so much. But, it's only money. If I can't pay Turner, then so be it. I may lose the gallery but that won't be the end of the world. But if you allow yourself to be seduced by Carter's promises – and just how do you know that he *will* actually pay up to keep you quiet? – you'll be just as bad as him. I'll be equally guilty and we'll both lose everything. I can't believe you can have been so stupid.'

Giles paused before continuing.

'There'll be no arguing about this,' said Giles speaking slowly and clearly and leaving no room for doubt. 'You can, if you wish, delay talking to Nightingale until Monday, though I wouldn't have any compunction about calling him immediately – any delay could reflect badly on you. What is certain is that under no circumstances will I accept Carter's 'hush money' – I could never live with myself and you know, really, that you couldn't either.

Giles again paused, holding Stephen's gaze.

'What you must do – and which won't break your word - is to call Carter and tell him that we will not be accepting any 'cut'. I guess it'll have to wait until later in the morning – it's after one o'clock now,' said Giles, glancing at the clock on the top of the low bookcase behind where Stephen was sitting.

'The only options that must be left open to him are either to come clean about what he's been doing and suffer the consequences – though from what you say he might not see this as a very attractive choice – or cancel the deals with Difesa Composita, Comparmour and ArmorTech in the next 48 hours. If he does this before Monday morning, you could still stick to your promise to say nothing. Of course, I expect he'll have some awkward explanations to make to the three companies and I don't suppose TDU will be particularly pleased when they find that there's been some, shall we say, 'poor management' of the contract negotiations, but that's up to Carter to resolve.'

Stephen remained silent for a few seconds after Giles had finished speaking. He took a deep breath and his whole body seemed to relax.

'Yes, of course - you're right,' he said in a voice that sounded both fatigued and relieved. 'I can't imagine why I thought I could agree to take the money. I was thinking of you and the gallery, but clearly I've been stupid! Of course we can't get involved in this – I'm sorry I got as far as even contemplating it.'

Stephen paused and smiled at his partner.

'However, I will keep my word about talking to him before I say anything to Nightingale. If Carter sees sense and sorts out the mess, I won't need to. I think we should get some sleep and give Carter a call later and tell him what his options are. He either doesn't go through with his scheme and I say nothing or he continues and I go to the University and tell them everything. If he uses the next day or so wisely he can extricate himself from most of the shit he's got himself into.'

'Thank goodness you've come to your senses,' said Giles. 'I personally think you should call the police now, but I understand you've given your word and I guess a short delay won't be a problem. I think you might need to reconsider your timing about talking to Nightingale when you've spoken to Carter, but let's see. It's very late – let's get some sleep.'

*

Stephen woke at a quarter to eight after a surprisingly untroubled sleep. His conversation with Giles in the early hours had gone a long way to calming him after the strain he'd felt about being party to a crime, even if it was to help his partner. Giles was already up and about – he would be driving to Oxford to open the gallery in about forty minutes – and Stephen could hear him in the kitchen preparing breakfast. Stephen quickly showered and shaved and joined Giles soon after eight. As he entered the kitchen, Giles handed him the handset of the phone that sat on one of the beech work surfaces that extended along two sides of the kitchen.

'You know what you've got to do,' said Giles quietly. 'Best to get things moving.'

Stephen nodded in agreement.

'I'll use my mobile,' he said. 'I've got Carter's home, office and mobile numbers in memory. I got him to give them all to me in case anything urgent came up about the contract licence negotiations out of office hours. I'll try his home number first.'

Stephen's thumb ran over the surface of his smart phone as he brought up Carter's home number on the screen and touched the 'Dial' icon. The number he'd dialled rang. He knew from experience that Carter had no answer phone at his home, so he let the number ring for almost a minute, but there was no reply. He next called Carter's office number at TDU with the same result even after a longer period of the phone ringing at the other end. He then tried Carter's mobile only to receive a voice response telling him that, after a dozen rings, the caller could not take the call at the moment. Stephen tried all three numbers again but with the same result.

'No answer from any of these,' he said to Stephen. 'I'm sure the home and office numbers are correct. He may have changed his mobile recently, though that doesn't seem likely.'

'Well, you've got to speak to him,' said Giles. 'I think you should go and see him. You really do need to tell him what you've decided.'

Giles paused before continuing.

'Look, time is getting on – I must go, the traffic will be getting up if I don't. Give me a call when you've spoken to him and tell me what he says. And don't worry – this can all be sorted out.'

Stephen looked at Giles and smiled.

'Yes, you're right,' said Stephen. 'I'll just have a glass of juice and some toast and then I'll drive to his house – it's only about a half-hour from here to Shellington. If he's not there, I'll go to TDU. Perhaps he's there already undoing all the mess he's been trying to make. Let's hope so, at least.'

*

It was almost ten thirty when Stephen's Mini drew up outside Robert Carter's small but attractive house. It was made of brick under a tiled roof with a garage attached on one side and had been built some twenty years ago on the edge of Shellington village. He'd hoped to have been there a good hour earlier but an accident on the main road about three miles from the turning to Shellington had brought traffic to a virtual standstill. He'd crawled along, continually stopping and starting and with no real option other than to be patient, since there was no easy alternative route he might have taken, frustrating as it had been.

Stephen got out of his car, walked up the tarmac drive and rang the doorbell, noticing as he did so that a newspaper was sticking out of the letterbox. After a few seconds, during which time there was no sign of any movement in the house, Stephen rang again but with the same result. Curious, Stephen pulled the newspaper from the letter box and, noting it was today's Times, bent down, pushed open the letterbox with one hand and looked through the aperture. There was little to see other than a small hallway with two or three doors leading off it. The one facing the front door was open and revealed part of the kitchen. There appeared to be no-one around, at least downstairs. Stephen pushed the newspaper fully through the letterbox and heard it land inside the door before taking a few steps back and looking up at the first floor. Stephen wasn't sure how many bedrooms there were – three he thought – but the curtains at every window he could see at the front of the house were undrawn. Stephen wasn't sure whether Robert Carter garaged his car overnight, so, as he made his way to the pathway beside the garage that led to the rear of the house, he glanced through the small window in the side-wall of the garage. The garage was empty. Stephen continued along the path and found himself on a small paved patio at the rear of the property. The kitchen window was fitted with venetian blinds whose slats were open allowing Stephen to look in. The kitchen was empty and there was no sign of any recent activity – certainly no signs of breakfast having been prepared and eaten there that morning. A glance up at the first floor windows at the back of the house showed that they too were undrawn.

With a sense of mounting disquiet, Stephen walked back down the drive to his car. Carter's house was not particularly close to any others – the nearest was about 50 metres away and Stephen didn't feel that much would be gained by asking these not so near neighbours if they knew anything about Robert Carter's whereabouts. He couldn't, in any case, imagine that Carter would have much to do with any neighbour, even if they were rather closer than was the case here.

Stephen got back into his car, started the engine, deciding as he did so to go to TDU to see if Carter was there. If he was finalising details either about carrying through with his plan to defraud or, as Stephen hoped, abandoning it and cancelling the bogus contracts, it could well be that he'd need access to documents and contact information that were only available in his office. Remembering the main road hold-up, Stephen decided to stick to the back roads to get to TDU – it would be a slightly longer journey than by the main road but it was likely to be much quicker this morning.

The journey took about twenty minutes and Stephen noted that it was past eleven o'clock as he parked in his usual spot in the TDU car park in which a handful of cars were to be seen. He went immediately to the TDU Headquarters building where, even though it was a Saturday morning, he found that the main door was open. This wasn't particularly unusual since sometimes senior headquarters staff took the opportunity a quiet morning offered to spend an hour or so catching up on business left over from the week that was best done without any interruption. Stephen climbed the stairs to the first floor, turned right at the top and walked along a short length of corridor which then turned right as it led to Carter's office. He was not surprised to find that the door to the outer office where Jean Blair worked was open, but he was not expecting the door of Carter's office to be slightly ajar. Even when Carter was in there during the working week, he habitually kept the door shut. Stephen entered Carter's office, hoping to see Carter seated behind his desk. The office was empty and the desk cleared of any papers. This in itself was not unexpected – Carter was known to be adherent to the 'clear desk' policy favoured by military colleagues at TDU.

Stephen walked round the desk to look out of the window overlooking the car park designated for use by HQ staff and which was slightly separate from the main car parking area. There was no sign of Carter's car either in his usual parking space or anywhere else as far as Stephen could see. He turned away from the window and noticed that the large filing drawer in the desk was partly open. This seemed odd – Carter's tidiness regime also extended to keeping filing systems closed when not in use and certainly locked at the end of the working day. Given the circumstances of his search for Carter, Stephen had little hesitation in pulling the drawer open to its fullest extent and reading the tabs on the dozen or so suspension files it contained.

The tabs on the front ten or so files were exactly what Stephen expected to see. There were files with tabs reading 'Staffing Projections', 'External Expenditure', 'Main Contract Income', 'Staff Contract Renewals' and 'Current Contract

Income' among others. One was labelled 'Current Grant/Travel/Conference Requests' from which Stephen lifted out a number of folders. These had headings related to contract and grants for which other members of the academic staff were tendering and he noted among them a newish-looking one labelled 'Carswell: Australia' and another 'Simmonds: Vehicle Ride'. There was also a folder labelled 'Wright: Armacomposta licence' and the letters 'AC' in the top left-hand corner, which contained the documents with which he had become familiar during the negotiations with for the licence.

At the rear of the drawer was an untabbed suspension file. Stephen looked inside and saw three buff-coloured folders. He lifted the file from its suspension rail and placed it on Carter's empty desk to allow him to inspect the contents more closely. The three folders were labelled 'CA', 'DC' and 'AT' respectively. He opened the one with 'CA' on it and saw that it contained the pages that he had seen and read yesterday lunchtime when Carter had revealed his scheme to defraud. There were, in addition, a number of other sheets that were printed copies of e-mails sent by Carter to Comparmour or received from Comparmour by Carter. Some related to the initial negotiations between TDU and Comparmour which should have ended when the decision to accept the offer from Armacomposta had been taken. Instead, it was clear that negotiations continued after that date and had resulted in the 'contract' that Carter had drawn up with the Australians. The other two files labelled 'DC' and 'AT' told the same story.

'Why on earth are these here?' thought Stephen to himself. 'Surely he wouldn't have left them here either if he was planning to go through with his plan or if he was going to resolve the mess?'

Stephen debated what he should do with these files before deciding that, on balance, it would be best to leave them where they were for the moment. He replaced the folders in the suspension file and put the file back in the drawer which he then closed.

His overriding concern was to locate Carter and ascertain what he was planning to do, but he wasn't sure what he should do next in order to locate him. Lost in thought,

Stephen left Carter's office, walked through the secretary's room and out into the corridor and turned towards the stairs. Just as he reached the turn in the corridor he was roused from his thoughts as he bumped hard into someone coming along the corridor from the direction of the stairs, causing whoever it was to drop what looked like an A4 envelope.

'Gosh, I'm so sorry,' said Stephen automatically, looking up in surprise. 'I didn't see you………Oh, it's you, Frank! Are you OK?'

Frank Hargreaves looked equally surprised as he recognised Stephen.

'Yes, fine, thanks,' replied Frank, bending to pick up the envelope. 'Probably my fault - I wasn't expecting to meet anybody coming the other way.'

Frank stood up and smiled at Stephen.

'What are you doing here this morning – you're allowed to take some time off, you know!' he said amicably.

Stephen quickly collected his thoughts and decided that he wouldn't tell Frank the real reason for his presence in the building, at least not just now. He felt he needed a little more time to decide what he should do next and without involving anyone else.

'I came in to pick up some notes for a lecture early next week,' said Stephen. 'I was out at a seminar for part of the week and I forgot to take the stuff home with me last night. I'd just put the notes in my car when I suddenly thought I'd come up here on the off chance that Robert Carter might be in, but there's no sign of him. I wanted to check a detail with him about the armour licence. It's not important and, in any case, the contract has been sent out now. It can wait until Monday.'

'I'm not surprised that he's not here,' said Hargreaves. 'I often come in for an hour or so on a Saturday morning – it's a good time to sort out things for the following week – but I've only very occasionally seen Robert here on any Saturday. I think he likes to switch off from TDU stuff at the weekend.'

'Understandable,' replied Stephen. 'I'd rather not be here, myself! I don't plan to look at the notes until Sunday evening – I've got one or two jobs to do back at home.'

'I'm on my way to put this envelope on the Provost's PA's desk – a few thoughts about my ideas for more formal arrangements with a couple of Australian Universities - so he'll have it first thing on Monday,' said Frank, 'then I'm off home. Enjoy the rest of your weekend.'

'You, too,' replied Stephen, as he walked to the stairs while Frank Hargreaves continued along the corridor to the Provost's office which was a couple of doors away from Carter's.

Stephen Wright left the headquarters building and walked towards his car. He was about to reach for his keys when his phone gave a couple of electronic beeps indicating the receipt of a text message. He took the phone from his pocket and, with a couple of passes of his thumb over the screen, the new text appeared.

> 'I've been foolish. Will cancel contracts by Sunday evening at latest. Will confirm. Carter'

Stephen read and re-read the text with a growing feeling of relief.

'Thank goodness he's seen sense', was his immediate thought. 'Let's hope that the matter can be finished without any real damage being done.'

He touched the 'Reply' icon and created a message in response:

> 'Good. Confirm all actions taken by 6.00pm Sunday or authorities will be alerted. Stephen.'

Stephen touched the 'Send' icon, unlocked his car door and got in. He sat behind the wheel for a few moments as he tried to think through what had happened in the last hour or so. Carter's whereabouts were concerning him, even though he'd just received the text. If he wasn't at his house and wasn't in his office here, where was he? Stephen speculated that he might be trying to make personal contact with the three armour companies, perhaps by going to their UK offices – a couple were in west London and the third in Bristol – but he dismissed the idea. It was, after all, the weekend and it was unlikely that the offices would be open. It was much more likely that Carter was compiling what Wright hoped would be suitably carefully-worded e-mails to send to the overseas headquarters of the three organisations. These messages would have to be skilfully composed, explaining the situation, maybe claiming some sort of bureaucratic blunder for having taken the negotiations so far towards completion, but having the result that TDU was extricated without damage from any contractual commitments. Stephen hoped that Carter's experience in the financial world would enable him to prepare the required messages. Stephen knew that Carter, like other senior TDU staff, had remote access to the University's e-mail system so that these messages could be sent using Carter's laptop which Stephen knew Carter always carried with him. Maybe Carter had just decided to get away from home and TDU so that he could work on unravelling the mess he'd created without fear of interruption. Perhaps he'd checked into a hotel last night in order to work undisturbed?

Stephen comforted himself that it would appear that Carter had come to his senses and was in the process of resolving the situation. Though he would still have liked to have confronted Carter today, at least by setting a deadline for tomorrow, there would still be time to take action if matters didn't proceed as he hoped. The text seemed to indicate that action was being taken

Stephen started his car and drove out of the car park, intending to do a few maintenance jobs at home and forget about Carter for a few hours. He'd talk to Giles in the evening.

*

After saying goodbye to Stephen, Frank Hargreaves continued along the corridor, past the Chief Finance Officer's room, and arrived at the door to the Provost's PA Marion's office which visitors had to pass through before entering the Provost's room that was rather bigger and better appointed than the office of any other member of TDU's staff. The door to Marion's room was unlocked and Hargreaves entered. He hesitated for a second or two in front of Marion's desk as if uncertain whether he should leave the envelope after all, before peeling off a Post-it note from a block resting on the left of Marion's desk adjacent to her computer monitor. He also took a pen from a number in a pot next to the Post-it notes and wrote:

> Marion – Please make sure Prof N sees this first
> thing Monday. Thanks, Frank H [Sat @ 11.15]

He stuck the note on the front of the envelope which he placed on the seat of Marion's desk chair so that she could not avoid noticing the envelope on Monday morning and turned to leave the office. He walked along the corridor, past Carter's room, down the stairs and paused for a few moments in the HQ entrance lobby, thinking to himself that he'd done all he could to sort things out, before he went out of the building and into the car park.

*

In the materials laboratory, Dan Parker was taking a break from preparing his final experimental sample and was standing by the window as Frank Hargreaves walked to his car. Dan looked at his watch and decided that, if he got a move on, he could complete the strain-gauging of this, the last of his ten samples, and take it and a couple of others he'd completed during the last two days out to EDER before lunch. As an authorised EDER user he was provided with the range gate's security code. He also had a key to the EDER demonstration hall, so that he would be able to take the three test pieces in the back of his car, leave them locked up in the hall for the rest of the weekend and then drive home.

He couldn't get Robert Carter out of his mind – the letter he'd received from the Finance Office which had been signed by Carter had upset him – he really did need to speak to him. Ever since he'd received it on Thursday, Dan had been thinking about how to respond. The letter bluntly informed him that, unless funding was in place to support him when his current contract ended, he should expect to leave TDU. Dan had found this bald statement unreasonable, particularly when he had received a number of assurances from Stephen Wright that funding issues needn't concern him and that matters were well in hand to secure the necessary backing for him to continue his work. He had trusted Stephen to sort out his future funding - there were several sources that he knew Stephen Wright was approaching – and he thought the tone of the letter unacceptable. The fact that Stephen was away both on Thursday and yesterday hadn't helped his state of mind.

Though his initial anger had subsided since Thursday he still felt he needed to have a talk with Carter and explain exactly his understanding of the situation which had so many implications for him. As he worked, he thought that he'd best wait till next week and talk with Stephen Wright first, though the thought of a chance to put his side of the argument to Carter in person did have some attraction.

He was pleased at the thought of a free afternoon – there were a number of things he needed to do before the end of the day, not least of them some food shopping which had been neglected this week because of the time he'd had to spend on various tasks in the lab in preparation for his sessions on the range. As well as sample preparation he'd also had to undertake some calibration of the instrumentation he'd be using as well as deal with more enquiries about projects from several MSc students.

He had agreed with Simon Davies, the Warrant Officer who took day-to-day responsibility for the running of EDER, that he would do some setting up for his initial couple of experiments in the demonstration hall first thing on the Monday morning while Simon was conducting a short demonstration for the benefit of the EOT and Protective Structures students in the hardened building. Dan thought the demonstration was concerned with the performance of different types of cutting charges to show the Munro effect in which explosive pressure waves were focussed to an intensity where they could be used to cut through materials like steel. Simon had assured him that it would take only about 45 minutes, so he would be able to start in the hardened building by about 10 o'clock. As he considered the time and effort he'd put in to preparing his samples – this was the second Saturday in a row that he'd had to be in the laboratory to complete a part of his preparations – it occurred to him that each of the actual high explosive tests on the samples would be all over and done within the matter of a few milliseconds.

Dan returned to the laboratory bench and continued with the fiddly and time-consuming task of attaching the last of the six piezoresistive dynamic strain gauges that would be used to record the dynamic response of the pieces of composite material when they were loaded by the blast wave from charge of plastic explosive detonated at a distance of only 400 millimetres from the material's surface. After working for about half an hour the gauge had been positioned, stuck down with fast curing adhesive and had had wires attached to connect the gauge to a strain gauge signal amplifier which would then communicate with a digital recorder to store the strain-time history for later analysis.

Dan got up from the bench and, tearing a sheet of bubble wrap from a roll that was tucked underneath the bench, carefully wrapped up the sample, making sure that the delicate wires were protected from accidental knocks and scrapes. He placed the newly-wrapped sample on top of two other similarly protected specimens before tidying up the bench space where he'd been working. He completed his clean-up, put on his jacket and carefully picked up the three samples – they weren't particularly heavy or cumbersome – and went out of the lab, turning the light off and closing the door before making his way to the stairs. He was walking across the car park towards his car when he heard a voice.

'Hi, Dan – you're keen!'

Dan looked up to see Gill Neville getting out of her car which she'd just parked a couple of spaces away from his own.

'Hello, Gill,' replied Dan with a smile of recognition. 'I've just finished the last sample for my trials on Monday, so I thought I'd take them over to the EDER now – it'll save time on Monday morning. What are you doing here?'

'I'm meeting Chris – he said he needed to finish off a lecture he's been working on for the last couple of days and then we're going to have a pub lunch. It's such a nice day, we thought we'd go to The Swan and then walk along the river afterwards.'

As she was finishing speaking, she raised her hand and waved to someone behind Dan.

'Here he is,' said Gill, smiling, as Chris Wells, who had just come out of the Horrocks building, walked towards them. He kissed Gill and smiled at Dan.

'Lovely day – hope you're not going to be working all day, Dan,' he said.

'I'm just going to take these samples to EDER ready for Monday,' replied Dan, no longer smiling knowing that Gill would be spending the rest of the day and probably the rest of the weekend in Chris's company. 'I think I'd better get a move on.'

Dan moved towards his car as Gill got back into hers and Chris got into the front passenger seat. As Gill pulled out of the parking space, she waved at Dan. He didn't return her wave – she assumed he had his hands full in placing the samples safely in the boot of his car.

With the samples carefully stowed, Dan got in, started the engine and prepared to move off. He checked to his left and right and edged forward, but was obliged to pause as a car approached from the right, passing in front of him, heading out of the car park. He recognised the driver as Michael Carswell – the second time he'd seen him this morning - and raised a hand to him in acknowledgement. Though he had had relatively little contact with Carswell during his time at TDU, Dan had consulted with Michael on a couple of recent occasions about some problems he'd been having with the software he planned to use in the analysis of his experimental data. Carswell had offered sensible and helpful advice about how the difficulties might be resolved. Carswell returned Dan's wave and continued towards the car park exit.

Dan pulled out of his space, thinking that it was a bit unusual for so many academics to be on the campus on a Saturday morning – he'd noticed both Prof Frank Hargreaves and Stephen Wright's cars in the car park earlier and now he'd seen Gill Neville and Chris Wells as well as Michael Carswell – but taking some comfort from the fact that there were others at TDU who seemed to be working as hard as he!

As he approached the entrance to EDER, Dan brought his car to a halt, got out and punched in the lock's security code on the keypad attached to the gate-post and pushed open the metal gates. He drove through, stopped again, pulled the gates to and locked them before continuing along the tarmac road to the demonstration hall where, earlier in the week he had put his other samples. He parked as close as he could get to the door of the hall, got out of his car, unlocked the hall door and carried the three samples in.

*

Though it was now almost lunch-time, it had been quite early on Saturday morning that Michael Carswell had arrived on campus, parked his car and walked towards the Horrocks building and his office. As he strolled across the tarmac he mulled over the events of the week. What had appeared to be an impending disaster for his research and the fear that his efforts might at best already be in the public domain and at worst be regarded as plagiarism, could now be turning into an excellent opportunity to develop both his research and give a boost to his academic profile. He realised that his introversion had increased over the last couple of years and this episode had made him realise the need to be less defensive about his work and more confident about his abilities.

After his discussions with Graham Dowell and James Schofield earlier in the week he had been engaged in further e-mail exchanges with Stuart Young at DSTO in Australia. Young continued to encourage him to formalise future collaborative efforts including the arrangement of a visit to Australia both to cement the link between the particular programmes of software development at DTSO and TDU and to promote a more general collaboration. It seemed to Michael that this would be in ideal opportunity for him to widen his horizons – he'd never travelled outside Europe before – and to further the aspirations of TDU in developing links with Australian Universities and research establishments could, as the expression went, 'tick a number of boxes'.

He'd risen early on Thursday morning and, before going to TDU, had spent a couple of hours at home in preparing an outline proposal, including some rough costings, to undertake a trip to Australia as soon as possible, preferably later in the year or early in the New Year. He felt that both his and the Australian work was at the stage where, though a lot of useful dialogue could be done using electronic communications, face to face discussions would be a valuable complement to these exchanges. He'd managed to secure a meeting with Robert Carter after lunch on Thursday where he had outlined his proposal and, in particular, how such a venture might be funded. Michael had several possible sources in mind, some of which were under his control, while some would need University and possibly MoD approval.

Michael had, frankly, been a little disappointed by the Head of Finance's response to his outline which he, Michael, felt could be a significant benefit to TDU both in the short and long terms. Carter had listened to his ideas and had promised to review Michael's draft proposal before the weekend but he had also indicated that, as it stood, it rather lacked what Carter described – in somewhat uncharacteristic language Michael thought - as the 'wow factor'. Michael felt disappointed by this less than wholehearted endorsement, but later reflected that it was probably Carter's job to be something of a devil's advocate when it came to assessing requests for the significant expenditure of University funds.

However, despite this rather discouraging assessment of Michael's proposal, Carter had offered to suggest how the proposal should be developed and improved and, perhaps most importantly, see what funding might be available to support the enterprise.

Michael had left the meeting with Carter in a slightly less optimistic frame of mind than he'd hoped. Nevertheless, some of his concerns were dispelled when he received an e-mail from Carter on Friday morning containing a series of recommendations and suggestions about how the proposal might be altered to improve its chances of being funded. Carter had suggested that it would be worth emphasising the urgency of the requirement for the visit, stressing particularly the benefits that could accrue to both TDU and MoD, if the project was able to benefit from the input of Australian expertise at relatively little cost. He'd also suggested obtaining a commitment from the Australians about the nature and level of collaboration and support they were prepared to offer. This, Carter had written, could only strengthen Carswell's case. Without making any promises as to whether such modifications would ensure success of the application, Carter wrote that, if Michael could get a detailed proposal to him at the beginning of the following week, he would make it his business to discuss it with the Provost and the head of MoD's financial team, who was also based in the TDU Headquarters building.

For his part, Michael had spent quite some time at home on Friday evening in developing his proposal and he had come to TDU this morning to get hold of some detailed information which he had in his office. He was beginning to feel even more confident that his proposal made a good case for support both technically and financially. He believed that he taken on board Carter's comments and both the quality and importance of his proposal had been enhanced and he was feeling confident that it would be supported in principle and, more importantly, financially. The question of the Australians' commitment needed to be addressed and he planned to send a couple of e-mails to his Australian contacts, indicating the urgency of his questions and hoping to get a response early in the week to add to his submission.

It could only be a good thing to have Robert Carter's support and it crossed his mind to see if Carter was in his office and have a word with him to see if he was on the right lines with his amendments. Frank Hargreaves had mentioned in the past that Carter very occasionally called in for an hour or two on a Saturday. This thought also reminded Michael that it would be important to apprise Frank Hargreaves of his actions – the past two days he'd been rather hectic as he'd worked on the proposal and he'd not had the chance to speak with Frank. He would remedy this first thing on Monday.

Michael reached his office, unlocked the door and entered. He turned on his computer, logged on and opened the e-mail he'd sent to himself earlier in the morning with the attachment containing the latest version of his proposal.

*

As Michael Carswell was re-reading the latest version of his funding proposal and making a final check of the text of the e-mails to Australia, Alex Simmonds, in his office a few doors along the corridor from Michael, looked at his watch, saw that it was nearly midday and decided that it was time that he was heading home. He'd decided that he'd pop into his office on the spur of the moment, having been into the village to pick up a newspaper and one or two items that Meriel had forgotten to include in yesterday's big weekly shop. Fortunately, the small Co-op convenience store in Sherington's high street had all the things on the list that Meriel had given him. Since it was only a five minute walk to the pedestrian entrance to the TDU campus, he'd decided to go and to check his e-mail, hoping for a reply to one he'd sent to America the evening before to Mike Kuszczak, the Vehicles Congress administrator. Alex was asking about one or two details of the financial support that the Congress was offering him in his role as keynote speaker. Alex knew that his travel and accommodation costs would be covered, but he needed to know if he would still be liable for the full conference fee. It wasn't a problem if he had to pay, but he'd need to factor it into the budget that he would need to present to TDU. He certainly didn't want to give the Finance Officer any excuse to reject his application. He'd got a few trips lined up and Carter, though he'd not rejected them, had been a bit lukewarm about a couple of them, suggesting that the returns on the outlay weren't as much as they should be. He'd need to talk with Carter sooner rather than later about this matter – it would be a pity to miss out on what promised to be some interesting and enjoyable visits.

There was a new message from Kuszczak which answered almost all the points he'd raised – he would still pay a conference fee but it would be reduced to reflect his contribution to the event. Alex felt a certain satisfaction that his presence at the Congress was being so highly valued. He printed off Kuszczak's message and then retrieved the conference budget document. He adjusted the conference fee figure to accord with what Kuszczak had told him and was pleased to see a small but worthwhile reduction in the funding he was requesting. He thought it might be worth taking the document over to TDU HQ while it was fresh in his mind, so he slipped the papers into an A4 envelope, wrote 'Attn: Robert Carter Head of Finance TDU' and sealed it. He turned off the computer, locked his office and left the Horrocks Building, calculating that he'd be home by half-past twelve and in plenty of time to drive his sons to the rugby club in Farlington where Philip and Paul were junior members. The senior side were playing against a team from Oxford this afternoon and the boys were keen to watch. Tomorrow morning they'd be back at the club again playing in a mini-rugby tournament competing against two or three other local clubs. He headed towards TDU Headquarters with the envelope in his hand.

A few minutes later, as he walked across the corner of the car park heading for the footpath that would take him back to the Sherington entrance, he noticed a familiar car pulling up nearby. He acknowledged a friendly wave from Kevin Varney who got out of the car and walked over to him.

'I forgot to prepare a couple of pages to be used at the EDER demo I've arranged for first thing on Monday, so I thought it would save a lot of rushing about on Monday if I did them now,' said Kevin. 'We were passing anyway and it'll only take a few minutes.'

Alex saw that Kevin's elder son – Jack, he thought his name was – was sitting in the passenger seat.

'Hi, there,' said Alex, directing his greeting to the boy before turning to Kevin. 'Never let it be said that we academics aren't a conscientious lot with all this Saturday working!'

'I try to avoid it if at all possible,' replied Kevin with a smile. 'But it'll save a lot of hassle on Monday if I do this now.'

Alex said his goodbyes to both Kevin and his son and continued his walk – at a slightly brisker pace after his encounter with Kevin - towards the exit gate onto Sherington High Street. As he rounded the bend just before the gate, he saw in front of him a group of people who were just in the process of leaving the campus. On seeing Alex, one of them gave a wave and called a friendly greeting.

'G'day Dr Simmonds – nice day for a stroll!'

It was Graham Dowell who spoke and it took only a second or two for Alex to realise that the group comprised the six members of the Protective Structures MSc – Graham Dowell, Grant Thompson, Philippe Giraud, Alfred Leng, Karl-Heinz Schmidt and Miles Cowley together with Bronwen Dowell, Jen Thompson and a woman he didn't recognise.

'I don't think you've met my fiancée, Nicky,' said Miles Cowley.

Nicky, an attractive brunette in her late twenties, smiled at Alex in acknowledgement of the introduction.

'No, I haven't,' replied Alex. 'Pleased to meet you, Nicky. Where are you all headed?'

'No prizes for guessing, really,' replied Grant. 'We thought we needed to establish a precedent for course gatherings and, since Nicky's here this weekend and everyone else is around, a pub lunch seemed a good idea. We thought we'd try the Buckley Arms – Chris Wells was saying they do decent food.'

'Yes, it's good – I'm sure you'll like it,' said Alex.

'Would you like to join us?' asked Philippe. 'If not for lunch, then at least for a drink?'

'Very kind,' replied Alex, 'but I'm late as it is and I've got to take my two boys to watch a rugby match this afternoon.'

As they continued walking, Alex exchanged pleasantries with other members of the group before bidding them good-bye as they reached the entrance to the Buckley Arms. Alex continued his walk home, looking forward to the afternoon with Philip and Paul.

16

Sunday 18th September

Sunday started as a bright and sunny morning and, though the forecast suggested that there might be a shower later in the day, staff and students at the Defence University looked forward to a pleasant continuation of the weekend before the realisation that a new week of work was shortly to begin all too soon took hold.

For David Burgess, thoughts about the upcoming week and the problems and activities it might hold didn't generally enter his head until well into the evening when he and Anna had had something to eat and were settling down for an hour or two of undemanding television. It was only then, as he sat watching a programme about antiques or a rather 'soapy' period drama, did he give some passing thought to what he needed to do in the following week. On this occasion, as the credits rolled at the end of a documentary on African wildlife he remembered that he said he'd go out onto the EDER with the MSc students to view the demonstration of cutting charge technology that WO2 Davies was running for Kevin Varney first thing in the morning. He also reminded himself that James Schofield had expressed an interest in coming along to witness the demonstration.

*

James Schofield had spent the morning doing some tidying up in the garden before enjoying a delicious family lunch with Laura, Sam and Rachel and Laura's sister and husband who had travelled over from their home in a village near Bath. After lunch all six of them had enjoyed a favourite circular walk on footpaths around the village.

*

In Sherington, Alex Simmonds, after taking his sons to Farlington, watching them play for the Club's Under-13s team against Wantage Under-13s and driving them home – and all before mid-day - suggested to Meriel and the boys that it might be nice to have lunch out somewhere. He said it would be a good way to celebrate his recent Washington conference invitation and the family had readily agreed. After one or two disappointments - a couple of their favourite pubs were fully booked - he managed to get a table at an inn he'd been intending to try out for some time. It was a bit further from home than the other places he'd called, but the menu sounded interesting and the location, by an attractive stretch of river, worth the journey.

*

Professor James Nightingale and Delia enjoyed a leisurely breakfast in their Cardiff Bay hotel before checking out at about 11 o'clock for the drive back to TDU. As they drove, they discussed the performance of Rigoletto by the Welsh National Opera that they'd attended at the Millennium Centre the previous evening, agreeing that it was one of the better productions they'd seen.

*

Frank Hargreaves backed the car out of the driveway and asked Elaine if she thought they'd got everything they needed. They'd had a call from their son in London on Saturday evening who'd asked them if they could come and help with a bit of DIY in his newly-acquired flat in Clapham. Harry was generally more than capable of tackling mending and fixing jobs, but he said he really needed two pairs of hands to complete the installation of new kitchen worktops. Elaine never needed to think twice about whether she wanted to see Harry. As for Frank, he thought that some manageable DIY and a pub lunch with his son might be a welcome distraction after the week he'd had. He'd got his toolbox and portable work-bench in the car and felt that, together with the tools he knew Harry had, he'd have all that was necessary for the work that Harry wanted done.

*

By twelve-thirty George Hambidge and Mary had completed the round of fourballs in the Club's monthly competition. They'd comfortably beaten their opponents – Bill and Joy Tresham, a couple who'd only recently joined the club – and were looking forward to pre-lunch drinks in the clubhouse.

They planned only a snack since they were scheduled to play another match at two o'clock. George knew that yesterday Mary had prepared a casserole for them to eat after the important business of golf was over for the day, so a sandwich and some fruit would suffice for now.

*

Michael Carswell knew that he'd probably done as much editing as he could of his research proposal, but still couldn't resist looking at it once again. He had been surprised by Robert Carter's response to his work – he'd not had much to do with Carter for most of his time at TDU and though Carter was clearly reluctant to commit any TDU funding without very good reason, the advice he'd offered had been Welcoming. Tomorrow he would seek a discussion with Frank Hargreaves to apprise him of his intentions and formally submit the document to the University, more confident than ever that it would be viewed favourably.

*

At nine o'clock Chris Wells quietly got out of bed and went to the kitchen to make tea. Ten minutes later he returned to the bedroom to find Gill Neville awake and sitting up. She smiled at him, accepted the mug he offered her and asked him what he had in mind for the morning. His reply seemed to please her and it wasn't until gone eleven-thirty that they set off on the four mile walk to the pub on the river that Gill had booked on Friday which, she had assured Chris, did excellent Sunday roasts.

*

Dan Parker couldn't help feeling a little apprehensive about the experiments scheduled for Monday morning. He resisted the temptation to go back into his lab and possibly out onto the EDER again just to make sure that he'd got everything he needed by way of equipment. When he'd delivered his final test samples to EDER yesterday, he'd thought that those he'd delivered earlier in the week had been moved from where he'd originally put them. However, he'd examined them carefully and found that all was well. It was likely that Simon Davies had moved them to make sure they suffered no mishap during a demonstration that Dan knew Simon had conducted for the Ammunition Technicians Course on Thursday afternoon.

*

For MSc students, Sunday was often a time to catch up on various assignments and pieces of coursework and, for those on the Protective Structures course, this Sunday was no exception. Kevin Varney had distributed a set of tutorial problems which were designed to consolidate and reinforce the material presented during the previous week of lectures and practicals. He had requested that solutions be submitted *via* the University's computerised coursework collection system by lunch-time on Monday. So, after a pleasant and relaxing Saturday, Grant Thompson, Graham Dowell, Philippe Giraud, Alfred Leng, Karl-Heinz Schmidt and Miles Cowley variously felt obliged to set aside Sunday papers, shorten training runs, curtail shopping expeditions, bid farewell to a visiting fiancée, and bring to an end calls to a wife and fiancée back home and get down to solving energy-balance equations relating to the detonation of high explosives.

*

Kevin Varney, the initiator of this particular analytical challenge, was feeling relieved that the previous intense week of teaching seemed to have gone well. He only had one more morning of contact with the MSc class before he would bring the module to a close and issue the final assignment that would form part of the assessment. His only regret about the coming week was the prospect of marking the tutorial work he'd set. He'd promised feedback to the students before the end of the week and this would involve a certain amount of juggling of other commitments to fit the chore of marking into his schedule.

He did, however, take some comfort from the fact that he'd only be dealing with the MSc cohort on Monday. The visitors taking the module as a short course had left on Friday since some of the material being covered on Monday morning was of more sensitive nature than the rest of the module and included some restricted components. He'd had a specially-prepared unclassified session with the short course participants on their own after lunch on Friday afternoon in which he had presented a 'sanitised' version of the session planned for Monday. After this, the course ended except for a final hour which had been devoted to a question and answer session.

Questions tended to be very specific and directed at determining just how the material presented on the course could be applied directly in a particular participant's company or establishment. Kevin found such questions difficult to deal with on occasion – it seemed to him that he was in some ways being asked to justify what he'd been teaching. He sometimes got the feeling that, unless the answer was exactly what the questioner wanted to hear, he was, somehow being implicitly criticised for the course not having delivered the solution to a particular participant's problem.

Despite the problems he might face in the coming week, Kevin was determined to enjoy his Sunday. He'd promised Jack that, after lunch, he'd go for a bike ride with him and, since his wife, Jo, had also said she'd come too, he set about checking tyre pressures and generally making sure the family cycles were in good order.

*

In the cottage in Sixhampton, Stephen Wright and Giles Mitchell spent the morning and most of the afternoon going over and over the events of the previous two days. Neither could quite comprehend the situation that had developed these last forty-eight hours. Stephen was pinning his hopes on Robert Carter himself resolving the situation that he had created. He was willing him to undo the mechanics of the fraud that he had been in the final stages of perpetrating and as a result save himself and the University – and Stephen and his colleagues in particular – from what would, at the least, be considerable embarrassment and, at the worst, could be professional ruin.

Stephen continually checked his phone, desperate get a call from Carter, or at least, a message of some sort. It was almost five-thirty when Stephen's phone buzzed indicating an in-coming text message. With mounting apprehension, Stephen touched the screen's message icon and saw the text was from Carter. It read:

ALL the money in my account. Sorry! RC

Stephen showed the screen to Giles who, as he read the message, looked as distressed as his partner.

'Ring him,' said Giles. 'Find out just where he is and what he's up to. You might still be able to talk some sense into him.'

Stephen dialled Carter's number but, as on every other occasion he'd called during the last two days, the call went straight to a messaging service.

'Well, that's it,' sighed Stephen. 'I'll have to do something about this now. It seems that he really has gone and done what he said he'd do. Everything he told me about reconsidering must have been just a ploy to gain time.'

'So, what are you going to do?' asked Giles. 'I think you need to contact the police immediately.'

'First I think I'll talk with Frank Hargreaves. He knows Carter as well as anyone and he is my boss,' said Stephen. 'Once he knows the situation we can contact the police. We could go to the civilian police but I think it might be better to inform the MoD Police first – Inspector Jarvis is the senior officer on the campus – and then take it from there.'

Giles looked somewhat dubiously at Stephen, clearly thinking that any delay in starting to track down Carter would not be a good thing, but he said nothing.

*

Stephen's first call to Frank Hargreave's home number was answered after five rings by Elaine Hargreave's voice asking him to leave a message. His second call to Hargreave's mobile phone was answered after only a couple of rings by Elaine.

'Hello, Elaine, it's Stephen Wright here,' began Stephen. 'Sorry to trouble you on a Sunday evening, but something's come up and I need to talk to Frank rather urgently.'

'Oh, hello, Stephen,' replied Elaine. 'We're in Clapham at Harry's flat. Frank's in the middle of some DIY in the kitchen. Can he call you back in a few minutes?'

'OK,' replied Stephen, relieved to have traced Frank, but frustrated at having to face a delay before talking to him. 'It is rather important, but I guess it can keep for a few minutes. Make sure he gives me a call.'

'I will,' said Elaine. 'I think he'd nearly finished what he was doing – I'll make sure he calls.'

Stephen said goodbye to Elaine and looked at Giles who had been pacing the room as he listened to Stephen's side of the conversation.

'He'll phone,' said Giles. 'Don't worry – a few minutes won't make too much difference to the situation. It'll give you a chance to think what you're going to say to him.'

'Yes, I guess so,' said Stephen. 'I'm really not sure how he'll react to what I have to tell him. Let's have a glass of something while we're waiting.'

'Good idea,' said Giles, pouring two glasses of red wine from an already open bottle on the kitchen table.

Stephen had just raised his glass to his lips when his phone rang.

'Stephen? Frank here. What's the problem? Elaine said you needed to talk to me urgently. I guess it must be serious for you to call on a Sunday evening.'

'Thanks for calling, Frank, and sorry to break up your Sunday,' said Stephen. 'What I have to tell you is important and could have serious consequences if it's not handled correctly.'

There was silence at the other end of the phone.

'Frank – are you still there?' asked Stephen.

'Yes – just reaching something to sit on while we talk – I've been doing some rather strenuous DIY in the kitchen with Harry and I'm feeling a bit stiff,' said Frank, who paused before continuing. 'Right then – what's this problem?'

Over the next ten minutes Stephen proceeded to give an account of his recent dealings with Carter which, for the most part, Frank heard in silence, only making occasional interjections, mainly expressing disbelief at what he was hearing.

'The last thing was a text from Carter that effectively says he's gone through with the fraud. He told me the money wouldn't be transferred until tomorrow, but it seems he lied about that – I can't deal with this on my own any more,' said Stephen.

When Stephen finished speaking there was a second or two of silence at Frank's end of the phone.

'Christ! I'm just shocked,' exclaimed Frank, sounding agitated. 'I can't believe it. Just give me a second to think.'

A few moments passed before Frank spoke again.

'OK. I think the first thing to do is what you suggested and contact the MoD police. Tell them what you've told me. I'm sure that whoever is on duty – it'll be one of the sergeants, I guess – will contact Jarvis and we'll take it from there. I'll leave here as soon as I can and meet you at TDU. I guess it won't be much before 9.30 though - Sunday evening traffic is usually pretty dire here. Is that OK with you?'

'Yes, fine Frank,' replied Stephen. 'See you later. I'll call the police now.'

*

It was getting on for ten o'clock when Frank Hargreaves walked into Stephen Wright's office at TDU. He looked tired and rather drawn, a product, Stephen guessed, of a busy day of kitchen carpentry, a tedious drive through south London traffic and the prospect of an unfolding crisis awaiting him at TDU.

'Frank,' started Stephen, 'I think you know Inspector Jarvis?'

Hargreaves nodded to the dark-haired middle-aged man sitting in the seat across from Stephen's desk before replying,

'Yes, of course, we've had a few encounters over the past few years – mainly to do with undergraduate pranks, as I recall,' said Hargreaves with an attempt at levity. 'Have you told the Inspector what's going on?'

The police inspector, dressed in navy needle-cord jeans and a grey sweatshirt, turned his attention to the notebook he was carrying.

'Yes, Prof, Dr Wright has given me a good account of the situation and I've already been in touch with the police in Oxford. They're sending a team down here shortly. In the meantime they've alerted all ports and airports with a description of Carter and details about his car to try and trace Carter's movements and find where he's gone.'

'OK,' replied Hargreaves. 'I understand why you've had to alert the civilian police, though I was hoping it might be possible to keep the situation under wraps with you and your MoD guys for a while. It may be that nothing criminal has taken place yet and Carter may be just playing some game…….'

Hargreaves voice again trailed off.

'I'm sorry, Prof,' interjected Jarvis, 'but, from what Dr Wright has told me it appears that Carter is, at the very least, intending to defraud some rather substantial international companies of significant sums of money. It's possible that he hasn't fully carried out his plan, though his text to Dr Wright this evening seems to indicate he's done what he said he'd do. In any event, I don't have the resources or indeed the authority to manage this sort of investigation. Though Carter's plan has been initiated at an MoD site, any effects are going to be felt outside of TDU..........'

Jarvis paused as his mobile phone, which was resting on Stephen Wright's desk, rang. He picked it up, touched the screen and listened. After a few seconds he spoke.

'Right, sarge.' said Jarvis. 'Bring them to the main entrance reception in the HQ building where I'll meet them together with Prof Hargreaves and Dr Wright. Just give us five minutes to get there.'

Jarvis ended the call and said, 'That was Sergeant Jones at the Police Lodge. Two detectives from Oxford CID have just arrived. I'm afraid you'll have to tell your story all over again, Dr Wright. They'll want to hear it straight from the horse's mouth, so to say.'

The three men left the office and walked the short distance to the HQ building. Both Jarvis and Hargreaves had keys to the main door, so gaining access was no problem, and a few seconds later they were in the reception area of TDU's HQ, which was located near the entrance to the Staff Common Room, awaiting the arrival of the Oxford police officers.

Within a minute, a uniformed MoD Police sergeant entered accompanied by two men.

'DCI Brown and DC Evans, sir,' said Sergeant Jones, addressing Jarvis.

'OK, thanks, sergeant,' responded Jarvis. 'You can leave us to it for the moment. I'll call you if I need you.'

Jarvis introduced himself, Hargreaves and Wright to the two newcomers. One of them – older and taller than his companion and with a head of short-cropped grey hair – introduced himself as Detective Chief Inspector Geoff Brown while the younger and rather shorter blond-haired man said he was Detective Constable John Evans.

It was Brown who spoke first.

'I got the gist of the situation from Inspector Jarvis, but I think I need to hear the story from you, Dr Wright, since I understand it was you who first became aware of what was going on and alerted Prof Hargreaves to the situation. Is that correct, sir?'

'Yes, absolutely,' replied Stephen. 'I'll tell you all I know, but I find it hard to believe what's happening. The last text message was a real shock – it seems to confirm he really has taken off with an awful lot of money, though where he might have gone I can't begin to guess……..'

'Let us worry about that,' interjected Brown. 'With the information that Inspector Jarvis has provided about your colleague Carter we're conducting a check on all recent departures from UK ports and airports. If he's left the country via a normal exit route we'll know where he's gone and will alert the appropriate authorities there. Our checking and monitoring system is pretty sophisticated and I'd expect that we'd have some firm indication of his movements within an hour or so. Now, perhaps you could tell me and my colleague the story in full, by which time we may have some definite news about where he's gone.'

DC Evans took out a reporter's notebook and a pen from his jacket pocket and looked expectantly at Stephen Wright.

'Well, it's hard to know quite where to begin, but I guess that Carter must have been working on his scam for quite some time,' began Stephen. 'I've been developing a new lightweight composite armour system – the sort of thing that might be used to make clothing that would provide protection against a range of ballistic threats – and, as it turned out, the techniques my team and I developed were very effective. We had an advisory panel acting as a sort of sounding board for the duration of the project. The panel was comprised of people from MoD research establishments and other universities with knowledge and expertise in the field of protection and the UK-based representatives from four international armour manufacturers – Armacomposta based in Brazil, ArmorTech from the States, Difesa Composita who are Italian and based in Rome and Comparmour who are Australian.'

'No UK-based company, then?' interrupted Brown.

'No, there wasn't,' replied Stephen. 'The UK's expertise tends to lie in the development of the materials themselves, rather than the exploitation of them in specific applications. The materials used in our new system are of UK manufacture and with UK Patents but they're not new or particularly unusual – it's just the way they are configured that is special. The four companies I mentioned would likely be obliged to purchase the materials to make the new system from UK sources.'

In response Brown nodded and indicated that Stephen should continue.

'The four companies were all interested in the system we developed and each expressed an interest in acquiring an exclusive licence to allow them to manufacture the system. Each of the four was adamant that there should only be one manufacturing licence issued at least for the first three years, arguing that an exclusive licence and the monopoly that would result would ensure an excellent return. We, for our part, were delighted at such a level of interest and decided that we would enter into separate negotiations with each of the four companies and select the bidder that would be the most beneficial to TDU.'

Evans looked up from his notebook.

'You mean that you were looking for the largest possible licence fee?' he asked.

'Well, yes, of course,' said Stephen, feeling a little uncomfortable at the tone of the question, 'though there were other considerations, too. For example, the prospects of undertaking further developmental work, funding new research students and acquiring new pieces of equipment.'

'I understand,' said Brown. 'Please continue.'

'Negotiations must have started about six months ago,' resumed Stephen. 'All four companies were invited to submit proposals about acquiring the licence to manufacture. Everything was done in the strictest confidence by Robert Carter. He was very clear in his dealings with the four companies that no hint of what each individual proposal contained should be made known to the others. A deadline was set for the submissions and we received them all just over six weeks ago. A date was also set for the announcement of the granting of the licence – it was to be next Tuesday, the 20th September. Robert Carter and I reviewed them all and during the course of our assessment of the proposals – which took two or three weeks – we had to ask each of the four companies for clarification and explanation of some aspects of their proposals.'

'What sort of clarification?' asked Evans. 'Surely the biggest up-front payment would have determined who gained the licence?'

Again Stephen felt somewhat uneasy at the tone of Evans' question.

'Well, it's true that each submission included a significant cash payment, but there were other aspects to each bid, particularly the issue of royalty payments based on the number of units sold – each company made different proposals – and about issues such as providing more research studentship funding.'

Stephen paused, but neither of the two policemen seemed to want to make further comment, so he continued speaking.

'Carter and I decided that the best overall bid had been submitted by Armacomposta from Brazil and they were informed of our decision about three weeks ago. They were required not to announce their acquisition of the licence until the deal had been completely finalised, funds transferred to TDU and the licence agreement had been signed. As I said earlier, the formal announcement was to be next Tuesday. All four companies had, as part of the negotiations, agreed not to reveal the result of the negotiations until the announcement.'

Stephen paused before continuing.

'Last Friday lunch-time I had cause to go and see Carter in his office. He wasn't there when I arrived, but his secretary suggested I went in and waited for him. His desk is usually clear of any paperwork when he's not at his desk, so I was surprised to see quite a few documents on it. My eye was caught by something that looked familiar – the licencing agreement documents for Armacomposta, which I'd been involved in preparing and had read several times. Then I spotted a similar-looking set of documents half-hidden under the Armacomposta papers. They were identical to the Armacomposta set but for the name of Difesa Composita. As I looked further I saw that there were similar sets of papers for ArmorTech and Comparmour. I was shocked by what I was seeing and trying to figure out what was going on when Carter came into the office. He was very calm as he explained to me what he'd done. It was simple, really. Because the negotiations with the four companies were conducted in complete secrecy – none knew what the others were proposing – and there was no way the three 'losers' would know who had won the contract until the announcement was made, Carter had continued to negotiate with ArmorTech, Comparmour and Difesa Composta after I had agreed with him that we should licence Armacomposta. He had continued negotiating with the other three and had basically got all four companies to pay for the licence. Each believed they had won the race – each had been in quite detailed discussions about their individual bid with Carter and there was no reason to doubt that, when Carter informed them they would get the licence, they had been successful. The secrecy clause in the contract was actually of the greatest help to Carter at this stage – he knew that each of the four would keep quiet about their winning bid, knowing that it would be announced with something of a fanfare on September 20th.'

'So why didn't you take steps there and then to stop Carter in his tracks?' asked Brown. 'It seems to me you would have had every reason to reveal what you'd found.'

Stephen shifted in his seat before speaking.

'Well, Carter made some suggestions to me about how I might benefit from his actions. My immediate response was to reject his offer which was to help out with my partner's current financial troubles, but then I started thinking about Giles......' Stephen's voice trailed off.

'Go on,' said Brown.

'Then Carter started to tell me about how he had advanced leukaemia and how his time was short and I began to think that maybe he deserved a chance to resolve the situation he'd created and not implement the final phase of his plan. I can't honestly say that he gave any indication that he might reconsider his plan, but my mind was in turmoil – I just needed to get away and I thought that, since any payments and announcement wouldn't happen until Tuesday, there'd be time for him reconsider and put a stop to the business, so I gave him till Monday morning before I'd take any action. I know it was a stupid thing to do.'

Stephen looked at the two police officers but got no reaction from either, before he continued.

'I was planning to discuss what I knew with Giles – my partner Giles Mitchell who owns an art gallery in Oxford – on the Friday evening but he was dining with clients until late and didn't get back until after midnight. When I told him about Carter and what I'd done, he was furious and said I should call the police immediately. Eventually he accepted that, since I'd given my word about my Monday deadline, I should first call Carter. We both thought that we had time before the fraud actually happened. By this time it was about two in the morning so we decided to wait until later to call Carter. I tried unsuccessfully several times on Saturday morning before I drove to his house in Shellingford. He wasn't there – and nor was his car – so I drove here and went to his office. He wasn't there either, but I was surprised to find the documents I'd seen the day before in a file in his desk drawer. I was wondering what to do next when a text came through to my phone. It was from Carter's mobile – I checked the number – and it said that he'd reconsidered and that the deals he was planning were being called off and that everything would be resolved by Sunday evening at the latest. This was such a relief, but I though it worth texting back to say that I'd expect confirmation from him by six on Sunday evening that he'd resolved matters. Then at half-past five this evening I received this text.'

Stephen took his phone from his pocket and with a few touches of the screen brought up the message: ALL the money in my account Sorry! RC. He showed the screen to Jarvis who was standing behind the seat where he was sitting and to Brown and Evans who were seated on either side of him. Evans jotted down the words of the text in his notebook. Frank Hargreaves remained in his seat opposite Stephen and the police officers with his head in his hands.

'I can't believe this is happening,' said Hargreaves in a voice that betrayed the fatigue clearly evident in his body language. He raised his head and added, 'The whole business sounds like a real mess – it's going to drag TDU through the mire when this gets out.'

'We'll worry about that in due course, sir,' said Brown in a sympathetic tone to Hargreaves before turning back to Stephen Wright.

'It does look that he's carried it through to the end,' said Stephen. 'He seems to have lied to me about the Tuesday deadline and he's got the money already.'

'It sounds as if he might just have been stringing you along,' said Brown. 'You really should have called us in earlier……..'

Evans' phone rang and Brown paused.

'No sign anywhere, you say?' said Evans. 'And you've checked airports and seaports. OK, thanks, but let me know if anything turns up. In the meantime, I need a check on the call register for Carter's mobile phone over the last 48 hours at least.'

Evans motioned for Stephen to show him the text from Carter which displayed Carter's number and read it out to the person on the other end of the phone.

'OK, if we have to wait till morning, so be it, but as quick as you can, please.'

He ended the call, put the phone in his pocket and spoke directly to Brown.

'Well, sir, there's no indication so far that he's taken either a flight or a ferry during the last 48 hours, though there are still a few possible departure points to check We've also been checking airport and ferry terminal car parking, but so far there's no indication that a vehicle with his registration has checked in during the last day or so. They'll contact the phone network provider about his recent call register, but we won't get that immediately.'

'OK, thanks, John, we can afford to wait a little while for the phone information. As for there being no trace so far about any flight or ferry departure by Robert Carter then I suppose he may have fixed himself up with a false passport,' said Brown, 'though from what you have been telling me about him he doesn't seem quite the type to have had the contacts necessary to arrange that sort of thing. Of course, he may just be spinning a yarn and he's still very much in the country and all this talk of foreign climes could just be a blind.'

Both Stephen Wright and Frank Hargreaves remained silent, both apparently at a loss as to how to respond.

'Right, gentlemen,' continued Brown. 'I'd like you to show me his office and the documents you've been referring to and then I think we'll call time on this for the moment.'

Hargreaves and Wright led Brown, Evans and Jarvis to Carter's office which looked just the same as when Stephen had last seen the file of licence documents on Saturday morning. Stephen opened Carter's desk draw, took out the file of documents and passed them to Brown.

'As you'll see, ' said Stephen, 'each of the four sets of documents to the four companies is essentially the same in format, the only differences between them being in the amount of money that each company would be contracted to pay. It adds up to well over a million pounds in all.'

Brown took the documents and placed them in a large clear plastic bag that Evans handed to him.

'We'll get these looked at later this morning and continue our checks to determine if Mr Carter really has left the country. If he hasn't left then he might take a bit more finding, but we will locate him,' said Brown. 'He may just be lying low somewhere relatively near biding his time before leaving – but we'll find him. We'll get back to Oxford and be in touch later in the day.'

17

Monday 19th September am
WO2 Simon Davies walked the thirty yards from the demonstration hall to the entrance to the EDER test building, unlocked the box by the door which contained switches to the hardened lighting system inside, turned the lights on, entered the test chamber and stopped. In the centre of the chamber, lying on the foot-thick layer of coarse sand that covered the floor was a body.

Davies' training as an ammunition officer immediately asserted itself. He showed no hint of panic and made no sudden movements as he assessed the situation. The body was lying on its back and appeared to be that of a middle-aged man. Looking around the chamber, Davies noticed that the sand layer on the floor, which was usually raked over after any explosive test, showed signs of disturbance between the entrance to the building and the body. Davies' immediate thought was that the body had been dragged across the floor from the entrance, because there was some indication of two parallel tracks in the sand which could have been made by the legs of the man lying in the middle of the chamber. There was also a flattened area on either side of these marks, though there seemed to have been some attempt to obliterate any disturbance of the sand between the entrance and where the body lay. Davies wondered why the rake, kept in a shallow alcove just by the entrance hadn't been used to remove signs of disturbance. There didn't appear to be any other marks on the rest of the sand, which otherwise looked untouched after its last raking.

Stepping carefully on raked sand, Davies approached the body. With a shock he realised he recognised it to be that of a TDU academic or administrative staff member whom he'd seen around the campus but couldn't immediately put a name to. He bent down and placed a couple of fingers on the neck of the body – it was cool to his touch and he could detect no sign of a pulse. He stood up and was in the process of carefully retracing his steps to the entrance when he heard a cheery voice outside.

'Mr Davies? Is that you? I'm coming in.'

Simon Davies recognised the voice of Kevin Varney, who appeared at the entrance to the test chamber just as he took his last careful pace back.

'Hope you've got……,' Kevin Varney's voice trailed off as he saw what was in the middle of the chamber. 'Christ - that's Robert Carter! What's going on? Is he dead?'

'Yes, I'm afraid so,' said Davies. 'Robert Carter, you say – the University's Finance Officer? - I recognised him, but couldn't put a name to him. Stay back, Kevin, and keep your class out of here – I need to make a phone call.'

Kevin Varney had recovered a little from the initial shock of seeing Carter's body and moved back out of the test chamber, followed by Simon Davies who ran across to the preparation room where there was a phone.

Outside the test building were the MSc students, for whom this session was to be the last demonstration on Kevin's explosives module, together with David Burgess and James Schofield. The group looked enquiringly at Varney as he emerged, pale-faced from the EDER building.

'What's going on, Kevin?' asked David.

Kevin collected himself for a moment before replying.

'There seems to have been some sort of an accident in the test chamber. Mr Davies is trying to sort it out………..'

'What sort of an accident?' interrupted David Burgess. 'It seems a bit early in the day for there to have been *any* testing in the chamber. There's nobody been hurt, has there?'

James Schofield was just about to speak but he was interrupted by the arrival, at some speed, of two of the MoD Police vehicles stationed on the campus. Four uniformed officers got out and started to talk with Simon Davies who had emerged from the preparation building when he heard the cars arrive.

*

It was just after 9 o'clock and, in TDU's Headquarters building, Frank Hargreaves and Stephen Wright were both sitting in Prof James Nightingale's office awaiting the arrival of Detective Chief Inspector Geoff Brown and Detective Constable John Evans. After the policemen's departure in the early hours, Stephen and Frank had both gone home to get some sleep, agreeing to be back on the campus by 7.30. The meeting with Nightingale had started soon after eight, following Hargreaves' call to Nightingale at his home at seven o'clock.

Wright and Hargreaves had recounted to Nightingale the events of the previous weekend. Nightingale had listened with a growing sense of disbelief, anger and fear: disbelief that Robert Carter, one of his most trusted lieutenants in the University, could have perpetrated the crime that Stephen Wright had been describing, anger that the effects of this crime would not reflect well on him or the University and fear that his new appointment as leader of the Universities Funding Council might somehow be jeopardised by any ensuing scandal at TDU.

Stephen had reached the point in his narrative where, in the early hours, the two Oxford policemen had taken away the four sets of licencing documents for examination and it had been decided that further steps in any investigation at TDU itself should wait until the morning, when there was a knock at the office door and Marion, the Provost's PA entered.

'Detective Chief Inspector Brown and Detective Constable Evans are here, Prof,' said Marion, 'together with Inspector Jarvis.'

'Bring them in,' said Nightingale, glad that he'd at least got the gist of the story from his own colleagues before he had to talk with the police.

The three policemen were ushered in by Marion who then left, carefully closing the door behind her. Introductions were made and Brown, Evans and Jarvis were invited to sit at the table that Nightingale used to chair the numerous meetings that generally filled his day. When all six men were seated, Brown spoke.

'Professor,' he began, addressing Nightingale, 'I'm sure you've been apprised of the situation by Professor Hargreaves and Dr Wright.'

Nightingale nodded before speaking.

'If what I've heard is true, I find it hard to believe. Robert Carter is one of the staff in whom I have always had implicit faith. This is absolutely the worst possible time for a scandal involving the university. There's so much going on that Robert Carter was heavily involved in – not least of which is a planned link-up with a number of Australian university and research organisations. So important for TDU and Carter was an important factor in the negotiations………'

'That's as maybe,' interrupted Brown, 'but all indications are that his attempt to defraud these four armour manufacturers has been planned for quite some time.'

'What do you mean 'attempt to fraud'?' said Frank Hargreaves. 'Surely the fraud has been executed and Carter is sitting somewhere with a large pile of money in some obscure bank account?'

It was Evans who spoke next.

'Yes, Professor Hargreaves, that's what we did indeed expect to find, but our investigations so far suggest otherwise. We've not been idle since we left you earlier this morning. We've been in contact with all of the four companies involved in Carter's plan. We first tried to contact the four UK representatives – the ones who were part of Dr Wright's advisory panel – and were partially successful. We got to speak with the UK agents of Armacomposta, ArmorTech and Comparmour – though they weren't too pleased about being woken in the early hours! - who then made contact with their parent companies. Contacting the Italians was trickier – the UK rep seems to be out of the UK, but we did eventually track him down and he's been speaking with his bosses.'

Evans paused and Brown continued.

'It seems that all four of these organisations were indeed under the impression that they - and they alone - were being awarded the licence to manufacture Dr Wright's system. They had all complied with the confidentiality clauses in negotiating the contract and were all planning a Press Release to announce their success.'

'You say '*were* planning'?' interjected Nightingale.

'That's correct,' said Brown. 'They were all planning to make a public announcement on Tuesday when the licence agreement was to have been officially in place and the money had been transferred. Nothing had happened at their end to change this arrangement. They'd certainly not had any word from Carter about making any alterations to the arrangements – either to bring the payment date forward or, as Dr Wright was hoping, to cancel everything.'

'Does this mean that none of the four companies has transferred the money?' asked Nightingale with a growing sense of relief, thinking that maybe things weren't going to be as bad as he'd feared.

'That would seem to be the case,' replied Brown. 'But the fact remains that there has been an attempt to defraud on the part of Carter and we need to find him. So far our enquiries at ports and airports have drawn a blank, which probably means he's still in the country. We've also been unable to trace the phone which Carter used to send the texts to Dr Wright. It seems it's an unregistered, cheap 'pay as you go' job that is virtually impossible to trace. When we checked the number of the phone that sent the texts, it turns out it's not the number that people here used to call him on his mobile – the number on his business cards. Dr Wright just used the 'Reply' option to respond two texts and didn't need to retrieve Carter's 'normal' number. Wherever he is, we're not going to find him from mobile phone records, it seems.'

As Brown paused, Jarvis' phone rang. He listened for a few seconds before ending the call.

'That was one of my sergeants calling from EDER, the University's explosives range,' said Jarvis. 'It looks like the mystery of Robert Carter's whereabouts has been solved. WO2 Davies opened up the EDER building a few minutes ago to prepare for a demonstration for a class of MSc students and found a body in the test cell – the early indications are that it's Robert Carter.'

The other five seated round the table greeted Jarvis's news in stunned silence. Stephen Wright's jaw dropped, Frank Hargreaves put his head in his hands and James Nightingale raised his eyes to the ceiling. The two Oxford policemen exchanged glances before Brown spoke.

'This puts a rather different complexion on matters,' he said. 'If you'll excuse us, gentlemen, perhaps Inspector Jarvis could take us to the explosives facility, please?'

All three policemen rose from their chairs and departed, leaving the three TDU academics still seated. A few seconds elapsed before James Nightingale spoke.

'What on earth are we going to do now?' he asked. 'Matters seem to have gone from bad to slightly better – at least from what Brown and Evans said about the licence business – and back to considerably worse. We need to keep a tight lid on all of this until we know where we stand.'

*

Nightingale's hopes of keeping matters as confidential as possible were progressively destroyed during the course of the morning.

A police medical team arrived from Oxford within an hour of Brown, Evans and Jarvis arriving at the EDER building and viewing the body that Kevin Varney had confirmed as being that of Robert Carter, and made an initial inspection of the body. The police pathologist, a middle-aged man by the name of Fielding and who had completed over twenty years with Oxford police's forensic and medical service, offered the opinion to DCI Brown that the cause of death appeared to be a blow to the back of the head which may have resulted in skull fracture and possibly cranial haemorrhaging, though a full post-mortem investigation would be needed either confirm or deny this view. When pressed by Evans, a reluctant Fielding said that the time of death could have been 48 hours, or maybe a little more, previously. This opinion suggested that Carter had died either late on Friday or early Saturday morning.

The arrival on campus of an ambulance was a further barrier to maintaining any level of discretion around the unfolding situation. A forensic team, in a couple of large vans with police markings, then arrived at the Headquarters building. One of the vans and two officers left shortly afterwards, headed in the direction of Robert Carter's house in Shellington, while the three officers that comprised the other team began their search of Carter's office. The whole campus could not but be aware that something unusual was happening on the site and by mid-morning the campus rumour mill was grinding rapidly with speculations, claims and counter-claims about what was taking place.

The Provost managed to speak with DCI Brown as he was directing the team who were working in Carter's office and proposed that he should try and provide some clarification to all on the campus about the situation.

'I think it would be a good idea to provide the grapevine with something factual about what's going on rather than allow uninformed rumour. I propose that I and the senior military office on the campus, Brigadier Williamson, send an e-mail to all TDU staff and students and the military staff – the IT people here can do this quickly and easily - and it will quell the sorts of conjecture that my secretary is reporting to me.'

'That is probably a sound idea,' said Brown, 'but you need to be circumspect in the words you use – it is vital that information is kept to a minimum at this stage until we know more about how Carter died.'

'I am aware of the need for discretion,' responded Nightingale, 'so I have drafted this message, which the Brigadier has approved, which I hope you will agree will offer some rationale to what's going on.'

Nightingale passed the sheet of paper he was holding to Brown, who read:

'The presence of both civilian police and medical services on the campus this morning has given rise to speculation about the cause. At this stage, I can only report that there appears to have been an incident on the explosives range that has resulted in a fatality. The formal identification of the victim of this incident is currently under way. All staff and students and requested to go about their normal duties and to cooperate fully with the police in their investigations.'

'That seems fine, Professor, at least for the moment,' said Brown handing the paper back. 'When we've completed our search of Carter's office we'll need to start asking your colleagues some questions to try and determine Carter's movements since he was last seen. Stephen Wright saw him on Friday afternoon and this has been confirmed by Carter's PA, Mrs Jean Blair. She tells us that she saw that Robert Carter was still in his office at four-thirty when she left for the weekend – she went into his office just prior to her departure and asked if he needed her to do anything before she left. He said no and wished her a pleasant weekend.'

'It might be worth checking with the Officers' Mess about Friday night,' said Nightingale. 'Robert Carter lived alone and I know that he occasionally used to take dinner in the mess though less recently than in the past, I believe. He'd formed the view that the mess wine cellar had little to tempt him these last couple of years. He was something of a connoisseur of fine wines and I'm afraid the mess's standard fare generally disappointed him these days.'

'A good suggestion, Professor, I'll get one of my men to talk with the mess manager right away,' replied Brown. 'For the moment, though, I need to see what, if anything, Mr Carter's office might have revealed.'

*

Mon 19th September pm

It was just after a hastily-eaten sandwich lunch and DCI Brown and DC Evans were standing in Carter's office. Evans, consulting a small notebook, was describing to Brown the outcome of the search of Carter's office that had just been completed.

'Well, sir,' started Evans, 'for the most part, the guys have found nothing particularly out of the ordinary. He was known to be a meticulously neat worker and, at the end of the working day operated what the military here refer to as a 'clear desk' policy – a bit of basic security to ensure that all documents are at least put away out of view and locked up if they could in any way be considered as dealing with sensitive topics. So, all of the University's financial documents – and there must be hundreds – are kept in filing cabinets with security locks that can only be opened by entering the right code on the dial on each. There are two cabinets in here and a further three in the outer office where Jean Blair works.'

Evans pointed to one of the cabinets with its rotatable dial set in a numbered wheel – turning the dial to the appropriate numbers in the correct sequence unlocked the cabinet.

'Carter, of course, had the code for each cabinet and so had Jean Blair. She tells me that the codes were changed, but not very often. The cabinets' contents weren't considered to be particularly sensitive and, anyway, it was all backed up electronically on the university's secure server. As far as she was able to judge, there was nothing either missing or unusual in any of the cabinets.'

Evans paused while he turned over a leaf of his notebook.

'As we know from earlier this morning, Carter also had a filing drawer in his desk. Mrs Blair says that she didn't have a key to this drawer which contained files that Carter was currently working on. He liked to ensure that only he had ready access to items that might have a certain sensitivity. It's no surprise that he would keep the licencing documents in this drawer which was invariably locked with a key kept on a fob that he carried around with him.'

'Well, he made a slip-up on Friday, then,' interrupted Brown. 'Stephen Wright says he found the four sets of licencing documents all over Carter's desk and on Saturday when he came here looking for Carter, the desk drawer wasn't even shut, let alone locked.'

'Maybe he was getting a little overconfident – after all, his plan at that stage seemed to be operating perfectly. However, it must have come as something of a shock to find Stephen Wright reading what until then he'd been so careful to conceal,' suggested Evans. 'Leaving the drawer unlocked for Wright on Saturday morning to find that the files were still there is even odder. I wonder what happened that led to Carter failing to secure the drawer, or at least removing the incriminating documents?'

'We know that 'something' happened, but not 'what',' said Brown. 'Let's hope we find out 'what' soon! The campus is really buzzing with rumours and, though Nightingale has sent a message to all staff to 'Keep calm and carry on', the sooner we can resolve this matter the better.'

'There are other items in Carter's filing drawer that might have a bearing on the case,' said Evans, 'though I'm not sure how or if even they do.'

Evans walked over to the desk, opened the drawer, and pulled out four files labelled 'Staffing Projections', 'Staff Promotions', 'Staff Contract Renewals' and 'Current Grant/Travel/Conference Requests'.

'There are several more files here besides – mainly dealing with income and expenditure prediction and pretty dull stuff – but these deal with matters directly involving staff. For examples, there are requests for money to travel to conferences, documents relating to employments contracts and files dealing with potential new contracts. Quite a few of these have been annotated by Carter and his comments are, more often than not, less than complimentary about the person who has, say, submitted a request for funding or is in the process of renewing a contract of employment. Look here......'

Evans paused, opened a file labelled 'Simmonds: Vehicle Ride' and saw that the file contained a number of applications for financial support to participate in international conferences in Europe, Australia and the United Sates. Evans leafed through the papers and drew Brown's attention to a number of pencilled notes in the margins of several pages. Brown saw where Evans was indicating and read: 'Another waste of university money!', 'Hargreaves needs to curb AS's wanderlust', 'How can such a minor talent be so sought-after?' and 'He needs taking down a peg or two – this is just a 'jolly''.

Brown read the name on these various applications and commented, 'Robert Carter doesn't seem to be very supportive of Dr Alex Simmonds, does?'

'Neither is he of Dr Michael Carswell either, it would seem,' added Evans, passing a second file to Brown.

Brown leafed through the three or four pages the file contained and which seemed to be making a case for a funded visit to Australia in the quite near future. Brown saw that the documents were dated just before the weekend and that there were a number of pencilled comments in a hand that matched an example of Carter's writing that Jean Blair had provided them with when the office search had been instigated.

'"A very weak case for support", "Needs a lot of additional detail" and "Will the University ever recoup this outlay?"', Brown read out to Evans. 'That last comment is written against the sum that Dr Carswell claims is needed to support him – not a very encouraging set of comments.'

Brown paused and turned to the last sheet in the file.

'Here's something a bit more positive, though,' he said. 'Carter's written at the end of the document: "Help MC to fix this submission?" Sounds as if Carter might have been planning to be a bit more positive about this application, despite his misgivings.'

'Maybe,' interjected Evans, holding up the file marked 'Staff Contract Renewals'. 'But not for these two colleagues. There are a couple of files here, one referring to a Dan Parker – a research student in Stephen Wright's group – and the other about a Dr Gill Neville who, if I read this correctly, was awarded her PhD last summer and has been appointed as a Teaching Associate, also working with Stephen Wright. Parker's contract term is due to end soon – March next year - and there's a copy of a letter here to Parker from Carter saying that the term won't be extended. The file about Gill Neville shows that she's on a one-year contract due to end next summer. Carter's hand-written note on one of the documents says that any extension could only be contemplated if there was firm evidence of substantial funding to support her. He doesn't seem to be particularly keen to help the academic and research staff here, does he?'

'Possibly not,' agreed Brown, 'though he might just be erring on the side of caution about spending the University's money. There's another file here about staff promotions – the last academic who came up before the promotion board a couple of months ago was Dr Kevin Varney. He didn't get his promotion and Carter's comments in the file – look here..........'

Brown held out a sheet from the file he was holding to Evans.

'............aren't terribly flattering about Varney's prospects. This note says he'll need to triple his research and consultancy income if he's to have any chance of promotion but, because Varney is "lacking in any great initiative". Carter doubts he'd ever do it. A bit scathing, I'd say.'

'Carter seems to be more enthusiastic about getting money in than shelling it out,' commented Evans.

Brown broke off to stifle a yawn. Almost immediately Evans did the same.

'I only managed three or four hours sleep last night – a couple before we were called here and a couple in my chair back at base while waiting for calls from the Brazilian and US companies,' said Evans.

'Same for me,' offered Brown, looking at his watch that showed it was approaching four o'clock. 'I think we should finish up here for now, drive over to Carter's house in Shellington to see if they've found anything interesting and then call it a day. First thing tomorrow we'll see where we've got to in determining Carter's movements from Friday afternoon and decide on our next move. We should also have the lab report on Carter by then.'

18

Tuesday 20th September am

It was about a quarter to nine on a cool and crisp Tuesday morning at the Oxford police headquarters when DC John Evans knocked on the door of his boss's office. Almost immediately he heard DCI Brown's voice calling to him to enter.

'Good morning, sir,' said Evans. 'Did you sleep well?'

'Not too bad, thanks John,' replied Brown, 'though I did wake up a couple of times thinking about what happened to Robert Carter. I've been in since about seven-thirty reading over the statements we've taken so far and waiting for the lab report on him. I've just got it here – they e-mailed it to me about ten minutes ago and I've just printed it off. Here's a copy for you – it makes interesting reading.'

Brown passed three stapled-together A4 sheets which Evans took and began to read. There was silence in the room for five minutes as Evans read his copy of the *post mortem* report while Brown made a few pencilled notes on his.

'So,' began Evans, 'the initial estimate of time of death was about right – early Saturday morning sometime between seven and ten, the report says. It wasn't the crack on the back of the head that killed him though.'

'That's what the report concludes,' agreed Brown. 'He did get a bash on the head, but it seems that it may have just knocked him out rather than caused his death. I don't suppose the impact did him much good, but there were other more powerful factors involved, mainly associated with Carter's illness and his eating and drinking habits.'

'As you'll see from the report,' continued Brown, 'Carter was overweight, unfit and with a liver that seems to have been working hard to deal with the significant amount of alcohol that he'd been enjoying over many years. He was known as something of a connoisseur of fine wine who appreciated not only the quality of what he drank but quite liked it in some quantity. As you saw yesterday, there is an extensive and, as I gathered from one of the forensic team who examined the house and who's a bit of a wine buff, quite impressive wine cellar. There were certainly plenty of bottles both in a temperature-controlled cabinet in the utility room at the house and a large number in the racks installed in a big under-stairs cupboard. Though he was never seen in public to be the worse for wear drink-wise, I guess he was in the habit of opening a bottle at home in the evening and drinking it all himself – OK on occasion, I suppose, but I'd say it was both a regular and frequent thing for him.'

Brown paused and looked at Evans.

'Yes, I see that the lab report comments on the poor condition of his liver,' said Evans. 'What about his eating habits? When we went to the house yesterday, I didn't get the impression that much cooking was done in the kitchen.'

'He was a regular diner in the mess,' said Brown. 'He'd eat lunch every day and dinner on three or four times a week where he was rarely known not to fill his plate………'

'So - he ate and drank a bit too much?' interrupted Evans. 'That's not an uncommon situation for a middle-aged bachelor in a fairly sedentary job like Carter's.'

'True,' continued Brown, 'but, as the report indicates his heart seems to have been in as equally bad nick as his liver. The report suggests that during the course of whatever happened that resulted in him ending up on EDER, he had a heart attack but with 'complications'.'

'What do you mean 'complications'?' asked Evans.

'The lab's not quite sure just yet, but I'm hoping to hear from them once they've got information from Carter's GP,' replied Brown. 'We know from Stephen Wright that Carter had told him that his time was getting short because of his leukaemia which seems to have been an unusual variant of the disease and largely unresponsive to any drugs currently available. Carter was apparently able to manage, more or less, the symptoms by the regular and frequent taking of a number of medicines. We don't know what these were yet, but we found a pill-box in Carter's jacket pocket which had separate compartments for each day of the week, with each day divided into sections for morning, afternoon and night doses. There were fourteen large sections, so that up to a fortnight of pills could be available and ready to take. The lab says that compartments up to and including the morning of Friday 16th September were empty, but those from Friday afternoon onwards were full with four different small pills in each. The box is only the size of a mobile phone, so easy to carry around and keep to hand. There was no sign of any mobile phone, neither his usual one nor the one used to send the messages to Wright.'

'So, Carter didn't take any pills from after lunch on Friday,' commented Evans. 'Why didn't he take them? It must have been a routine procedure for him……'

Evans was interrupted by the ringing of Brown's office phone. Brown picked up the handset.

'DCI Brown here.'

A pause ensued while Brown listened to the caller, before saying, 'OK - thanks for that. It's as well to know what the pills were for and to have an informed view about Carter's general state of health.'

Brown put the phone down.

'That was DC Jameson,' said Brown. 'I asked him to liaise with the lab and, on the basis of what they told him about Carter, speak with Carter's GP. He managed to meet with him – Dr Vijay Singh whose surgery is in Farlingon – before he started to see his patients this morning.'

'So, what did he have to say?' asked Evans.

'Carter was very sick with his leukaemia,' said Brown. 'Dr Singh said that what Carter had told Stephen Wright about his prognosis was not far off – Singh thought he had a year, fifteen months at the most. He also said that he'd tried over the years to get Carter to improve his eating and drinking habits – from well before the leukaemia appeared about a year or so ago – but Carter was unwilling to take heed of Dr Singh's advice. Singh had told Carter that he was a likely candidate for a heart attack if he didn't modify his diet and take some exercise and in danger of liver failure if he didn't moderate his drinking habits. When the leukaemia was confirmed, Carter said that he saw no point in any change – he was going to die anyway - so he might as well carry on as he had been since he'd nothing much to lose.'

'What about the regime of pills?' asked Evans.

'Well, Dr Singh said that the combination of drugs that Carter was taking – four different pills three times each day – were meant to slow down the rate at which the leukaemia was progressing,' replied Brown. 'He started taking them about a year ago and without them he'd most likely be dead already.'

'What could have been the result of Carter's failure to take the pills after Friday morning?' asked Evans. 'Surely a few missed pills won't have led to his death in what was rather less than a day?'

'No, of course you're right on that,' said Brown. 'Singh said that a failure to take a couple of the scheduled doses would have had an effect after a few hours and could have produced a feeling of disorientation and tiredness. He'd probably have needed help to take his missing doses. If he had taken the two lots of tablets that he should have had between Friday lunchtime and his estimated time of death sometime on Saturday morning, he'd most likely have re-established some sort of equilibrium. Singh expressed surprise that Carter had missed not one, but two doses – he was sure that Carter wanted to prolong his life-style for as long as possible and had always been very careful to take his drugs.'

'Did Singh offer any view as to whether Carter's failure to take his medication could somehow have brought on a heart attack?' asked Evans.

'Jameson asked just that question,' replied Brown. 'Singh's view was that, if something had caused Carter's general stress levels to rise, then a combination of several factors surrounding his state of health could have brought it on.'

'Well, we know that he was under stress by virtue of the scam he was about to pull off and this stress can only have been increased by his encounter with Stephen Wright,' offered Evans.

'Again, that's true,' said Brown, 'but according to Wright, Carter seemed exceptionally calm when he found him in his office reading the contract documents and seems to have remained just as calm as he put the various ultimata to Wright.

I think it must have been some later event that put him more in danger of an attack. Maybe someone he had dealings with later in the day on Friday or on Saturday morning.'

'That's possible,' conceded Evans. 'But who else could have known about what Carter was planning? Keeping matters secret seems to have been pretty well-handled by Carter - up until Friday lunch-time at least.'

'Of course, it may not have been anything to do with the licence fraud,' suggested Brown. 'By all accounts Carter wasn't much liked – respected, maybe, but not much liked – and he may have had a meeting with any number of people who might have wanted to take issue with him on a number of matters: overseas trips, research and employment contracts and there may have been other things as well.'

'Yes, I recall that Nightingale was quick to mention the potential link-up with several Australian organisations – it seemed to be at the forefront of his mind when he heard about Carter,' said Evans.

'I think we need to get down to TDU,' said Brown. 'Though it may be that Carter's death was not the result of a criminal act, it seems clear to me that someone has gone to considerable lengths to keep Carter's demise hidden for as long as possible and we need to find out why. For that reason, I think we'll play down the cause of death for the moment – I think we'll stick with 'death due to suspicious circumstances' and make whoever has something to hide sweat a bit.'

'Good idea, sir,' replied Evans. 'It seems to me that there was no great love lost between Robert Carter and several members of the TDU staff. It would be nice to see if we can determine exactly the circumstances of Robert Carter's death. All we really know is that he died sometime early on Saturday morning, probably as the result of a heart attack brought on by a combination of a failure to take his prescribed medication, a general level of unfitness – not helped by a blow on the head at some stage - and, most likely, a raised stress level. *Something* happened to him to cause his death.'

19

Tuesday 20th September am

There were quite a number of both military and academic staff in the Common Room as David Burgess and James Schofield entered at about a quarter to eleven. There were several groups of staff dotted around the room and it was evident from the comments that David and James picked up as they got their coffees that the talk was mainly of Robert Carter and what had happened to him the previous weekend. There was an air of expectation and slight unease in the room – or so David, at least, felt. The police had spent a long time on the campus the previous day following the discovery of Carter's body on EDER and staff knew that there would be significant police activity at TDU today.

James and David were taking their customary seats in the 'Civils Corner', when George Hambidge, who was sitting facing one of the large windows overlooking the visitors' car park, spoke.

'Those two who were here yesterday are back, then,' said George. 'A bit late in the day – I'd have thought they'd have been here at the crack of doom.'

'Maybe there were things they had to do back in Oxford – they always say that the police are overwhelmed by paperwork whenever any crime is reported or investigated,' offered James.

'Perhaps they've….,' said David but his words were cut short by George Hambidge.

'They were quite busy yesterday,' said George. 'Soon after lunch-time there were forensic people in and around Carter's office as well as out on EDER and there were a couple of uniformed civilian police helping Jarvis's MoD guys - taking statements from Mr Davies and the others who were out on EDER when Carter was found.'

'How do you know all this?' asked James Schofield. 'I thought the police looked to keep what they do fairly low quiet.'

'Yes, but people talk!' replied George. '- and I had a session with some of the MSc guys at the end of yesterday afternoon and they were only too keen to tell me all about their encounter with the gentlemen of the constabulary. The police also spoke with staff in the mess before they finished last night.'

'How do you know that?' asked David, as he sipped his coffee.

'Mary played golf yesterday afternoon and decided to go out for something to eat with her partner and their opponents after the game, so I stayed on after my lecture with the MSc class, did a bit of marking – an undergraduate practical on telemetry, which was a depressing hour or two – and then decided to have dinner in the mess.'

George Hambidge paused to sip his coffee before continuing.

'I was chatting with one of the mess stewards – Les Kenneally – you know who I mean? – he's been there a long time. He said the police had been asking whether Robert Carter had dined there on Friday evening. Les told me that Carter was a regular diner, but not often on a Friday. Les said that Carter was in the mess on Friday and that he'd noticed him simply because it was unusual for him to have been there on that day. Les didn't think that there was anything unusual about Carter's behaviour and he didn't speak to him. By the time the mess staff had cleared up Carter had left – he'd had a coffee in the reading room and Les assumed he'd driven home.'

'I supposed the police are trying to trace his movements over the weekend,' said David, finishing his coffee. 'James and I were questioned yesterday morning because we were at EDER when Mr Davies found the body. I couldn't tell them anything, really. I'd not seen Carter since some time last week – I haven't had many dealings with him recently.'

'Same here,' said James. 'I haven't spoken with Robert Carter for a while. I do know that Stephen Wright was planning to see him on Friday afternoon in connection with the licencing of his body armour design, so I guess that Carter was just working a normal day on Friday. His eating in the mess might have been a bit unusual – maybe he had stuff to finish off on Friday and he thought he'd have a mess dinner rather than look after himself?'

'Must go,' said George. 'Time to discuss the mysteries of telemetry with the second year – they won't be too pleased about the marks they've got!'

'You're a hard man, George!' said James who rose from his seat, as did David Burgess. All three academics left the Common Room and returned to their offices.

*

It was just after eleven o'clock when DCI Brown and DC Evans entered the small meeting room in the TDU HQ building that Professor Nightingale had made available to them as a base. Brown took a number of files from his brief case and laid them on the table. He opened one of them and pulled out a couple of pieces of paper.

'This is the report I mentioned to you on the drive down, John,' said Evans. 'It's a summary of what the forensic team found at Carter's house yesterday.'

Evans took the sheets and read them both.

'Their investigation doesn't seem to have thrown up anything particularly untoward, given we know what Carter was planning to do last weekend,' said Evans.

'Yes, you're right,' replied Brown. 'It looked like the suitcase on the bed in his bedroom was pretty much packed and ready to go. His passport and a mix of US dollars and euros – about two thousand pounds worth in total - and a one-way Channel tunnel ticket were in a drawer of the bedside table. The team also found his 'normal' mobile phone in the drawer.'

'So it looks as if he was fully intending to go home at some stage to collect his stuff before taking off,' commented Evans.

'Looks like it, yes,' said Brown. 'The forensic boys didn't find anything else that seemed relevant to Carter's demise. They've not located his car, though, and there've not been any sightings of it – I can't believe it's too far away from

TDU. I think we'd better start talking to a few more of Carter's colleagues and see if we can figure out where he went after dinner on Friday. The period between about half-past eight on Friday 17th and up to about nine or ten o'clock on Saturday morning is unaccounted for. If we can determine what he was doing for those eleven or twelve hours we'll be a lot better off towards finding what happened.'

'If it wasn't for the fact of him being found on the explosives range, you'd say that his death was 'natural causes' – he was an unfit, middle-aged man with a heart condition, a liver that was in a poor state and a serious illness whose treatment he seems to have temporarily neglected,' offered Evans. 'Any one of those things could have killed him at anytime, I guess. But something unusual must have happened which led to him being where we found him and with a bash on the head to boot. Someone else must have been involved – that's the person we need to find.'

'That's it in a nutshell,' said Brown. 'Let's go and talk to Carter's colleagues. I think we need to start with his PA…' Brown consulted his notebook, '....Jean Blair and, of course, Stephen Wright. They may have been his last contacts during the working day. I think we should also talk with Professor Nightingale and his PA – Marion, I think I heard him call her.'

*

Tues 20th September pm

It was just after one-fifteen when Jean Blair knocked on the partly-open door of Marion Jones' office and went in.

'They've gone, then?' asked Jean directing her question to Marion who was sitting behind her desk eating her lunch and just about to open a pot of strawberry yoghurt. 'I had them with me for a good half hour earlier. What did they ask you?'

There was no need to identify who 'they' were – everyone on the TDU HQ building knew that the two policemen were continuing their investigations and talking with staff.

'They wanted to know if I'd seen Robert Carter after lunch last Friday and, if so, if I knew what he'd been doing that afternoon,' replied Marion.

'That's the way they started with me,' said Jean. 'I told them that I'd been in my office all morning and even stayed there to eat my lunch. Sometimes I go out and do a bit of shopping in the Co-op in the village, but not last Friday. Mr Carter went to have lunch in the mess at about half-past twelve and didn't get back until about half-past one and was only in his office a few minutes before he went out again – I think he said he'd left something in his car. Just after he'd gone, Dr Wright arrived to see Mr Carter and I suggested that he went into his office to wait. I think Dr Wright wanted to finalise some details about his armour contract. I'd been doing a lot of work with Mr Carter on it these past few weeks. Anyway, Mr Carter was back about five minutes later and I told him that Dr Wright was in his office. He seemed a bit put out, but didn't say anything, and went in to his office and closed the door – he always did that – didn't like anyone to hear what went on in there! After a few minutes Mr Carter put his head round the door and asked me to call you to say that he'd be a bit late for his meeting with the Provost. They must have been in there for a good half an hour or more. As it turned out, Dr Wright came out of the office just after twenty past two. He did say goodbye to me on his way out, but he was a looking a bit upset, I'd say - I don't know why. Anyway, about five minutes later Mr Carter came out carrying a couple of files and said he was off to his meeting with the Provost. He looked pretty much the same as always – if he and Dr Wright had had some disagreement, it didn't show. He came back at about three thirty, asked me to type up a few notes he'd made at the meeting with Prof Nightingale and went into his office.'

'Mr Carter got to Prof Nightingale's office at about half-past two. We exchanged a few words and then he went into Prof's office,' said Marion. 'A couple of the military arrived for the meeting shortly after and I didn't see Mr Carter until the meeting ended just before half-past three. I thought he was looking a bit tired but that's probably not unusual after a meeting with Prof…..'

Marion's voice trailed off a little guiltily, as if she was afraid the Provost might overhear her.

'I sorted out the notes as he'd asked me and, when I'd finished, saw it was almost time to stop so I took the documents into him – that was at about half-past four – asked if he needed anything else from me before I left – I finish at a quarter to five on a Friday – but he said no and wished me a pleasant weekend,' said Jean. 'He seemed quite OK, sitting at his desk just as normal. I couldn't really say he looked particularly tired – but it was the end of the week and we're all ready to stop by then, aren't we?'

Jean paused and smiled before continuing. 'I left the building at about ten to five after I'd closed down my computer and I was home by five-fifteen, I'd say. I certainly didn't see Mr Carter after I'd said goodbye on the Friday or at any other time over the weekend. He only very occasionally came in at the weekend, because, on rare occasions, he'd have work for me the very first thing on Monday morning, saying he'd been in for an hour or two on Saturday morning. He never asked me to come in - he probably knew I'd refuse!'

After a pause Jean asked, 'So what did they ask you?'

'I didn't have much to say, really,' replied Marion as she finished her last spoonful of yoghurt and put the pot into the waste paper basket beside her desk. 'I just told them that I'd seen your boss when he arrived for the meeting at about two-thirty on Friday afternoon and when he left at about half-past three. I went home not long after that. Prof had said I could leave early because I needed to pick up my car from the garage in Farlington – it had had its annual service – and they close at about four-thirty on a Friday. I had a courtesy car from them for the day to get in here. I didn't set foot in the place again until Monday morning when all this started......'

*

Prof James Nightingale unlocked the front door of his house which was just a six or seven minutes walk from his office and on the edge of the TDU campus.

'Delia, I'm back,' he called, followed by, 'What a morning!'

Delia Nightingale emerged from the kitchen, smiled and said, 'You'd better come and tell me all about it, then. Lunch is just about ready.'

Nightingale tried to take lunch at home at least a couple of times a week – just to get out of the office, really, and have a break from phone calls, meetings and reading documents. He found it therapeutic to talk about his morning with Delia and enjoy what he always knew would be a good lunch.

'I've had the two policemen in with me for getting on for an hour this morning,' Nightingale began. 'They were asking whether I'd seen Robert Carter after the meeting I'd had with him and the Brigadier and his adjutant on Friday afternoon.'

He paused before continuing.

'I had to tell them that I had. I went along to his office at about a quarter to five after both Marion and Jean, Robert's PA, had gone home.'

Delia looked at her husband, noticing his agitation as he spoke.

'What's so unusual about that?' asked Delia. 'You often needed to talk to Robert out of normal office hours.'

'Yes, of course,' replied Nightingale, 'but on this occasion the subject of our conversation was a bit 'awkward', shall we say.'

'Go on,' said Delia. 'What did you talk about?'

'About the University Funding Council appointment and my plans for a formal link with ADFA in Australia,' replied Nightingale, 'and the comments that Robert Carter had been making about me in relation to them.'

'Comments about you?' said Delia Nightingale. 'What sort of things?'

You know I'm trying to set up a formal research link between TDU and ADFA – that was one of the purposes of my visit there last year,' said Nightingale.

Delia nodded.

'Well, it seems that Carter had been having exchanges of e-mails with quite a number of people in Australia. He'd been in discussion with someone at Melbourne University in connection with Frank Hargreaves' plan to set up a Research Network in the area of physical security – protective structures, you know the sort of thing Frank's lot does. I was cross about that when I first heard Frank talk about it, but I think we've come to an understanding about how his plans with Melbourne and mine with ADFA could complement each other rather than be in competition. Then Carter had been liaising with someone at the Defence Science and Technology

Organisation in Salisbury – in South Australia – about a proposal for research collaboration between Michael Carswell in Frank's department and the team at Salisbury who are developing software similar to that which Carswell has been producing under an MoD contract. He'd also had some dealings with the organisers of a conference at the University of Adelaide which Alex Simmonds is planning to attend. Carter always felt that Alex went on rather too many - and quite expensive - conference trips and I guess may have been trying to see what the cost of sending Alex to Adelaide might be before Alex started getting serious about advances for travel and conference fees.'

Nightingale paused as Delia placed a bowl of steaming hot home-made soup in front of him. He nodded his thanks, before continuing.

'Although it's a huge country, the Australian defence and university community is relatively small and close-knit. Something happening in one place soon gets heard about in lots of others. It seems that Carter's enquiries were fairly common knowledge – nothing sinister about them, of course, Robert was only doing his job. However, it seems that Robert's counterpart at ADFA got to hear about his enquiries and couldn't help apprising Robert of an embarrassing little incident when I was at ADFA last year.........' Nightingale's voice trailed off.

Delia looked up from her soup

'Come on, spit it out – what 'embarrassing little incident'?' she asked.

'At the formal dinner in the ADFA mess,' began Nightingale. 'I guess I'd drunk a bit too much of the excellent Coonawarra Shiraz they were serving and I made a few – shall we say 'uncomplimentary' - remarks about how UFC operates and how it needs a good shake-up and how, when I'm in charge, things are going to change with a lot of dead wood being cut out. I think I may also have said something about how I had to take the financial admin people here to task when I first came to TDU to improve the way they did things.'

Delia said nothing, though she did sigh.

'Anyway, late on Friday afternoon I found an e-mail addressed to Robert Carter that had been 'cc'd' to me. It was from ADFA's Chief Finance Officer telling Robert all about my gaffe and wondering if anyone here knew about what I'd been saying about UFC and, of course, TDU. I don't know how it happened that I was an addressee – I guess that guy at ADFA must have inadvertently copied me in. I feature several times – and in a rather uncomplimentary light - in the message, so he may have put me as an addressee without consciously registering that he had.'

Nightingale paused and drank a spoonful of the cooling soup.

'I went straight to Carter,' continued Nightingale. 'He'd just read the message himself and knew immediately why I'd come to see him – he'd been surprised that I was an addressee, but thought it might have been a bit of devilment on the part of his ADFA contact. Robert was looking a bit washed out, I thought - it was late on Friday - but he was still determined to make me feel really awkward about the contents of the message. He kept on saying that it wouldn't do for the present incumbents at the UFC to find out about my very clearly expressed attitude towards them. He said that what I'd said about what they do and the way they do it didn't seem to him to be entirely complimentary. Also, he wasn't best pleased that his department had featured in my comments about 'shake-ups'. He didn't, I suppose, directly threaten that he would make the email contents more widely known, but he certainly enjoyed making me squirm.'

'But you didn't do anything, James, did you?' asked Delia in a tone that betrayed her anxiety.

'Of course not,' replied Nightingale. 'What do you take me for? I was feeling angry at Robert's malicious teasing - but I was convinced he was only teasing. I actually apologised for the comments I'd made in regard to TDU that were, at least indirectly, critical of him. After I'd extracted an assurance that the contents of the message would go no further, I left him in his office – he just sat there throughout our meeting, smiling and knowing what damage he could cause me.'

'And you told the police all of this?' asked Delia.

'Yes, of course, though I didn't enjoy the experience. It's the truth of what happened on Friday afternoon and Robert

Carter was sitting at his office desk when I left him at about six o'clock. That was the last time I saw him.....'

Again Nightingale paused.

'But.............?' said Delia.

'The police wanted to know if I'd gone back to see Carter later in the evening or early the following day. They could tell that I was upset by the way Carter had hinted at spreading word of my indiscretion wider and wondered if I'd thought to go and discuss matters with him again,' said Nightingale.

'Well, they just need to come and talk to me then,' offered Delia. 'I can tell them exactly where you were from when you got in – about half past six I think it was - because The News Quiz was just about to start on the radio – and you were in all evening. After we'd eaten, you watched a rugby match on TV – Bath against London Irish, if I remember correctly - while I finished the crossword in the Telegraph. I went up to bed at about half-past ten and you followed about ten minutes later.'

'Yes, they might well come and talk to you,' said Nightingale rather resignedly. 'I swear that Friday evening at six o'clock was the last time I saw Robert Carter.'

*

It was almost two-thirty when, after a lunch-time pint and sandwich in the village, Brown and Evans knocked on the door of Stephen Wright's office.

'Come in,' called Stephen and the two policemen entered.

'Sorry to disturb you again, Dr Wright,' began DCI Brown, 'but we do need to go over events from the last time you saw Robert Carter on Friday evening to when you called us on Sunday night.'

'OK, but I don't think I can tell you anything more than I've told you already,' Stephen replied.

'You may think not,' said Brown, 'but you'd be surprised how often a little extra detail gets remembered in the retelling of a series of events. Let's start from the time you met Carter in his office just after lunch last Friday.'

*

It was a little after three o'clock when the two policemen returned to their room in TDU HQ.

'Well,' began Evans, 'Stephen Wright's account just now tallies in almost every particular with what he told us earlier. I don't think he can have had contact with Carter after Friday afternoon, other than the text messages on Saturday morning and Sunday evening. Of course, he should have contacted us as soon as he got wind of what Carter was planning, but I think he believed he'd talked Carter out of it and things could be sorted out internally.'

'I think you're probably right,' said Brown. 'Stephen Wright is really only guilty of naiveté, perhaps an excess of trust in Carter and loyalty to TDU.'

Brown paused and looked through his notebook before continuing.

'There *was* one small detail different in what he told us just now compared with his earlier account: he didn't mention that he'd seen Professor Nightingale on campus on Saturday morning when we'd talked earlier. It may not be significant, of course.'

Both Brown and Evans consulted their notebooks again before, at Brown's suggestion, Evans wrote on the whiteboard attached to one of the walls of the room, the names of those who had either been on campus or had been seen on campus that Saturday morning who had been mentioned to them by Stephen Wright and the others who'd given statements since Monday morning.

'Stephen Wright said he'd not spoken to many people that morning,' commented Brown. 'But he did see several others besides, either on foot or in their cars.'

Evans finished his writing and both policemen considered the list.

'So – let's see…,' said Brown. 'Prof Frank Hargreaves, Dan Parker, Dr Gill Neville and Dr Chris Wells, Dr Michael Carswell, Dr Alex Simmonds and Dr Kevin Varney who was with his son and Prof James Nightingale. Wright didn't mention him when we spoke earlier and neither did Nightingale indicate that he'd been out and about on the campus on Saturday.'

'Yes, I see that,' said Evans. 'But Stephen did say that it was not unusual to see Nightingale on campus at weekends – after all he lives only a short walk from this building. He may have been out for a stroll.'

Brown continued reading from the whiteboard.

'Then we've got a whole gaggle of MSc students and their wives: FLTLT Graham Dowell and his wife Bronwen, FLTLT Grant Thompson and his wife Jen, Maj Philippe Giraud, Capt Alfred Leng, Maj Karl-Heinz Schmidt, Maj Miles Cowley and his fiancée Nicky.'

'Dowell and Thompson are the Australians in the MSc class – maybe they know something of the armour work that Stephen Wright has been involved with?' suggested Evans. 'Maybe they had some knowledge of Carter's involvement with the Australian armour manufacturer – what are they called?'

'Comparmour,' offered Brown. 'It's possible, I suppose. The Australians were out on EDER when Carter's body was found. According to the officer who took statements from all of those who were out on the range that morning, the Australians seemed as bemused as anybody by what had happened. It might be worth speaking with them again, I guess.'

'Of the three academics in the group who went out to EDER on Monday morning – Dr Kevin Varney, Dr David Burgess and Dr James Schofield – the last two don't seem to have been anywhere near TDU at all over the weekend. In the statements we took on Monday, both said they were home in good time on Friday and spent Saturday and Sunday with family and friends. We've got plenty of corroboration that that's just what they did from their neighbours and others in the two villages where they live. They don't seem to be involved in any way. We need to talk to Kevin Varney again – he was on campus on Saturday morning and we know that he'd crossed swords with Robert Carter recently over his failed promotion bid.'

'Let's just review what we've got so far,' suggested Evans.

Brown nodded.

'We know Carter ate dinner in the mess on Friday evening and it was assumed by mess staff that he'd then gone home,' said Evans. 'The guards on the gate don't recall Carter's car leaving on Friday evening, but that doesn't mean he didn't – it was, after all, dark and cars exiting the campus don't get anything like the attention that those coming onto the site receive. The car must have gone at some stage, though, because it's not anywhere on the campus as far as we can see – I've had men looking for it all over the campus.'

'The fact that Carter was found on Monday morning and the time of death has been estimated as sometime on late Friday to early Saturday morning makes me think that Carter never left the campus after his dinner,' continued Brown. 'Maybe he went back to his office in TDU HQ, perhaps to pick up something he'd forgotten earlier. Or, maybe he met somebody…..?'

'The fact that Carter's car is nowhere on campus and it wasn't logged in by security on the gate as having come onto the campus for a second time after Carter's arrival on Friday morning, suggests someone was aware that something had happened to Carter and, for whatever reason, thought it better to get the car off campus,' said Evans. 'That could have happened either late Friday night or early on Saturday morning.'

'My betting is that the 'something' happened early on Saturday morning. We know Carter was alive up to about eight or eight-thirty on Friday evening which was when he left the mess after dinner,' said Brown. 'Our investigation of those we think may have had business with Carter weren't at TDU on Friday evening, certainly not as late as after eight o'clock.. I just wonder whether, after his meal and the events of the day, some of which must have rattled him somewhat – particularly Stephen Wright's lunchtime call - Robert Carter was feeling worried about whether his plans would after all succeed. He may have been feeling ill – his failure to take his medication is likely to have been because of the day's upheavals – and, thus, as Dr Singh suggested he could have been feeling disoriented and fatigued. Maybe he just fell asleep in his office…..?'

'If so, his car would have stayed on campus all night,' said Evans. 'So who moved it and where is it?'

'If we can determine the answer to those two questions, I think our problem will be pretty much solved,' replied Brown, with a smile.

'OK,' said Evans. 'Assuming nobody met with Carter before Saturday morning who do we need to talk to in more detail about what they were doing on campus on Saturday morning?'

'We need to talk to Professor Nightingale again to see what he had been doing when Stephen Wright saw him. Professor Hargreaves also needs to be questioned again – Stephen Wright met him not far from Carter's office at about a quarter past eleven, after he'd found Carter's office empty. Then there are those who Carter seems to have somewhat 'rubbed up the wrong way' recently – Michael Carswell who seems to have had a mixed reception from Carter to his research proposal, Alex Simmonds who doesn't seem to have been Carter's flavour of the month with his conference travel plans, Kevin Varney whose promotion prospects seem to have taken a dent recently, possibly on the basis of information supplied to the promotion board by Carter.'

Brown turned to another page in his notebook before continuing.

'Then there's Dan Parker, the research student who had been told that his employment would be terminated after Christmas – seems a bit harsh when he's in the final stages of his PhD programme, wouldn't you say?'

Brown looked up at Evans, who nodded.

'Dr Gill Neville is a new academic on a one year initial contract that Carter's file suggests would not be extended when the year ends - again a bit severe, I'd say. I should imagine that Stephen Wright would be very much opposed to losing either Parker or Neville: they seem to be an integral part of his team,' continued Brown.

'Chris Wells was on campus with Gill Neville on Saturday – they seem to be something of an item,' interrupted Evans. 'Wells is a very new member of staff and doesn't seem to have had any dealings with Carter since the start of the new academic year a few weeks ago. Wells said he'd spoken once very briefly to Carter in the Common Room on his first day here. I don't think he has any links or involvement with Carter that should concern us.'

'I think you're right,' said Brown with a nod. 'Of the MSc students who were on campus on Saturday morning, I think only the two Australians – Dowell and Thompson – would be worth another talk, simply because they have links both with ADFA and with the wider Aussie defence community.'

'The only other person whom we've not spoken with at any great length is Stephen Wright's partner Giles Mitchell,' said Evans. 'His financial problems seem to have been a crucial factor in Stephen Wright's reaction to Carter's offer on Friday afternoon. Mitchell's response seems to have been one of horror that Wright might ever have contemplated accepting what Carter was proposing, but it might be worth having another conversation with him.'

'So............let's see,' said Brown as he wrote in his notebook. 'We need to talk to Prof Nightingale and Prof Hargreaves, Dr Alex Simmonds, Dr Michael Carswell, Dr Kevin Varney, Dr Gill Neville, Dan Parker and Giles Mitchell and the two Aussies – Thompson and Dowell. Let's hope that one of them can shed some light on Robert Carter's Saturday morning.'

Brown looked up from his notebook and Evans glanced at his watch that showed the time as a quarter to four.

'I suggest we divide the interviews up between us,' said Brown. 'We can each have one of Jarvis' MoD officers with us when we have our chats – I suggest starting with Simmonds, Carswell, Varney, Neville and Parker. Then we can call in on the Australians in married quarters on campus on our way out and make an appointment to see Giles Mitchell either in Sixhampton this evening or in Oxford at his gallery tomorrow. Maybe leave the two Profs until tomorrow.'

In the corner of the room there was a phone and a TDU telephone directory. Evans found the numbers for the first five on Brown's list and began dialling. After a few minutes and several calls later he turned to Brown.

'Well, I managed to find four of them – all but Parker, in fact - and fixed up to meet Simmonds and Carswell at four o'clock in their offices and Neville and Varney at half-past four in Neville's office and in Varney's lab,' reported Evans. 'I've also spoken to Inspector Jarvis and two of his chaps will be here in a couple of minutes.'

While Evans had been on the internal phone, Brown had been using his mobile.

'Giles Mitchell says he's meeting with a potential buyer after the gallery closes this evening,' said Brown. 'He won't be back in Sixhampton until late – he thinks he may be entertaining the client to dinner in Oxford. He suggests meeting him at the gallery tomorrow just before he opens up – I've said we'll be with him at nine o'clock.'

Brown was interrupted by a knock at the door and two uniformed MoD police officers entered.

'Ah – good! Thanks for getting here so quickly. One of you go with DC Evans and one of you come with me, please. We're just going to have a chat with one or two of the academic staff and I'd thought that the presence of a uniformed officer might serve to concentrate the minds of our interviewees, if you see what I mean?'

Both the MoD officers smiled at Brown in acknowledgement.

'OK, let's go,' said Brown. 'This shouldn't take long. I'll talk to Simmonds and Neville and you take Carswell and Varney.'

20

Tuesday 20th September pm
Alex Simmonds rose from his seat behind his desk, shook DCI Geoff Brown's hand and gave a nod to Brown's uniformed companion before inviting them both to sit.

'What can I do for you, gentlemen?' said Simmonds. 'I thought I'd covered everything you were interested in when I spoke with one of your officers yesterday.'

'Just one or two points of clarification, that's all,' said Brown with a reassuring smile. 'When you came onto the campus on Saturday morning, you told my officer that you'd gone to your office to check your e-mails, hoping for some response from America about an upcoming conference – is that correct?'

'Yes, that's right,' replied Simmonds. 'I got to my office round about half past ten. There was an e-mail from the conference organiser – he was giving me an update on the level of financial support that they were offering me.'

'Was it good news?' asked Brown.

'Not bad, actually,' replied Simmonds. 'I'll still have to pay a conference fee but with some discount because of my contribution to the conference.'

'I only ask because I believe that you and Robert Carter have had some, shall we say, 'discussions' recently about the amount of financial support you've been applying for in order to attend what seems to have been quite a number of conferences over the last year or so. I believe that you are well-known among your colleagues as an enthusiastic conference delegate,' said Brown in a friendly tone.

'I'm not quite sure what you're suggesting,' said Alex, suddenly on his guard. 'All my conferences and overseas trips are fully costed and approved before I make any move to book flights or accommodation or pay any fees. It's true that Robert Carter was wont to query every item of expenditure I proposed and it was something of a game between us to ensure that I presented a watertight case for support which he would inevitably query. It was a sort of ongoing duel, you might say.'

'What about your latest 'duel'?' asked Brown. 'Did you have a watertight case to present to Robert Carter?'

'Pretty much,' replied Simmonds with a smile, relaxing a little. 'As I said, the e-mail indicated that I'd have to request a slightly reduced level of support from the University and I didn't think a reduction, even a small one, would be a problem! In fact, after I'd read the e-mail I reworked the figures and also added some further text – highlighting how my contribution to the conference would reflect well on TDU - in my 'Case for Support' to present to Carter – of course, circumstances mean that I've not been able to do that.'

'You didn't consider taking your revised documents over to TDU HQ on Saturday so that Carter would have them in front of him first thing on Monday morning?' asked Brown.

'The thought did cross my mind,' replied Simmonds, 'but I abandoned the idea. In fact the envelope with my revised request is here.'

Simmonds took a buff A4 envelope from a small pile of papers resting on his desk before continuing.

'I expected Carter would want to dispute my figures and it's far better to do these things in person, face-to-face. I did walk in the direction of HQ with the intention of leaving the stuff on his PA's desk, but time was getting on and I thought better of it. It had taken longer than I thought to make my amendments and I needed to get back home.'

'So, just to be clear about timings,' said Brown. 'You arrived on campus at about ten-thirty, having done a bit of shopping in the village, and went directly to your office where you turned on your computer, checked e-mails and then made some changes to your request to TDU for financial support. You abandoned your idea of taking the envelope over to Carter's office because you thought a face-to-face meeting would be a better tactic and, anyway, you needed to get back home because of family commitments.'

'That's about it. In the event I took this envelope home with me and brought it back on Monday morning,' agreed

Simmonds. 'On my way out I met Kevin Varney and his son in the car park and had a few words with him. Meeting him rather decided me not to take the envelope over to HQ – time was pressing and, anyway, just after I'd said goodbye to Kevin, I was hailed by a big group of MSc students – all those who are doing the Protective Structures course – and a couple of wives and – oh, yes - the fiancée of one of them. It must have been about twenty past twelve. We had a brief chat – they asked me if I'd like to join them in the pub, but I declined – I didn't want to disappoint my sons. I was home soon after half past twelve.'

'Just one more question, Dr Simmonds,' said Brown. 'Did you notice anyone entering or leaving the TDU HQ building while you were on the campus on Saturday?'

'Not that I recall,' replied Simmonds. 'I did see a couple of other people, but not to speak to. Dan Parker was around, I recall. I saw him near HQ but whether he was going in, coming out or just passing, I couldn't say. Dan was getting ready for some work on EDER this week, so I understood from Stephen Wright, and I guess he was using a quiet Saturday morning to finish his preparations – he's got a reputation for being very conscientious. I can't see what business he'd have in HQ. As I was saying goodbye to the MSc students, I noticed Michael Carswell – he was walking in the general direction of HQ but he could just have been heading to his car. I saw it when I arrived, parked between the Horrocks Building and HQ. I don't know how long Michael had been in – he may have been in his office which is a few doors away from mine – but I didn't speak to him.'

'OK,' said Brown, getting to his feet. 'You've been most helpful, Dr Simmonds. We'll leave you in peace now!'

Brown and the uniformed officer shook hands with Alex Simmonds and left. Simmonds sat back down at his desk, opened the envelope containing his revised funding request and wondered when and to whom he should now give the document.

*

While DCI Brown was talking with Alex Simmonds, a few doors along the corridor DC Evans, accompanied by another of Inspector Jarvis's MoD policemen, was talking with Dr Michael Carswell.

'What time did you arrive on campus on Saturday morning, sir?' began Evans.

'Quite early,' replied Carswell, 'because I was anxious to have everything I'd been working on at home the previous evening incorporated into the funding proposal that I'd been discussing with Robert Carter as soon as I could and while all was fresh in my mind. I think I arrived on campus at about eight o'clock – I remembered thinking that there were quite a number of cars in the car park so early and on a Saturday, too. But then, with a lot of people living on the campus in the mess and in married quarters, I guess there are always a fair number of cars around even at weekends.'

'You went straight to your office after you'd parked, did you sir?' asked Evans.

'Yes, I just wanted to get on with the task as soon as I could,' replied Carswell.

'Why did you need to come in at all?' continued Evans. 'Didn't you have access to all the information at home?'

'I thought I did,' replied Carswell. 'However, whenever I work at home, I invariably find that I'm missing some vital piece of information that can't be got at remotely – perhaps a document or a name or a telephone number. There were several things I needed and it was just easier to come in to get hold of them.'

'You were in your office soon after eight, you say. When did you leave?' asked Evans.

'It took longer than I'd thought to make the amendments and write my e-mails. It must have been about a quarter past twelve when I left,' replied Carswell. 'I remember glancing at the clock on my computer just before I closed it down.'

'Were you in your office all the time you were on campus, sir?' asked Evans.

'Mostly, yes,' replied Carswell. 'After about an hour I thought I'd have a coffee – there's a machine outside the lecture theatre on the ground floor here, but it wasn't working, so I went into the HQ building where there's another. I was only out of the office for about ten minutes.'

'Did you see anyone when you went to get your coffee?' asked Evans.

'I think the only person I saw was Dan Parker – he's one of Stephen Wright's research students. I saw him just as I was leaving HQ. I said a 'good morning' and I think that's all he said in reply,' answered Carswell.

'Did he go into the building, do you remember?' asked Evans.

'I'm not sure – he may have done, I suppose, but I can't quite think why,' replied Carswell. 'Research students don't have many dealings with the powers in HQ. They're most involved with their supervisors and other students in their research areas.'

'You said you were 'mostly' in our office – when else were you not?' asked Evans.

Carswell gave a slightly embarrassed smile before replying.

'I'd had a mug of coffee before I left home as well as a bowl of cereal. I'm afraid that together with the rather unpleasant drink from the coffee machine, I needed the loo. The nearest one is on this floor at the end of this corridor. I must have been out of the office for five minutes - not much more.'

'When you'd finished what you'd planned to do to your funding proposal, what then?' asked Evans.

'I did consider taking it over to HQ to leave on Carter's PA's, desk but then thought better of it – I still had to incorporate stuff about what commitments the Australian would make and I'd not have had those until Monday morning at the earliest. I thought it best to present Mr Carter with the full and finished proposal and arrange to discuss it with him in person. So, I turned off the PC and left for home.'

'Did you see or meet anyone after you'd left your office on your way to your car?' asked Evans.

'There were a few people about, I recall. I recognised a group of our Structural Protection MSc students headed across the far end of the car park towards the footpath that leads to the exit that brings you out in the village. They'd just moved out of view when I noticed Kevin Varney talking with Alex Simmonds by Kevin's car. After a second or two they split up and Alex went the way the MSc group had gone and Kevin walked away from me towards HQ – he was carrying something, but I'm not sure what. I don't think he saw me. I got in my car and drove home where I spent the afternoon.'

Evans rose from his seat, offered his hand to Michael Carswell and said, 'Thanks for your time – you've been very helpful. We'll let you get on now.'

Evans and his companion left Michael Carswell sitting at his desk. When the office door closed, Michael took a folder marked 'Australian Proposal' from a desk drawer, opened it and wondered how he might go about getting approval for his ideas now that he'd lost his important, though albeit initially reluctant, supporter.

*

It was just coming up to five o'clock when the Oxford policemen, having parted company with the two MoD officers, returned to the room in HQ. Both sat down at the table in the centre of the room and consulted their notebooks, recounting the essence of their conversations with Alex Simmonds and Michael Carswell earlier.

'Gill Neville really didn't have much to say,' began Geoff Brown. 'She and Chris Wells seem to have 'a thing' going and she spends as much time at his place in the village here as she does at her house in Farlington.'

Brown paused and looked at Evans who was smiling broadly.

'Something funny?' asked Brown.

'Not really, sir,' replied Evans. 'Other than that Chris Wells seems to be a quick worker – he's only been on the staff here for less than a month!'

'Must be his charisma – or a meeting of like scientific minds,' said Brown.

'And bodies, too….,' added Evans with another grin.

'Quite likely,' said Brown. 'Moving on………..'

'Yes, sir,' said Evans, suppressing his grin.

'Gill Neville says that she and Chris Wells spent the night together at his flat in the village. She says he got up at about eight, made her some tea and then made himself some breakfast before leaving her to walk to TDU. He wanted to finish off a lecture he was going to give on Monday morning.

She finished her tea, listened to the bedside radio, got up at about half-past nine, showered and made some breakfast for herself. She'd agreed to pick up Wells soon after noon and, since she had some time to spare, she thought she'd try and finish the novel that she'd been reading. She says she set off in her car – Wells doesn't have a vehicle – and arrived on campus at about twelve o'clock. She'd gone into the guard house reception because her car pass was due to expire at the end of the month and it was a convenient time to be issued with another. I've checked with reception and indeed she's logged as having signed for a new pass at five past twelve on Saturday.'

Brown paused and turned over a leaf of his notebook before continuing.

'She parked near her lab to wait for Chris Wells. While she was waiting she spoke with Dan Parker who was carrying test samples out to his car which was parked a couple of spaces away from her. She didn't have time to say much to him because Chris Wells arrived. She thought that Parker seemed a little subdued when she first saw him but thought that was because he was preoccupied with his big EDER trial on Monday. He was apparently taking his last samples out onto the range then.'

'That's interesting – so someone seems to have been on EDER on Saturday morning which is when it appears likely that Carter's body was put there.' said Evans. 'I think we need another word with Mr Parker.'

'I agree.' said Brown. 'He didn't mention his Saturday EDER visit when we were questioning all those who'd been on the range on Monday morning. He turned up just after Carter's body had been discovered – he was due to start his experiments after Kevin Varney's demonstration session. The officer who interviewed him didn't think he was anything other than surprised and shocked by the news of Carter's death. He said that he'd not had the opportunity to do any setting up for his experiments in the test building because of the MSc demo. If he'd set out any instrumentation it would likely have been damaged by Kevin Varney's tests.'

'Did Gill Neville know anything about what she needed to do in order to have her contract renewed?' asked

Evans. 'Carter's notes were very definite about the conditions she'd need to meet if she was to continue in her employment.'

Brown paused before replying.

'I asked if she'd had many dealings with Carter during her time at TDU. She said that she'd spoken to him only on a couple of occasions and both those times she'd been with Stephen Wright who was, as we know up until last summer, her PhD supervisor. She said that Stephen dealt with Carter about all aspects of her employment contract. Stephen had made it quite clear to her that it would be necessary to have a good level of contract and consultancy work in place when her contract came up for renewal so that there could be no grounds for the University and Carter refusing to renew her employment. She and Stephen had had several discussions about how such funding could be obtained and they were in the process of talking with a number of potential sources. She seemed very sanguine about the process and didn't display anything particularly negative in relation to Carter – I think Stephen Wright had reassured her that the situation was under control and Carter was, after all, only doing his job.'

Brown stopped while he consulted his notebook.

'There was one other thing.............Yes, here we are,' said Brown. 'Gill Neville said that, on their drive to their pub lunch Chris Wells commented that he'd seen Frank Hargreaves coming out of the Horrocks building as he was going in. They'd greeted each other briefly but Hargreaves didn't stop to talk. We know that Professor Hargreaves was on the campus and in HQ later in the morning because he met with Stephen Wright but, from what Gill Neville says, he must have been there earlier. We might ask Frank Hargreaves to give us a bit more detail about his Saturday morning – he may have seen something that might be important.'

'Anyway, it doesn't sound as if Gill Neville has any serious issues with Robert Carter's approach to her employment contract,' said Evans. 'I got a similar sort of feeling about Kevin Varney. He was on the campus on Saturday morning but only for fifteen or twenty minutes. He did, though, go into HQ building to do some photocopying. Apparently one of the clerks in the ground floor offices is notoriously slack about both locking her office and turning off the photocopier at the end of the day. Kevin – who had his son with him and wanted to be away quickly – gambled on being able to use this copier rather than gain access to his departmental photocopier which would have taken longer to get to and would have needed a while to warm up before it would be ready to copy. Anyway, he was in luck – the office was open and the photocopier still on - and he was headed back to his car after about ten minutes. He said he'd had a few words with Alex Simmonds just after he'd parked his car and, as he came out of HQ, he'd seen Dan Parker.'

'Dan Parker seems to have been around a lot on Saturday morning, doesn't he?' said Brown. 'Did Kevin Varney have any comment about Carter? I know he was there with WO Davies when Davies found the body – he seemed pretty shaken up by the discovery from what Jarvis's men said - which is what you'd expect.'

'Varney did volunteer that Carter was not at the top of his 'favourite people' list because he knew that Carter had not been on his side at his recent promotion board,' said Evans. 'Carter had asked more questions that anyone else on the board about the funding opportunities that Varney was pursuing. He'd made it quite clear that there weren't enough and their value was not sufficient. Varney was upset that his academic credentials were considered secondary to his money-generating potential. He said he'd come out of the board fuming about Carter's attitude but, after he'd calmed down, forced himself to acknowledge that maybe Carter did have a point and Varney has apparently already started to be rather more proactive in his search for contract monies.'

'It seems to me that the four we've spoken with this afternoon and also Chris Wells – and we might need to talk with him yet – don't seem to have done anything or seen anything that might link them to Carter's death,' began Brown. 'Alex Simmonds acknowledges that Carter could be a bit of a bastard about his conference funding requests but regarded their dealings as something of a battle of wills – a duel or a joust. Michael Carswell was initially upset by Carter's view of his Australian proposals but Carter seems to have been more constructive and encouraging later in their exchange of views. I can't think that Carswell would contemplate doing any harm to Carter – he seemed to be becoming something of an ally. As for Gill Neville and Kevin Varney – both seemed pretty calm about the way Carter was addressing the contract renewal and promotion issues. Neville has confidence in Stephen Wright and her ability to attract significant funding and Kevin Varney's failed promotion board seems to have galvanised him into action.'

'I agree,' responded Evans. 'The person we need to chat to now is Dan Parker – let's see if we can find him in his lab. He wasn't answering his phone when I called earlier.'

'OK, John, let's both of us see if we can find him,' said Brown.

21

Tuesday 20th September evening

It was approaching six o'clock on a beautiful autumn evening as Brown and Evans walked from HQ towards the Horrocks Building and Dan Parker's materials laboratory. The sun was still strong but low in the sky and cast long shadows of the two officers as they made their way along the tarmac path that cut through the grassed area that bordered the car park. They had almost reached the entrance to the Horrocks Building where the materials laboratory was located, when Dan Parker emerged carrying a number of substantial-looking books under his arm. He stopped when he saw the two policemen.

'Mr Parker?' said DC Evan. 'Could we have a word, please?'

'Yes, I guess so,' replied Parker, in a slightly reluctant tone. 'Will it take long, only I need to get over to the Library to return these books and they close at half six.'

'Only a few questions, that's all, just to clarify a few points,' said DCI Brown. 'Why don't we walk with you over to the Library, so as not to delay you.'

Parker nodded his assent and the three men set of to walk to the TDU Library located on the edge of the campus not far from where the main block of married quarters was sited.

'It must have been a shock to you yesterday when you arrived on EDER to start your tests,' began Brown, looking questioningly at Parker.

'I couldn't think what was going on,' replied Parker. 'I'd arranged with WO Davies to start my test programme after Kevin Varney's demonstration had ended. There didn't seem much point in getting out onto the range until that was due to end – I'd done all the preparatory work on my test samples and just had to set up the instrumentation in the hardened building. I couldn't do that until Dr Varney had finished – his demonstration would have generated fragments that could have been potentially damaging to my gauges. I expected to see people on the EDER but certainly not police cars. When I asked one of the MSc students what was going on I was shocked to hear that WO Davies had found a body in the EDER building.'

Dan paused and shifted the books he was carrying from under his left arm to his right before continuing.

'I heard someone – not sure who it was - say that it was Robert Carter, the University's Chief Finance Officer,' continued Parker. 'One of the MoD police officers told everyone to stay on the EDER and suggested that we move into the viewing area – it's like a small grandstand with a few seats where you can observe open air demonstrations taking place on the range.'

'Yes, I know where you mean,' said Brown encouragingly. 'What happened then?'

'After a short time I saw you and your colleague arrive,' Parker nodded towards DC Evans, 'together with the MoD Inspector – I think his name's Jarvis?'

'That's correct,' replied Brown. 'Then what?'

'Well there was a bit of a delay before two of the MoD policemen spoke to each of us in the grandstand in turn, asked us to identify ourselves and whether we'd noticed anything out of the ordinary on the EDER that morning,' replied Parker. 'I told them that I was scheduled to carry out a series of tests in the building that morning and showed them my test pieces in the preparation building. When all of us had given the information asked for, we were allowed to leave and told to expect to be asked a few more questions when things had become clearer about what had happened.'

'The samples that you were going to test – when did you bring them out onto EDER?' asked Brown.

'It was over the course of the previous week – some went out on Wednesday, some on Thursday and couple on Friday morning,' answered Parker. 'It had taken longer than I expected to get them all ready, but by Friday evening all but three were on the EDER and I decided to come in early on Saturday morning to finish them and take them out. I think I was in the lab soon after seven-thirty. I thought it would take me a few hours to finish and I wanted to be home by lunch-time. Because preparing these samples had taken so long, I've been working quite late each day and needed to catch up on a number of things at home – I hadn't been shopping for over a week and was running low on lots of things.'

'So, you were in your lab all morning from seven-thirty until you took your last test pieces out to the EDER?' asked Evans.

'Yes, more or less,' replied Parker.

''More or less', you say?' asked Evans. 'Does this mean you weren't in your lab all morning?'

Dan Parker hesitated before responding and seemed to be choosing his words carefully as he replied.

'I had something else on my mind as well as the test samples......,' he began. 'I'd had a letter…'

'Go on,' said Evans encouragingly. 'What letter?'

'A letter from the Finance Office, signed by Robert Carter telling me that once my present contract runs out it won't be renewed,' replied Parker. 'It seemed very clear that a decision had been made and wouldn't be changed. I was very upset by it – Stephen Wright - my supervisor - had given me no indication that this might happen. I have started to write my thesis but there's a lot to do yet. These were the last experiments, but there'll be a lot of work to do in analysing the results. I was hoping for at least a three or even six months extension to complete the thesis. It could be very difficult to finish it if I wasn't allowed use of the facilities here. I tried to talk to Stephen on Friday but I didn't manage to get hold of him. I'm sure he would have been just as shocked as I was – he'd always told me that anything up to a six or even nine month extension would be no problem to put in place, since he was confident that he had the necessary funding.'

Dan paused as the trio reached the entrance to the Library building and looked at his watch that showed that it was twenty minutes past six.

'We'll just take a seat here while you go and return the books,' said Brown, indicating a small area equipped with a wooden tables and benches where TDU Library users could sit while taking a break from their studies and drink a coffee available from a machine located in the library entrance foyer.

Parker nodded in assent and disappeared into the library, returning five minutes later empty-handed. He sat on one of the empty bench seats near the two already-seated policemen before speaking.

'I'd noticed when I arrived that Mr Carter's car was in his normal parking space outside the HQ building. I think that Prof Hargreaves' car was there as well, though he usually parks near the Horrocks building. I've often seen him in on a Saturday morning – I think he likes to do a bit of admin when it's quiet. It's generally just research students like me who seem to keep odd hours,' said Parker with something approaching a smile. 'I went to my lab and started work, but I kept thinking that it would be good to speak with Carter face-to-face about the letter and, if he was in his office, I could put my case to him about the possibility of an extension to my contract. I resisted the temptation for a while but then felt I just had to go and speak with Carter. His car was still there so I went up to his office- the door was open - but it was empty. It looked as if he'd been there recently because there were papers on the desk that I suppose he'd been working on. Anyway, he wasn't there, so I went back to my lab thinking I'd go over later to see if he'd returned.'

'What time did you go to Carter's office?' asked Brown.

'I think it was a short time after eight o'clock – I had a radio on in the lab and I think there'd just been a news bulletin when I left the lab,' replied Parker.

'What about the next time?' asked Brown.

'That must have been getting on for nine o'clock. The office looked pretty much the same as when I went first, so I thought he might still be around – he's known to be strict about leaving stuff on desks and I assumed that he'd be back to clear the papers away at some stage. When I headed back to my lab I saw that his car had gone – I was sure it had been there when I went into HQ. I thought perhaps that, if he'd had an early start, he'd gone to have some breakfast in the mess and I'd just missed him. I thought it might be worth another try later, so I went over again at about ten o'clock. His car still wasn't there, but, since I was there, I decided to go up – daft idea really. I guess I must have just missed him again because this time his desk was clear.'

When Parker said this, Brown caught Evans' eye.

'So you think that Carter left the campus sometime between your second visit at nine o'clock and your third call about an hour later?' suggested Evans.

'I suppose so, yes,' replied Parker.

'Why didn't you telephone him to see if he was in, rather than keep traipsing over there each time?' asked Evans.

'Because he wouldn't have answered – all calls went to his secretary. You could never get to speak to him unless he wanted to talk to you,' replied Parker.

'So what did you do then?' asked Brown.

'I went back to my lab and finished my last sample,' replied Parker.

'Did you see or talk to anyone on Saturday morning?' asked Brown.

'There wasn't anyone about early on,' said Parker, 'but as the morning wore on there did seem to be a few people about. I saw Prof Hargreaves – I said I'd seen his car. He was walking near the HQ building and Dr Carswell was entering the car park. When I was taking my test pieces out to my car to take out to the EDER, I met Gill Neville.'

Parker paused and, when he continued, his mood seemed to have become rather subdued.

'I started to chat to her but didn't get to say much before Chris Wells turned up. He never seems to be more than a few yards away from her at any time of day,' Parker paused.

'Is that a problem?' asked Evans.

Parker let a few moments pass before his response.

'Well, it shouldn't be, but it is,' he said. 'Gill and I get on well and I've been trying to get her to come out with me these last few months. I thought I was starting to get somewhere with her when along comes Chris Wells and she seems to have lost what little interest she had in me. I was hoping that Wells would be just a passing fancy and that she'd return to behaving towards me the way she used to. This letter from Carter was the last straw – the prospect of me having to leave the university was a bloody miserable prospect. I'd never get another chance with her.'

Parker stopped, has face somewhat flushed.

'Sorry – I shouldn't have told you that – very embarrassing,' he muttered.

'Don't worry, Mr Parker, what you've said will remain confidential,' said Brown reassuringly. 'What did you do when you'd parted company with Gill Neville and Chris Wells?'

'I drove onto the EDER – as an authorised user, I have the security code for the lock – stopped the car, opened the gate, drove through and stopped again so I could close the gate,' continued Parker. 'I also have a key to the preparation room where my other samples were, so I opened up and took the last three in. I locked up and drove back to the campus. I had to go through the same procedure to drive out. It was getting on for lunch-time, so I decided to drive home.'

'Did you notice anything unusual on the EDER that morning?' asked Brown.

Parker paused for a moment, clearly trying to recall anything out of the ordinary, aware of the purpose behind the policeman's question.

'I can't think of anything – it all looked pretty much as it usually does. The site is kept pretty tidy and everything out there has its proper place. The only think I did notice was that the sand and gravel at the entrance the hardened building was a bit more scuffed up than usual – but a lot of people had been on the range the previous week and, though that area is usually raked over at the end of a session, it sometimes gets overlooked – I've been guilty myself – particularly on POETS day……..'

'POETS day?' said Evans.

'"Piss off early tomorrow's Saturday",' said Brown with a grin.

Evans smiled in response before saying, 'So the next time you were on the EDER was when you turned up for your tests yesterday morning?'

Parker nodded in response.

'OK, thanks for talking to us. You've been very clear about your Saturday and what happened on Monday morning. We ought to let you go now – time is getting on,' said Brown.

Parker shook hands with the two policemen and set off back towards the main car park. Brown looked at his watch, saw that it was coming up to a quarter to seven and the shadows had lengthened further.

'Well, Mr Parker seems to have had an interesting Saturday morning,' ventured Brown. 'The business of the Carter's car and the state of his desk is intriguing. I think something must have been going on from about the time that Dan Parker arrived on campus on Saturday to when he said he was last in Carter's office at about a quarter to eleven. I wonder if he's telling us the complete truth about his morning? He could have seen Carter early on, confronted him and maybe argued with him about his contract. Dan Parker seems to have been under both professional and personal stress these last few days. He finds that the preparation of his samples is taking longer than he expected and he's got the pressure on to be ready for a limited time slot to test his samples. And……Gill Neville seems to be slipping through his grasp.'

'If she was ever anywhere near his grasp,' commented Evans. 'He may be deluding himself about the way Gill Neville feels – or felt – about him.'

'Maybe,' replied Evans. 'However, he may have let his feelings get the better of him and got Carter annoyed by his protestations about the contract issue. We know that Carter was likely to be in a somewhat unstable state having missed taking his medication. I'm wondering now if he'd spent the night in his office if he was feeling tired and disorientated as Dr Singh suggested he might be.'

'I was beginning to wonder that myself. Are you suggesting that Dan Parker attacked Carter in his office?' asked Evans.

'Well, if not attacked, then at least provoked a response from Carter that alarmed Parker,' replied Brown.

'You think that it was Parker – for whatever reason – who removed Carter from his office, took him out to the EDER and then moved his car?' asked Evans. 'It seems a bit unlikely and, anyway, I'm not sure why he'd do anything like that – it seems far more likely to me that he'd have called for assistance if Carter's state of health had taken a dramatic turn for the worse while he was arguing with him. He doesn't seem the type to try and hide what may have been just an unfortunate series of events.'

'You may be right,' commented Brown. 'It is a possibility though, but, as you say, unlikely from what we've seen of Dan Parker. It's something to bear in mind, though.'

Brown paused and looked at his watch.

'Since we're so close, a brief visit to the two Aussie MSc students might be in order – just a quick chat then home, I think.'

*

DCI Brown and DC Evans walked the couple of hundred yards or so to the front door of Graham Dowell's married quarter. Evans rang the bell and the door was opened a few seconds later by Graham Dowell himself.

'Good evening, Flight Lieutenant Dowell…,' began Brown.

'Graham, please!' interrupted Dowell, who recognised the two officers from yesterday's events. 'What can I do for you?'

'Just a quick word or two about the business on the EDER yesterday,' said Brown.

'No worries!' replied Dowell before adding. 'Come on through. Grant and Jen Thompson are here. We're all just having a drink on the patio. Grant was with me on the EDER yesterday, so you might want a word with him too.'

Brown and Evans followed Graham Dowell through the standard MoD magnolia painted hallway into the kitchen at back of the house and out onto a paved patio bathed in the last of the day's sun.

After introductions and the arrival of a can of beer for each of the two policemen – both felt they could claim to be more or less off duty now – Brown pulled out his notebook.

'We know that both you and Grant were out on the EDER yesterday morning and we've seen your accounts of what you witnessed there,' began Brown, 'but I wanted to ask you both a few questions about something that you, as Australian officers, might be best placed to answer.'

Both Dowell and Thompson looked a little surprised before Grant Thompson spoke. 'Not sure what we can help you with, but we'll try to if we can.'

Dowell nodded in agreement.

'I think Jen and I might make ourselves scarce while you gentlemen talk shop,' said Bronwen Dowell. 'We'll be in the kitchen or the living room if you need us for anything. OK, Jen?'

Jen Thompson smiled her agreement and both women took their half-full glasses of white wine and went into the house.

'OK,' said Graham Dowell. 'How can we help?'

'You know that it was Robert Carter, the University's Chief Finance Officer, who was found in the EDER building yesterday?' began Brown.

Both Australians nodded.

'We're trying to work out how he came to be there and have been looking at the work he'd most recently been involved in to see if it has any bearing on the situation,' continued Brown. 'There are two matters we thought you might have some knowledge of. The first is the proposed link between TDU and Australian universities – Melbourne and ADFA in particular – and the Defence Science and Technical Organisation. Both Prof Nightingale and Hargreaves were involved in these discussions as well as Robert Carter. The second is the contract for the manufacture under licence of the armour system developed here at TDU by Dr Stephen Wright. Can you tell us anything about these with your, as it were, 'local knowledge'?'

'Robert Carter was involved both in the proposed academic links and with the commercial contract issues,' added Evans, being careful not to give anything away, particularly in relation to Carter's involvement with the potential armour contract fraud.

'Both Grant and I know a bit about the academic links, particularly the one with ADFA – we're both ADFA old boys and still keep in touch with what's going on there,' said Dowell. 'I know that it was Prof Nightingale who was pushing for a formal link with ADFA and Prof Hargreaves who'd been working with Melbourne Uni.'

'At the Welcoming Party a few weeks ago it was clear that Prof Hargreaves hadn't been keeping Prof Nightingale fully up to speed on his negotiations with Melbourne,' said Grant Thompson.

'The atmosphere was a bit frosty when the subject of Melbourne was raised. I think Prof Nightingale felt that Prof Hargreaves was trying to steal his thunder,' said Dowell. 'I heard from my ADFA contacts that Prof Nightingale wasn't terribly complimentary about some aspects of the operation here – I heard he'd had a couple of glasses too many at dinner one night and was telling anyone who's listen how he'd had to make lots of changes at TDU when he took up his post to get the place running properly and how he'd be doing the same when he started his work with the UK universities financial body – the Funding Council, is it? I understand that he had a bit of a go at TDU academic departments in general and the Finance Office in particular, though I don't know if any of this got back to Mr Carter or if it has any bearing on Mr Carter's death. I don't really know anything specific about Prof Hargreaves' work with Melbourne Uni and their plans for a research network in the security area other than ADFA knew that Hargreaves had been in Oz and had raised the issue of TDU, Melbourne and ADFA working together.'

Dowell paused and drank some of his beer before continuing.

'I've also had some dealings with DSTO since I've been here,' he said, 'trying to help Michael Carswell with a mess he thought he'd got himself into with a piece of MoD research he'd been doing. He thought he'd plagiarised work that is currently going on at DSTO in Salisbury, South Australia – I was working there before I came here. I put him in contact with a couple of key people there and he seems to have resolved the problem – which actually wasn't a problem, if you see what I mean. His work complements rather than copies the stuff DSTO are doing and now he's keen to get together with DSTO to push the work on, so much so that I think he's working on a funding proposal to travel to Oz soon – I guess Mr Carter will have been involved with that?'

Brown nodded in tacit understanding of what Dowell had been saying.

'What about the TDU – Australia armour contract links? Do you know anything about these?' asked Brown.

'I can probably answer that,' said Grant Thompson, 'though I'm not sure I've got that much to tell. I knew that Comparmour – they're the biggest armour manufacturer in Oz – were expecting – or at least hoping - to be awarded the sole manufacturing licence. I don't know if their expectations were realistic, but the gossip had got out to us in Kabul when I was nearing the end of my tour, so there may have been something in it. But then again, there also seem to be other companies in the competition for the licence. Giovanni Corradi, the Italian on the Ordnance MSc was saying that the Italian outfit Difesa Composita was also very much in the running. I did hear mention from one or two other Aussie sources that there may be a couple of other firms also in with a real chance of landing the contract. It all seems bit confused and unnecessarily complicated – but I suppose it's all being done as 'Commercial in Confidence' with everybody expected to keep their own secrets! Whatever the true situation, I imagine that Mr Carter must have been pretty heavily involved with sorting out the contract, whoever was going to get it.'

'That's something of an understatement……,' began Evans, before a sharp look from Brown caused him to fall silent.

'That's all very interesting background information,' said Brown, 'and I'm sure that it will prove very useful to us, so thanks. And thanks for the beer – but we must make a move.'

Brown and Evans rose, shook hands with Dowell and Thompson, passed through the kitchen where Bronwen Dowell and Jen Thompson were sitting at the large kitchen table with the Dowell's two boys who were tucking into a large pizza each.

'Got to keep the beasts fed!' said Bronwen with a smile at the two boys who seemed to be about ten and seven years old. 'You gentlemen are welcome to stay for a bite of supper – there's enough for about ten here.'

She indicated a large saucepan from which rose the unmistakeable aroma of bolognaise sauce.

'Tempting!' replied Brown. 'But we must be off - but thanks for the offer.'

The two policemen left the house, walked back across the campus as the final rays of sun faded and got into their car.

'An interesting day,' commented Evans as he drove the car through the security barrier at the exit to the campus and onto the Oxford road.

'Yes, indeed,' responded Brown. 'We need to think hard about what Dan Parker told us earlier – his account sounds plausible and if what he told us is the truth, then our conversations with the two professors tomorrow might be interesting. The timescale that Parker outlined – providing it's correct, and there seems to be a number of other accounts that support it – suggests to me that Alex Simmonds, Michael Carswell. Gill Neville, Chris Wells, Kevin Varney and the MSc cohort can be pretty much ruled out of any involvement with Carter between the time after he left the mess on Friday night and fairly early Saturday morning.'

Evans nodded in agreement before adding, 'Of course, we're also going to talk with Stephen Wright's partner, Giles Mitchell, tomorrow morning at his gallery in Oxford. It'll be interesting to hear if he has anything to add to what Stephen Wright told us about the events of last weekend.'

'Yes,' said Brown. 'It will be worth talking to Giles Mitchell. But for the moment all I can think of is the prospect of getting home and having something to eat – let's not worry about TDU any more until the morning.'

22

<u>*Wednesday 21th September am*</u>

It was just coming up to nine o'clock on Wednesday morning when DCI Brown and DC Evans tapped on the door of The Mitchell Gallery in the centre of Oxford. Giles Mitchell was clearly expecting them and opened the door within a few seconds of their knocking. He bid them welcome, closed the door after them, ensuring that the sign on it still showed 'Closed', and shook hands with the two officers.

'How can I help?' began Mitchell after Brown and Evans were seated opposite his desk located at the rear of the gallery. 'This whole business with Carter, the contracts and then finding Carter dead has been a great shock to Stephen – he'd been working a lot with Carter in the preparation of the licence contract which would have brought a lot of money to the university and quite a lot to Stephen himself – but I suppose he's told you all of this?'

Giles Mitchell paused and looked expectantly at the policemen.

'Dr Wright has given us a very full account of what happened between him and Carter on Friday afternoon. He told us how he was very keen to discuss the situation with you because of the proposal that Carter had made about money........,' began Brown.

'And I told him straight away to forget it,' interjected Mitchell. 'I can't imagine what he must have been thinking about. It's true that I do need to raise money – and quite a lot it is too – to pay off my former gallery partner, but the plan that Carter outlined was not the way. As matters stand, I've done some unexpectedly good business these last few days. The reason I couldn't meet you last night was that I was with a client. He was interested in three pictures that I was beginning to think I would never sell, but last night I did – and the return will be good. I was gambling on Thurston – he's the artist –

coming back into vogue when I bought them almost a year ago. Over the last few months he's been regaining some of the popularity he enjoyed a decade or more ago– nothing spectacular, mind – but then, almost out of the blue, one was sold in New York last week for over $30,000 and now everyone wants to own one. My client knew I'd got three and we did a deal which meant he got them at rather less than he might have paid elsewhere and I got a great deal more than I'd paid for them last year. Though it'll be a bit tight, I think that, between us, Stephen and I will be able to get hold of the all money I need. That man Carter could have ruined everything, if Stephen had accepted his offer – I was fuming about what Carter had tried to do. And so, I..........'

Mitchell paused in his narrative, looking somewhat uncomfortable.

'And so you..........what?' asked Brown, looking steadily at Mitchell.

Giles Mitchell shifted in his seat before reply, 'And so I went to see him –Carter that is.'

Both Brown and Evans stared at Mitchell.

'Go on, sir,' said Brown.

'Stephen was exhausted after he'd told me about what Carter had been doing and needed to sleep. He went upstairs first and, when I followed about ten minutes later, he was already fast asleep. It was then that I decided to go and see if I could find Carter and confront him, so I left Stephen asleep and drove over to Carter's house in Shellington – there was no traffic so I was there in under half an hour.'

Mitchell shifted in his seat before continuing.

'The house looked empty – there was no car in the driveway and all of the curtains were undrawn. There were certainly no lights on. I suppose it was only then that I realised that Carter really had gone and done what he was planning to do and that I'd been foolish to think that I could have done any good by trying to see him. I felt a bit stupid, to be honest.'

'What did you do then?' asked Brown.

'I drove home,' said Mitchell. 'I'd only been away for just over an hour. Stephen was still asleep when I got into bed and when he eventually woke up, I didn't say where I'd been.'

'You didn't consider looking for Carter at TDU after you'd been to his house?' asked Evans.

'It didn't seem very sensible – it was about two o'clock in the morning,' replied Giles. 'I don't have a security pass to get onto the campus and, anyway, it seemed to me that it would be better to let things lie until the morning. I really thought he'd gone. By that time I'd calmed down anyway and thought it better to talk with Stephen again before doing anything else. Well, Stephen woke at about twenty to eight and set off for Carter's house at about nine o'clock. I didn't say I'd already been to Carter's house – I thought it better to let Stephen go and, anyway, Carter might have returned home. I had to go and open the gallery and didn't see Stephen till the evening when he told me about what he'd found in Carter's office and the text messages from Carter.'

'Didn't you think it strange that Stephen didn't call the police on Saturday?' asked Brown. 'He surely.......'

Mitchell interrupted him saying, 'Stephen genuinely believed that Carter would undo the sequence of events that he'd set in motion. He wanted to give Carter a chance both to preserve his personal reputation and the good name of TDU. It was only on Sunday evening that he realised that his trust in Carter had been misplaced. That's when the events with him first calling the MoD police and then, of course, you, started to unfold. I know Stephen regrets delaying calling in the police.......'

'But that's what he should have done on Friday afternoon, for goodness sake,' said Brown in an exasperated tone. 'However, we're where we are and have to deal with the matter as it is and not as, perhaps, we might have liked it to be.'

Brown rose to his feet. Evans stood up too.

'You've been most helpful, Mr Mitchell,' said Brown. 'I just wish your partner had been a little less trusting - we may have avoided the need to be investigating a death.'

*

On the drive from Oxford the two policemen speculated about the events of the early hours of Saturday morning. They were getting on for halfway to TDU when Evans, who was driving, said, 'Of course, Mitchell might not have gone straight back home to Stephen Wright after he'd been to Carter's house. What if he continued to look for Carter and did go to TDU.............'

'But he has no security pass,' said Brown.

'He could have taken Stephen Wright's with him,' suggested Evans.

'Both he and his car would have been noticed – there can't be much coming and going at that time of the morning,' interrupted Brown, 'and one of the security guards would certainly have mentioned it.'

'What if he left his car outside the campus and walked in through one of the pedestrian gates? After midnight they're not manned. There's an electronic system – each security pass has a chip - when the gate senses it, it unlocks. Mitchell could have gone to Carter's office and confronted him, assuming he was there all night.'

Brown paused before replying, 'Well, John, I can just about allow that you may have a point but, as Mitchell said, his visit to Carter's house was driven by his feelings of anger towards Carter which seem to have dissipated when he started thinking a bit more rationally about why he was looking for him. Besides, I don't see how he can have had anything to do with getting Carter out onto the EDER. He may have 'borrowed' Stephen's campus security pass but I'd be pretty sure that he wouldn't have the code to access the EDER and, anyway, he'd have had to have driven Carter's car to the EDER, parked it back outside HQ and then later in the day somehow moved it off the campus – and he was in the gallery in Oxford on Saturday morning. Then there's the business of the text messages from Carter's phone on both Saturday morning and on Sunday evening. It seems clear that they can't have been sent by Carter who, we believe now, was lying in the EDER building from quite early on Saturday morning.'

'I'd forgotten the text messages,' admitted Evans. 'It's difficult to see how Mitchell could have sent them – particularly the one on Sunday evening when he was with Stephen Wright. Maybe he had help later in the day – from Stephen?'

'I can't see it,' replied Brown. 'This is all getting a bit too complex. For Giles Mitchell to be more deeply involved with Carter's death seems totally unrealistic. But.................. let's keep it at the back of our minds for the moment. I think it might be worth thinking more about what Dan Parker told us yesterday.

'You think he might be involved in Carter's death?' asked Evans.

'Well, we know he had been upset by the letter from the Finance Office, signed by Carter,' began Brown. 'He'd not been able to talk to Stephen Wright who, most likely, would have offered him reassurances about his future. He seems to have been further upset by the fact that his – probably rather timid – efforts with Gill Neville seem to have been scuppered by the arrival of Chris Wells and his mind may have been in something of a turmoil on Saturday morning.'

Brown paused as Evans pulled out to overtake farm tractor that they'd been stuck behind for ten minutes before continuing.

'What if Parker did meet Carter soon after eight o'clock in Carter's office?' said Brown. 'We are fairly certain that Carter never left the campus after dinner on Friday, but went back to his office, possibly feeling unwell after missing some of his medication, and fell asleep. Maybe Parker woke him and something happened to Carter – he was a sick man anyway, hadn't taken his pills, was likely feeling tense about the execution of his fraud and this tension was further increased when he realised he'd spent the night at TDU when, I guess, he'd planned to be long gone.'

'So you think maybe that Carter collapsed or fell or even died in his office when Dan Parker arrived to confront him about the letter?' said Evans. 'What then?'

'Maybe Parker panicked if Carter collapsed,' began Brown. 'Parker's a fairly strong looking chap – he could have carried Carter down to his car……..'

'But why on earth would he do that?' interrupted Evans. 'Why go out to the EDER? Someone in such a panic would have just left, surely? There weren't any people around at that time and Parker could just have gone back to his lab and calmed down. He seems to have been fairly calm when he did go out to the EDER later in the morning,'

'Good point,' admitted Brown. 'It doesn't seem to pan out as a particularly realistic course of events. Maybe we'll have a better idea after we've spoken to the two profs.'

As Evans turned the car into the entrance to TDU a few minutes before eleven o'clock and drew to a halt in front of the security barrier, Brown was deep in thought. He was mulling over the meeting with Giles Mitchell which had given further support to the notion that Robert Carter had not made it back home from the campus on the night of Friday 16th September. He agreed with the view that Evans had expressed on the drive that Stephen Wright had been far too trusting in his dealings with Carter. He had to concede that, although Dan Parker may well have been angry with Carter about his future, any direct involvement in his death seemed unlikely.

A few minutes after they'd been checked in, Evans had parked the car outside the TDU HQ and was following Brown into the building.

*

Marion Jones knocked on Prof James Nightingale's office door, opened it and took a step into the room.

'DCI Brown and DC Evans to see you, Prof,' said Marion.

James Nightingale looked up from the papers on his desk.

'OK, show them in,' he said rather wearily.

He stood up to greet the two policemen, shaking hands with both before asking them to take a seat.

'How can I help, gentlemen?' said Nightingale with a watery smile.

'Just one or two points of clarification, sir, if you don't mind,' began Brown. 'After your slightly – shall we say – fractious meeting with Robert Carter on Friday evening, you say you went home for supper with your wife?'

'Yes, that's correct,' replied Nightingale.

'You didn't, by any chance, go out again later and walk over here to continue your 'discussion' with Carter?' continued Brown.

'Certainly not!' said Nightingale vehemently. 'I'd had enough of the man – he'd said things to me earlier in the evening that I'd found hard to take. I'd even made myself apologise to him - even though his malicious teasing fell just short of out and out blackmail – and I was feeling pretty sore. But, after something to eat, I'd calmed down, and even managed to relax in front of the TV – Bath against London Irish on BT Sport. Delia – my wife – will confirm all of this. I didn't go out again that night.'

'We may have a word with your wife, sir,' continued Brown. 'Tell us what you were doing on Saturday morning. Did you come here?'

Nightingale paused before replying in a tone that clearly indicated his displeasure at being asked these questions.

'No, I did not come here on Saturday morning. If you are implying that I sought him out on Saturday morning, then you're wrong. I had no thoughts about seeing him again until, at the earliest, Monday morning when we had a Finance Sub-committee meeting scheduled for 10 o'clock.'

'We do have a witness who saw you near this building fairly early on Saturday morning,' said Brown.

'I greatly resent your line of enquiry,' said Nightingale. 'I've told you that I did not come here on Saturday. For your information, I was out walking – our house is, as you know, on the campus and only a few minutes away. I enjoy an occasional cigarette, but Delia refuses to allow me to smoke in the house, so I took a stroll to have a smoke. When I'd finished, I went home. I admit that it crossed my mind to go and see if Carter was in, but when I saw that there was no car in his parking space, I gave up on the idea. I'd anyway have been surprised to have seen him in on a Saturday. The only car I recognised was Frank Hargreaves', I recall - Frank often seems to pop in for an hour on a Saturday morning.'

'So, after your smoke you walked home?' said Brown. 'Then what did you do?'

Nightingale, perhaps realising that he'd somewhat overreacted in his earlier response, replied less tetchily.

'My wife and I tackled the Telegraph General Knowledge crossword – it didn't take us long! Then we got ready to drive to Cardiff. We had tickets for the evening performance of Rigoletto at the Millennium Centre and had a hotel booked near Cardiff Bay. We had a bite of lunch and then set off a bit before two o'clock.'

With a thin smile he added, 'I can give you the name and address of the hotel so you can check.'

Nightingale pulled a pad of paper towards him, wrote briefly and passed the paper to Brown.

'Thank you, sir,' responded Brown. 'We'll do just that. We need to get as clear a picture as possible of what happened here last Saturday morning.'

*

After leaving the Provost's office, the two policemen returned to their temporary office to compare notes.

'It doesn't seem like Nightingale did much other than have a quiet ciggy and do the crossword on Saturday morning – at least in the first half of the morning,' said Evans, consulting his notebook.

'On the face of it, that would appear to be the case,' replied Brown, 'but we do need to check his movements – we'll talk to his wife and check on the Cardiff hotel after we've had a word with Frank Hargreaves. If he can't give us anything useful I don't know who else we can talk to.'

Evans called Hargreaves number. The call was diverted to the Civil and Military Engineering Department's office where a secretary informed him that Prof Hargreaves was lecturing until noon but should then be free.

Evans looked at his watch that showed the time as five minutes to twelve, before saying, 'He's lecturing until twelve, sir, but free after. If we walk over to his office in the Horrocks Building now, we should be able to catch him before he gets involved in anything else.'

At just after twelve o'clock the two officers arrived outside Frank Hargreaves' office in the Horrocks Building and were pleased to see Hargreaves headed towards them from the other end of the corridor. His pace seemed to reduce a little when he recognised who was waiting for him but, by the time he reached his office door there was a smile on his lips.

'A final year undergraduate lecture on the stiffness method for analysing statically indeterminate structures successfully delivered,' said Hargreaves, 'but possibly not received with all the understanding I was hoping for. Still, there's plenty of time for them to get to grips with the technique before the summer exams.'

'Sounds too complex for me,' said Brown in response, 'but maybe you can deliver something to us that we can understand!'

Hargreaves unlocked his office door, and went in, followed by the two policemen. He put the file he was carrying down on his desk and sat down, inviting Brown and Evans to sit in the couple of chairs positioned opposite.

'How can I help?' began Hargreaves. 'I thought I'd told you everything I know about this bloody awful business.'

'You've been most helpful, already, sir,' said Brown, 'but you may be able to help us in understanding some of the information we've gathered since we last spoke with you on Monday.'

Brown paused and looked down at his notebook before continuing, 'We understand that you often come onto the campus on Saturday mornings?'

'Yes, that's right,' replied Hargreaves. 'It's generally pretty quiet on a Saturday and it's a good opportunity to finish off the things that I didn't get done during the week. I don't live far away and I'm rarely here for more than an hour and am sometimes back home before Elaine – that's my wife – is up and about. She's a primary school teacher and likes to have a bit of a lie-in on Saturday morning.'

'What brought you in here last Saturday, sir?' asked DC Evans.

'As I said,' replied Hargreaves, 'just a few things to finish off.'

'What time did you get in on Saturday?' continued Evans.

'I can't quite recall,' replied Hargreaves. 'I was here certainly at eleven-fifteen because I looked at my watch so that I could put the time on a note I'd written to Prof Nightingale's PA that I left on her desk.'

'Would you mind thinking back, please sir?' continued Evans. 'It may be quite important.'

'Well………..let me see…….maybe about a quarter to ten or maybe ten o'clock?' replied Hargreaves who seemed to be somewhat discomfited by the question.

'Are you sure it was as late as that?' pressed Evans. 'It's just that we have a witness who says that your car was parked outside the HQ building at about seven-thirty on Saturday morning.'

Hargreaves shifted in his seat and appeared to be struggling for a response, before, after a pause of a second or two he said, 'OK, yes, I was in quite early on Saturday – I think I got in at about a quarter past seven - I had things I needed to do that couldn't wait until Monday and could have taken a while to finish.'

Hargreaves paused and his tension seemed to have lessened.

'What might these things that couldn't wait have been?' asked Brown, taking over from Evans.

Hargreaves again paused before replying, 'Things to do with my Australia plans and things to do with what I hope will happen when the Provost leaves to take up his post with the Universities Funding Council.'

'Please, go on sir,' said Brown encouragingly.

'Nightingale and I had had a bit of a disagreement about how to manage the links with Australia that we are both working on individually. There was a slightly embarrassing moment or two between us at the Welcoming Party on the ninth which resulted in the Provost requesting a meeting with me the following Monday – that was the twelfth. Anyway, we had our meeting and Nightingale made his position perfectly clear. He had firm ideas about how the links with Australian Universities should be managed and also about how it would be important for me to present a united front with him about these matters if I was to have any hope of succeeding him as Provost. We parted amicably enough, but Nightingale made it clear who was to be calling the shots in future. I suppose he had a point and that both for my own good and for the good of TDU it would be sensible if we were seen to be singing from the same hymn-sheet. So Nightingale asked me to set out in some detail the extent of my dealings with the Australians and provide him with a report before the end of the week. As it turned out, my week was inordinately busy and I didn't get to finish my report, so I thought that I'd get in early on Saturday, complete it and deliver it to the Provost's office so he'd have it on his desk first thing on Monday morning.'

Hargreaves paused and seemed relieved to have got this off his chest.

'I'm sorry I've been a bit vague about my timings on Saturday,' he continued. 'I think I feel a bit embarrassed having Nightingale put me in the position where I've had to explain my actions. He can be rather arrogant when the mood takes him – and I guess I may have been trying to play down in my own mind the sort of humiliation I felt at having to justify myself to him. I've had to admit to myself that I've got to 'play the game' to help my efforts to become the new Provost when James Nightingale goes. It's something I've hoped for for a long time.'

'I can see that the situation must have been a bit awkward for you,' said Brown. 'None of us like to feel that we're being criticised unfairly. So - you delivered your finished report to Prof Nightingale's PA's office and then left for home?'

'Yes, that's about it,' agreed Hargreaves. 'When I got home at about twelve, Elaine had been up and about for a long time – in fact she was wondering why I'd been so long.'

'While you were here, were you in your office all the time?' asked Evans.

'Mostly,' said Hargreaves, 'though I did go and get a cup of coffee from the machine in HQ, but I can't recall the time exactly - maybe about nine o'clock or a bit after. Of course, I went over to HQ again to deliver my report and bumped into – literally – Stephen Wright.'

'What did you talk about with Dr Wright?' enquired Brown.

'He told me that he'd called in to pick up some notes for a lecture he was working on - he'd forgotten to take the stuff home with him on Friday – and that he thought he'd see if Robert Carter was in. I told him that I'd rarely seen Carter in his office on a Saturday. I think Stephen was a bit anxious about his armour contract – with some justification it would seem,' said Hargreaves.

Evans and Brown nodded in acknowledgement of Hargreaves comment.

'It must have been a terrible shock for Stephen to have found out what Carter was planning to do,' continued Hargreaves. 'His attempts to dissuade him seem to me to have been well-intentioned but rather naïve – it's a pity he didn't blow the whistle when he found out what Carter was about on Friday afternoon. To have received that text from Carter on Sunday evening – "ALL the money in my account" - and he even had the cheek to put the 'all' in capitals – must have been sickening for Stephen.'

'That's as maybe,' said Brown. 'At least, in the event, the fraud didn't take place. Our main priority is now to determine how Carter came to be dead in the EDER building. We may need to ask you one or two more questions, but we've taken up enough of your time for the moment.'

Brown rose from his seat, offered his hand to Hargreaves and, together with DC Evans left Hargreaves seated at his desk, looking calmer than he had been during the whole conversation.

As the two officers walked back to the HQ building, Evans said, 'The prof seemed pleased to have 'come clean' about what he was doing here on Saturday morning. It can't have been easy having his Australian plans sort of taken over by Nightingale in order not to queer his pitch in relation to his bid to become the new Provost.'

'I think you're right,' replied Brown. 'Academics in my limited experience are very full of themselves – keen to promote themselves and their ideas – they're not the best of team players. Hargreaves must have found it galling to have to concede ground to Nightingale to keep his ambition of becoming Provost on track.'

'Do you think we're any further forward in finding out what happened to Carter?' asked Evans.

'I'm not sure,' replied Brown, 'but a bite of lunch in the Buckley Arms might be just the thing that'll aid us towards a solution of this mess.'

23

Wednesday 21th September pm

Over plates of beer-battered fish and hand-cut chips served with a generous helping of mushy peas and tartare sauce, accompanied by pints of the pub's own microbrewery bitter, Brown and Evans discussed the three interviews that had filled their morning.

'If we accept that Carter was in his office on Saturday morning after having spent the night there because he was feeling too unwell to make it home, we seem to have everyman and his dog on campus at some time on Saturday morning. Not just keen students anxious to advance their studies, but academics all apparently pursuing their careers with commendable care and diligence,' commented Evans, raising his half-empty glass to his lips.

'Do I detect a certain note of cynicism in your tone, John?' asked Brown with a smile. 'I agree with you that we seem to have most of the staff and students at TDU on our 'suspects' list – OK, an exaggeration – but the cast of characters is impressive. They all seem to confirm each other's movements that morning.'

Brown paused with his glass half-way to his lips. He put the glass down before continuing.

'Something has just struck me – there was something we heard this morning that, as far as I can judge, could only have been known to Stephen Wright. There was a detail this morning that was known by someone who shouldn't know it.'

'Have I missed something this morning?' asked Evans.

'Yes, and so had I until now – I told you a good lunch would do the trick,' replied Brown. 'Let's finish here and get back onto the campus.'

*

A telephone call had established that the person Brown and Evans wanted to talk to was in his office and at just after two o'clock the two officers were once more sitting opposite Prof Frank Hargreaves in his office.

'Just a small point from our conversation this morning,' began Brown. 'You said that it must have been 'sickening for Stephen' to have received the text from Carter that read "ALL the money in my account". Tell me how do you know what was the wording of the text that Stephen received and, more particularly, how did you know that the word 'all' was in capitals?'

In the chair opposite Frank Hargreaves visibly paled before replying, 'Because Stephen told me that's what the text said.'

'I'm not sure that's quite correct, sir,' said Brown. 'In our discussion with Dr Wright he says that, when he was speaking with you on Sunday evening, though he told you the essence of them, he didn't read out to you the two texts he had received from Carter on Saturday morning and Sunday evening verbatim – he was using his mobile phone to speak with you on Sunday and that would have been difficult while the phone was in use on a call. When we arrived at TDU on Sunday night, Stephen Wright did bring up the second text message on his mobile phone, but only showed it to Inspector Jarvis, DC Evans and me. You were there with us, sitting opposite, but the screen wasn't shown to you and neither did you make any move to see it yourself or ask what it said.'

Hargreaves pallor increased and beads of sweat appeared on his brow.

'I think that the reason that you didn't press to see the precise words of the text was because you knew what they were – because you sent them,' said Brown. 'Would you like to tell us just what happened on Saturday morning, Professor Hargreaves?'

Any thought Hargreaves may have harboured of disputing Brown's suggestion visibly evaporated – Hargreaves shoulders slumped and he began to sob silently. Several seconds elapsed before Hargreaves spoke.

'I knew I couldn't keep it hidden,' he began. 'It's been hell these last few days. I wanted to tell you but couldn't.'

'Perhaps it would be best if you told us now,' said Brown in a gentle tone. 'Just tell the truth.'

Hargreaves composed himself, pushed his shoulders back and seemed to be in a much calmer frame of mind.

'I suppose it was several things that started me off,' began Hargreaves.

'Started you off on what?' interrupted Brown.

'The business of the armour contract,' replied Hargreaves. 'There'd been a lot of talk both among staff and even among some of the MSc students about the destination of the contract to manufacture Stephen Wright's new armour system. I heard staff talking about it in the Common Room and students talking about it between lectures. There seemed to be a lot of rumours going the rounds and I wondered why. I know the business of commercial confidentiality seems to do strange things to people – perhaps they like the idea of secrets - it makes things more exciting, maybe. But in this case it seemed a quite straightforward commercial bid had become very confused. When Stephen Wright began the process of getting his armour system into commercial manufacture, he naturally approached the four companies who'd provided support in the research programme - CompAmour, Armacomposta, Difesa Composita and ArmorTech. I'd got to know the guys who came to Stephen's progress meetings – they'd come into the Common Room for coffee – and they seemed pretty open about their interest in the armour system and, when the competition to acquire the licence opened, they understood the rules of the game.'

Hargreaves paused, took out a handkerchief and wiped his brow before continuing.

'We've been involved in this sort of competitive tendering many times over the years here, but the stories surrounding this particular business seemed to be very convoluted. I thought I'd call in a few favours from my military colleagues – we've got lots of former TDU students in quite senior positions both here and overseas – and from many and various commercial and academic contacts who work in the general area of security and protection. I had it on good authority from Stephen Wright that Armacomposta were the preferred bidders and that the other companies had fallen short. However, from information I got from my various contacts it became apparent that, depending on who I spoke with, each of the other three firms also were regarded as the preferred bidder. This all seemed very unsatisfactory and totally unlike any bids that Robert Carter had been involved with previously. On every other occasion matters had been handled impeccably – no cause for concern at all – all done by the book. The last bit of information came to me in an e-mail from one of my Australian sources who knew something about the Comparmour bid and I knew that something wasn't right. Anyway, it was clear that all four companies regarded themselves as the preferred bidder and were expecting to have the award of the licence announced round about now. I decided that I'd need to talk to Robert Carter on Monday morning and thought that, if I came in early on Saturday morning, I could finish off my report for the Provost, deliver it to his office and leave Monday clear.'

Hargreaves paused again to ask Brown if he could have some water, indicating that there was a water cooler in the Department's office two doors away. Brown despatched Evans who returned a minute or so later precariously carrying three full plastic cup. Hargreaves drank most of his in one go before continuing his narrative.

'When I got in I was surprised to see Robert Carter's car parked outside the HQ building. I thought this was odd – I'd rarely ever seen him here on a Saturday. I parked near his car and went up to his office – though the HQ building is generally opened by the security staff at about eight o'clock it was locked at seven-thirty but I have a key and let myself in. I found Robert Carter sitting slumped in his office chair – he looked pretty rough and it seemed that he'd just woken up. He seemed rather disorientated and confused. I got him a cup of water from a dispenser outside his office and, after he'd drunk it, he seemed a little better. I asked him if he'd been here all night and he said he had – something about having had dinner in the mess and needing to pick up some documents after and not feeling well because he'd forgotten to take his medicine. I wasn't sure what he meant by that then, of course – and he was rather incoherent. After a few minutes when he just sat in his chair, he seemed to be in less of a state. I said that, if he felt up to it, I was hoping he could clarify the rumours about Stephen Wright's armour contract. I don't know why I said what I did – Carter was clearly still in a pretty poor state and how I thought he could answer what I thought were tricky questions, I don't know. It was an ill-judged move on my part, but I really did want to know what had been going on, probably because I thought it could have a bearing on my future plans.'

Hargreaves paused again and finished off his water.

'The mention of the armour contract seemed to galvanise Robert. He stood up – he seemed a bit shaky, I thought – and said he needed some fresh air. He suggested I drive him out onto the EDER. He said that if I wanted to talk about things like armour and protection it would be better to find somewhere quiet and where better than the place where a lot of the testing had been carried out. He said he'd never actually been there in all his time at TDU and it might be his last chance. I had no idea what he was talking about, but thought it best to go along with him. We walked out to my car – he still seemed somewhat unsteady – and I drove out to the EDER. I have the security code for the gate, so it wasn't a problem.'

'What time was this?' interjected Brown.

'I think it must have been about a quarter to or ten to eight,' replied Hargreaves.

'Carry on, sir.' said Brown.

'When we got to the EDER, we got out and Carter leaned on the car and seemed to be a bit more himself. He asked me what I wanted to talk about. I put to him what I'd gathered, namely that all four companies each expected to gain the armour licence. Carter's reaction was extraordinary – he became extremely animated and started to tell me how he'd set up the scam, how Stephen Wright, James Nightingale and all the armour firms had been duped by his scheme. He said that after all his years of being told what to do and how to do it by people he'd lost all respect for, he was now going to show everyone just how clever he was and how stupid and greedy they were. He said that Stephen Wright had found out the previous afternoon what he was planning, but he was like all the others. It seems to have been quite a conversation between Robert and Stephen. He said that he'd offered to cut Stephen in on the deal and that Stephen had been on the point of accepting his offer, but pulled back at the last minute. He said that Stephen eventually went away convinced that he'd persuaded him to abandon him plans and save the good name of Nightingale and TDU. He said that Stephen was expecting a message to confirm that he'd undone all his plans. He seemed to find this very amusing and the telling of it provoked a burst of almost hysterical laughter. He then said that if he'd offered to cut me in on the deal, I'd have accepted - because I was just as greedy as all the others. Towards the end he was extremely agitated – he was red in the face, he was covered in sweat and his shirt was soaked. When he'd finished I knew everything about what he'd done and was planning to do – I felt shocked and disgusted by it. He looked and sounded quite demented. I thought the best thing to do would be to get him back in the car and get him to a doctor. I tried to take him by the arm and guide him to the car – while he'd been ranting he'd been walking around. He shook me off the first time I approached him, so I tried again and took hold of his arm. He started to push me but then stopped and grabbed at his chest. As he did so he seemed to lose his footing and fell. We'd moved off the tarmac where the car was parked and were standing just on the gravel apron surrounding the EDER building. He fell backwards and I think he hit his head on the concrete kerbing of the tarmac. He went down heavily and just lay there unconscious. I thought I'd killed him!'

Again Hargreaves paused, seeming calmer than at any point during his narrative as if the telling was easing his anxiety.

'What then, sir?' prompted Brown gently.

'I panicked,' said Hargreaves. 'I just panicked. I couldn't think straight. I really thought I'd killed him.'

Hargreaves shifted in his chair.

'All I wanted to do was pretend it hadn't happened. I wanted Carter out of my sight and, I hoped, out of my mind. I didn't even check to see if he was alive – I don't think he was, but I should have checked.......... I should have checked.'

Again Hargreaves paused.

'He was quite a weight, but I managed to drag him into the EDER building and left him there in the middle lying on his back. I noticed the marks I'd made on the sand inside the building and scuffed them out and tried to do the same to the gravel outside the building. Then I must have started to think a bit more clearly because I realised that I had to move Carter's car off the campus. I went back into the EDER building and found his car keys in his jacket pocket. I also found his mobile phone, so I took that as well. I scuffed out my footprints again and drove back to HQ, locking the EDER gate after me.'

'What time did you park your car back at HQ?' asked Brown.

'It was nine o'clock,' replied Hargreaves. 'The car radio was on and the nine o'clock news bulletin was just starting as a parked. I went straight to Carter's car, started it and drove out of the campus.'

'What were you planning to do?' asked Brown.

'Just hide it somewhere,' replied Hargreaves. 'Just get rid of it so I'd have time to think about what to do. I was still in a funk – but I told myself I needed to get rid of the car. It's pretty rural round here and I knew that one of the farms bordering the campus had some disused outbuildings less than a mile from the main entrance. It took three or four minutes to get there. There's an old barn with a big door and I just drove the car in and left it at the back of the barn. There were some old tarpaulins lying about so I covered the car up as best I could – it only took a couple of minutes and when I left the car, it was pretty well hidden. Then I walked back to the campus – it only took about fifteen minutes - and let myself in through the pedestrian gate using my pass – I didn't speak to anyone and no-one challenged me. There's not the same number of security guards on duty at weekends as in the week and the only one I saw was dealing with a vehicle when I walked in. I went back to Carter's office in HQ and found all the stuff about the four different contracts spread all over his desk. I thought it would be best to tidy it all away – Robert Carter was very strict about operating a clear desk policy – so I put the papers in the files and put them back in the filing drawer of his desk, though I'm not sure whether I fully closed the drawer, I was still in a state.'

'What time was this?' asked Brown.

'It must have been nearly ten o'clock,' replied Hargreaves.

'So what then?' said Brown.

'I went to my office to try and calm down,' replied Hargreaves. 'What had happened didn't seem at all real and I thought if I tried to do something 'normal' maybe I'd be able to get things back into perspective. So, I set about putting the finishing touches to my report for the Provost. I did manage to concentrate – anything better than thinking about Carter lying out there on the EDER. I finished my report at about twenty past eleven and thought I'd better deliver it to the Provost's PA's office. I had to go past Carter's office and as I was approaching I saw Stephen coming out of it. He didn't seem to be looking where he was going and he walked into me. He knocked the envelope with my report in out of my hand. We had a brief chat – Stephen confirmed he was looking for Carter and I said I'd rarely seen him in on a Saturday – and said goodbye. I went to the Provost's office to leave my report on Marion's desk. It suddenly came to me that I could buy a bit more time to try and come to terms with what had happened out on the EDER, so I took Robert Carter's phone out of my pocket – it was a model similar to the one I have, so I knew how to use it – found Stephen Wright's number in the phone directory and sent a message to Stephen.'

'"I've been foolish. Will cancel contracts by Sunday evening at latest. Will confirm. Carter",' interrupted Evans reading from his notebook, then looking up at Hargreaves.

'Yes, that's what pretty much what I sent,' said Hargreaves. 'I think he must have got it before he left the campus, because I quickly got a reply from Stephen saying that Carter should confirm that all had been resolved by six on Sunday evening.'

'What did you do then?' asked Brown.

'I needed to get away,' said Hargreaves. 'I wanted to be anywhere but here, so I went home. Things seemed easier to deal with away from TDU – I had other things to think about at home. Elaine wanted me to go shopping with her that afternoon and in the evening we had a call from my son Harry in Clapham asking if we could come down to help with some DIY and I spent part of the evening getting together things to take with us. The situation with Carter was to some extent pushed to the back of my mind.'

'But you must have had some thoughts about it because you sent the second text on Sunday evening,' suggested Brown.

'Yes, you're right,' conceded Hargreaves. 'While I was busy with the work it wasn't so bad, but as six o'clock approached I couldn't get Carter out of my mind. I knew I had to tell someone what had happened, but I still needed time to think how to explain. I thought I could gain a bit more time and remembered the deadline Stephen had specified. At about half-past five I went out into the yard at the back of Harry's flat and sent the message about 'all the money' to Stephen.'

'Where's the phone now?' asked Evans.

'Smashed up in a ditch somewhere between home and here,' replied Hargreaves. 'Soon after I had taken the call from Stephen in Harry's flat, Elaine and I set off for home. I dropped her there at about half past nine and drove here. On the way I stopped in a quiet lay-by and smashed up the phone with my hammer – I still had my tools in the boot – and scattered the pieces in the ditch between the lay-by and the hedge – it didn't look much like a mobile phone when I'd finished. I got to TDU just before ten o'clock and spoke with Stephen and Inspector Jarvis….and then you gentlemen arrived.'

Hargreaves fell silent for a moment and looked across his desk at the two officers.

'What now?' asked Hargreaves wearily.

'You didn't kill him, sir,' said Brown. 'Robert Carter was sick man – unfit, overweight with a heart condition, not to mention the fact that he was suffering from advanced leukaemia and was only being kept alive by a cocktail of drugs. This scam was his way of putting two fingers up to the establishment who he thought hadn't appreciated his talents as well as they might. The post-mortem gives the cause of death as a heart attack with 'complications'. He could have died at any time and this likelihood was considerably increased by his failure to take his full quota of medication in his last twenty-four hours.'

On hearing this, Frank Hargreaves slumped back in his seat, his frame convulsed by silent sobs. After a minute or so during which both policemen sat silently, Hargreaves spoke.

'What are you going to charge me with?'

'Well, you've certainly done things that you shouldn't have done, sir,' replied Brown. 'The most serious, of course, is that you failed to report Carter's death on Saturday morning. You also misappropriated Carter's car and destroyed his mobile phone. You've been wasting police time in that your actions have prolonged this investigation which has been going on for two and a half days now, though I guess we'd have needed quite a lot of that time anyway to sort out the machinations of Carter's plan, so maybe you haven't contributed to too many wasted hours.'

Brown paused, looking across at Hargreaves who seemed to have regained some of his poise on hearing what Brown had to say.

'I think,' continued Brown, 'we will have to charge you with something but, given the circumstances, maybe we can allow a certain academic licence in the matter.'

EPILOGUE

Robert Carter's death had been registered as due to 'natural causes' and his funeral service took place at the Oxford Crematorium. The congregation was small, the only family member present being a distant cousin who'd not seen Robert Carter for over twenty years. The eulogy was delivered impeccably by Professor James Nightingale who spoke warmly of the great contribution the Chief Finance Officer had made to the Technical Defence University over many years.

*

Professor James Nightingale ceased to be the Provost of the Technical Defence University at the end of the academic year to take up a new appointment as chairman of the University Funding Council. His concerted campaign of the autumn and winter had served to reassure his future Council members that any apparently derogatory comments he may have been reported as uttering about the Council and its members had been greatly exaggerated. They did not reflect the high regard he had for the Council and the work it did and he hoped that, if he were appointed as the new Chair, they would work together to enhance the profile of United Kingdom universities worldwide.

*

Professor Frank Hargreaves was charged with failing to report a death and wasting police time and was fined for both offences just before Christmas. Early in the New Year Frank Hargreaves and his wife left for a three month sabbatical in Australia in the knowledge that, on his return he would be regarded as the principal candidate to take over from the current Provost at the start of the next academic year.

*

Dr Stephen Wright engaged on a frantic round of 'commercial in confidence' discussions with the four companies tendering for the new licence and managed to persuade the three losers in the competition to stay keen on future cooperation. This situation was somewhat helped by the promise of manufacturing sub-contracts from licence winner Armacomposta who realised that they would not be able to meet the increasing world-wide demand for the new system on their own.

*

Mr Giles Mitchell forgave his partner Stephen Wright for contemplating accepting Robert Carter's financial inducements, particularly when Stephen received his *honorarium* from the university for the successful completion of the licence contract negotiations. With Stephen's money, the sale of the Thurston paintings and another couple of lucrative deals – the Garnetts bought two more pictures from The Mitchell Gallery – he was able to pay his former business partner Edward Turner all that was owed.

*

Dr Michael Carswell completed his request for support to visit Australia to further his modelling work in close collaboration with DSTO and had the foresight to take his proposals directly to the Provost. Prof James Nightingale, anxious to draw a veil over recent events, approved the award without hesitation, using it as a vehicle to demonstrate how outward-looking the University was in seeking to develop its academic staff and their research. Michael travelled to Australia on the same flight as Frank and Elaine Hargreaves.

*

Dr Alex Simmonds, aware that the Provost seemed anxious to promote the world-wide credentials of the university, submitted a further request for support for conference participation. He'd never visited China before and his attendance at the Third Beijing Symposium on Vehicle Dynamics could only be of benefit to TDU's international profile.

*

Dr Gill Neville received reassurances that her initial one-year contract would be extended. Indeed, her former supervisor's diligence in maintaining the momentum of his armour research and development secured a sizeable percentage of her salary for a further three years.

*

Dr Chris Wells continued to learn about TDU's unique ways. He delivered a successful lecture course and was pleased by the good marks his students obtained in the quite testing exam he set. His submissions for both UK Research Council and commercial funding of his materials research were progressing. He was seeing a lot of Gill Neville, and had moved in with her in Farlington.

*

Mr Dan Parker – or Dr Dan Parker as he became after the graduation ceremony in late July the following year - was another beneficiary of his supervisor's ability to attract funding. He was awarded a two-year extension to his contract and was pleased to welcome a new postgraduate research student to Stephen Wright's group. Amy Greene and Dan had been spending a growing amount of time together both on campus and off.

*

Dr James Schofield was both surprised and delighted by his appointment as acting head of the Civil and Military Engineering Department during Frank Hargreaves absence. He quite like the taste of power which he exercised with consideration and, with gentle pushing from his wife Laura, decided to apply for the post on a permanent basis when, as was expected by most at TDU, Frank Hargreaves became Provost.

*

Dr Kevin Varney, over the following couple of years managed to attract a number of sizeable contracts in the area of the safe disposal of time-expired munitions and had three journal papers accepted for publication. He was successful at a second promotion board convened in the following academic year.

*

Dr George Hambidge decided to take what the university referred to as a 'voluntary early severance package' and left full-time employment with the university at the end of the academic year before being re-engaged as a consultant just two months later. His time on the golf course increased and, given that he reckoned his net income was now more than when he was working full-time, he indulged himself and Mary in new sets of clubs and the occasional Portuguese golfing holiday.

*

FLTLT Graham Dowell, FLTLT Grant Thompson, Maj Miles Cowley, Capt Alfred Ng, Maj Karl-Heinz Schmidt and Maj Philippe Giraud all graduated with MScs in Protective Structures. As the cohort predicted Karl-Heinz Schmidt was awarded the prize for top student. As they had expected, Dowell, Thompson, Ng and Giraud were returning home to take up posts that would make significant use of their newly-acquired knowledge. As he had expected, Miles Cowley was given a non-technical post at a training establishment.

*

Dr David Burgess continued with his teaching and research and his administration of the Masters course. He'd always wanted to write a 'campus novel' and thought the events of the past few weeks could provide a basis for such a book.